'Brilliant! *The Institution* will grab you from the first page and not let go until the final paragraph. The novel finds author Fields, a master of psychological suspense, in top form as she spins a harrowing, non-stop story populated with complex, fully formed characters – notably Connie Woolwine, a true hero for the ages! I'd say the novel is the perfect weekend read, except it won't last that long; you'll consume it in one sitting.'
Jeffery Deaver

'Criminally compulsive, claustrophobic and captivating, *The Institution* is Helen Fields at her just-one-more-chapter best. A word of warning, though – don't get a manicure before opening it, your nails will be ruined long before the book is finished! Watch out for this one, it'll do big things.'
Neil Broadfoot

'I was gripped from the start. Scary, tense and totally absorbing, I just couldn't put it down. Wonderful.'
Simon McCleave

'A wonderful, compulsively gripping rollercoaster of a read.'
Liz Nugent

'Wow… what an absolutely pulse-pounding, stay-up-all-night read this was. Bravo, Helen Fields!'
Cass Green

'A superbly written thriller – intense, disturbing and atmospheric – Helen Fields delivers!'
Alice Hunter

'A remote location, a race against time, a terrifying cast of killers and decidedly shifty staff members combine to create a claustrophobic nailbiter carried by Helen Fields's customary propulsive prose. Unease drips from every page.'
Douglas Skelton

'An extraordinary novel that drew me in and spat me out, utterly exhausted. It's the ultimate locked room mystery that terrified and enthralled me in equal measure. You'll love it!'
Marion Todd

READERS LOVE *THE INSTITUTION*

'A remarkable premise... **dark and terrifying!** *The Institution* had me committed to finishing it from the first chapter!'
NetGalley Review, 5 stars

'Haunting, scary, shocking... an unputdownable novel.'
NetGalley Review, 5 stars

'What a story!!!! I couldn't put it down – it gripped me from the opening chapter... WOW!'
NetGalley Review, 5 stars

'Dark, atmospheric, creepy and hauntingly good... it kept me guessing until the end. I loved it.'
NetGalley Review, 5 stars

'A very dark and exciting read! If you want to stay up all night *The Institution* is for you!'
NetGalley Review, 5 stars

'This book is absolutely brilliant. Right from the first chapter, it jumps right off the page.'
NetGalley Review, 5 stars

'Terrifyingly brilliant. An absolute must-read for those who enjoy dark psychological thrillers.'
NetGalley Review, 5 stars

'Helen Fields's talent for creating atmospheric thrillers **knows no bounds. This is a real page-turner...** I absolutely loved it!'
NetGalley Review, 5 stars

'Another powerful, mind-blowing read. It will keep you super glued to the pages.'
NetGalley Review, 5 stars

'Full of tense moments which kept me on the edge of my seat. As always, a five-star read from Helen Fields.'
NetGalley Review, 5 stars

Helen Fields studied law at the University of East Anglia, then went on to the Inns of Court School of Law in London. She joined chambers in Middle Temple where she practised criminal and family law. After her second child was born, Helen left the Bar, and now runs a media company with her husband David. The DI Callanach series is set in Scotland, where Helen feels most at one with the world. Helen and her husband are digital nomads, moving between the Americas and Europe with their three children and looking for adventures.

Helen loves Twitter but finds it completely addictive. She can be found at @Helen_Fields.

THE
INSTITUTION
HELEN FIELDS

avon.

Published by AVON
A division of HarperCollins*Publishers* Ltd
1 London Bridge Street
London SE1 9GF

www.harpercollins.co.uk

HarperCollins*Publishers*
Macken House, 39/40 Mayor Street Upper,
Dublin 1 D01 C9W8, Ireland

This paperback edition 2024
24 25 26 27 28 LBC 6 5 4 3 2

First published in Great Britain by HarperCollins*Publishers* 2023

A catalogue copy of this book is available from the British Library.

ISBN: 978-0-00-866115-1 (PB)

Typeset in Sabon LT Std by Palimpsest Book Production Limited,
Falkirk, Stirlingshire

Printed and bound in the United States

This book is produced from independently certified FSC™ paper
to ensure responsible forest management.

For more information visit: www.harpercollins.co.uk/green

For Grace, Martha and Esther

With thanks for lending me your mum from time to time

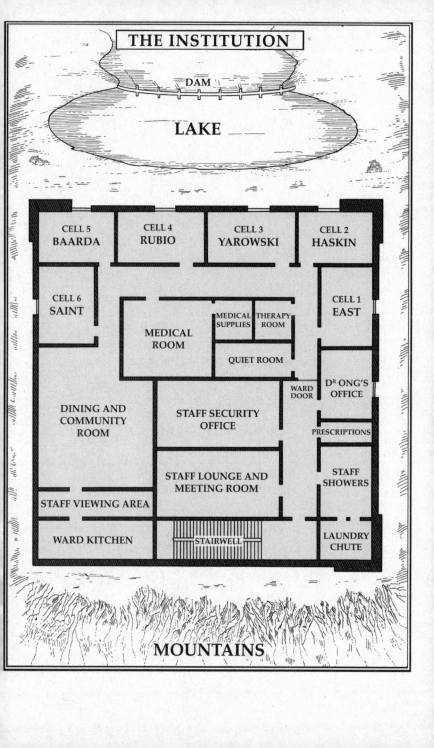

Chapter 1

The dead often made more compelling company than the living. That had been Connie's experience. They told their story plainly, without subterfuge or hyperbole, and they asked for remarkably little in return. Justice, perhaps, or to protect others who might follow the same path, though this particular body was going to make greater demands on her, and rightly so.

Dr Connie Woolwine gripped the corpse's hand with her own. In life, the two of them might have been friends, bonded through a mutual love of medicine and helping the hopeless. In death, the common denominator was the baby one of them had carried and whom the other had been engaged to find.

'Who took her from you, Tara?' Connie asked. 'How could they have been so cruel?' She ran gloved fingers over the dead woman's hair, admiring the silken mass, bobby pins still stuck randomly here and there, where a struggle had loosened her bun. 'Do you mind if I look at what they did to you? I'll be gentle. You can trust me.'

Connie gave it a moment before folding down a section of

1

the sheet that covered Nurse Tara Cameron's body, and was reminded of a childhood game played in a group. Each player had a piece of paper and a pencil. One person drew feet, folded the paper over and passed it on, the next drew the legs and folded it again and so on until there was a whole body waiting to be revealed in all its ridiculous, hilarious jollity. Not so the picture unfolding before her eyes now. Connie let the injuries – the brushstrokes of murder – tell their story.

Tara's face was relatively unmarked, unless you counted the mascara that had bled down from her eyes, the wet blackness dripping outwards to leave sad trails across each temple. The young woman had been on her back as she'd died and she'd been conscious for most of it, crying both for the loss of her child and for her own impending end. She would have had more than enough medical knowledge to understand that there was no way of surviving what was happening to her.

Almost invisible, mistakable to the untrained eye as faint lipstick smudges, was the reddening that extended from each corner of her mouth.

'Was that the first thing they did? Gag you?' Connie asked her, running a fingernail over the minuscule abrasions the material had left. 'It must have been, or you'd have called for help.'

A tiny, dark stud sat in her left earlobe. Connie ran her thumb over it, wondering who had given Tara the earrings, and when. The surface came away as the glove left the jewellery, and suddenly it was a diamond stained with a droplet of blood. There was no such stud in the right ear, and the possible explanations for that were many, but Connie could almost see the gag being pulled roughly off and catching on the jewel, popping it from the butterfly clip that held it in place.

Neck and shoulders next. The clear, bloody circle shapes of

two fingertips sat at the side of Tara's neck, a moment frozen in time as her attacker felt for a pulse. Connie already knew they would find no prints in the blood. Whoever committed this atrocity had worn gloves. Nothing had been left to chance. Only the smallest detail, unforeseeable, had left Tara's corpse recoverable in the way it had been.

Her shoulders, undamaged, unblemished, spoke volumes about Tara's life. At thirty years of age, her skin tone was healthy, her flesh firm and unmarked. Thin white lines from shoulder to breast evidenced a bikini worn somewhere hot. She'd liked being outside, enjoyed the feel of heat on her body. It was a hopeful thing, to holiday. A passing of time in the belief that you had enough of it left to simply enjoy, to forget yourself a while and be frivolous. Connie wondered what Tara would have done with that vacation time if she'd known what fate had in store for her. Spent it with family or putting her affairs in order? Written letters to those she loved, to help them through the coming darkness?

Another downward fold of the sheet. Breasts unharmed, just starting to swell with first milk. Speckled with blood that had dried to minuscule, blackening flakes and left her smooth skin roughly textured. To the sides, her upper arms reflected cruel fingers that had clenched hard enough to leave bruises, the ghosts of a man who had been swift and merciless in restraining her. Thumb marks on the inside of her arms, fingers on the outer flesh. Tara had looked him in the face then, known the man who would go on to kill her. His face would have been as close as Connie's was to Tara's now.

There would almost certainly be some clue on the body. Trace DNA from skin cells, a drop of sweat, a fleck of saliva shed in the physicality of the attack. Technological advancements had rendered every body a forensic map waiting to be

3

discovered, a trail of touches, kisses, slaps and scrapes. One big chemical party. If only there were time for such discoveries to be made.

But there wasn't. Connie checked the clock that ticked away at her from the cream-tiled wall, and forced herself to hurry along. She was short on minutes. Next fold. Lower arms, ribcage, stomach, abdomen. She steeled herself. The further down she looked, the bloodier the residue. Tara's loose skin flopped and sagged around her belly, crinkling where it had been suddenly spared its former swell. It wasn't a beating. There was no evidence of blunt force. This was something altogether worse.

At the base of Tara's abdomen a single slash had been made, roughly seven inches long, just deep enough to part the skin and reach the muscles. Tiny, regular wounds around the edge showed where clamps had been applied to hold the skin back and facilitate internal access. From there, the cuts were layered until the womb was accessible. And that was most of the story. Not all of it, but most.

Tara's body had been violated, her baby taken. The womb that for thirty-six weeks had been the ideal nest and transportation system as the baby readied itself for the outside world, had been vandalised and robbed. It was by no means a professional job, but it wasn't a bad effort. Someone had done their homework. A teacher grading their work would have given them a B for effort and a C+ for the final product, and that was enough to perform a non-consensual caesarean section.

It was called foetal abduction, and it was possibly the worst crime imaginable as far as Connie was concerned. No small claim given how high her professional experiences had set the bar. It was murder, too, but that hadn't been the attacker's primary motivation.

The corpse was little more than collateral damage from the main event.

No effort had been made to close Tara's wounds. She'd bled to death as the baby had been prepared for removal from the building. Silenced, bound by the wrists and held down, Tara had been far too awake as the most precious thing in the world had been stolen from her.

Connie put one gentle hand over the wound as if wishing she could turn back time, tempted to grab the lips of it and close the gaping hole. As if closing it could return the baby to its loving mother's body.

Tara's hands were swollen. The surgery, for anyone sick enough to call it that, had taken some time. Connie walked her own fingertips, centimetre by centimetre, down Tara's left hand, probing the bones gently. Only a full post-mortem with X-rays would be conclusive, but she felt sure there were fractures beneath the crimson blooms on the skin. The narrative of those injuries was expanded by her nails, snapped and split, bloody and blackening.

'You fought so hard,' she soothed. 'I hope you know that you did all you could for your baby. Some fights are unwinnable. Your attacker was too well prepared.' Connie patted the corpse's hand as her own grandmother had patted hers when she'd needed comforting. You learned how to love early if you were lucky, and those skills either stayed with you for life or eluded you forever. Connie wondered what Tara's baby was seeing and learning in the first few tender, precarious hours of life. Probably nothing good.

From there on down, little new information presented itself. There was some bruising on Tara's legs, again around the ankles, which also appeared to have been bound. Tara's body hadn't yet reached the extremes of discoloration that the days after death would bring, so soon had Connie been called in

5

following the discovery. Time being of the essence was a grotesque understatement.

The mortuary suite door creaked, jammed, was thumped and finally gave way. It had hardly been used in years and the fabric of the building would clearly have preferred the area to remain sealed, but needs must.

'Dr Woolwine, I'm Kenneth Le Fay. We were wondering if you were nearly finished?' a man asked.

'Nearly,' Connie said.

'So . . . how long? Only the family is waiting in my office. I don't know if you were made aware but the consultant paediatrician takes the view that the baby cannot survive more than seven days, having been removed in such a traumatic manner, and it's already more than a day since it happened.'

'That's the timeframe I expected,' she said. 'After that, the trail will have gone cold anyway.'

'The body will need to be moved, discreetly, but soon. Arrangements have been made.' His voice was harsh in his throat and she was reminded of the sound of an insect rubbing its back legs together. Mr Le Fay's gaze lingered where Connie was holding the dead woman's hand. He was unable to keep the surprised distaste from his face.

'My methods can seem unusual,' Connie said. 'But profiling is all about making connections, both between the facts of the case, and between myself and anyone involved. It all helps me move closer to a resolution.'

'I was warned that you can be a little . . .' He seemed unable to find the right word to finish the sentence.

'Don't worry about it, Director. I'll be right out.' He forced the door to open a little wider and extended his arm to encourage Connie to leave. She didn't move. 'Privacy would be best.'

He sighed, but left her alone without argument. Connie

didn't hold it against him. Kenneth Le Fay was the head of a busy, specialised mental health hospital that housed high-security patients. This wasn't the first death on his watch, nor would it be his last, but it was certainly the one that was going to cause him the most sleepless nights.

'I've got to go,' Connie told Tara, folding the sheet section by section back over her cold flesh. 'I'm going to do what I can. No promises – it wouldn't be fair to make any – but I'll get started today and I'm going to give it everything I've got. For what it's worth, I believe your baby's still alive right now. I'm so fucking sorry this happened to you.'

She stroked Tara's hair once more and leaned over her forehead, tempted to kiss the smooth skin and wish the poor young woman into a sounder sleep. The inevitable transfer of DNA prevented her from being so careless.

'I'll come see you again when all this is over, and I'll have more time to spend with you then. Don't give up hope.'

The helicopter that delivered Connie before she'd examined Tara's body had flown through a series of meandering valleys, following the path of rivers, bothering only deer and goats, all of which had passed her by as she concentrated on her brief and made notes in her head. They'd bumped over rough air as she'd begun analysing the workings of a mind capable of such an atrocity. The pilot had said nothing since lifting off other than to issue standard safety instructions, and Connie had appreciated the opportunity to gather her thoughts, until he patted her arm and pointed up into the distance as they rose vertically up over a vast dam wall.

'Holy shit, that's . . .' Connie hadn't known what the right word was. Terrifying, awesome, stunning, horrific. Strangely stately. Some would even consider it beautiful.

7

Below them there was nothing but a flat expanse of water reflecting the myriad greys of the sky. In the far distance, the clouds made secrets of the mountain tops. But in between the two stood an affront to nature, yet in many ways it seemed a perfect fit for the unforgiving landscape. A building featuring three square towers – the tallest in the centre – appeared to dwarf the scene.

'You're lost for words, right? Everyone is the first time they see it. I'm glad all I ever do is drop people off or pick them up and leave again. That place scares the crap out of me.'

Connie had read that it began life as a fortress, the towers rising up from the valley's end, each joined to the next by lower-level structures that combined to give the place a vast, sprawling look, as if the granite had risen up to grow unevenly, mimicking the mountains behind.

The Charles Horatio Parry Institution for the Rehabilitation of the Criminally Insane had made the fortress its home one hundred years ago, give or take. The ridiculous title had soon been abandoned in favour of the moniker 'The Institution' and thereafter speedily associated in the global consciousness with madmen and serial killers, attempts to temper insanity and make lambs of the lions within its infamous walls. Bedlam, Topeka, Broadmoor, Rampton – and The Institution. The names of such places were whispered, wide-eyed, and the subject of endless speculation the world over.

The square towers were fronted by a spiked-topped wall protecting against dangers, both incoming and outgoing. Behind it all, a single road snaked around the perilously sloping mountainsides to provide access for staff, supplies, maintenance vans and new patient arrivals. Not so many patients leaving that way. By reputation, The Institution boasted almost none. The men and women incarcerated there weren't the sort anyone expected to be made well enough to retake their place in a functioning society. The accommodation provided a home for life, however long that might be.

As they'd flown overhead in search of the cross marking their landing pad, Connie had noted a staff car park at the front, a contractors' vehicles bay to the side of Tower 1, and the separately housed incinerator, which allowed for waste disposal, to the side of Tower 3, making four ways a body could be removed from the facility, alive or dead. The only visible guard post was on the contractors' exit, so an amount of trust was exercised once staff had left the hospital buildings.

The towers themselves, the middle one the highest of the sky-reaching piles of grey brick, were tall enough to dissuade even the most desperate patient from attempting escape. Notwithstanding the drop, the windows were barred and the view alone would prevent the majority of people from considering an unauthorised excursion. Drowning one way, exposure and perilous falls the other. Hypothermia in any given direction in the colder months, until you could hitch a ride. Even then, when the alarm bells rang as they inevitably would sooner or later, with so few cars on that road, the culprit would be easy to identify. Unless the escapee had assistance from someone on the inside, as had undoubtedly been the case with Tara's murder.

Some staff member had been approached by an interested party and either bribed or blackmailed into leaving doors unlocked then smuggling the baby out. A staff member who was trusted enough on the wards to have access to keys and passcodes, with sufficient disregard for human life that even the worst atrocities were a bargaining chip.

Anything was possible.

There had been a time when Connie hadn't believed that, when she'd genuinely felt there was a cap to what one human could do to another, but that was in the dim and distant past before she'd worked as a profiler for police agencies across the globe. Before she'd obtained her degree in psychology and trained as a forensic psychologist. Back in the days when she, too, had been incarcerated in an institution more attractive (and more costly) than this, but in all the ways that actually mattered, the same as the one she stood in at that moment. What she knew better than anyone was that there was good and bad in everyone, stored as a form of potential energy waiting to explode into life given only the right catalyst. That no one could ever be trusted in their entirety. That the essence of being human was to harbour one's darkest desires beneath a façade of normality and routine. Some could hide it and control it; others could not.

That special understanding of human nature was why Dr Connie Woolwine was there. It was why she'd made the difficult decision to forgo a trip to support her mother while her father went into hospital for an angiogram. It was why she'd cancelled a date with the only man who'd expressed an interest in her for as long as she could remember. According to her mother she 'pushed people away'. It was the reason she'd stopped thinking about vacation destinations – Bora Bora, Australia and Marrakech would all still be there next year. Work was her reason for existing. *It might,* a voice whispered in the darkest depths of her brain, *be literally the only thing you live for.*

And at that moment in time, Connie's ability to do that work, her natural ability to read people, was everything. The only thing between her and locating Tara's baby was a ward full of convicted serial killers and psychopaths.

Chapter 2

Connie let herself into the office at the very rear of the administrative complex without bothering to knock. The security staff had simply noted the tag dangling from the lanyard she'd wrapped around her wrist and allowed her to enter unchallenged. The secretarial assistants had been given reasons to be absent from their desks.

Four people got to their feet as she entered the large suite with its picture window looking out at the base of the mountains behind. Kenneth Le Fay walked out from his substantial desk, meeting her in the middle of an enormous rug that was desperately trying – and failing – to give the room a warmer air.

'Dr Woolwine,' he said. 'Join us.'

She reached out to shake his hand and caught the look on his face, remembering his last view of her clutching the fingers of the young dead woman. He turned abruptly, jamming his hand into his pocket instead.

'Death is rarely contagious,' she murmured as she passed him.

The youngest of the three strangers stepped forward. He was almost as pale as the woman Connie had just left.

'Will you be able to help? Do you have any idea who did this or how to identify them?' he asked.

'This is Tara's husband, Johannes Cameron,' Kenneth Le Fay introduced them. 'Also Keira and Francis Lyle, Tara's parents.'

'I'll do my best to help but nothing is certain. The window for retrieving the baby safely is short,' Connie said.

'Just one week,' Francis Lyle agreed, 'and that's if there were no additional complications with the birth that would further impact our granddaughter's health.'

'Aurora,' Johannes interjected. 'Tara chose the name. I'd prefer that we use it.'

Francis Lyle nodded. 'Aurora, yes. I spoke to a paediatrician as soon as we heard what happened. She said that in her experience non-parents would be poorly equipped to meet the child's needs outside of a medical setting. Given that Aurora was removed early from . . . from our daughter . . .'

'I understand,' Connie said. 'We should assume that we have only five days from now. May I see the ransom demand?'

Francis Lyle lifted a sheet of paper from the edge of Le Fay's desk and handed it to her. 'They sent it via my accountant, who is also a close personal friend.'

Connie read the printout of the email aloud.

'"Purchase five million Crater Coins in batches. Transfer into digital wallet – details attached. On receipt we will notify location of baby."'

'Cryptocurrency. Clever. Almost untraceable,' Connie said. 'Are you going to pay it?'

'The police have advised not to. They say paying a ransom makes it no more likely that a loved one will be returned,' Le Fay said.

'We're paying it,' Francis Lyle added in a tone that was designed not to be disagreed with.

'Will the police oversee the currency exchange? They're going to need to follow the money, or its equivalent in this case.'

'The police have agreed to work with my accountant, who will be handling the purchase and transfer. We've already set up our own digital wallet. Rest assured from our end, every currency transfer will be made on time. The resources have already been set aside. The kidnappers will not be given cause to harm the baby.'

'All right,' Connie said. 'I understand your decision. This is a particularly precarious situation, though. Forgive me using such a blunt phrase, but has there been any proof of life provided?'

'There was a video attached to the email. We took a still from it. Here.' Francis Lyle handed her a second sheet of paper.

The baby's eyes were tightly shut. She was wrapped in a plain white towel, just her tiny face and arms showing. It could have been any newborn baby anywhere, but for the fact that in the corner of the shot was a section of a face that belonged, unmistakably, to Tara Cameron.

'Police are tracing the email?' Connie asked.

'We were told it went through an onion router,' Johannes said. 'It's been pinged back and forth across the world so many times, there's no hope of tracing it.'

'Were you able to communicate the fact that you'd received the email and that you're intending to pay?' Connie asked.

'Yes,' Johannes said. 'And we've demanded a new video every day with proof of the date.'

'Good. Send the videos on to me, if you don't mind. I need to see whatever the police are seeing. It might be that there's a detail from some information I've picked up here that the

13

police won't have realised is relevant.' Connie handed the paperwork back.

'I want to see her,' Keira Lyle shouted. All eyes turned to her. 'I want to see my daughter. Here, now. I don't want to wait. She needs me.'

Francis Lyle sighed and reached a hand out towards his wife, who took a step away from him.

'Darling, everyone has agreed how this has to happen. We'll be able to see Tara when she's been removed from the site.'

'She saw her!' Tara's mother pointed a shaking finger at Connie. 'She came here on a helicopter and walked straight to where my daughter is. This is insane. We should just let the police in and arrest every person in this bloody place until we find out who killed her.'

'The priority has to be getting Aurora back,' Francis said. 'The police believe that if they move in too fast, whoever is holding the baby might panic and kill her, or just leave her somewhere to die.'

'None of our patients are going anywhere,' Kenneth Le Fay added. 'Not only that, but any member of staff who left unexpectedly this week would effectively be admitting their part in it. We need inside information. That's what Dr Woolwine is offering us.'

'But she's dead. My baby's dead. *My* baby. Why can none of you hear me?'

Connie walked between the two men, who were overwhelmed by the need to find the missing baby and too shocked to be able to comfort their respective wife and mother-in-law. She took hold of Keira Lyle's hands and gripped them hard, stepping inside the invisible circle of the woman's personal space, commanding her attention.

'Tara wants us to find her baby,' Connie said. 'She needs

you to be strong for just a little bit longer so we can help Aurora.'

Keira Lyle began to sob.

'I went to see her for two reasons. The first was to see for myself what I'm dealing with as I try to find the people who ended your girl's life. I don't want you to see her right now, and I already know from the bond you and your daughter clearly shared that Tara wouldn't have wanted you to see her like this.'

'I can't do this.' Keira hung her head and let heavy tears fall onto their linked hands. 'Please. Please find another way. I need to hold my baby.'

'I know,' Connie said. 'But the second reason I went to see Tara was to figure out what she wanted us to know.'

'Stop, I'm begging you. I don't want to hear any more.'

Connie gave the woman's hands a gentle shake. 'Your daughter fought the people who did this to her. She fought hard, even when she knew it was too late to save her own life. She did her very best to save your granddaughter. Other people might have been paralysed by fear or by pain. They might have let themselves be swallowed by the enormity of what was happening to them. But not Tara. I believe she was extraordinary. In my experience, most extraordinary women have extraordinary mothers. Will you help her, when she needs it most, Mrs Lyle? One last deep breath, grit your teeth and push through, to get Tara what she wanted? To do all we can to get Aurora safe?'

The sobs trailed off. Her whole body was shaking violently, but Keira Lyle forced her head up.

'It hurts so much. I won't survive it,' she said.

'You'll have a better chance of surviving it with your granddaughter in your arms,' Connie said. 'I promised Tara we'd try to make that happen.'

'Did you . . . did you talk to her?' For the first time, her hands gripped Connie's in response.

'I did. I held her hand the way I'm holding yours now. I smoothed her hair just like you must have done a thousand times. I told her I wouldn't rest until I found the people who'd hurt her.' Another cry burst from Keira's lips. 'Will you tell me what she was like? Anything you can think of. It'll help. Let's sit.'

She led Keira to a small sofa by the fireplace and sat next to her, keeping their hands linked, maintaining the contact.

'I begged her not to work here,' Keira began. 'I hated the thought of her being in this place with these people. The worst thing is, I think I was waiting for something to happen. I . . . I wanted to be proved right so she would come to me and tell me she was leaving.'

'Of course you did,' Connie said. 'What mother would want their daughter to be around such dangerous, sick people? You were protecting her.'

'But I feel like maybe I—' She broke off abruptly, her mouth a circle of dawning horror.

'You didn't bring this into existence,' Connie said. 'You didn't open some door into a world where this happened. That's not real. It's your brain trying to make you responsible. Almost all parents who lose children experience a false guilt complex. I can help you get through that later, but for now you need to trust me and believe me when I say you have to control your demons. They will use your grief against you. I'd like to hear about Tara's qualities. Her personality.'

'She was convinced she was doing good here,' Johannes Cameron said from the place he'd taken at the picture window, his back to them all. 'That's why she wouldn't leave. You weren't the only one who begged her to, Keira. I tried to make her promise me that after the baby was born, she wouldn't come back.'

'She was bright enough to have become a doctor,' Keira said. 'She went to the best schools, always worked hard and did well. When she chose nursing, I told her she was wasting her intelligence, but this was what she wanted. Just to care for people. She said that her own life had been so full of privilege and blessings, the only possible means of balancing the scales was to find the most needy, the most rejected, dejected members of society, and to help make a change.'

'And away from work? What were her passions?' Connie asked.

'Crafting,' Johannes answered softly. 'I always thought she was wasting her time but really it was just her way of detoxing from the things she dealt with here. When we married, she handmade all the wedding favours, personalised them for every guest.'

'How beautiful,' Connie said. 'Any close friends outside of the family? Did she socialise a lot?'

'She did until she fell pregnant. Tara started nesting early. Since the day she found out we were going to be parents, she did nothing but decorate the nursery, obsess over her health. She took up pregnancy yoga. She started coming home more often, too. Before, she would stay here maybe three nights a week between shifts. The hospital is so remote that it made sense, and I was away a lot with work.'

The air filled with an awkward silence.

'I should have protected her better,' Johannes said. The words were quiet but the self-loathing was at screaming pitch.

'From her career? From her right to make her own choices? Your wife didn't want you to protect her from those,' Connie said.

17

Kenneth Le Fay's landline gave a low purr. He strode to the desk and took the call, then replaced the receiver before tapping some keys on his laptop. An image of the exterior of the building came to life as a laundry van performed a three-point turn to back into the opening garage doors.

'The police have arrived,' he said. 'There's a pathologist in the van with them to supervise the removal of Tara's body. The officers have a map of the building and they've been left a set of keys in the garage. That van is on loan from our usual laundry contractor so we've minimised the number of people who know what's going on.'

'Good,' Connie said. 'Obviously the people involved in Tara's death will be expecting some sort of investigation or intervention, and there's no way of avoiding their suspicion of me, but that shouldn't stop me from at least being able to exclude other players. The police are conducting their own external investigation in tandem while I do my work in here.'

'How do you . . . forgive me for saying this, the police said you were the best in your field . . . but it seems a little vague. How do you psychologically profile someone to the extent that you can tell who's guilty and who's innocent?' Francis Lyle asked.

Connie was ready for it. The question wasn't unreasonable. Psychology and its practical applications were often regarded as hocus-pocus in a consumer, tech-driven world, and even she'd learned most of what she knew about the subject outside of a classroom under unusual circumstances.

'Psychological profiling is a science to the extent that it has its roots in understanding human behaviour, sociology, how the brain works, having a good knowledge of psychiatry and criminology. But I understand that it seems more like guesswork from the outside. I can guarantee you, it isn't. We look for

18

patterns, anomalies. Most people give away information about themselves when they're trying their hardest to hide it. It's true that my job usually involves deriving information from crime scenes, communications, by looking at the similarities between crimes such as location, victim type, methodology et cetera. To that extent, this is a very unusual situation. But please remember that on this occasion I'll be dealing with a closed circle of potential culprits. There are five patients on the wing who had immediate access to the area where Tara was killed. In addition there are eight members of staff on that wing with access to the keys, all of whom have accommodation on site.'

'But you'll be undercover. It's not as if you can just question these people and assess their responses,' Francis Lyle continued.

'Not overtly – you're right about that – but we obtain information when people talk naturally, when their guard is down. You own several successful businesses, Mr Lyle, and I'm sure you didn't get where you are today without being able to assess people's faces and body language, and learning to read between the lines.'

Francis Lyle considered it and gave a slight nod.

'I'll be liaising with the police and yourselves,' Le Fay added. 'You'll be given Dr Woolwine's mobile number to pass on any vital information. Please do restrict your contacts with her to that purpose. I will be undertaking regular debrief sessions with you, circumstances allowing, and I'll be available twenty-four hours a day to provide assistance.'

Connie checked her watch, discovered it was already nearly noon, and stood. 'I should get started,' she said.

'Give me your word you'll find the people who did this,' Keira Lyle said. 'I need an assurance that if we do this, if we put our faith in you, there'll be justice for my daughter.'

'I can't promise you that, Mrs Lyle. It would be a lie. But

this is your best chance at getting your granddaughter back alive. That one thing, I know.'

Connie left them in Le Fay's office, each stood awkwardly alone, as if stranded on separate islands just too far to swim to one another. Unexpected grief was like that. It left its victims too raw for them to want to be touched by anyone at all.

'Dr Woolwine!' Connie turned in the doorway to listen to whatever Johannes Cameron wanted to say to her. She anticipated either a threat or a plea. That was what she would have been issuing in his shoes. 'Tara loved music. Johnny Cash, Neil Diamond, Tom Petty, Bruce Springsteen. She sang to herself all the time, even when she didn't realise she was doing it.' His voice trailed off and he gave a final, weak shrug. 'Help bring my daughter home. I don't want her to die in a stranger's arms.'

Chapter 3

As she dropped her bags at reception, where she officially signed in, a teenager ran over, grabbed her by the hand and shook it vigorously.

'Welcome to The Institution,' he said, beaming. 'I'm Boy, and I'm an official visitor guide. How may I assist you today?'

Even in the terrible circumstances, Connie couldn't help but return his smile.

'Thank you, I'm going to be working on the top ward of Tower 2. Can you give me directions?'

'I'll take you,' he said. 'That's my job. Well, one of my jobs. I do lots of different things here. Come on, it's this way.' He motioned and she followed.

'So, Boy?' Connie asked as they walked down a long window-less corridor. 'Is that your actual name?'

'My parents couldn't agree on a name, and they argued over it so much my father suggested they just call me Boy, and my mother was so angry with him that she went and registered it to annoy him.' He grinned. 'I don't mind. You get used to

21

anything after a while. Can I ask why you're not wearing a uniform? Everyone wears a uniform here.'

'I'm a therapist rather than a nurse or a doctor, so my role is a little different,' she explained. 'Do you like working here?'

'My mother worked here. When I turned sixteen she managed to get me a job here too. It's okay. Every day is different. Sometimes I show people around. Other times I assist the porters or the handymen. My favourite job is when I get to help in the creative unit.'

They reached a lift obviously designed to take a full-sized stretcher if necessary and Boy pressed the button for floor three.

'Tell me about the creative unit,' Connie said. 'What happens there?'

'Director Le Fay says the arts are good for the soul. We have music and dance teachers, art and pottery classes, poetry and short story writing. The patients seem to really enjoy it. It's the only time they get to spend long periods off their wards unless they're seeing their lawyers or getting their monthly visit.' He dropped his voice to a lower pitch in spite of the fact that it was only the two of them in the lift. 'Most of them don't get many visitors. It's a long way for people to come. This place is pretty remote.'

'I noticed,' Connie replied, smiling. 'Can I ask how old you are?'

'Seventeen,' he said. 'Apparently nineteen is when you stop growing so I have two years to reach my full height. I want to be really tall. How tall were you on your nineteenth birthday?'

'I was . . .' Connie paused as she considered her nineteenth birthday. It wasn't a happy memory and she'd spent a considerable amount of time burying it. 'I didn't measure myself. I guess I was the height I am now, so five foot seven, and I was in a place quite like this, in fact. So there you go, we have something in common. Does your mother still work here?'

'Oh no, she left pretty soon after I started. She told me I should stay, though. Steady jobs are hard to find. I get free accommodation, all my meals cooked and my washing done. It meant my mum could let out my room at home, so she didn't need to work as much any more, which was good.'

Connie studied Boy's open smiling face, spattered with freckles that would have been much more pronounced in sunnier climes, the innocence that would die a little every year and turn to cynicism as he finally realised how his mother had played him.

'Do you have friends here, Boy? People you like to hang out with?'

'Oh, I like everyone really,' he said. 'I mean, mostly. You can't like everyone, so I just avoid the people who . . .' He stopped talking and tilted his head to one side. 'It takes all sorts – that's what my mother always said.'

They climbed out of the lift and he motioned towards a door.

'These are the Tower 2 stairs. We have to walk from here. We're in the base of the tower now. Do you know that parts of The Institution date back nearly two hundred years? I think that's amazing. I like to touch the old stonework and imagine other people doing the same years ago. Building this place, putting stone on stone, all the things that must have happened here.'

'Do you know how many patients live here in total?'

'Up to two hundred and forty,' he said proudly. 'I know all about it. We can have one hundred patients in Tower 1 – those are the ladies' and elderly care wards. Another hundred in

Tower 3 – that's all men, but they're less high risk. The serious ones are in Tower 2. They only let thirty-six people live in that whole tower, even though it has the most space.'

'How many wards are in Tower 2 then?' Connie asked.

'Six,' he said. 'They're not allowed to come out of their tower to the arts and music rooms, not even for exercises. They have to have bigger rooms and their own community spaces. There are more staff up there too.'

'I'm impressed,' Connie said. 'You know about everything here. What about you? Where's your home?'

'Um . . .' He looked up into the vast stairwell as if trying to remember a particular detail. 'I'm not sure. It's difficult to go home now that my room is let, and my mother has her new boyfriend staying so it's not really convenient. Say, do you like chocolate brownies? On Mondays, the cafeteria always makes a fresh batch and they'll warm them up if you ask. If you're going to be busy today, I'll put some aside so you can try them. They go pretty fast if you're late to dinner.'

Connie breathed a sigh of relief at finding some purity within the gloom of the building's purpose. 'That would be great. How many floors up do we have to go for the top ward?'

'Heaven,' Boy said, giving her a heavy wink. Connie was reminded of a character from a 1940s movie indicating to a naive audience that some tomfoolery was afoot.

She played along. 'Heaven?'

'You'll see,' he said. 'Follow me.'

He raced ahead of her up flight after flight until they reached a locked doorway where he pressed a buzzer. A few seconds later the lock released and the door clicked open. Boy stepped back.

'You're not coming in?' Connie asked him.

'I'm not allowed on this wing. You have to have special

security clearance to be in here. I hope you'll stay. You're nice to talk to.'

'So are you,' Connie said, having to restrain her hand from reaching out to smooth his messy hair. 'I'll try and catch you later for those chocolate brownies.'

She stepped further inside and the door clicked shut. A nurse appeared from a side room, rubbing her eyes and yawning.

'They're all waiting for you in the staffroom,' she said. Her hair was dark but prematurely streaked with white, and her shoes were stained with dirt that she had clearly lost the battle with cleaning. 'I'm Dawn Lightfoot, ward nurse. Better hurry. We don't have long before drug round.'

Connie followed her. Notwithstanding the age of the building and its rough exterior, internally it could have been any modern-day hospital save for the additional security measures. All the doors were metal with dual locking systems, one manual, one electronic. Panes of glass within doors contained thick wire mesh so no hand could reach through even if the glass itself were smashed. Cameras were perched high in the corners.

'You'll be given a safety briefing once Director Le Fay is done. We shouldn't keep him waiting. Keep questions to a minimum. It's a busy shift and we're one member of staff down. There's work to be getting on with.'

'Got it,' Connie said, following Nurse Lightfoot into a small staffroom featuring individual plastic seats along one wall, a television on the next, opposite which there were two long sofas, and on the last, a large noticeboard in front of which Kenneth Le Fay was talking to a tall, thin Asian man in the most pristine suit she had ever seen.

'Let's get started. Please do have a seat,' Kenneth Le Fay said. 'Thank you all for coming up this afternoon. I appreciate that many of you are not currently on duty but there are some pressing matters to attend to.' His voice was confident but his hands hung awkwardly by his sides, tightening into fists then flexing. Connie willed him to relax. 'As you know, Nurse Cameron was due off on maternity leave at the end of this week. She had something of a scare last night. We believe it was a blood pressure issue and she is now in a specialist gynaecological hospital getting the best care, but she's been advised to rest while they assess the baby's health. I'm asking you to give her some privacy. I'm sure she'll be in contact after the baby is born.'

Connie forced herself to keep her eyes on Le Fay. She desperately wanted to check the faces of the other people in the room. It was sufficiently hard to feign shock convincingly that reading their expressions would have been a good head start, but that would have meant breaking character. Not only that, but Connie was certainly being watched herself. Looking around at that particular moment would have blown her cover immediately.

'Is she going to be all right? It's close to her due date. She should never have kept working this long. I did tell her,' Nurse Lightfoot said.

Le Fay didn't miss a beat. Connie was impressed. 'I've been assured by her husband that there's no imminent danger to the baby and that Tara is feeling quite well now. No need to panic. I'm afraid I will have to ask you to cover her shifts until we can get a replacement, which as you know takes time given our remote location.'

'Will we be paid overtime rates for the extra shifts?' a man asked. He was broad enough to fill both his own chair and half of the one to his left, tall enough that Connie estimated she would only reach to the centre of his chest when standing, and he had the nose of either a boxer or a contact sports player. Connie was willing to put good money on him being an orderly.

'I'm sure we can reach some sort of accommodation, Tom,' Le Fay replied, his irritation not even vaguely hidden.

The callousness wasn't a surprise to Connie. In her experience, two types of people worked within the in-patient mental health sector – those who believed they were doing good and following a calling, and those who were in it for the cash. There was no middle ground.

'Now to the reason I'm here today,' Le Fay continued. 'You'll have noticed that there is a new person with us. I want to wish Dr Connie, as she prefers to be addressed, a warm welcome.' He wasn't doing a bad job of pretending they'd never met but the indifferent audience helped. There was no reaction at all to his welcome. 'What you're about to be told goes beyond our normal expectations for patient confidentiality and into the realms of national security. Dr Connie is here as a specialist therapist for a patient who will be arriving today. She has been appointed by the army and will be here for a month or so while the patient settles in. I expect you to help her in whatever capacity she requires, to give her the access she needs, and to follow her instructions. I'll hand over to Dr Ong for the clinical introduction to your new patient.'

There were some moans and a few mutters. A couple of staff members were checking their watches. Kenneth Le Fay stepped aside and Dr Ong took up a more commanding position in the room, file in hand. Connie stayed very still and very quiet. Her self-imposed brief on the first day of any active investigation was to watch and learn. Taking centre stage from the get-go would ruin everything.

'Thank you, Director Le Fay. The first thing you'll notice is that, unlike our usual guests, this patient has not had a well-publicised trial. In fact, if the military have done their job properly, you won't have heard of him at all. That stems from the fact that Patient B was tried by courts martial and assessed by army doctors and psychiatrists.'

'We have to call him Patient B?' Nurse Lightfoot asked.

'Just until Dr Connie has been able to complete a ward assessment. Should Patient B become a long-term guest on the ward, we will be given additional information about him, including his full name. The decision was made by the military authorities, in case Patient B needs to be moved elsewhere. It saves releasing potentially sensitive information twice,' Ong explained.

'So why isn't he in a military prison?' Tom asked.

'Because military prisons don't cater well to the criminally insane, and because it may well have been his experiences while posted abroad in the military that caused his psychopathy. In those circumstances, it was felt more appropriate to take him out of the military environment to see if any measure of improvement could be made.'

'What did he do?' a female nurse asked.

'He tortured, maimed and murdered twelve people during his army posting. Those people were detained legally for questioning but then Patient B became involved. The first few were accepted as accidental killings, then other deaths were investigated and a pattern emerged. Eventually a commission was set up and a trial resulted.'

'Yes, but what exactly did he do to his victims?' the nurse persisted. 'Sensitive information or not, you know we're entitled to that when we work on this ward, Dr Ong. We have to care for these prisoners—'

'We refer to them as patients or guests, Nurse Madani,' Dr Ong interjected.

28

The nurse sighed. 'I hadn't forgotten.' She gave a brief shake of her head. 'But if I'm going to be in a room with Patient B, I need to know what to look out for.'

Dr Ong flicked through the file. It contained only the bare minimum of information. Connie had checked it herself and knew he wasn't going to find the answer to the question in the hastily compiled pages.

'Perhaps, Dr Connie . . . ?' Ong invited her to step in.

Connie remained in her seat. No point standing up and giving everyone the impression that she was any sort of authority figure.

'I'm limited in terms of what I can tell you,' she said. 'My only notes are that Patient B has substantial weapons training, obviously. He used both physical and psychological forms of abuse on his victims. There were chemicals involved in some of the deaths, both forcibly ingested and used to cause external burns. Sleep deprivation, waterboarding, although Patient B used vinegar rather than water. Some body parts were crushed or severed. That should give you the picture. I'm here because we believe there are other victims and we'd like Patient B to start opening up to us. He's spoken very little since his arrest, and my therapeutic role is to work with him to settle him here, and move him forward. That will include working with you to ensure he is given appropriate care, and I will also need to assess anyone else – other patients included – before Patient B has contact with them. He can't be kept in solitary confinement – socialisation will be important – but he needs to avoid being triggered.'

'Just another day with the whack jobs,' Tom said.

'We don't speak like that on our ward,' Dr Ong said swiftly, casting a concerned look at Director Le Fay. 'I will have overall control of Patient B's care in terms of ordering medication and treatment. The military are hoping to see some improvement in Patient B over time, so the work we do here will be on show. I hope I can count on all of you to prove that The Institution is a medical facility rather than just a place of incarceration.'

'Well said,' Le Fay added. 'Now I know you all have a busy shift ahead so I'll leave you to get on. As always, my door is open. Feel free to raise any concerns with me directly.'

No one responded. Le Fay stuck his hands in his pockets and strode from the room. Dr Ong held up a palm, waited until the external door could be heard opening and closing, then lowered his hand.

'Please do not raise pay issues with the director. The work we do here is a vocation, not just a job. I expect our primary focus to be on positivity. Best foot forward, everyone fully engaged. Right?'

There was a vague mumble from the staff.

'Good,' Ong said. 'Nurse Lightfoot, I'm leaving Dr Connie in your care today. Make sure she's familiar with our procedures and introduce her to our other guests. They should have a chance to get to know her if she's going to be a regular face on the ward. Thank you all.'

Ong left swiftly and for a few seconds no one moved or spoke.

'I'm not doing any extra fucking night shifts,' a man announced. Connie glanced at his name badge. Tom Lord certainly wasn't afraid to state his case. 'We'll be at capacity again with this Patient B up here, and it's going to set all the other bastards off again. I say double their meds and stop pretending we can fix the fuckers.'

'Like you work so hard when you're on duty,' Nurse Madani said. 'It'll be the nursing staff who end up with the extra shifts, so quit whining.'

'Really?' another man joined in from the corner where he'd been sitting quietly, prying dirt from his nails with a toothpick. 'You think you do the hard work on this ward? You give them their pills, take their blood pressure, wield the odd needle and think that's you doing what needs to be done. One of them deviants so much as sneezes near any of you and it's me and Tom who get called in to restrain them. When did you last get head-butted or pissed on during a fight?'

'That's enough, Mr Aldrich.' A woman stood up, her dark pixie-styled hair brushed forward onto her perfect skin. She was no more than five foot three, but commanding. Cool bordering on indifferent to the argument. 'You're on a shift, so do the work. Nurse Lightfoot, give Dr Connie . . .' she drawled her name in a manner close to, but not quite, patronising '. . . the procedures tour. Everyone else, inmates to attend to.'

Connie remained in her seat until everyone else had left the room.

'Who was that?' she asked Nurse Lightfoot as they walked the corridor to the security office.

'Dr Roth, senior ward psychiatrist. She's not like Dr Ong. Don't use the words "guest" or "patient" around her. She's very clear that the primary purpose of this ward is to keep the world safe from the men in here, not to treat them and make them safe for release.'

'Thanks for the heads-up,' Connie said. 'Anything else I should know about Dr Roth?'

'Never disagree with her. She hates it with a passion. And believe me, you do not want to get on her bad side. I'd sooner go a round with one of the patients than with Roth when she's in a temper. She'll fuck with your head.'

31

Chapter 4

'So that's the meds cupboard. It's kept locked. Every item has to be accounted for, and there have to be two medically qual-ified staff present at all times when meds are being signed out of cabinets. You don't have prescribing authority so you won't be allowed in there.' Nurse Lightfoot waved her hand at the locked door. 'That way is bathrooms, lockers, changing rooms. There are plenty of spare uniform items around in case, you know, one of them decides to give you a yellow shower or shove their fingers down their throat and aim it at you. Happens on a daily basis, so don't take it personally.'

'I won't,' Connie said. They moved along.

'In there is the laundry. Takes bedding, patients' clothes, towels. Staff uniforms if we have to change mid-shift.'

'We're in Tower 2. How does it get across to the laundry vans?'

'Down a chute from here to the bottom of the tower, then across on a conveyor belt and into the vans. Is that a particular concern?'

'Patient B has certain well-developed military skills. I have to eliminate any possible escape routes as part of my assessment.'

Nurse Lightfoot gave a disinterested nod. 'Which part of America are you from?' she asked as they strolled along the corridor.

'Massachusetts. Martha's Vineyard. Haven't lived there for years, though,' Connie said. 'How long have you worked here?'

'At The Institution or on Heaven Ward?'

'Both.'

Nurse Lightfoot unlocked the door labelled 'Security' and held it back for Connie to enter. 'Five years in total; only two years on this ward. I'll be applying for a promotion soon.'

'On this ward?' Connie asked.

'On whichever ward has a vacancy. The only thing that makes doing this job worthwhile is the money. The pay isn't as good on any other ward, but if I went into a more senior role in one of the other towers, I could earn the same and keep my sanity.'

Connie nodded as she walked in and did a three-sixty, staring at the restraints and quasi-weaponry on the walls.

'How often does this stuff get used?'

'That really depends on the staff member on duty. Some are better at talking a situation down than others. If either Tom or Jake is left to make a decision without a doctor or nurse present they'll usually opt for a restraining jacket and the quiet cell. The jackets are hard to get on a patient when they really lose it, though, so occasionally we have to resort to the distance tranquilliser.'

Connie started at the wall where four padded jackets were hung, sleeves too long to leave the patient's hands free to scratch and hit, with long straps to bundle the body up and prevent self-harm. The distance tranquillisers were essentially dart guns, more familiar in a big-game veterinary practice than a hospital, but they would do the job in an emergency if a patient got hold of a weapon and couldn't be restrained. There were stab vests on the wall, too, and helmets to protect the staff in a riot.

'Access onto the ward is double security, using both your pass and then inputting a five-digit code. Memorise this.' She slid Connie a small square of card. 'It changes every Monday morning. The code means patients can't get out by just grabbing a pass from a staff member.'

'Can the doors be operated remotely from in here?' Connie asked.

'Sure. There are a few specific events that carry special orders. In the event of a fire in the block, all the security goes to manual with traditional keys rather than electronic.'

'So there are keys to all the doors as well?'

'There are. Master keys are on the back of this door and staff members inside the ward carry a set at all times in case of a power outage and a delay before the generators kick in. If there's a riot, there's an immediate lockdown and the security system will—'

A harsh, low-toned beep came from a panel on the wall, which began flashing. Nurse Lightfoot clicked the computer mouse, bringing a screen to life, but the four-way view down corridors appeared quiet.

'Shit, stay here,' Nurse Lightfoot said. 'Tom needs help.'

She opened a drawer, pulled out a syringe and headed out of the door. Connie stepped into the doorway to watch her go through into the ward, punching in the number and flashing her pass over an electronic pad on the wall. The lock clicked open and Nurse Lightfoot was gone.

Back inside the security office, the screen showed her

disappearing along the first corridor then taking a left. She reappeared on a different section of the screen. For a moment she was gone again into a room, depriving Connie of a view, until Tom Lord stumbled out of the same doorway, his back hitting the wall. He stayed upright but only just, then another body came flying out of the room to disappear off down the corridor. Nurse Lightfoot reappeared to check on the orderly.

Together, they followed the patient, not bothering to run. Connie sat in a tatty chair before the screen and leaned forward to watch what would unfold. Tom Lord was big, but apparently not as unstoppable as his frame suggested, or perhaps he'd simply lost the will to keep fighting. That could happen in high-security institutions. Connie had witnessed it first-hand, and it was dangerous for a plethora of reasons but not least because that was when people got sloppy. Apparently Dr Ong was very good at maintaining a level of kindness and respect for his so-called 'guests' but he was failing to notice the signs of burnout in his team.

Back on screen, the escapee was desperately trying different doors as he ran the corridors. Connie sat back in the chair, unconcerned. Whoever he was, he had a smile on his face. However hard he was rattling door handles, the look on his face was that of a naughty child, perfectly aware that he wasn't going to get away with the behaviour for very long, but carrying on just because he could.

His joy was directly proportionate to Nurse Lightfoot and Tom Lord's ennui. They plodded along the corridor towards him, neither bothering to speak. There was no sound with the visual, but their mouths were closed and Tom looked utterly bored.

The thump on the far side of the ward door came at the same moment Connie saw the escapee throw himself against

35

it on camera. She remained in her seat for the better view, but could hear muffled voices now to accompany the images.

'Benny, come on. There's no point making things worse,' Nurse Lightfoot told him.

Tom was stepping forward slowly, arms outstretched and ready to wrangle.

'You're mean,' Benny replied. 'And you're supposed to call me Mr Rubio, if that's what I want. Dr Ong says we're to be treated with respect.'

The sneer on Tom's face widened.

'All right then. Mr Rubio, I'm going to ask you to turn and face the wall, hands laced on your head. We'll get you back to your suite—' Nurse Lightfoot slightly inclined her head, underlining the irony of the last word '—and give you something to take the edge off your anxiety.'

'Don't want anything. Don't need anything.' Rubio was screaming now and thumping his hand against the glass in the ward door to emphasise his words. 'Get Nurse Cameron. I'll do what she tells me. She's not rough like him!' He pointed in Tom's direction. 'Or nasty like you!' He aimed a shaking finger at Nurse Lightfoot.

Rubio's voice was querulous and mewling, his bottom lip stuck forward to a much greater degree than could have been natural, eyebrows knotted together into the most dramatic of frowns.

'Nurse Cameron isn't on shift,' Tom said. 'You know the rules. You deal with whoever is here, and it's not up to you to make demands. Either comply now or it's quiet time.'

'No! No quiet time. I won't go. I won't!'

Connie let the scene drift on as she looked around the security office. Alongside the jackets and tranquilliser guns there were soft handcuffs, ankle spacers, a couple of hoods, bite guards, two tasers and two batons. And that was all before she got a look inside the drug cupboard. She'd seen less impressive weaponry inside some police stations. To be fair, most of it was there in the event of a riot or a hostage situation. No one was taking any chances.

Connie looked back to the screen. Tom was only three feet in front of Rubio now, with Nurse Lightfoot right behind him brandishing the syringe. Rubio was crying, shaking his head back and forth, and sending a spray of mucus into the air. What went on inside most high-security psychiatric units was depressing and predictable in equal measure. Staff and patients would play out the same routines over and over again, until someone broke.

In the distance, at the far end of the corridor, another doctor exited from a room accompanied by the other orderly, Jake. Rubio froze, staring at the newcomers. Tom took the opportunity to lunge forward rugby-tackle-style, head low into Rubio's chest so he couldn't be bitten or head-butted, pinning Rubio's wrists against the wall.

Nurse Lightfoot stepped in, needle aimed straight into the fleshy upper section of Rubio's arm, and they waited. Connie counted. Thirty seconds later Rubio's struggles ceased and he flopped against Tom, not unconscious but drained of both the desire and ability to protest.

Quiet voices took over once more, and Connie could hear nothing but indistinct murmuring as Jake stepped in. He and Tom shared the burden of the body weight, supporting from either side, and manoeuvring Rubio back to his room. The doctor, a man with pale shining hair and the sort of profile that would make for a dramatic camera shot, issued a command to Nurse Lightfoot. She backed away immediately and followed Rubio down the corridor.

Connie stayed in the chair.

The ward door swished open then clicked shut and the doctor, fully kitted out in scrubs, stethoscope around his neck, hands still gloved from whatever procedure he'd been undertaking, stepped into the security office.

Moving to the desk next to Connie, he leaned against it, legs outstretched and arms crossed, staring at her.

Connie smiled and nodded then returned her attention to the screen. The doctor stayed like that, watching her for three minutes. Connie was checking the passing time on the security screen clock.

'I never met a woman who could remain quiet that long,' he said. 'Are you self-possessed or just stubborn?' His accent was Slavic, his voice deeper than she'd imagined given his slim frame and aquiline features.

'Is there a home screen where I can click onto different camera views, or is this all you get?' was Connie's response.

'Okay, you're making a point. We'll do it your way. No, there are no cameras in the individual rooms. Privacy and human rights issues, if you can believe that. The men we house here are considered the most dangerous in The Institution. They've all earned their serial killer badge and they do not let us forget it. But even so, us watching their private moments, nakedness, using the shower – any of that can get us sued. Same goes for the quiet rooms and medical treatment rooms. There's a feed that goes into the community area but that camera has been out of action for a couple of months. My turn, where was your last posting before this?'

'With the military. I'm not allowed to discuss any of the details. Why wasn't the camera replaced, Doctor . . . ?' She let it hang.

'Sidorov. You can call me Vassily.'

38

'You're Russian?' Connie asked.

'I'm from Belarus originally, but I studied medicine in England. How long have you been posted here to . . . sorry, what was the brief again? I didn't really understand your purpose earlier.'

'Yes you did,' Connie said. 'I'm guessing you get bored easily and play with people. Make them feel they owe you an explanation, a reaction, placation, words.'

He gave a low whistle. 'Do you normally do that with a crystal ball in front of you? I'll admit, it's fun. I'm just not sure what the professional context is.'

Connie stood and dusted crumbs off her trousers that someone had left on the chair seat.

'What's the full professional context of your job? This is a psychiatric ward. What do you do here, exactly?'

He stood, too, making himself taller than her again. Connie did her best to contextualise the behaviour. It was a relatively small community at The Institution. Its remote location meant that everyone lived in. The stressful working conditions guaranteed that everyone was looking for a way to release their frustrations and tension. Working within the arena of psychosis was disturbing. But no matter how many different colours she tried to paint it, Dr Vassily Sidorov was still fundamentally just an egocentric jerk.

'Dr Ong says we have to balance the mind with the body. If either one is sick, then the other cannot be healthy. These patients don't take proper care of themselves. Exercise is limited in here; they have strange diets, self-harm at every given opportunity. There's more than enough to keep me busy. Why don't we talk some more tonight, after the shift? I have a good selection of wine or spirits – you really shouldn't drink the vinegar they'll give you downstairs – and I can brief you on all the patients.'

'That's against my rules, I'm afraid. For therapeutic reasons, I do my best to find out a patient's history from them directly. It gives me a much greater insight into why they did the things they've done, seeing the world through their eyes. But I appreciate the offer.'

She studied him. He was a good-looking man with decent facial symmetry. Many women would find him attractive, which probably meant he could be both lazy and rude.

He shrugged. 'They'll all lie to you. I don't see how you can provide any level of therapeutic service without knowing the full background of a patient. More Victorian parlour games?'

She smiled. 'You know the thing about those parlour tricks? We use the term so dismissively, as if it was all just a crude charade. But the people who made their names and their fortunes had a particular skill set. They could read faces, get people to impart information without ever understanding that they had. Palmistry, conjuring spirits, telling the future, reading cards – all required a remarkable level of applied psychology. They were artists. Leaders in their field.'

'So you think you can get these men to tell you their stories, open their hearts to you, and somehow you'll be able to separate the truth from the lies, understand their reality? It's that simple?'

Connie glanced at the screen. Nurse Lightfoot was making her way back down the corridor towards the ward doors.

'I'm guessing you were an only child,' she said.

Dr Sidorov raised an eyebrow at her. 'Fifty-fifty odds,' he said. 'Either I was a sole child or I was raised with siblings. That's not psychology. It's chance.'

'Maybe so,' Connie said. 'Or maybe my job is the same as yours. A patient sits down, tells you their symptoms. Some of them you discard as being irrelevant; some you know they're exaggerating because they make no sense or because the patient seems insincere. But a few of the things they describe form a picture in your head. They make sense in the context of one particular organ system or a specific disease. You cut through the extraneous information and narrow down those parts that make sense and feel real. Our jobs are the same, Dr Sidorov.'

'Not at all. What my patients describe to me actually makes them sick. There's a physical, provable manifestation with evidence.'

'And what those patients describe to me also makes them sick. Sick enough to maim, torture, kill. I'd call those physical, provable manifestations. Wouldn't you?'

Nurse Lightfoot came through and knocked on the security office door before entering.

'Coast's clear,' she said. 'If you're ready, Dr Connie, I'll give you a tour of the ward. As soon as you're done here, that is.' Her gaze didn't quite meet Dr Sidorov's.

'We're finished,' Connie said. 'Thanks for the offer of a drink. Maybe when I've settled in.'

Nurse Lightfoot negotiated the ward door for her, making sure it was fully shut before whispering as they made their way down the corridor.

'He hit on you already? That must be a record. Normally he manages to wait until the second shift before asking a new staff member out.'

'Did he do the same to you?' Connie asked.

She reddened notably and brushed something invisible from her cheek. 'I probably should have been a bit wiser. You think I'd have learned by now. I'm not some kid.'

'Hey, I'm sorry, did something happen? I wasn't prying.'

'No, no, it's fine,' Nurse Lightfoot said, stopping halfway up the corridor. 'You'll find out anyway. They make you sign a

41

contract when you work here saying you won't have relations with any other staff members. They're terrified of lawsuits and harassment claims. But this place is like the world's worst cruise ship. None of the luxury, all the close quarters. When you're off shift there's nowhere to go and nothing to do. It's lonely. Lonely people do stupid things.'

'That they do,' Connie said. 'Does Dr Sidorov do that a lot?'

'I would say the less accessible you make yourself, the more attractive you are to him. He certainly loses interest quickly enough when you respond to his advances.'

'Thanks for the warning,' Connie said.

'One other warning while I'm at it: if the lighting on the ward turns from white to red, it means there's a lockdown emergency – a riot or a fire, something like that. Get out fast. They use lighting here rather than an alarm because the alarms tend to set the patients off straight away, and if you were in a community area at that moment, you'd suddenly be very vulnerable. The patient doors have a backup battery lock so even if the mains power goes out, they'll be unlocked to avoid having patients stuck in their rooms with a fire. The ward door will remain locked though. You'll have to get off the ward; don't wait for anything.'

'Got it,' Connie said.

Except it wasn't quite as simple as that. She'd been expecting any number of hurdles when she arrived. It was her first under-cover assignment, her first time living under the roof of a mental health facility for many years, and there was time pressure and the emotional issue of a missing baby. But this problem was the one thing she couldn't ask anyone to help her with. Connie's eyesight was limited to black, white and shades of grey. It was possible that she might notice a change in the tone of the lighting, but until she saw it happen and was aware of it, she couldn't be sure.

She said nothing to Nurse Lightfoot about it, nor would she mention it to anyone else. Achromatopsia was rare, and hers was incurable. Two years earlier some bulldog of a journalist had decided to write an article on forensic profilers and her name had made its way onto the list. Worse than that, a little invasive snooping and the writer had also found out that Connie suffered from a lack of colour vision, which made her personal journey all the more interesting to report. That article had left her vulnerable. Even without knowing her real surname – the one on her ID tag was false – typing in the terms 'Constance, psychologist, achromatopsia' was going to yield results. So unless she wanted her cover to be blown with a simple internet search, absolutely no one could find out.

Chapter 5

Connie moved along the corridor, pushing away the thought that she wasn't properly prepared for undercover work, and that it was hard to imagine a situation more precarious than being in a series of locked rooms, in a hospital prison tower, with some of the most dangerous men in the world. She focused instead on baby Aurora, on the ticking clock, on what was at stake if she failed.

'What's an average day like here?' she asked.

Lightfoot laughed. 'An average day? You mean every day. These patients don't get day trips. Moving them around makes them agitated, gives them ideas. It's better just to keep them in their routine. It's less risky for us.'

'So they don't exercise?'

'There are occasional yoga and Pilates sessions conducted in the common room, two patients at a time, on a rota basis. It's hard keeping the instructors, though. There aren't that many people chasing their zen to a place that houses the criminally insane. Anyway, their day is pretty much based around three

44

meals, same time, same place, same seating plan. They're allowed two library books each week. A list is sent around detailing what's on offer and they have to order a month in advance. Medical appointments are in the morning. There are individual and group therapy sessions, mostly in the afternoons. Structured art sessions, socialisation or entertainment in the evenings – heavily supervised, of course. They have to keep their rooms tidy, and we're supposed to do a check each morning, but honestly, unless something's really out of order, why bother?'

'Who cleans the ward?' Connie asked.

'Nursing and orderly staff. We don't use auxiliaries up here. The threat level's too high.'

'Are you not in danger? Surely any of these men could snap at any time. That must make for a very stressful working environment.'

'That's why they keep so few patients on each ward in Tower 2. Anyone working here has special training that includes self-defence, crisis management and situation defusion. But mostly, these men know they're going nowhere. They get out of the ward? So what? They've got to get through the tower, out of the base building, navigate a way either to cross the dam or get through the mountains. It's pretty hopeless.'

'Aren't you concerned that a hopeless man with nothing to live for might kill just for the fun of it?' Connie asked quietly.

'Thanks for that,' Lightfoot said, raising one eyebrow momentarily. 'Remind me not to come to you for therapy.'

'I'd apologise, only it seems to me that particular threat is the one that needs to be addressed.'

'And not thinking too hard about it is the only thing that keeps me sane. Did you have any other burning questions?' Lightfoot put her hands on her hips.

'Sure, I understand there's a communal area. Could I get a look at that?'

'Follow me.' Nurse Lightfoot took the lead. 'There are six patient suites on the ward. Five were already occupied. Your patient will be the last. It's all set out in a U formation. The stairs you came up and the staff only areas are along the rear wall of the tower. The communal room is at the back of the ward, no windows because of the rear structure, and it has no access out except to the area beyond the common room where there's a small kitchen. To leave the ward, you have to retrace your steps through this corridor—'

'Nurse Lightfoot,' Dr Sidorov called from behind them. 'I need to take bloods from each patient for a meds check. Can you assist? I'm sure Dr Connie can find her way around. It's not as if she can get lost.'

Nurse Lightfoot raised her eyebrows at Connie.

'I'll be fine,' Connie told her. 'You go. I know the code to get out.' She waited until the corridor was clear before continuing.

Her first impression was that the ward was surprisingly quiet. Now that Rubio had been sedated, no one was shouting or calling out. Nothing was being rattled or banged or broken. There was no background elevator music jingling through tinny speakers. Connie had been in psychiatric units and prisons all over the world and the one thing she'd never heard in any of them, at any time of the day or night, was silence. A single bead of cold sweat trickled, insect-like, down her spine.

One of the patients' doors was open as Connie walked past. She stopped, retraced her steps and put her head through the doorway. No one was in.

It was simple and functional, as she'd expected. The door had a thick glass panel at eye height with a shutter that could be closed from the outside as required. A single bed was bolted to the wall, fashioned from a single piece of metal from which no parts could be removed to make a shiv. There were similar shelves on the walls, on which were sat some photographs, maps, a small painting, and various arts and crafts projects. There was a desk with an attached stool, upon which sat a pad of paper and some small pencils. Off to one side was a bathroom without a door containing a shower, toilet and sink. No frills, but it was an en suite, and more than most hospital prison cells could boast.

But the thing in the room you couldn't drag your eyes away from, the thing that overwhelmed the senses and dwarfed everything else, was the view. In spite of the notably thick glass, in spite of the metal poles embedded into the concrete outside, you couldn't help but be drawn to the vast, flat lake reflecting the moody sky. In the distance, the dam wall rose majestic and impenetrable as if it had been dropped there from space. More overwhelming than anything else was the sense of being suspended above the earth. Whispers of mist rolled past, chased by the soft whistle of an icy wind.

'Heaven Ward,' a soft voice said behind her. 'Do you think they call it that to reflect the view or just to be plain cruel?'

Connie turned slowly to find a man in a tight grey T-shirt, a number printed on it in black, and loose jogging trousers, leaning against the doorframe.

'I suspect it's neither,' she replied. 'Just high up.'

He smiled revealing perfect teeth above a square jaw, lighting up pale eyes that Connie assumed were blue, contrasting arrestingly with his dark, unruly hair. Had he not been incarcerated, his skin would have been tanned. He had the unmistakable look of someone who loved the outdoors and was happiest shirtless and shoeless.

'I'm Vince East,' he said. 'You probably shouldn't be in here. The usual occupant of this cell is not someone I'd think of as kind to women. Or to anyone really, but especially not women.'

'Thanks for the advice. I saw the view and it drew me in. My own fault. So which cell is yours? If that's the terminology you prefer.'

'I'm in number 1. And yes, it's a cell. Doesn't matter if they call it a room or a suite or anything else. These are cells because that's what we've all earned one way or another. I'd rather not pretend that I've done anything other than deserve this. Sorry, I don't know your name. You're not in uniform but you're definitely not an inmate.'

He stepped forward and held out a hand to shake hers. Connie stared at it, took a silent breath and held it, but stepped forward and shook it anyway.

'I'm Dr Connie,' she said. 'Pleased to make your acquaintance, Mr East.'

His grip was firm but not inappropriately so. He kept hold of her while he continued to speak.

'What is it you do here, Dr Connie? The name's a little twee, to be honest, but I don't think anyone's going to be complaining.' The compliment was drily given and he dropped her fingers as he finished his sentence, stepping back again to give her space.

Connie wondered if he was trying to be controversial, or if his unfiltered honesty was natural. 'It is twee, I agree, but there's a reason for everything. I'm here as a therapist, really for one specific patient, but I'll have time on my hands and the ward doesn't have anyone else filling the position at the moment, so my metaphorical door will always be open.'

'Well, for starters, don't say that to anyone else. You'll never have a moment's peace. Offering attention to a bunch of bored psychopaths and expecting them to use it purposefully is like offering a mouse to a cat and hoping they'll become friends.'

'Where do you fit in on the mouse-to-cat spectrum? Are you not one of the bored psychopaths?'

His hands were hanging loosely at his sides. He'd moved out of the doorway so she could get past and he had his back up against the wall to keep maximum distance between them within the cell. His tone was light but respectful. East was doing everything right.

'Are we in a session already?'

Connie shrugged. 'If you like.'

'Okay then, I suppose I think of myself as being like an addict. Just because you're not actively engaged in something doesn't mean you're cured. Always in recovery, right? So with that in mind, I guess I'm a recovering psychopath. I went through some things, I responded by taking my fury out on some people – and there's no punishment adequate for taking a life, I know that – but I'm doing my best to be mindful, to think about the effects of my crimes, and to find better ways of processing my anger and my pain.'

Connie remained quiet.

'Too practised? Not sufficiently shame-filled?' he asked.

'Too soon,' she said. 'What's the food like here?'

East sighed. 'That's what you're interested in?' Connie waited. 'It's the sort of food I'd expect badly drawn cartoon characters to be given to eat.'

She laughed. 'Thanks for the image. It's clever.' East grinned and pulled his shoulders back, pushing out his chest. So he liked compliments, Connie thought. It was often the case that the most charming people needed praise. She filed him in her mind as at least a little egotistical. 'Well, I should be going. Still lots to see.'

Jake the orderly appeared. 'Vince, you know you're not allowed in any room other than your own, and you were only given permission to walk the corridor unaccompanied on the basis that you wanted to use the toilet in your cell.' He caught sight of Connie. 'For fuck's sake. You're in a different cell with a new, unaccompanied female staff member? Even if she doesn't know better, you do. Off we go.'

'You shouldn't refer to Dr Connie as "she", and I was protecting her. There are some dangerous people in here,' Vince said, exiting slowly, hands on his head.

'Right, and you're not one of them? Does the nice lady know what you're in for? Not sure she'll feel like standing around chatting when she does.'

'It's fine, I'm done here anyway. Thank you both for your assistance.' She left Jake still admonishing Vince and moved along.

On the opposite side of the corridor was a medical room. Connie put her ear to the door and listened carefully for voices before knocking gently then using her pass on the electronic pad and entering. She looked around for CCTV cameras but saw none and concluded that Sidorov had been telling her the truth about patients' rights. The medical room wasn't subject to external surveillance.

Where the patient's room had been crude and bare, the medical facility was state of the art. It might have been any other medical suite in a private facility but for the restraints that would fit over ankles, wrists, waist and head when necessary. Other than that, there were surgical lights, instrument trolleys, a flat screen set up for reading notes and viewing X-rays, steel shelving with stacks of medical equipment, a sterilising unit in the corner, and a double-locked cupboard labelled 'anaesthetics and sedatives'. On separate trolleys were a defibrillator, and an electroconvulsive therapy machine.

In a secondary room, there were washing facilities, a rack of fresh scrubs, a plastic couch for quick, non-invasive examinations, and a desk for making notes. Beyond that was a cupboard, door half open, containing cleaning equipment.

Connie made sure the medical room door was locked from the inside and began a closer inspection.

The metal gurney was spotless, but then surgical equipment was designed to withstand any amount of blood and facilitate an easy clean-up. There were no instruments left in the sterilisation unit, which would also have removed fingerprints, DNA and any other trace evidence. There were no dirty scrubs left in the laundry basket, and that was because the laundry basket was missing. It had been found next to the chute that had dumped Tara's body into the waiting laundry truck, where a particularly astute driver had heard the sound of something far too big and heavy to be normal arriving in the body of his truck. The next sixty minutes of that driver's life were ones he would never forget, but more importantly he'd recognised Tara, realised the baby had been taken, and asked to speak with Kenneth Le Fay immediately to seek advice on what to do. As far as anyone else knew, the body had not yet been discovered.

It made sense that this was the room where the forced caesarean had taken place. Anywhere else on the ward and it would have been impossible to clean up. Not only that, but the surgical room had soundproofing, necessary during some procedures to minimise disturbance to the rest of the ward. That would have taken care of the possibility that Tara would slip her gag or that the baby might cry.

Connie took five sets of scrubs in a neat pile from the medical supplies room, and hopped up onto the gurney. She lay on her back and pushed the scrubs under her top until they were resting on her abdomen, then pushed her ankles apart to where the restraint straps were, likewise her wrists. She stopped short of putting a gag over her mouth, but otherwise she was in exactly the position Tara would have been.

Tara had known that room. She would have known every piece of equipment it contained. Each scalpel, saw and syringe. It occurred to Connie that unless her attacker had stated his purpose, Tara might have assumed something else initially. Rape, probably, perhaps followed by a sexually driven murder. It was unlikely that she would have known what alternative horror was about to befall her right away.

Connie listened to her body. It was incredibly uncomfortable, just with a pile of scrubs pressing on her bladder. Her back was protesting after sixty seconds, and that was without a baby pressing down into her. The lighting above was harsh, and Connie turned her head to the side, following the action through step by step. If it had been a patient who'd performed the quasi-operation, he was either loaned a security pass to get into the medical room, or the door had been propped open enough to prevent the lock from engaging. Had he gone into the medical room in advance to prepare, or had someone done that for him? Certainly the laundry trolley had to have been left in advance. There was no other way of transporting Tara's body afterwards.

Connie waited there long enough that Tara's stoppered screams bulged painfully in her throat, then climbed down from the table, leaving only the pile of scrubs where Tara's abdomen would have been. She moved to stand at the end of the table, pulling a pen from her pocket to hold in place of a scalpel.

'I've taken all your lower clothes off to get easy access to your bump. So here we are: you strapped to the table, legs apart; me here holding the sharpest object I'll have had in my hand for years. You can't fight, can't scream. And yet I don't rape you, not even just to mess with your head.'

Connie mimed making the incision, realising she would have to touch other parts of Tara's body – the legs, the bump itself – to steady the hand on the blade.

'From most cutting angles, I can't see your face, so that makes it easier. I can pretend I don't know you. I can forget that you were the kind one.' Connie took a step back and looked around. 'Did I put something over your face, so I didn't have to see you at all? Much easier, then, to pretend that you're nothing to me. I think I did.'

Connie got back to the business of performing the caesarean. Her hands were shaking just pretending, just imagining it.

'It's stressful. I'm trying not to hurt the baby. The baby's the prize. I know the clock's ticking. But this is the first time I've been allowed to indulge myself for probably years, and I want to remember every second of it. If this is all I've got, if I never get out of here, I need to savour the moment.'

She dropped the pen, nauseated, shook her head to clear the picture from her mind.

'Did you masturbate, you sick fuck? I believe you did. You covered her face to make her nothing more than a hunk of meat in your mind, then you finished yourself off while she was bleeding to death, as the baby lay wrapped in whatever sheets you'd been given for the purpose.'

Connie took a deep breath. 'God, Tara, I hope the last sound you heard wasn't that. I hope it was Aurora crying, so you knew she was alive and fighting.'

Connie gave a small sigh as she put the scrubs back where they'd come from, noticing as she did so a grate in the centre of the slightly inwardly sloped floor and a hose curled on the wall ready for sluicing. From her pocket, Connie withdrew a small evidence bag and a long swab. She took gloves from a box on the wall, knelt over the grate and pulled until it finally gave way. Focusing on the rim of the grate where tissue could more easily get caught beneath the metal lip, she ran the swab around and picked up whatever samples she could get. There would inevitably be more than one DNA source in there, but what she needed was confirmation that Tara's blood had been spilled in that room.

She had until Saturday, at best, to help find baby Aurora, but after that the police would need to build a case, which was why she'd agreed to gather whatever evidence she could whilst undercover. It wasn't her normal job, but she'd been part of enough investigations to have a good idea of what to do and where to look.

Sealing the evidence bag with the swab inside, Connie pocketed it again and refitted the grate into the drain. She put the gloves she'd used in her pocket rather than in the clinical waste disposal, in case the unit had only just been emptied, and closed all the cupboard doors she'd opened. At the door she turned to check everything was as she'd found it.

The shadow snagged in her peripheral vision just as she was reaching for the door handle. Only a millimetre out of place, just fractionally off perfect, but that was enough. Most of the time, almost all the time, her lack of colour vision was a handicap, but in her line of work, her brain worked to compensate for the absence of hues. It saw form and lines more acutely, noticed angles and shadows more fully. There was a shadow to the left edge of the grate, the slimmest of lines on the white floor that shouldn't have been there if the grate were flush in its setting.

On her knees once more, Connie lifted the metal a second time, more carefully now. She'd swabbed the rim of the grate past which Tara's blood, if she were correct, must have flowed, but not the very corners. She considered donning a second pair of gloves but decided against it, needing the undiminished nerve endings in her fingertips to feel inside the drain.

She found the culprit in the far corner, the object that had lifted the grate to that minuscule degree from its proper seat. Pinching the thing between thumb and forefinger as hard as she could to prevent it from dropping, unrecoverable, into the depths of the drain, Connie placed it gently onto a section of tiling. It was grubby and had loose hairs wrapped around it, but closer inspection revealed it to be an earring back.

The room felt suddenly colder, the evil of what had happened there seeping into her veins.

Hand shaking, she took the evidence bag out once more, added the butterfly clip, and put it back in her pocket before getting her eye to the ground and looking around for the missing earring stud. There was every chance it was in the drain, or possibly it was in the laundry truck where Tara's body had landed, maybe somewhere in between. It certainly wasn't on the medical room floor. Of course, there was one other option. Someone on the ward might just be holding a trophy. The idea of it made every muscle in her body seize up.

Connie slipped quietly out into the corridor, intending to head for the community room. It was time to introduce herself formally to the patients she hadn't yet met and make a plan for a therapy session with each of them.

'Dr Connie,' Nurse Lightfoot called from behind her. 'You're wanted in the quiet room.'

'Is there a problem?' Connie asked.

'Just normal procedure. Whenever we get a new arrival, Dr Ong has them spend the first twenty-four hours in the quiet room. Patients tend to go through a disruptive period when they first come onto the ward, so it's considered a pre-emptive measure. Dr Ong is about to sedate Patient B and he needs access to the detailed medical records to ascertain what the best medication might be. He's asking that you attend immediately.'

Chapter 6

Inside the quiet room – no more evolved than the padded cells of Gothic fiction – was a crowd of people. Dr Ong was issuing orders to a group of nurses, orderlies and men who had clearly been tasked with delivering Patient B to the ward. In the far corner, barely visible, face pushed in to the wall, was a man in a restraint jacket. He stood perfectly still, ignoring the fuss, as if resting.

'Is there a problem?' Connie asked again.

'Dr Connie, we couldn't find you. That's always concerning when you're on a ward of this nature. It would be better if you didn't leave the side of your escort. During the day, many of our guests walk around the ward without being monitored. I was concerned for your safety.'

'I'll remember that,' she said. 'Is there a problem with Patient B?'

The delivering orderlies exited, leaving only the ward staff in control. Still Patient B did not move or speak.

'I appreciate that the military authorities have reached a

special accommodation with Director Le Fay regarding this guest, and I'm more than happy to be working on his recovery with you, but it's my policy to sedate for the first twenty-four hours. Do you have a medication list for him? I haven't even been informed of his allergies yet. I was assuming that I'd be able to access his detailed records as soon as he was placed in my care.'

'He doesn't look as if he needs sedating,' Connie said, frowning. 'There's no evidence of distress or dangerous behaviour, and I can tell you that since his incarceration he has required no sedation at all. He's compliant.'

The muscles at each corner of Ong's jaw flexed. 'This is for Patient B's own good. I find that any change of environment, staffing, routine, can set off psychotic episodes. I don't want him to hurt himself or anyone else. By far the best way to begin our journey together is to ensure that each guest is relaxed and stress-free.'

As much as she wanted to object, she had no grounds for complaint. Early sedation was by no means an unusual policy, whether patients needed it or not. It was as commonplace in psychiatric units as giving food and water. It made life easier for staff and certainly reduced self-harm rates. Ong was a by-the-book kind of psychiatrist, and the only way to deal with him was to respond in an equally standard fashion.

'I understand completely, but his medical doctors have expressed concerns about his blood pressure when sedated. It's part of the reason I was briefed to facilitate handover. Patient B and I have been undertaking some hypnotherapy to ensure his continued cooperation.'

'I had no idea the military was using hypnotherapy. I'm glad to hear that. It's a valuable tool when used with other more traditional psychiatric medicine.' He looked appreciative.

'Would you allow me to watch sometime? It's not something we currently use on this ward but I'd love to keep an open mind about the benefits. Perhaps you could try it on a couple of our guests who suffer from anxiety and we'll see how efficient it is.'

Connie gave a gracious smile, as unlikely as she thought it was that any staff member on Heaven Ward except Ong would consider hypnotherapy a useful tool. 'I'd be happy to. If you don't mind, I'll conduct a session now privately with Patient B. As you say, new environments can prove disconcerting.'

Dr Ong responded by waving his arms for everyone to leave.

'Let's talk in more detail about our new guest when you've finished. I'll be in my office.'

'Sure,' Connie said. 'And if the viewing flap could be closed, please? I need privacy for hypnotherapy sessions. Distractions undermine the process.'

A minute later they were alone. Connie waited until the door was locked and the glass was completely covered. Even so, she counted half a minute before speaking, to reassure herself that she couldn't hear any footsteps outside the door.

She put her hands on her hips and looked him up and down. 'Got to tell you, I prefer that outfit to those ridiculous tweed jackets you like. Maybe I should leave you in here a while. Consider it fashion school.' Connie gave him a broad smile.

Patient B huffed. His voice had the sort of depth that made it hard to hear his words when he was speaking quietly but made people need to cover their ears when he was shouting. 'Do I need to remind you that some of us weren't flown here, VIP style, in a helicopter, but had to endure a six-hour journey in a prison van, wrists and ankles cuffed for authenticity? I'd appreciate access to a bathroom fairly soon.'

Connie undid the straps that were holding his arms in place behind him, releasing him to stretch and flex.

'Hey, you okay? It's good to see you, Baarda. I love the new haircut. You missing the curls?' She was laughing, but her voice was soft. Double-checking there was no one looking in, she stepped forward and wrapped him in a tight hug, before releasing him and moving an appropriate distance away.

'Whose idea was it for my undercover character to be military?' He ran a hand over the new buzzcut that had replaced short dark curls, greying at the sides.

'It was the only option,' Connie said. 'There aren't that many serial killers whose trials stay out of the news. Psych unit staff always do their own research on a new patient. We had to come up with a reason why there wouldn't be any information available on the internet, with the added benefit of the fact that the military machine was able to kick in quickly, no questions asked. Have you really not been allowed a restroom break since your arrival?'

'The jacket comes with the added indignity of an adult nappy, and if you ever refer back to it again, our partnership will be extremely short-lived. Tell me how you've been getting on.'

They sat down on the floor, face to face, close enough to share whispers and for the appearance of a mocked-up hypnotherapy session should anyone decide to open the glass to check up on them.

'I met the family. They're genuinely distressed, no signs that any of them are involved. They're in shock and torn between grief for Tara and desperation to get baby Aurora. You're the kidnapping expert. Have you ever dealt with a foetal abduction before?'

'No. In the Met, I dealt with babies stolen from maternity wards, taken out of cars when a mother was distracted, from a pram in a supermarket, but never this. What are they asking for?'

'Funds in the form of cryptocurrency, something called Crater Coin. The police are checking it out and Director Le Fay can feed back any information during our debrief. He's the only person inside The Institution who knows everything that's going on. If he comes to see you, you're safe to talk as long as no one else is in the proximity.'

'Got it,' he said. 'Listen, Connie, don't hate me for saying this. I know you're good at your job. There's no better profiler out there, as far as I'm concerned. But undercover work is—'

'Brodie, I swear if you tell me how dangerous this is, I will call Ong back in and let him fucking sedate you.' She raised her eyebrows and shook her head at him. 'Of all the police I've worked with over the years, you were the only one who didn't just see some skinny girl who was out of her depth. That was exactly why I asked you to be my partner. Being six foot three and solidly built isn't the only solution for being able to handle yourself in difficult situations,' she said.

'Have you even seen their files yet? Being able to handle yourself is not going to be enough with these men. I had an hour to skip through at the most superficial level, and even I'm concerned about being in here after nearly thirty years on the force. Don't underestimate what you're dealing with.'

'You don't think you should have tried to persuade me not to do this a bit earlier?'

'I believe I did,' he said.

She gave him a mock-serious look. 'And how did that work out?'

Baarda shrugged and cricked his neck. 'As usual, you didn't take any advice from anyone. So what's the plan?'

'I'm going to be on the ward as many hours as I can without

61

arousing suspicion. You'll be assigned a room soon and I'll try to persuade Dr Ong to bypass the usual first twenty-four-hour procedure in here. There's some heavily supervised socialising in the community room, mainly mealtimes and evening sessions. So far I've seen a patient called Benny Rubio attempting a doomed escape, and talked briefly with Vince East but not in depth enough to form any opinions. One of my concerns is the level of threat the staff here are facing. We came into this worrying about finding the perpetrators, but someone here has been allowed to kill and there's no guarantee they'll stop at just one victim.'

'But you can't warn anyone without jeopardising the operation,' Baarda said. 'I agree, the threat is real, but I don't see how to mitigate it.'

They froze in tandem as the door rattled.

'Breathe in, hold it, relax your face, your neck, your shoulders. Keep your body loose but your mind present, just like we practised,' Connie said loudly. Footsteps faded away and they reverted to their reality, each breathing a sigh of relief. 'I need you to be my ears. I can assess the staff and patients, build up a picture of their likely motivations and triggers, but they're not going to let their guard down in front of me. The patients have to believe you're one of them, and the staff have to find you unthreatening, relatively speaking. I don't want you high on their agenda this week.'

'Believe me, I'm not going to be drawing attention to myself. What's the regime like here?'

'Dr Ong seems to think he's running a treatment unit, but the rest of the staff don't have any illusions about the fact that this is just containment. They call it Heaven Ward because it's the highest in any of the three towers, but also, I suspect, because no one's getting out of here alive. Nurse

Tara Cameron seems to have been popular although I haven't gotten very deep into that yet. Staff have been told she's gone off on early maternity leave and is on bed rest, not to be contacted. Tara's philosophy seems to have been closer to Dr Ong's than anyone else. In the usual way of things on a psych ward, the staff members who have the closest contact with the patients are the ones who're the most exhausted and cynical.'

'Security systems?' Baarda asked.

'Pretty basic because of the environment. Security here takes care of itself. Everyone lives on site during shift periods and all staff have access to the ward. CCTV isn't recording, it's just running in the hallways and public areas for monitoring.'

'What about personal protection? Do you have anything on you?'

'My wits,' she said, wryly. 'And my not inconsiderable charm. In addition to that, I've smuggled my cell phone in for evidence gathering, but if anyone finds that on me it's likely to be cover blown. It's not a mistake any half-decent professional would make, and it's a clear breach of the rules.' She checked her watch. 'Mealtime in the community room. There's a schedule on the staffroom wall. Let's see if I can't get you out of here to join the others. We need to get started tonight. Clock's ticking.'

Connie stood and offered Baarda a hand to pull him up. He took it but kept hold of hers when he was on his feet.

'There's a lot of pressure on you, Connie. I don't want you blaming yourself if this doesn't work out. Profiling in the outside world when other people are conducting an investigation and you get the time and space to immerse yourself in all the facts is one thing, but in here, assessing and assimilating as you go, keeping your guard up all the time . . . I'm really not sure this is possible. Add to that the fact that you're hardly, well, typical in terms of your approach.'

'I'll take that as a compliment,' she said, with a playful toss of her hair.

'Connie, I'm serious. You're unconventional at best, and at the outside edge your methods are sometimes viewed as quite bizarre. You won't be able to behave like that here.'

She let out a breath. 'Yeah, I know. I'm playing a standard, run-of-the-mill therapist type, especially given the military connection. Do nothing to make yourself stand out, first rule of undercover, right? Although it did give me some insights earlier in the medical room. I believe that whoever did this to Tara covered her face so they didn't have to deal with any emotional connection they had to her, and I also think they probably masturbated once they'd finished. Means that maybe there'll be some semen DNA on the body or on the other sheets in the laundry found with the body.'

'You may well be right, but it won't be probative,' Baarda said. 'I'm guessing these guys end up with that sort of DNA all over these sheets on a regular basis.'

'Ugh, thanks for that.' She wrinkled her nose. 'But you're right. That's going to be the whole issue here. Any DNA they find on Tara's body could have gotten there a dozen different ways.'

'That's just one of the reasons why this is going to prove virtually impossible in the timescale. I don't want you putting too much pressure on yourself.'

'You Brits are such pessimists,' Connie said, smiling. 'I need the challenge. If I can't think on my feet and respond to different situations, I'm no use as a field psychologist. Might as well head straight for academia and wait to collect my pension.'

'Is everything okay?' Baarda asked, his voice no more than

a half-whisper in the claustrophobic cell. 'I mean other than this case.'

She filled a pause with a casual shrug that she knew wouldn't fool Baarda. He could read her too easily. 'The usual stuff. My dad's in hospital for an angiogram investigation this week. I'm hoping they don't find anything serious. I've had a complicated relationship with my parents for my whole adult life. I guess I always thought they should have fought harder to keep me out of the psych unit. I haven't had a holiday for . . . I have no idea how long. I was just about to actually start working on my personal life. And I'm still glad we're here because this matters. It really, really matters, but I'm fucking terrified of what'll happen if we fail.' Connie stopped herself. She was sounding self-pitying, and she hated that. 'On top of all that, I'm really not enjoying having to squash the more sarcastic edge of my nature and pretend to be compliant. Not sure that part of my cover is going to last long.'

'Connie,' he said softly. 'Your father will be fine. Angiograms are safe, routine procedures. I'll take you on holiday myself when we're done here. I'll kidnap you if I have to. Having a personal life isn't something you should work on. It's best when it happens naturally. But we should talk about the real issue here. How are you feeling being in a place like this again? On the ward. Behind locked doors. You coping?'

Connie pulled her hand gently from Baarda's grip. 'Hadn't given it a thought,' she lied. 'This is a million miles from my experience of a psychiatric hospital. I don't want you worried about me this week. Neither of us have the bandwidth to be concerned for the other. Ears open but don't be too fast to socialise. Let them come to you. Now let's go.' She nudged him lightheartedly with her elbow. 'I can't wait to see what you're having for dinner.'

Chapter 7

The community room was brightly lit to make up for the lack of natural light, which only served to increase the starkness of the room. On the right, as they entered, small tables were bolted to the floor with a stool either side, also firmly attached to the infrastructure. The left of the room featured three large sofas and two armchairs. At the far end was a reinforced glass screen behind which two nurses and both orderlies were gossiping and sipping drinks.

As Baarda walked through, conversation stopped. There were three men present on the sofas. Neither Benny Rubio nor Vince East were anywhere to be seen. Connie walked behind Baarda, keeping her distance. At her entry, the staff began to stand and busy themselves.

From behind the glass, Tom pressed a button and his voice was projected into the main communal area. 'Take your assigned chair for dinner, Patient B. You're in 5. No one gets served until everyone is seated.'

Baarda kept his back to Connie and walked forward,

66

inspecting seats as he went. The numbers had been crudely painted onto each stool. At his place, he stood over the stool and waited, back ramrod straight, head up, eyes on no one in particular. He played military well, as Connie had known he would. It might have been his English public-school bearing, or the constant watchfulness that years in the police force had bred into him, but he was believable as a former army officer. Only time would tell if he managed to convince anyone he was also a sadistic murderer with PTSD who had witnessed too much human destruction after too many tours.

One by one, the other patients in the room walked to their assigned places and began to sit down. After a minute, only a wiry, elderly man was still seated on the sofas reading a newspaper.

'Gregor, take your seat please. You know the rules,' Tom said. His voice was weary. There were sighs from the other patients, too, but no one spoke.

Connie took the opportunity to walk through and let herself into the staff area, watching the situation unfold. This was one patient she already knew something about. His trial had been reported globally, his fall from grace nothing short of spectacular.

'Gregor, put down the newspaper and move. The meals are getting cold.'

He looked up over the top of the newspaper and glared through the glass in Tom's direction before returning his focus to whatever article he was reading.

'Does he do this often?' Connie asked the room.

'Often enough for him to know how it's going to end,' Nurse Madani said. 'Come on, Tom, put us out of our misery. Once dinner's served I'm off shift.'

'Gregor, last warning. You're not making yourself any more popular.' Tom yawned as he took his finger off the speaker button. 'How many years do you figure he has to live? I mean, he's sixty-nine, already been locked up in here a decade, gets no exercise. Am I going to get my pension before he finally gets what's coming to him?'

No one answered him. Connie watched the other patients' reactions. No one was getting upset. They all knew the drill. Sooner or later either Professor Gregor Saint would give in and move to his table or he would be escorted either to his cell or the quiet room, presumably with a little sedation for good measure.

'Just threaten his privileges, Tom,' Nurse Madani said. 'I'm so bored of his shit.'

'I'm going to count to three, Gregor,' Tom said. 'Then I'm withdrawing your reading rights for forty-eight hours. Let's see how you like that.'

The professor didn't move, but now the other patients were becoming restless, murmuring and starting to shift around in their allotted places.

Connie kept her eyes on Professor Saint's fingers, clenched white on the edges of his newspaper. The idea that he might lose his reading privileges had affected him, but still there was a fight to be had for something more important.

A door opened at the back of the staff area, and the psychiatrist Dr Roth entered.

'Is he playing up again?' she asked. 'He just got bad news. His last review has been externally verified. He's going nowhere. Deemed just as dangerous and sick as the day he arrived. Amen to that.'

Tom smiled broadly. 'In that case,' he said, pressing his finger back on the speaker button. 'Professor Saint, would you mind taking your seat at the table, please, so we can serve meals?'

The professor didn't miss a beat, on his feet immediately

and striding towards his stool. It was always useful to know what made someone tick, and Connie reminded herself to call him 'Professor' at all times if she wanted to stay on his good side. Like most serial killers, he was clearly narcissistic, although his status made him an unusual subject. Most psychopaths weren't able to function at quite such a high professional level.

As soon as they sat, Nurse Madani unlocked the staff area door and began wheeling in hot food. Connie took a seat in the corner, keeping a low profile as the men began eating. It was gammon and mash with a large serving of mixed green vegetables. There were no options, no sauces, no condiments. Cutlery was plastic, plates were thick cardboard. She made a point of not looking at Baarda's face as he ate.

They'd met on a case in Edinburgh two years earlier. A year later, aged fifty, Baarda had taken retirement from the police, and she had immediately poached him to join forces with her. Now they took cases as a team – him as an investigator, her as a profiler. They made a good, if unorthodox, pair. Baarda had been happy to travel, escaping the unhappiness of a bad marriage that was dragging itself out into an even worse divorce, and for her, travel meant not having to wonder why she'd never been able to find a relationship worth committing to for more than a month.

'Right, I want meds given straight after dinner – no delays tonight. They're not misbehaving yet, but having a new face on the ward is going to throw them all off. I want every one of them warned that disruption won't be tolerated,' Dr Roth said. 'You,' she aimed at Connie. 'I don't want you on the ward again tonight, either. It's hard enough keeping these deviants calm on a normal day. You walking around in your skinny trousers and your tight shirt isn't exactly helpful.'

Connie bit back her desire to explain that it was hard enough living in a world where sexual assaults were commonplace, without having women blame each other for inciting them.

'You have female staff members on the ward every day,' Connie commented, glad that Roth couldn't see her hands clenched into fists behind her back. 'Does their very presence cause problems?'

'Those issues are eased by familiarity,' Dr Roth said. 'And by knowing that if any of them step out of line, my nurses will not hesitate to request that a prisoner go onto a punishment regime. You, on the other hand, look like you're more likely to try and hug them better.'

Connie studied the psychiatrist. She was in her fifties, no wedding ring, no make-up. The cords in her neck were standing out as she spoke, in spite of her best efforts to sound casual as she laid down the law. She was making a few fair points, but aiming them in the wrong direction. Bad men did bad things either because they wanted to or because they couldn't help themselves, not because of anything a woman decided to wear. Even so, she supposed that on a ward it was sensible to take precautions.

'I've worked with high-security patients before,' Connie said. 'I can assure you, I won't be hugging any of them. I would like a chance to interview them tomorrow, if that's all right with you. I hope it'll give them a chance to ask any questions they want about Patient B as well as my presence, which should make the settling period faster.'

'Are we being audited?' Dr Roth asked. 'Is that what this is? Some sort of performance review? Are you going to be asking about the treatment we provide? Our contracts say we have to be given notice about any evaluation.'

Connie leaned forward in her seat and rested her elbows on her knees – a gesture designed to say, *I'm taking you seriously but I'm not a threat.*

'You think anyone actually cares whether or not you're providing these patients with a sufficiently nurturing environment? Or that there's an agency out there prepared to pay good money to send in undercover auditors? If I'm honest, I'm just a bit curious. Your unit houses some of the most dangerous men in the world. I'm a psychologist. How could I not be curious about them? It may not be the most professional of analogies, but kid in a candy store springs to mind.'

Dr Roth considered it. 'At least you're honest about it,' she said. 'You can see the professor and Benny Rubio in the morning. The others have treatments scheduled.'

'Treatments?' Connie asked.

She became aware of rising voices in the common room but was wary of looking too interested.

'Harold Haskin needs a tooth checked out, and Joe Yarowski needs an endoscopy. We could—'

Someone was yelling, a patient Connie didn't recognise. 'I want to know who he is and I want to know what he's done. This is where we live. You can't just bring someone in here without checking with us first!'

Jake, the orderly, was approaching slowly, hands raised, trying to defuse the situation. Baarda just carried on eating as if hearing nothing.

'Damn it, I knew this would happen,' Dr Roth said. 'Mealtime's over. Get cleared before the plates start flying.'

One by one the staff filed out into the large room. Only Dr Roth remained behind glass, ready to fire off an alarm if needed, Connie guessed, or perhaps just too senior to get her hands dirty.

Connie went with them, keeping her eyes on Baarda in case things got out of hand, even though she was perfectly well aware that he could handle himself. Getting into a physical altercation on the first day was likely to have Dr Ong reaching for the sedatives again.

'This man is Patient B,' she announced. 'His details will have to remain private as a matter of law. He's here to receive care and to be rehabilitated back into civilian life.' As for what he's done, that's just the same as everyone else on this ward. Murder. He's no different than any of you.' There were some huffs at that. Connie could have kicked herself. She should have seen that coming. Every psychopath she'd ever met had believed they were one of a kind, somehow removed from ever belonging to a category or type. She didn't want to irritate them at such an early juncture, not when she needed them to confide in her. 'It is important, of course, that you feel comfortable with Patient B here, so if you have questions, I'll be available in the next few days to answer them. Director Le Fay has agreed that I can assist with ward integration. So Mr . . .'

'Yarowski,' he said. 'Joe Yarowski.'

'Mr Yarowski. I will answer your questions in so far as I'm allowed to. Patient B is a very quiet man by nature. He won't be bothering any of you.'

Yarowski was breathing hard and staring, unblinking, at Baarda.

'I just want to eat,' Baarda said, turning his back on Yarowski and picking up his fork.

'You don't belong here,' Yarowski shouted. 'I can see it on you. Walking in here like you're on a fucking cruise ship. Why didn't we get any warning? That's what I want to know.'

He took another step towards Baarda, who quietly chewed a mouthful of food and pointedly didn't react, as Jake inserted himself between them.

Connie took a longer look at Yarowski. It was interesting

that he'd been the first to call out Baarda as an outsider – had he got some sort of sixth sense or had he been fed information?

'Enough,' Tom told him. 'You've interrupted dinner. That's against the rules.'

Yarowski began slapping himself in the face. Tom gave an exhausted shake of his head and started hauling him out of the door. The others went willingly as plates were cleared. Baarda remained where he was until Jake motioned for him to stand.

'Quiet room for you, pal,' Jake said as he took hold of Baarda's left arm.

'No. He needs to be taken to his cell. Dr Ong and I have agreed that there's no need for the usual twenty-four-hour settling routine.'

'You're not my boss, lady. I don't take directions from you.' He turned his head away from her as he began walking away, muttering, 'Not you and not any other fucking woman.'

Connie quickly scanned the area. The rest of the inmates had gone. The staff were busy pushing the trolley of dinner debris back into the staff area for return to the small kitchen area.

'Hey, Jake,' Connie said, stepping after him. His face was a picture of unadulterated loathing. Connie kept her voice so low he had to lean in to hear, and that was just how she wanted it. 'I could tell you that I have a direct line to Kenneth Le Fay and that's all the authority I need, or I could tell you that I've dealt with men just as dangerous as any you have here, and in much closer quarters with none of the support you have available. But I'm actually just going to explain that if I ever hear you talking about me, or any other woman, that way again, I will grab your testicles and keep twisting until there isn't a surgeon in the world who'll be able to get your pipes back in working order.' She moved further away and let her voice rise to its normal volume. 'You can take Patient B to his cell now,' she said sweetly. 'Thank you for your assistance.'

Jake's upper lip quivered with the effort of controlling what might otherwise have become a snarl, but he started moving anyway. Baarda gave her the briefest glance over his shoulder, inclining his head so slightly that no one but Connie would ever have been able to decode the message of solidarity. It had felt good unloading on Jake, better in fact than it really should have. Connie was finding playing nice absolutely exhausting, as necessary as it was.

All around the corridor, doors were banging shut. Connie left it a few minutes then walked along to check that Baarda was in his cell rather than the quiet room. She opened the eye grate on door 5 and found her partner lying on his bed contemplating the ceiling. They locked eyes and he gave her a small smile before she closed it again and set off for her room.

As she arrived back in her accommodation, she saw that she'd missed three calls from Johannes Cameron, and dialled his number immediately.

'Johannes,' she said as soon as he picked up. 'Is there news about Aurora?'

'The kidnappers sent an audio recording.' He was breathing hard and his voice was quavering. Connie could only imagine the effort it was taking him not to simply scream at her. 'In the background there was a broadcast from the BBC World Service and they said today's date. We could hear the sound of a baby crying over the top.'

'Can you play it to me now?' Connie asked.

'Sure, give me a moment.' Connie could hear keys being tapped on a computer. 'Here you go. I'll turn the volume up.'

A man's voice, with a slight South African accent, was saying the date and following it up with the news headlines, and across it all was a desperate screech that rose in pitch until a breath was taken, then it began again. Connie felt that scream in her gut. It made her head hurt and her eyes water. She had to find the baby, to hold her, comfort her, protect her. She needed to stop her crying.

'We don't know it's Aurora,' Connie said, speaking over the lump that had formed in her throat, 'but if it is, then that's a good strong cry. She's letting them know that she needs something. Warmth, food or changing. Keep hold of the positive there. Your daughter's not giving up.'

'I can't bear it,' he said. 'I've listened to it so many times and all I can think is, why is no one picking her up and cuddling her? Why am I having to listen to my baby cry through a recording that's come from God knows where?'

'As long as they're making contact, the plan is still progressing and that's good news for us. Don't forget, they need Aurora alive.'

'Yes,' Johannes said. 'I suppose so. And I actually phoned because I've been going through Tara's emails. There was a recent staff appraisal.'

'Conducted by whom?'

'Ong and Roth. It was faultless. The conclusion was that Tara should be working towards applying for a promotion in the future. They set her some goals and asked her to consider which continued professional training courses would be best for her this year.'

'No negatives at all on there?' Connie asked.

'None,' he confirmed. 'There was also a request from lawyers for a Joe Yarowski for her to speak at his next review hearing.'

'He's one of the patients on the ward,' she said. 'Did Tara reply?'

'She did. She told them she was sympathetic to Mr Yarowski's position and pleased that he seemed settled at the moment but that she wouldn't be able to recommend any changes to his current plan, and that they should approach one of the doctors instead.'

'That's interesting. I hadn't realised Yarowski's case was up for review so soon. He must have felt incredibly let down that she wouldn't speak for him. Furious, probably,' Connie said. 'Any other contact from the ward?'

'Only from Dawn Lightfoot. She's one of the other nurses,' Johannes said.

'Yeah, I've met her. What did the email say?'

'I'll read it to you.' More keyboard tapping. 'It was from a little over a month ago. She says, "Dear Tara, I'm emailing because it's so hard to talk on the ward and it's not the right place anyway. I wanted to say I'm so pleased you're having a baby. I know you're planning to come back to work after six months and I just don't think that's a good idea. A baby should have a mother at home full-time. Lots of people say that's an old-fashioned view, but I think a baby can only thrive with its mother there. You've been a good nurse and I know you care about your work, but being a part of your child's life is much more important. So just think about it. You might regret it if you don't. I hope I'm not out of line, but I don't want you to mess this up. Sometimes we only get one chance. See you next week on the early shift! Dawn".'

Connie rolled her eyes and gritted her teeth. It wasn't the right moment to let herself be influenced by personal politics, but the mummy-belongs-at-home perspective made her blood boil. And to express it to a colleague was extraordinarily brazen. 'Did Tara talk to you about that?' Connie asked.

'No, and I looked in her sent items and it seems she didn't

76

respond. I think she probably read it and decided to ignore it. Tara was never going to be swayed by what anyone else thought.'

'It's a pretty bold thing to write, telling someone what they should and shouldn't do.'

'It is, and I suspect Tara didn't tell me about it because I'd have been cross. There's been some vying for position on the ward. They were all hoping Nurse Casey would leave. Tara implied that he's one of those work-to-rule types, never doing a single thing more than the bare minimum. His position is a pay grade up from the other nurses. I suspect they all want his job, and that this is Lightfoot's way of trying to get Tara out of the running.'

'Did Tara want the job?' Connie asked.

'Not for the money, but she'd have applied if only to make the ward a better place.'

'Of course. Thanks for letting me know. And call again, any time.'

'Has there been any progress so far?' he asked.

'It's been a useful day,' she said. 'But I'm just getting started. Try not to listen to that audio too many times, okay?'

Johannes Cameron rang off and Connie scrolled through her emails to the first request she'd received to help find Aurora. The lead detective in the case had attached a photo of Tara recent enough for her baby bump to be showing, as she held up a handful of daisies to show to the camera. The abundance of life on display made Connie feel almost queasy. The loss of a woman like that was a terrible thing. Tara had loved life, and it had been stolen from her for no other reason than to line someone else's pockets. Connie flexed her shoulders up and down, then shook them. The fury she felt would turn to frustration unless she kept working, kept trying to solve the puzzle. She moved position to look for her laptop, only to find her hand on her abdomen. Rather than pull it away she stared at it for a few seconds, wondering when she'd put it there and what it meant.

A case involving a missing baby was new to her. Slightly older children, yes. Awful cases. Devastating. All the time wondering what they were being put through. But this was something different. Like there was something missing from her, personally. *She's not my baby,* she thought. *I'm not cut out to be a mother.* How must it have been for Tara, the first time she felt that tiny creature kick inside her? Alien or comforting? A relief or a burden?

'All of it,' she said aloud, pushing her fingers against her flat belly, trying to divine some sort of maternal, ancient knowledge. None came. She withdrew her hand gently and reached it out to take hold of her laptop instead. She might not know how it felt to be a parent-in-waiting, but she could make up for that with the skills she did have.

Connie used the time before dinner to make notes on the staff members she'd met and what she'd seen of the patients. Most of it was too cursory to point in any particular direction. The email from Nurse Lightfoot felt pushy and inappropriate, but also desperate. Perhaps not as desperate as Joe Yarowski, though. Surely he must have felt he had a score to settle? Checking her watch once again – something Connie found herself doing several times per hour – she realised it was dinnertime. She didn't want to eat. It felt like a waste of precious minutes, doing any activity that didn't get her closer to Aurora, but eat she must. Just half an hour, she told herself.

'I won't be long, Aurora,' she said. 'I'm coming to find you. Stay strong.'

Chapter 8

True to his word, Boy saved Connie a place at dinner that evening, along with a plate of the famous chocolate brownies. He stood next to her as she tried them, shifting from foot to foot, anxiously awaiting her judgement.

'They're amazing,' Connie told him. 'But I don't think I'll sleep if I have any more sugar tonight. Could you help me finish them?'

'Well okay, but only if you're sure,' he said, reaching out a shy hand to take the remaining block of confectionery from her plate.

They sat together, chatting about The Institution and life there. In his own simple way, he described how small-scale power struggles became fierce battles, gossip was a staple for getting through long shifts and boring evenings, and working conditions were a constant source of complaint in spite of the better than normal rates of pay in a highly specialised industry.

Jake, the orderly, walked past deep in conversation with Nurse Madani. They spotted Connie with Boy and acknowledged her

79

with slight nods, but not before Madani's nostrils had flared and Jake had grimaced. Connie read their expressions as superiority and distaste respectively. There was a pecking order and a class system in play, she thought. In spite of their common problems and singular goal in that place, the worst aspects of society had been concentrated into their little community. That caused friction, and friction made people behave badly. She forced her focus back onto Boy who was still telling her about his world, which was a much more positive view of the place than was probably justified.

He liked having his own bedroom and bathroom but didn't like the towels, which were scratchy. He thought the food was good but the tap water tasted sour. He liked the fact that there was a library but hated when the last person to read a book had turned down the corners of pages to mark their progress. Most of all, he loved being given a uniform as his own clothes were tatty and he couldn't afford anything new or cool, so it was better to wear what everyone else was wearing. His innocent perspective was illuminating. She was starting to feel like The Institution was as much a prison for the people working there as it was for those they cared for.

After precisely thirty minutes, the hands of the dining hall clock moving way too fast, she thanked Boy for his company, made her excuses and rushed back to her room to continue working.

Director Le Fay visited her briefly at 11 p.m. looking thoroughly uncomfortable as he peered around her room, shaking his head and tutting. 'Oh dear, I'm sorry we weren't able to accommodate you better, and apologies for the lateness of the hour,' he began.

'I once spent two months in Alaska living in an unfurnished log cabin profiling a man who collected his victims' fingers and toes. Believe me, this is five-star accommodation compared to that.'

Le Fay gave an embarrassed nod. 'You'll let me know if you need anything, of course. I came to tell you that Tara's father received another contact from the kidnapper this evening.'

'I spoke to Johannes earlier,' Connie confirmed. 'He played me the audio file with the time and date.'

'This was different. A video. In it, Aurora appears all right, for now. She's tiny and the family's paediatrician says you can tell she was removed from the womb prematurely, but she was moving slightly. Her skin tone was not what it should be, and it seems likely that the baby is not getting sufficient nutrition.'

Shit, Connie thought. *Shit, shit, shit.*

'Can they tell how serious it is?' Connie asked.

'Their information is very limited from the footage. Suffice it to say, the paediatrician is rather talking in code. They're preparing Johannes and his parents-in-law for the worst without calling it inevitable. But time is of the essence. A fact of which I know you're all too aware. As far as the police go, they're looking carefully at the footage. There were fingers in shot pulling a blanket back from the baby's face and they appeared to be female and Caucasian, but that's all they've been able to take from it.'

Connie ran her hands through her hair, took in a deep breath and released it slowly.

'All right. The positive takeaway from this is that the kidnappers are making plenty of contact, which is hopeful. I guess they want to give Johannes and the Lyles plenty of reasons to comply rather than simply bringing in the police. Would you mind asking the paediatrician to contact me directly? I'd like to talk through the medical implications.'

'Of course. I'll arrange a conversation for some time tomorrow. How was your first day?'

Connie dug in her pocket. 'I found this earring back in the drain of the medical suite. I need you to get it to the police for evidence preservation, but also to double-check if it matches the one still in Tara's ear.' She handed the bag over. 'Other than that, Baarda was nearly sedated and kept in the quiet room for the first twenty-four hours, which would have been a nightmare. It was a struggle to persuade Dr Ong to do otherwise.'

'Yes, I thought that might be an issue but if I'd intervened it would have suggested I had access to better information than he, which would have been a mistake. I tell all my clinical ward heads that they are kings of their own domains. They all have different rules and processes to meet their particular patients' needs. I apologise. I should have warned you.'

'Not a problem. What we really need to figure out is how baby Aurora was removed from the site. How are the police getting on with tracing vehicle movements for the hours in question?'

He put his hands in his pockets and leaned against the wall. Connie could see her own fears mirrored in his eyes. 'We obviously know which registered staff cars left the facility but there are also contractors and visitors. I'm afraid this incident is raising some red flags in terms of security. The mountain pass throws up a lot of mud and debris. We don't use an electronic recognition package for licence plates – budgets don't allow it – so anyone bringing a vehicle onto the site simply fills in a form on arrival with the details. Of course, if the details they've given don't actually match the vehicle . . .' He looked sheepish.

Connie blew out a frustrated breath. She understood that

The Institution was in the middle of nowhere and that security largely took care of itself, but the protocols Le Fay had in place were lacking. 'Are you saying that no one actually checks these things?'

'It's not as if it's a busy city street with limited parking.' He shrugged.

Give me strength, she thought, the effort of keeping her face neutral only just short of Herculean.

'So then what's the procedure if a patient escapes?'

'Our security on the wards and within the buildings is sufficiently tight that we don't worry about the vehicles. I suppose we just never anticipated anyone on the inside being implicated in a security breach. Is there any other information that would help?' Le Fay asked.

'Staff files,' she said. 'All the ward staff are suspects. I'd like to find out more about them. If I ask too many direct questions it'll seem suspicious.'

'The police have applied for emergency court orders for the information to be released. You understand that I can't breach data protection rules until then.'

Connie folded her arms. 'A baby is missing and a woman is dead, Director. Release the information to me. We'll get the court order. No one ever needs to know the chronology.'

'I'm aware of the circumstances, Dr Woolwine.' It was the first time he'd spoken sharply to her. Connie watched as he wrung his hands, noting the smallest shake as he fought to control them. He was facing a monumental investigation into The Institution's practices once baby Aurora was found – dead or alive – and the stress was starting to manifest. 'But I cannot be seen to have acted with anything but absolute professionalism.'

'Absolute professionalism is doing whatever it takes to

prevent another life from being lost. But you must do whatever you can live with,' Connie said, trying to keep the frustration and contempt from her voice.

He nodded. 'I'll be going then.' Le Fay moved to the door, put his hand on the handle, then stopped. 'I'm not a medical man, you know.' He addressed his comments to the floor. 'When I saw Nurse Cameron's body it was . . . I couldn't process it. I'm an administrator, you see? I deal in procedures and rules.' He paused for Connie to give him something in return. She chose to remain silent. 'This may be a hospital environment, but really it's about containment. I've never actually seen a body before, let alone . . .' His breath caught in his throat, and for a moment Connie was reminded of Boy, of the sense of being small and lost and out of your depth. 'It was like someone snapped her in two.'

Connie walked up behind him and gently put her hand over his on the doorknob.

'You're in shock,' she said, her voice quiet now. 'We can't prepare ourselves for this. Not medics, not police officers, not pathologists. What we do is learn how to cope afterwards. Mainly that involves us finding someone we can talk to who's removed from the situation, find therapies that allow us time to process – fishing or knitting or photography, whatever's your poison. You reacted fast. You didn't just alert the whole place; you figured out that the baby had to be the priority. While your brain is trying to drag you back into that awful moment, you have to reposition your focus onto the positives.'

'I have no idea how to do that,' he said. The shake in his voice matched the one in his hands.

'All right,' she said. 'You'll need proper counselling later on, but for now just start with this. When the memory of what you saw grips you, I want you to repeat this phrase

84

until you retake control of your mind. "I reacted, I responded, I helped."'

'I'll feel ridiculous,' he said.

'To start with, maybe. But a mantra is not about you thinking about the words each time. It's about your brain performing another function as a reaction, and that will help dull the returning shock. Try it now.'

He sighed. 'I reacted, I responded, I helped. Honestly, I think this may work better with teenagers.'

'No,' Connie said. 'Teenagers' brains work completely differently. Say it again, but this time I want you to focus on what each verb means, on what you did.'

He shut his eyes as he said the words a second time. His voice was stronger, more controlled.

'That's it,' Connie said. 'Every time you have a flashback, you say those words and you don't stop saying them, either out loud or in your head, until you've reset your thoughts. Got it?'

'Got it,' he said. 'Thank you, Dr Woolwine. We're very fortunate that you were able to come.'

'Best reserve judgement until I get results,' she said. 'I'll check in with you again tomorrow evening.'

Tuesday morning came too fast after only three hours' sleep. Connie rose at 6 a.m. hoping that would be early enough to avoid the start of the daytime hustle and bustle so she could poke around as she liked without being observed doing so. There were no porters in reception, no staff on the front desk, only the water dispenser added to the atmosphere with occasional bursts of bubbles. She started in Tower 1, keeping her staff credentials on full display and acting as if she were perfectly entitled to be there – not that any of the few souls she saw bothered challenging her. The wards seemed quiet through their outer doors, the night staff due to end their shifts in an hour or so. The place was cold in spite of the radiators and lack of windows.

As she walked, footsteps echoing, Connie had a sense of being watched. She peered over the banisters on the stairwell, looking up and down, before realising she wasn't expecting to actually see anyone. It was as if The Institution itself, the very bricks and mortar, were following her progress. She shivered. By the time she'd been round all the common staff areas and finished in Tower 3, the place was just starting to come alive.

Director Le Fay wasn't wrong that the internal parts of the hospital were seemingly very secure. It was hard to imagine how any patient could possibly escape without inside help. Prisoner movements in or out of the wards were always accompanied by multiple staff members, including an orderly, as Baarda had been the day before. The alert system was well established. All of which just went to show that in both killing Tara Cameron and moving the baby, nothing had been left to chance. It had to have been planned in terms of equipment, personnel and vehicles. Most importantly, whoever had performed the caesarean had to be able to do so under time pressure. There were limits on the number of people you could draw into a serious conspiracy without information leaking. Two, usually. You might get away with three. More than that was unusual because then you really had to be generating a lot of money to make it worth everyone's risk.

Connie had dressed carefully for the day, choosing cream trousers and a tea rose pink shirt with tiny daisies. Pale pink nail varnish, hair tied back in a ponytail. She couldn't see the colours, of course, but she'd ordered clothes online that featured detailed descriptions and had learned over the years to always wear neutral colours below the waist that would never clash with her choice of shirt or sweater.

It didn't matter to her what colour she wore, but it did matter to other people. Colours were strange things and she had become increasingly aware of them since losing her rainbow spectrum. Some colours were obviously threatening or calming, sexual or Gothic, happy or sombre. But within the better understood social colour codes there were more subtle distinctions that could elicit nuanced responses. Today she was seeing both Professor Saint and Benny Rubio. Saint was from an academic background, and she thought the pastel colours would be a good match for the preppy, understated girls he would have admired from his own time at college as a student, times when he might have been happier than at his career's final, humiliating end. As for Rubio, with his tantrums and his childish manner, she could pass as gentle and motherly in the flowered blouse. Maternal.

It was Dr Roth who met her in the security area of Heaven Ward.

'I'd like to check in with Patient B before I do anything else,' Connie said.

'Not for the next two hours. He's with Dr Ong undergoing psychometric testing.'

'Psychometrics?' Connie couldn't keep the surprise from her voice. Psychometrics were most often used by employers during the recruitment process, to assess suitability for specific types of work, as well as applicants' motivations and values. It was starting to feel like the Heaven Ward staff had no real grasp of just how off-the-scale dangerous and deluded their patients were. 'That's more an outside-world application, surely. What's the relevance?' Connie asked.

'Dr Ong likes to persuade all of his so-called guests that

87

their lives here can still be useful. That might involve encouraging a certain creativity, skills, education, making a contribution to The Institution, taking responsibility for an aspect of life on the ward. All the artwork downstairs was done by patients, for example. Some of the furniture was made on site, not by anyone on this ward, of course. Offer any of these animals a screwdriver and you'd be dead before you could say "Phillips head". So if you're thinking psychometric testing's a waste of fucking time, you would be correct.' Roth took a long sip of coffee as she filled in a time sheet.

'What aspects of ward life are patients allowed to take responsibility for here?' Connie asked.

'Music choices in the common room, but nothing controversial. Wake-up calls, so one patient gets up earlier than the others and is tasked with getting the others up. If they're abusive or unpleasant about it, the privilege is moved to someone else. Choosing the film for movie night, although that's from a pre-set list of options. Games and puzzles is another one, although no one really wants that job. God knows what these animals do with the puzzle pieces when no one's watching.'

Dr Roth stood and reached up to pull a different form from a cupboard. Her sleeve fell backwards, revealing the upper half of a semi-circle of teeth marks on her forearm.

'You've got a biter here?' Connie asked.

'More than one,' Dr Roth said. 'It's just what happens when you take other weapon options away.'

'Which ones bite?'

'Benny Rubio and Harold Haskin. Watch yourself around them. You're seeing the professor this morning?'

'I am,' Connie said. 'Do you think he'll open up to me?'

'Believe me, with the professor, opening up isn't the issue.

88

The problem is shutting him up again. Speak of the devil, that's him in the bottom right screen in the corridor with Tom, and it looks as if he's already refusing to do what he's being asked. He starts that early in the morning and carries on right until he falls asleep. Good luck,' Roth said, an unpleasant edge of fake cheer in her voice. 'Tom'll be through to collect you when he's got the professor settled in the therapy room.'

Dr Roth exited, and Connie took a moment to study the body language of the men on the security monitor. The professor was gesticulating wildly, Tom's arms were folded tightly across his chest, cheeks sucked in, mouth in a slight pout. It was a scene they had no doubt played out hundreds of times. Professor Saint liked to be the dominant force in the room. He needed to be shown respect, craved admiration. That was what had put him in The Institution in the first place. Connie had pored over the trial transcripts, vivid beyond belief, and felt her blood chill in her veins as Gregor Saint's only surviving victim described his ordeal.

Chapter 9

GREGOR SAINT

The university was sufficiently prestigious that obtaining an academic position within its hallowed walls was the beginning of an extraordinarily stressful existence. One had to publish regularly in only the most respected of periodicals. One's students had to obtain top grades. There should be no scandal or drama within the faculty. Places on the course should be not only highly desirable but also actively fought over. And there should be an air of the mystical about the professors. Untouchable. Beyond mere mortals.

Earlier in his career, that catalogue of requirements had been easier to achieve. Since the 1990s, though, academics had inched round ever-decreasing circles into a less hallowed existence. Professor Saint blamed the tidal wave of smartphones that had overrun his college. At first it had been just a handful of students, those with wealthier parents and no student loan, flashing them around like a newly engaged woman with her diamond solitaire. Professor Saint had completely ignored the dreadful items at first. Then, like a virus, they had begun to spread throughout the student body. Worse, his fellow faculty members now peered into their tiny screens at any given opportunity. Gone was the collegiate chat over coffee. The sharing of articles, jokes about competitor colleges, all fallen prey to a handful of metal, plastic and glass.

He hated them so.

His policy was to exclude from his lectures any student seen with one in their hand or out on the desk, until the university told him to leave it alone. Most students were too scared of him to actively use the things when he was speaking, but now and then he would see them passing a mobile between themselves and smirking, deadening a few more precious brain cells with a cat video or a teenager swallowing some inadvisable object as part of a dare.

The professor thought it had bothered him at the beginning. He'd considered his anger to be fairly high on a score of one to ten. Then came the new appraisal format. In an app. In a 'click here, smiley face or frown, move the sliding scale' app. After all his years – his decades – of study and dedication and reading and writing and expertise, now his pupils could sum up his efforts and effectiveness as a teacher in an app. In real fucking time. During his lectures. They could give feedback, those imbecilic, immature, unkempt, uncouth morons, even as he tried in vain to educate them.

It was worse when he actually tried to see what all the fuss was about. There were photos of him with words on, videos that looped, all designed to portray him at his worst, delivered with mockery as the sole aim. In what universe did students think so little of their teachers that they behaved in so disgusting a way? He found it hard to recognise the world around him. Twice he was reported for swiping mobile phones from a student's hands, and forced to apologise. He was even expected

91

to pay the repair bills for the smashed screens, adding insult to injury.

Gregor Saint began wearing dark glasses and a hat through lectures. See how hilarious their videos were now his face couldn't be seen. Matters had come to a head when some idiot had forgotten to put their phone on silent during a lecture, and their chosen ring tone was the sound of a toddler having a meltdown. There was a moment of shocked silence, then one by one every student in the class had begun to giggle, which had become out-loud laughter, and finally something close to hysteria as the professor had stood there growing more purple by the second.

Eventually he had thrown a chair in the direction of the offending noise, and screamed at every single person in the room that they would all be failing his course. By the end of the day, every last one of them had put in a complaint about his behaviour. They had used their smartphones to do so, of course. There was an app the university had developed to allow them to do exactly that.

Professor Saint was given an official warning and put on professional probation that Friday afternoon. No one died until the following Monday, and he maintained in court that waiting a whole weekend without ending any of his students' lives showed just how remarkable his restraint was, in all the circumstances.

Later, fellow faculty members would say that Professor Saint had seemed unusually chipper in the coffee room that morning, compared to his mood over the previous several months. Rumour had gone around about the disciplinary proceedings and everyone had been expecting the worst, so it was with some relief that he had seemed resolved to do better, and was entirely pleasant and relaxed on the Monday.

Saint was seen walking to his rooms, newspaper under one arm, coffee in hand, smiling and greeting passers-by with an upbeat 'good morning'. One faculty member said afterwards they should all have known straight away that something was wrong. No one had ever seen him quite so happy.

He had killed his first victim by 10 a.m. A second by noon. A third around 3 p.m. The last of that day by 6 p.m. None of them lived in dorms, which meant housemates just assumed each had stayed late at the library, gone to a boyfriend or girlfriend's house, or had just gone out partying. Two of them were reported missing the next day, but it took another two days for police to find out that they'd been called in for a special meeting with the professor before going missing. Two other students had been reported as absent by then. All far too late to save not only them, but also the other six students Professor Saint had slaughtered over the Tuesday and Wednesday.

Only one survived to tell the tale. He made it as far as the courtroom where he gave evidence, lived to see Professor Saint deemed to be so mentally ill as to lack the capacity for a criminal conviction, whereupon he decided that stepping in front of a train was a better option than reliving the nightmare in his dreams every night. At trial, as Victim J gave his evidence, one by one the members of the public in the gallery exited rather than live his trauma through his words.

'The professor had put a note in my pigeonhole, where I picked up my post. It was typed and photocopied, but it had two areas where there was handwriting. The first was my name and the second was the time I was supposed to see him. That's why I figured it was nothing out of the ordinary, you know? There had to be loads of other people seeing him too. The heading on the note said it was a meeting for anyone with less than a fifty-five-per-cent grade on his course. I figured it would be a bit of a telling-off, some extra work, maybe some additional classes.'

J was two minutes early. Better that than late. As much as they all laughed at Professor Saint, J wasn't stupid enough to wind the old man up unnecessarily. He waited until 12.30 p.m. on the dot then knocked.

'Come,' Professor Saint called through the closed door. J gave a final, silent sigh and pushed the door handle down.

The professor was sitting at his desk in a window bay with a red pen in hand, hovering above a stack of papers. Every other teacher in the university was more than happy to accept coursework by email. Professor Saint preferred the old-fashioned method, and J had always suspected that was for the simple reason that he could plaster grades in large letters designed to be visible to everyone as they were handed back through the rows of seating.

Victim J stood, back to the door, waiting for the professor to be ready for him. The clock on the wall ticked through three excruciating minutes.

'Phone in the basket next to the door. No distractions. Then take a seat,' he was instructed.

He chose an ageing leather couch, knees pressed uncomfortably close to a large walnut coffee table upon which sat his last essay. There was no mark on it, as yet, nor any of the professor's usual scrawl and cutting comments.

'We should discuss your work,' Professor Saint said, standing and walking to the door that led into the corridor. The key grated as it turned in the lock. 'I dislike being disturbed,' he explained.

Victim J wanted to look back at the clock but didn't dare. The professor seemed to have an arachnid's array of eyes, always aware when someone in his class was chatting or looking at their phone.

'This essay does not, I fear, reach the standards of which you are capable. I am prepared to give you an opportunity to rewrite it before I mark it, if you can show me today that you have a reasonable understanding of the subject matter.'

'Yes, of course, and sorry. I mean, sorry about the essay. I did do the research and all the reading you set,' Victim J stuttered.

'I'm sure you did. I'm making myself accessible to you today to prove that I can be reasonable about such things. That was part of your complaint about me, I believe, in the student feedback you submitted.'

'Er, I'm not sure I remember. I . . . I definitely didn't mean to be rude.'

Victim J tried to get to his feet but the coffee table was in the way. Before he could slide out along the sofa, he felt a hand on his shoulder, patting gently.

'No, no. You don't need to get up. I'm not in the slightest bit put out. Feedback is good, no? It allows us to strive to be better. And you were only answering the questions the university asked you, after all.'

Victim J was glad when the professor took his long, bony fingers from his shoulder. The room was cold and a slight breeze was ruffling the papers on the coffee table. It made no sense, being November, and a colder than normal autumn at that. The professor was always moaning about the temperature in the lecture hall, and rarely appeared without a scarf and gloves.

'Let us begin with you reading your essay out loud. If you have not tried this method of self-critique before, I believe you will find it most helpful. It is easier to spot typographical errors, sentences that ramble, paragraphs that have no coherent structure. Here, take my pen.' The professor handed J his beloved red pen. 'As you read, I would like to see you mark your pages. If you yourself can identify the areas of weakness then I can be sure you have the potential for improvement. Do begin.'

Victim J picked up the paper and tried to keep the tremble from his fingers. It wasn't a terrible essay but it certainly hadn't been one of his best. He'd rushed the reading, probably not given any studies that week his full attention. Girlfriend problems had been sapping his energy, not that he could explain that to Professor Saint.

He tried to read the title but all that came out was a soft croaking noise. He coughed, tried again. Still nothing.

'Could I get some water, please?' he asked, turning to look at the professor who was standing behind the couch reading over his shoulder.

The professor sighed and glanced at the clock.

'Yes, but then we have to get on.' He went to a side table and poured a glass of water from a jug.

Victim J took a few gulps, cleared his throat once more, then began.

'To what extent do the limits of our own personal experiences define our understanding and application of philosophical arguments in the context of social class and education? The question is really an answer. We are all inevitably—'

The blow came from behind. There was no noise at all beforehand. No warning, no grunt of effort from Professor Saint. No movement of air in the millionth of a second before the chair leg hit him. The force of it took his upper body into the air, his legs pinned into place by the coffee table that suddenly seemed to have been placed there strategically.

J landed face first on the walnut wood. There was a moment

when he was concerned that he had knocked over his glass of water, followed immediately by the knowledge that he was going to die. That the professor had only invited him there to deliver the blow, and that more would follow. There wasn't any pain in his head at that stage, but there was an understanding that if he survived long enough, pain would come. Footsteps, muffled by the rush of blood in his ears, coming his way. A voice, the professor's, although he couldn't make out the words. Then a knocking sound.

At the door.

Victim J opened his mouth to speak, but the only issue was a bubbling stream of blood and bile. Knocking again followed by a voice, female, insistent.

'One moment please!' Professor Saint called breezily.

Victim J was aware of being pulled by the arms. His head hit the floor heavily and the rest of his body followed suit. After that, there was just a red-brown blur of movement, a door opening, then he was being hauled by the torso, lifted, dumped. But what flooded his senses was neither pain nor panic. It was the smell.

Growing up in a small town, his family had relied not on vast supermarkets but on local traders. Twice a week, a van would turn onto the high street and two white-suited men would jump out, nets over their hair, thick gloves on their hands. From the back of that van they would bring the carcasses of animals destined for the butcher's block and dinner tables. He'd forgotten the scent of cold blood until that moment. The coppery, meaty tang of mammal flesh.

For a second it was comforting. His mother was holding his hand as they passed the butcher's van, telling him not to look, reassuring him that it was all right, they would be past it in just a moment. In his final moment of consciousness, he felt his body roll and came to land with his face resting against something warm, soft. His last thought was that it had to be his mother's hair, and that – thank God – he was home with her, and safe.

As Victim J was sinking deeper into the gloom of swollen-brain sleep, the professor was wiping the blood spatters from the leather with a towel and throwing the chair leg, screws, bolts and all, into a closet. A minute later, a university administrator was asking Professor Saint if he had seen two students in particular who hadn't returned to their accommodation for more than twenty-four hours. Alarm bells had started to ring. The police were involved. Parents and guardians were on their way.

Professor Saint expressed concern then sympathy, explained that one of the students had attended an academic counselling session with him the day before but left perfectly happily with mention of meeting a group of friends at a bar, he forgot which one. The other girl hadn't turned up at all, and he had been intending to ask about her absence at the next lecture. He wondered if he could do anything to help. He suggested student hangouts known to him. He had noticed, he said, that the second of the two girls had seemed unhappy recently, flaky, accompanied by a sudden downturn in the quality of her work. Perhaps, he hypothesised, the course had become too much for her.

The administrator had shifted from foot to foot, eager to be out of Professor Saint's cold room, notes of their conversation scribbled onto a notebook in a pencil that could have stood some sharpening. There was a shard of glass beneath the professor's table, and she'd thought about mentioning it to the grumpy old bastard, but Professor Saint had made a complaint about her last year regarding the length of her skirts, so she kept quiet about the broken glass. If he cut himself on it, she figured, he probably wouldn't even bleed. For that you needed a beating heart.

On her way out of the professor's door, her smartphone beeped. She read the text, aware of the professor's hatred of mobile technology, and her heart sank.

'I'm sorry, Professor Saint,' she said. 'I know you're busy, but the police have just arrived and they're asking to see all members of the faculty in the coffee room to try piecing together a timeline of sightings.'

'It's really not convenient,' he snapped. 'I've told you all I know. Are you not capable of simply passing that information on?'

She took a deep breath and did her best to arrange her lips into the shape of a polite smile.

'The request hasn't come from anyone within the faculty,' she said. 'It's the police who have asked us all to attend. I'm not sure I have the authority to say you don't need to be there. Perhaps you could just come down, explain that it's inconvenient, and arrange to speak with them once you've finished your—'

She let the word hang, and the professor didn't feel the need to fill the space with any sort of explanation.

Professor Saint exhaled noisily.

'Well, all right, but it really is most inconvenient. I'll be right down. Let them know I haven't long to spare.'

The administrator didn't need to be dismissed twice, and she hurried along the corridor as quickly as she possibly could. Saint took his keys, locked the internal cupboard door behind which Victim J was lying, slowly dying, grabbed his coat and made his way out.

Victim J dreamed of mud, of quicksand, of being buried alive. It was thirst that woke him and a sense that someone was hitting his skull with an ice pick from the inside in a desperate attempt to get out.

As he opened his eyes in the near dark, his train of thought was this:

Oh my God, my head hurts. There's Olivia! What's she doing lying next to me? What's that smell? Oh Jesus, I'm going to vomit. (Brief pause for vomiting.) *I can't breathe. I have to get up. Why can't I? What's wrong with my legs?* (Reaches out one slow, aching hand to touch Olivia's face.) *Why won't she wake up? What happened? Oh fuck. Oh fuck he hit me. Where am I? Why can't I get up? What am I lying on? Help me, help me, help me. I have to get up. I'm going to die. I don't want to die. I don't want to die here. He killed Olivia. What am I lying on?* (A moment of silence, even inside his head, as he reached around to figure what the intermittently soft then hard mattress comprised.) *Fuck, oh fuck, not just Olivia. Shit, shit, shit.* (He reached out shaking fingers to feel all around and found himself to be lying on the back of another male student. There was someone with long braided hair lying halfway across Olivia, and a pair of boots sticking out crossways under both of them. Ahead, he could feel a hand but couldn't crawl closer to figure out who it belonged to. And there were more. A pile of bodies.) *Got to get up, got to get up, got to get up. Light switch, door, shout for help.*

But what if he was still out there? What if the professor was just waiting for him to try exactly that? Didn't matter. If he stayed in that room he was dead. If he opened the door and found the professor standing right there, he was dead.

Victim J took a deep breath, pushed himself up onto his elbows then began hauling his body across the corpses to the

100

door. The two metres he had to travel might have been two hundred. With each movement came a new discovery. Someone else's hand, foot, face. A shoe. A wallet. Someone had lost control of their bowels in the moments between suffering a blow and their brain quitting its functions. Victim J turned his face away and tried not to breathe through his nose.

He had no plan as he reached for the door handle. It seemed unlikely that he would be able to form the words required to beg for his life. There was no noise from beyond the door, but more than anything he hoped he wouldn't interrupt another student session and have to bear witness to someone else being slaughtered. And if the professor was standing there, waiting patiently to mock his desperate attempt to survive, he would just close the door quietly, lie back down and hope it would be over quickly.

Victim J turned the doorknob as slowly, as quietly as he could manage. It moved, a centimetre at a time, tantalisingly free, until it didn't. He tried it again. And again. By then he didn't care if the professor heard him. What did it matter? He was out of choices. He rattled it, thumped on the door. Tried to scream.

No one heard. No one came. Not even the professor.

His strength was failing and the head wound had opened up a little wider. Blood was trickling down into his eyes and finding tiny pathways to the corners of his mouth. Sooner or later he would have to deal with the professor's return.

Taking several deep breaths, J pushed himself up as high as he could with his useless legs – the cause of that didn't bear thinking about but either it was brain damage or a spinal injury – and felt the wall near the door handle for a light switch. It took two or three passes but then his fingers caught the edge of the plastic square. His heart leapt. He lit up the room.

And immediately wished he hadn't. The faces he had only barely been able to make out in the charcoal gloom were twisted declarations of agony now. There was a guy he'd shared a dorm with in his first year. He'd moved out pretty early on to find somewhere quieter to live, but he was nice enough. There was a girl no one had really liked. They'd all assumed she thought she was better than the rest of them. Now he wished he'd made time to find out why she seemed so cold and distant. Below her was an athlete, a young man who had undoubtedly been headed for greatness in one sport or another. Others he only recognised in passing.

But in the corner. Upright, against the join of the walls, was Lucy. Lucy who had made his knees weak with her smile because she had no idea how cute she was. Lucy to whom he'd sent an anonymous Valentine's card like some stupid fourteen-year-old, not because he thought she'd reject him if he asked her out, but because he wanted to wait. Not to have an idiotic college fling. Not to waste their words and their moments too soon. Because he thought that maybe he'd met the girl he wanted to marry one day. Lucy with a tiny tattoo of a bumblebee on her left shoulder that seemed to fly in and out of her T-shirt sleeve as she walked along, swinging her bag. Sometimes she sang to herself as she walked. He didn't think she was even aware of it.

Lucy had survived a while too. They had that, among numerous other things, in common. She had decided not to die lying down but sat up where a waterfall of crimson had cascaded over her shoulders and down the wall. Finally, she had reached up to leave one perfect handprint in blood next to her face.

Victim J tore his eyes from hers and looked around the room instead. There was nothing but bodies. No furniture from which to fashion a weapon. No hidden door. No shuttered window. And inevitably, infuriatingly, no phones in pockets. The professor had taken care of that as soon as his students had walked through the door.

He would be back, of course. Without being able to run, or even walk, and certainly not to fight, Victim J had to make a different choice. He needed to make himself invisible.

If Professor Saint looked really hard, took his pulse, opened his eyes, he would know immediately that he was faking; but playing dead was his only option and life suddenly seemed very precious indeed.

He reached a decision that felt simultaneously like cowardice and bravery, then he switched the light off once more. Victim J pulled himself back over the mound of corpses. He let his legs tumble behind him and did his best to control the roll. Then he manoeuvred himself sideways, grabbed the body closest to him, and pulled it on top of his torso. He made sure he could breathe, but kept his face hidden – that being the most likely giveaway if the professor came calling.

There he lay for one day more. At one point the door opened then closed again, but Victim J had no sense of time. He had either slept or fallen unconscious, waking briefly and crying, hoping he hadn't been overheard. The sadness of it all, the hopelessness, had returned and drowned him again.

At some point one new weight was added to the pile. Victim J had lain there waiting for movement, for a voice, a sign that this new victim had life in them yet, only to be disappointed.

When the police finally broke down the professor's door more than twenty-four hours later, Professor Gregor Saint was stretched out on the couch rereading a book he had written a decade earlier that was still – in his humble opinion – the definitive work in its field. The stink of decaying human flesh was so noticeable that it was a wonder the whole building hadn't complained about it.

They found all the mobile phones smashed to pieces in his desk drawer. The weapon, a vicious old rusty metal-and-wood chair leg, boasted the blood of every single victim. The bodies went untouched until they had been photographed from every angle.

Until, at the far end of the heap, in the darkest corner, a little finger could be seen twitching. A detective, a man hardened from years on the homicide squad, had screamed and cried before getting his shit together and racing in to uncover the still-living victim.

Alive, but not doing well. Desperately dehydrated, almost entirely unresponsive, covered in both his own blood and that of the people beneath whom he'd hidden. Head wound so cavernous you could see a shard of white skull in its depths.

An air ambulance had been called to take him to the nearest head trauma specialty unit. No one had expected him to survive the journey. Then no one expected him to survive the night. It was against the odds that he ever walked again, and yet he did. He survived it all.

Except the trial.

Where Professor Gregor Saint had sat and laughed and laughed and laughed.

By the time Connie had shaken herself from her recollection of the witness testimony, Professor Gregor Saint was waiting for Connie in the therapy room. It was furnished simply with two chairs and a small table between them. She had the emergency keys on her belt and her electronic key tucked in her pocket. No mobile phone hidden on her today, not when she was in such close proximity to the patients – especially this one.

He sat straight-backed pulling at the trousers of his daywear as if trying to make a sharp crease. Connie knocked and waited in the doorway.

'How quaint. We're starting with the pretence that I have the ability to invite you in or not, are we?'

'No,' Connie said. 'We're starting with politeness. It's how I was brought up and it's a hard habit to break. Would you rather I didn't bother?'

'Very clever,' the professor said. 'Appeal to my better-educated nature. You've read my file, then.'

'I read the court transcript. Do you deny any of it?' Connie sat down and watched as he shifted in his chair to face her more directly, his arms loosely crossed below the elbows and resting on his knees. No signs of stress. Dr Roth was right. He was enjoying the opportunity to talk.

'I deny that I'm a serial killer. Puerile label. I broke, that's all. Many people do in high-end professions.'

'But when you broke, you manifested your psychological symptoms by killing. That doesn't happen very often,' Connie said.

'Doesn't change the fact that I simply snapped. Not so much as a parking ticket before that, Doctor. Not a foot out of line. I snapped. I've healed. They say I'm still dangerous. What do you think?'

'Is this a test?' Connie asked. 'I think you like testing people. I think you like to assure yourself that no one else can match your intellectual standards.'

He gave a slight laugh, turning his head to one side as he did so, an affectation learned at soirees and academic dinners, the raised head was condescension, the side turn was dismissiveness.

Connie sat and waited for his answer. A few seconds later he shrugged and looked back at her.

'Where did you study?' he asked.

'Why does it matter?'

'Because it marks you. It tells me how hard you worked to get where you are. That matters.' He frowned and began picking at his trousers again.

Connie leaned forward to meet his intense gaze.

'So you're not a serial killer,' she mused. 'But spree killers are usually randomised. Unplanned, to a large extent. Your episode – shall we call it that?' The professor nodded. 'Your episode was planned to the minute. You spent a weekend with your calendar, sending out invitations to particular students, staggering times, making sure you could clean up between them, clearing your diary of all other matters. There was a suggestion you chose victims who didn't appear to socialise in the same groups so they weren't waiting to talk to one another about the session you'd invited them to.'

He gave a watery smile and flicked his fingers at her to continue.

'You believe you're not a serial killer because you were able to identify a moment when your life changed and you feel that your actions were beyond your control,' she said.

'Beyond my control? No, Doctor. I was clearly in control of my actions. But it was a version of me who existed then only, in that period. I had lost everything that was meaningful to me. Smartphones did that to me. Apps. Wi-Fi.' He extended the two syllables like a pantomime villain. 'Technology is a curse. Surely you understand that much at least?'

'In the wrong hands, certainly. But the people you killed

were little more than teenagers. We know, at that age, that self-control is a difficult thing to achieve. We understand the temptation to explore, to find distractions, to communicate endlessly as a way to self-validate.'

'Did you pause to ask yourself about the people I chose to spare?' Connie marked the phrase 'chose to spare' in her mind. 'Even in my darkest moment, I did not behave in a way that was entirely unconscionable. There were students in my class who did not consult their mobile devices during my lectures. Students who worked consistently hard. Who turned up punctually and appreciated the education to which they had been given access.'

'How do you feel about yourself for leaving those people alive?' Connie asked.

'Are we really still doing psychology 101? I'm disappointed.'

'You feel disappointed for letting people live?'

'Stop being silly. You know that's not what I meant. I'm disappointed in you for asking such an asinine question,' he said. Again with the raised chin, head turned off to the side.

'All right, no more silliness,' Connie said. 'I'm asking because it seems to me to be important where your focus was. Was it on rewarding students you perceived as deserving of life, or on punishing those you felt did not?'

The professor's eyes drifted off to the right as he considered it, and Connie watched his feet, which had turned in and rolled onto their outer edges. Confident toes that had been pointed straight for her now touching, protecting each other, forming a circle in which he sat. It was the first time she'd asked him a question he hadn't prepared for.

'Neither,' he said. 'I was thinking about myself in those last three days. How I felt. What I needed. I believed that it was them or me. If I hadn't killed those students the only alternative would have been to take my own life.'

His tone was deflated, earthy. Real.

'And when you were stopped, when the police caught you, how did you feel then?'

'They came sooner than I would have liked,' he told her. 'I had a few names left on my list.'

'What about during the killings? How did you feel in the moment that you took a life?'

He shook his head. 'As I told the police, I have no recollection of any of it. I just carried out the plans I made. It's as if someone else wielded the weapon.' He raised his eyebrows. It was a challenge.

'Is that the best you can do?' Connie asked.

One tiny section of the professor's upper lip flickered upwards in a snarl before he got control of himself. 'Relevance?'

'A spree killer might not remember individual moments, each death. They might have switched into an entirely different mode. But you waited between victims. Overnight, even. You hid the bodies. Reset your scene. Opened windows even though it was late autumn, to get rid of the smell of the decomposing bodies. So I don't accept that you have no recollection of how it felt to kill. Your hand wrapped around that old chair leg, you took aim knowing how it would sound, the damage it would do, how each body would crumple and fall. You did it over and over again. It's not really possible for you to have no conscious recollection with periods of complete lucidity and routine in between. I don't care if they accepted it at trial. I don't.'

'And I don't care what you think,' he retorted, nose elevated as he peered down at her.

'Yes, you do,' Connie answered. 'You care what people think of you more than anything else in the world. That's why every single one of the students you killed was selected: because they each gave you the lowest possible score on the teaching evaluations. I'm curious, how did you find out who'd given you the low evaluation scores? That information is usually provided anonymously.'

'Not quite. The university has to verify that the feedback is coming from registered students and that they are actually enrolled on the course they're commenting on. The faculty is, of course, supposed to treat the identification securely, but our administrator was less than careful with her password and she never attended work at the weekends.'

'So you actively pursued the information? That took some time and effort, risk too, using someone else's computer and inputting their password. That sounds very organised, and not at all like someone suffering from a serious mental illness.'

He crossed his arms more tightly, wrapping them hard around him like armour.

'You won't goad me,' he said, his voice dropping in pitch and volume. More like his one surviving victim had described it.

Connie stayed very still. She didn't want to break the moment. In spite of his insistence that he couldn't be manipulated into disclosures, she got the feeling that Saint was desperate to talk. Perhaps there was still something she could learn from him. 'Why is it goading you, to present you with the truth?'

He took several breaths, faster and faster, then stood abruptly. 'We're done,' he said. 'I'd thought it might be interesting, entertaining, to speak with you, but now I see you're just as much of a hack as the rest of the idiots here.'

'What's it like living here?' Connie asked, ignoring his outburst. 'How do you find the staff, for example? Are they kind, interested in you, easy to approach?'

His eyelids lowered over his eyeballs, leaving them at half-mast. He reminded Connie of a crocodile – watchful, patient, yet impossible to escape from once they had their jaws around you.

'Why are you here?' the professor asked. 'Why now?'

She kept her face relaxed, made casual eye contact with him, made sure the lie didn't show. 'To help a military man adjust into a different stage of his life. That's my responsibility, so I'd like to know what he can expect from the staff on this ward.'

'You're bright enough to assess the staff members here yourself. Why ask a murderer with a psychiatric condition?'

'Staff behave differently behind closed doors than they do around fellow team members. I'm asking for your impressions, your experiences of how you've been treated. How you've seen other patients treated. Is there any abuse?'

Professor Saint took a slow, deliberately audible intake of breath.

'Oh, Dr Connie, now there's a question. Is there any abuse? Where to start.' His anger was nowhere to be seen, now. Like any genuine narcissist, asking his considered opinion on anything beyond his own faults was an easy distraction. 'No one here is truly sane. Who comes to work in a place like this? We are, I am told quite regularly, the dregs of society. People so awful we don't even belong in a regular prison. My defence counsel told me this would be preferable to normal incarceration. I was persuaded to comply with psychiatric reports. Now here I am, no real hope of ever leaving, miles from civilisation. This is no-man's-land, Doctor. Tell me, how much money would it take to persuade you to leave whatever job you do now and come here to practise psychotherapy full-time? Twice your current salary? Three times as much? Four? Five?'

Footsteps now, in the corridor. Someone coming towards them fast.

'What's your point?' Connie asked quickly, all too aware of the imminent interruption.

'You already have it. No amount of money would persuade you to work here. Tell me I'm wrong.' Connie said nothing. 'The people inside these walls are broken. All of them. It's bad enough being here against your will. Imagine having so little to live for that of all the places in the world, you would choose to spend the precious years allocated to you in this godforsaken place.'

Connie nodded her understanding. 'About the abuse—'

Nurse Madani opened the door and poked her head in. 'Dr Connie, Dr Ong needs you to come. Patient B has been sedated.'

Connie was on her feet in a heartbeat, veins standing out in her neck. 'What the hell happened?' she demanded.

'I'm not sure. He must have become violent. Follow me please.'

'Sorry, Professor. We'll have to pick this up another time,' Connie said, walking quickly to the door.

'Don't believe anything they tell you,' the professor said as she left. 'Remember: truth can be witnessed, but it can never be told.'

Chapter 10

Baarda was in his room, not entirely unconscious but as good as, rolled onto his side in the recovery position, tongue lolling, breathing heavily. His T-shirt was ripped and there was an angry red mark on his cheekbone that would blacken later.

'What happened?' Connie demanded.

'We'd nearly finished our session when Patient B became angry and made physical contact with me. I had no choice but to sound the alarm and ask Tom to sedate him,' Ong said. 'I really am most surprised. He was stable and compliant this morning.'

'What did you give him?' she asked.

'An intramuscular anti-psychotic. It's our standard medication,' Dr Ong said.

'That can cause respiratory side effects,' Connie said. 'I want his vitals electronically monitored.'

'Of course, Nurse Madani will see to that.' The nurse disappeared out of the cell in the direction of the medical room. 'You know, I do wish I'd been warned that Patient B could be so reactive. I haven't been given a trigger list and you suggested yesterday that there were no concerns about his behaviour in incarceration. What I just witnessed was an incredibly scaled-up reaction with no warning signals at all.'

'It's not behaviour that Patient B has ever displayed before,' Connie said. 'Perhaps if you'd called me before ordering sedation, I could have de-escalated the situation. Surely you have a protocol that requires de-escalation efforts prior to sedation. Even the simple use of restraints. Intramuscular medication should be a last resort.'

Dr Ong gave her a concerned look. 'You do understand what we're dealing with here, don't you? These are patients who kill without motive, without notice—'

'How, exactly, did Patient B become violent?' Connie interrupted. 'And how did he sustain that injury if he was being sedated?' She was doing her best to keep her voice level, but a man she knew to be mild-mannered even faced with the most extreme provocation had been assaulted and drugged, which was not what she'd persuaded him to sign up for.

'I asked him if he had any children. He refused to answer. So I asked, if he did have children, how he would feel about the possibility that he might never see them, that given his crimes they might choose to disown him. He became agitated, physically at first, flexing his muscles, making himself look bigger. Then he responded with a barrage of abuse and began squaring up to me. I decided it was an alarm situation when he pushed me back against the wall.'

On his bed, Baarda was starting to groan. Nurse Madani entered, pushing a vital-signs monitor, rolling Baarda onto his back and strapping him to the bed before attaching the equipment.

'Is that when Tom came in?' Connie asked.

Dr Ong looked across to Tom who stepped forward, nodding.

'That's right. It was lucky Dr Ong was close to an alarm button. I assessed the situation as posing a direct threat to safety and security. When I asked Patient B to comply and allow a sedative to be administered he turned on me, which was when I defended myself and threw a punch. I had no options left. When Patient B went down, I immediately pushed the syringe into his thigh.'

'I see,' Connie said. 'Well, now that Patient B is restrained by straps the sedative is no longer required. I'd like an antidote to be administered so that I can assess his state of mind.'

'Can't be done, I'm afraid. He'll need close monitoring for the next four hours as it's the first time he's been given these meds here, and that monitoring requires patients to remain sedated so that they don't grab any of the medical equipment and harm themselves or anyone else,' Dr Ong said.

Tom Lord was smirking and Dr Ong was hiding behind policy. Most of all, Connie was unsettled by the sense that, at that moment, the person who had been most truthful with her on the ward was Professor Gregor Saint. *This stinks,* she thought.

She looked at her watch. 'Four hours,' she said. 'I'm due to interview Benny Rubio shortly. I'll go ahead with that as Patient B is to remain sedated, then I'll come back here to offer psycho-therapy once Patient B is fully conscious. I'm going to have to insist that he is not given any further medication until I've had an opportunity to conduct a full examination.'

'Nurse Madani will be checking on him regularly in the meantime,' Dr Ong said. 'I think in light of this behaviour I'll need greater access to this guest's offender information. I really can't manage this level of threat to my staff without being given full disclosure.'

'I'll request it,' Connie said. 'Bear with me. As ever with

military documentation, there will need to be redaction of sensitive information.'

'Of course,' Ong said. 'Tom, could you take Dr Connie to see Benny Rubio, please? And remain in the room with her. Mr Rubio is still on probation after his episode.'

'That won't be necessary. I'm well versed in self-defence and patient restraint techniques.'

Tom laughed out loud.

'Tom, please, that's rude,' Ong said. 'I appreciate the sentiment. I encourage all my staff to have an equally go-getting attitude, but Mr Rubio is often delusional. He can't be reasoned or negotiated with, and his track record is not pleasant when it comes to young women. I'm going to insist that you're accompanied by an orderly when with him.'

'So be it,' Connie said matter-of-factly. She knew she had to pick her battles. 'I'd obviously rather be safe than sorry.' She took one more look at Baarda as Nurse Madani made notes on a medical chart. As much as she hated to leave him, it was a waste of her time to sit and wait for him to regain consciousness. They'd known the risks when they'd agreed to take the case, and that meant putting Aurora first. 'Let's go.'

Tom escorted her back to the same therapy room where she'd seen Professor Saint, then disappeared to fetch Rubio.

Her approach to Benny Rubio would have to be substantially different to that she'd taken with the professor. Connie had already observed him being childlike and temperamental. Normally with a patient like that, she thought, a therapist would spend anything up to a month establishing a relationship, building trust, finding out his preferred language, testing a number of varied methods of communication. Here and now, it had to be fast-forwarded, and there was really only one way to do that, as much as she disliked the idea of it. With Tom in the room, the questions she could ask would be severely restricted; certainly she wouldn't be able to go into details about his treatment on the ward or his thoughts on staff members.

He appeared in the ward's standard T-shirt and loose jogging bottoms, but those were markedly bulging around his groin and backside. Tom noticed her quizzical look and explained before she could ask the question.

'He's wearing a nappy. You have good days and bad days, don't you, Benny-boy. Sometimes he just can't control himself; other times if he gets mad he'll just piss himself – or worse – so the nappy is necessary.'

'I can be naughty sometimes.' Rubio grinned. 'You're pretty. Yesterday your hair didn't look so pretty, but I like it today. Can I touch it?'

'You know you can't,' Tom told him, his voice sharp. 'Don't start with that or I'll take you back to your cell.'

Rubio stuck out his bottom lip and infused his voice with an extra whine. 'Not going back to my cell. I like the lady. I don't like you. You're mean.'

'I'm not in the mood, Benny,' Tom said, weary now. 'Sit still, listen and answer her questions. Last warning.'

Rubio pulled a face for half a second then turned his attention to Connie, sitting up straight, hands in his lap, adopting what he clearly thought was an angelic expression.

'What shall we talk about?' he asked her.

'I'd like to try something to make it easier for you to answer my questions, something to help you remember clearly without getting distressed or worrying about whether or not you're giving me the answers I'm looking for.' She kept her voice light and upbeat, as if she were trying to persuade a child, meeting Benny on his chosen ground. 'How would you feel about that?'

'Something new? Will it be fun? Will I get a prize?'

'I'm not allowed to give you any prizes, I'm afraid, but you might find it helps you relax. It should certainly help me understand you better, and I'd like to understand you, Benny. It must be hard to feel like no one here really knows what you've been through.'

'Sorry, but I can't have you suggesting that no one else here cares about—'

'Please don't interrupt,' Connie told Tom. 'I need silence.'

Tom Lord huffed but accepted the rebuke.

'Benny, have you ever tried hypnotherapy?' Connie asked.

'Like when you make people think they're a chicken or do funny dancing?'

'It's not really like that,' Connie said. 'With hypnotherapy you don't lose control of yourself at all. It's about putting you into a state that's so relaxed you can remember things more easily, talk about things that have happened without getting upset. When you come out of it, you'll remember it all. There are no tricks here. I'm not allowed to do this without your consent.'

He frowned. 'Will it hurt?'

Connie studied him. His facial expressions were exaggerated, bordering on the ridiculous. He spoke as if he were a child, yet he was quick enough to respond when he stood to lose a privilege. In the real world young children often took a lot more persuading. Benny Rubio was playing a part, without a doubt, and what she needed to figure out was how deep it went.

'None of it will hurt, but I'll be asking about the things you did that put you here.'

117

'Why can't you just ask me?' He folded his arms.

'I could, but I'd like to see it through your eyes as it happened. Is there a reason you don't want me to do that?'

He gave an exaggerated shrug. 'No reason. I told the police everything over and over and over. I never lied.'

'I'm sure you didn't,' Connie said. 'But sometimes our memories are clouded by the need to find the right words, or by people asking the wrong questions. Shall we try? If you get upset or you don't like it, you can tell me and we'll stop.'

Chapter 11

'Lean back in the chair,' Connie told him. 'Make sure your arms, head and neck are comfortable. You want to be entirely relaxed. When you're ready and your body is free of tension, I'd like you to close your eyes and concentrate on letting go of stress. Be aware of the top of your head, relax your face . . . your mouth . . . your neck. Remember that this is a safe space. Relax your chest, your arms, your stomach. Let your hands feel heavy, let them anchor you in this safe space.'

'Feels nice,' Rubio murmured.

'That's good,' Connie said, keeping her voice low. 'Relax your stomach, your legs, your feet.'

As she said it, Rubio's feet rolled to an open position and his breathing slowed to a rhythmic almost-snore.

'This is your safe space, Benny. Nothing here can harm you or touch you. You can tell me if you want to stop, or if you feel uncomfortable. Are you safe now, Benny?'

He turned his head a little to the left then a little to the right as if checking his environment.

119

'I am,' he said. 'I do feel safe here.' He gave a smile, his voice less childish now, more like a curious teenager, cautious but willing to give it a try.

'Benny, I want you to imagine that you're in a long corridor. It's wide with ornate columns and high ceilings. There are mirrors on either side, and the lighting is a warm orange glow. You're walking down the corridor thinking how beautiful the architecture is, drawn to the doors at the end. As you get near, the doors begin to open for you, inviting you in. This corridor is a safe space for you, Benny. There is nothing in here that can harm you. There is nothing behind the doors that can harm you. Are you safe, Benny?'

'I am,' he whispered.

'That's really good. You're doing so well. Now approach the first set of doors, walk as slowly as you like, take time to look around if you want. Check how you look in the mirror. Can you see yourself?'

'I can,' he said, his voice breathy, dreamy.

'Well done, Benny. Now keep walking, and see how the first set of doors starts to open as you approach. You don't have to do anything, don't have to touch anything. It's all being done for you. Tell me when you're walking through that set of doors.'

Connie sat quietly and waited. Rubio's hands flexed a little and his knees shifted.

'I'm going through now,' he said. 'I like the sound the doors make as they open.'

'What do those doors look like to you?' Connie asked.

'They're big and wooden, with brass handles. Like in a castle or something.'

'Like in a castle,' Connie repeated. 'You've gone through the number 10 doors and now you're in the next corridor. Just keep walking. Is the light a little dimmer in here, Benny, a more golden colour?'

'It is,' he agreed.

'Good. And when you look in the mirror are you a little younger do you think?'

'I . . . yes, I think I am. It's before they cut my hair when I got here,' he said, sounding surprised.

'But you're still safe, remember? Now walk along this new corridor. There's another set of doors at the end. Like the last ones, these will open as you approach. It's not too far now, not too many more steps. These are the number 9 doors. Go through them, Benny, and keep walking.'

'Okay,' he said.

'Good, Benny. Now the next doors are closer again. You can look around. It's beautiful in here, isn't it? Watch the mirror, see how you look now.'

He smiled, eyes still firmly shut.

'After this the doors will keep getting closer together. I'll count as we go through them. With each set of doors, each corridor, you'll get a little younger. Just a little, but you'll still feel like yourself and you'll still feel safe. Each corridor will be darker than the last, but it's a good darkness, like at the end of the evening when the fire is starting to go out and you're warm and comfortable in front of it, just dozing off to sleep.'

'Sleep is nice,' Rubio said. 'Lovely and warm now.'

'Number 8,' Connie said. 'It's pretty in here. Like a castle.'

'Castle,' he muttered.

'Number 7, 6, 5. We're halfway along the corridor now, Benny, and you feel so safe.'

He wasn't answering now. His mouth was hanging open and he was breathing as if he'd been asleep for hours.

'Through door number 4, a few more steps. The light in

121

here is red, Benny, the crimson glow of the last embers of the fire. Through door number 3. Well done. Just keep going. Number 2. You can see the final doors just ahead of you. This is your very safe place, Benny. You'll be able to see things but they can't touch you and they can't hurt you. Final couple of steps, the doors have opened, you're on the threshold, and you're through.'

Connie snapped her fingers and Rubio's breathing lightened, he shook himself slightly but his eyes remained shut.

'Where am I?' he asked.

'You're in the place where you did the things that the police didn't like, Benny. It's a place that was very important to you.'

'I know this place,' he said, full of wonder. 'I worked hard here. There were lots of things I wanted.'

'This place has all your important things, Benny. Things happened here. Can you tell me about them?'

'It's a lot!' he said, excited now.

'I want to know about the first thing you did that the police wanted to speak to you about. Can you tell me about it?'

'I can but . . . won't you get mad? Everyone else got mad when they found out,' he said, squirming in his seat, agitated.

'Benny,' Connie said. 'It's important that you listen to my voice. My voice tells you that I'm not angry, just curious. I won't get angry with you because you're safe here; this is your safe place. No one can hurt you here. I want you to breathe deeply and feel relaxed again.'

'I can do that,' he said, dropping his shoulders again and settling down.

'When you're ready then, Benny. Tell me everything you see, everything you feel, everything you do. Take your time. You're doing really well.'

'I'm at work,' he says. 'That's why it's so dark in here. There's a film playing but I'm not interested in the movie because I just saw a girl. She's beautiful. Not nasty-looking. Not too much make-up. Her clothes are nice and she has brown leather boots on with a mini-skirt. I like her hair. It looks like she just brushed it. Her perfume smells like summer.'

'What's your job, Benny?' Connie asked.

'I check people's tickets and I show them which row to sit in. Sometimes I have to clear up if they spill their popcorn and I hate that, but I like the cinema, and I like watching the people's faces when they're seeing the films.'

'How old are you, Benny?'

'I'm twenty-four. My dad used to say that was too old to be working in a cinema but I liked it. No one bothered me there.'

'That's good. It was a safe space for you, like this one. You're doing really well. Keep going,' she said.

'I try to talk to her as she leaves. I ask her if she enjoyed the film, but she just sort of smiles and walks away. She's with some other people and they're waving to her like they want her to hurry up.' His voice gets low. He covers his mouth and giggles. 'Her skirt his risen up a bit and it's caught on her tights. I see the top of her thighs from behind. Nearly her . . . you know, her panties.'

'How do you feel when you see that, Benny?'

Benny crossed his legs. 'I feel good but bad. Good but bad. I like it but I know I shouldn't.'

'Are you excited?' Connie asked.

'Uh-huh, that's right. I'm excited. Good but bad, just like before.' Another giggle, hand in front of his mouth.

'Good but bad, like before. Tell me about before, Benny. Tell me when you first felt good but bad. What happened?'

'After my mother died,' he whispered. 'That's when it started.'

'Nothing can hurt you here,' Connie reminded him. 'The memories are just memories but they're not painful in your safe place. How old were you when your mother died?'

A pause. 'Nine. Nine years and one week. She got ill at my birthday party.'

'I see. And how did you first come to have that good but bad feeling after your mother died?'

'They got me a nanny. When my mother died I stopped going to school. I cried and I got cross sometimes. The teachers said horrible things about me. So my father said I could stay at home. There were teachers – different ones on different days. And a nanny the rest of the time. The teachers went home after lessons but the nanny stayed because my father was away working a lot.'

'What was your nanny like?' Connie asked.

'Can't remember,' Benny said, too quickly.

'I think if you try harder you'll be able to,' Connie said. 'Look around now. You'll see something of hers. What is it you can remember? Sometimes there's an article of clothing or a piece of jewellery. Perhaps a song she liked or the way she walked.'

She gave Rubio the space to think about it for a few moments.

'She's here!' he shouted. 'You were right. She's hanging up her coat. It was cream and she always used to tie the belt loop so it circled at the back rather than doing it up at the front. Oh my gosh, she's pretty. She never yells at me. My mother used to have rules for everything, but the nanny tries to make things a game. *She* lets me touch her hair.' His voice was petulant as he said that last part. 'If I cried, she would cuddle me and we would watch TV together under a blanket. Her eyes were brown and they shone when she laughed. She told me a joke over breakfast every day. She would learn one in the evening just to make me laugh. She was so pretty. For a while. Then she wasn't pretty any more.'

'Why not?' Connie asked.

'I don't like this part,' Rubio said. 'It makes me unhappy. Do you want me to be unhappy?'

'No, I don't,' Connie said. 'But you're in a safe space. These are facts, not emotions. It's the past and it can't hurt you. Why wasn't the nanny pretty any more, Benny?'

He sighed deeply, sitting forward to lean his head on his hands, knees balanced on elbows, eyes still shut. 'My father came home.'

'Tell me about that.'

Benjamin Rubio Snr was an important man. He married well when he was a less important man and used his wife, as he used everything he found, to its best advantage. His wife was substantially older than him when they married, a decision he'd made consciously. An older wife meant that her own parents hadn't long to live, which meant an inheritance coming soon. Being of a certain age, she was keen to try for a child as soon as the honeymoon was over. Benjamin Snr had done his duty and implanted a son in his wife's belly to the delight of all involved.

His wife's father had contacts in the business world who helped with positions on various boards, the lending of vacation homes, membership to a private club. And as soon as the boy was born, his wife became obsessed with the child, leaving Benjamin to do as he pleased. The boy, though, was weak. He cried whenever his mother put him down and whenever his father picked him up. He cried when he was tired and when he was put into his cot. He cried to be read to then grabbed the book so no one could read to him if they tried. Benjamin

Snr shrouded himself in work and a professionally inclined social life that excluded his wife, and she wrapped herself in a boy who found her too much and not enough all at once.

When his wife died, Benjamin Snr managed to stay at home for a week then decided that a global tour of all the company pies he had his fingers in was overdue. He left the boy in the care of a nanny with good references who had no family commitments of her own.

Back at home, Benjamin Snr reasserted his authority. The boy needed strict bedtimes and boundaries. He shouldn't be read to at his age. Kisses and cuddles were for babies.

And the nanny – Benny's precious, beloved nanny who he'd had all to himself – didn't even try to tell Benjamin Snr that he was wrong. It was all yes sir and no sir and of course, Mr Rubio. No more blankets and movie nights for Benny.

He hated his father. He hated him a lot. He hated his leather wallet that smelled of cigar smoke, his handmade suits, his crisply pressed shirts, his cufflinks. No, not the cufflinks. He longed to steal pairs of the gold and bejewelled beauties. Which was why he'd been in his father's dressing room one day when his father had marched in, sat on the bed and begun taking his shoes off. Benny hadn't even known his father was in the house, and now he was hiding in a forbidden room, three different pairs of cufflinks heavy in one sweaty palm, too scared to exit for fear of his father's temper.

Instead, he crept backwards into the row of suits, away from the closet doors he'd left ajar, hoping his father would disappear to his study soon. That was when he realised his father wasn't alone in the bedroom.

Not at all.

He was barking commands at someone again, which was all his father ever seemed to do. Only these commands were foreign to him. It was a language Benny had never heard before, new words, grunts, demands. On hands and knees he crept forward to peer out, curiosity stronger than fear. There she was, his perfectly pretty nanny, in positions Benny had never imagined, doing things that made him feel good and bad at the same time. Touching his father in ways Benny was sure his mother never would have done.

She wasn't pretty any more. The nanny was disgusting and ugly and dirty, and all of that made him feel things he'd never wanted to feel but that he already knew he would feel, again and again.

He dashed tears away from his eyes, even as he knew he couldn't possibly stop watching, the edge of his elbow just nudging the door a millimetre wider. His father, sharp as ever, turned to look. Benny didn't know if his father had caught the white of one eye inside the wardrobe door, or heard his breathing, or just sensed he was there, but his grin widened and he did what he was doing with renewed vigour, forcing the nanny into ever more strange and sick gymnastics, seeming to enjoy himself all the more, as Benny watched and hated them and hated himself, and couldn't look away.

Later, when they were done, his father sent the nanny to her rooms and took himself off to his bathroom to shower. Benny crept out.

He put a note on his door saying he had put himself to bed and wanted to be left alone. His father didn't bother him and that was no surprise at all. But the nanny didn't bother him either, and Benny wasn't so sure how he felt about that. Was she sorry for the things she'd done and too ashamed to face him? Was she so obsessed with Benjamin Snr now that little Benny didn't matter at all? Had she even remembered that she was supposed to be putting him to bed at all?

He hadn't slept that night, not that he could remember. He'd sweated through his bedsheets, wished with all his heart that he'd never seen those terrible things, and found his mind constantly reconstructing the image of his nanny's naked body.

The following morning she had knocked gently at his door and tried to open it to find that Benny had pushed a chair in front of it.

'Can I come in?' she called softly.

'No,' he growled from beneath the duvet. 'Don't want you in here.'

'Benny.' She pushed more firmly, the chair squealing as it scraped across floorboards. 'What's wrong?'

She walked in and sat on the edge of the bed, putting a gentle hand onto the outline of his shoulder under the bedding.

'Don't touch me. I don't ever want you to touch me again!'

'Benny, what's going on? We've always been friends. Come on, there's breakfast downstairs. Your father's going away again later today so tonight we can choose a movie and things can go back to normal.'

He sat upright, fists hammering into the mattress.

'They can't!' he screamed. 'Not ever. I saw you. I saw the things you let him do to you. I heard the noises you made.'

The nanny stood and took a step away from the shrieking, incandescent boy on the bed.

'Benny, I'm so sorry. How did you . . . what were you doing? I wish you hadn't seen that.'

'So do I! Now I hate you and you have to leave because I never want to see you again. Not ever. You're disgusting.'

He jumped off the bed and pushed past her into the hallway barging open the door into his father's bedroom.

'Get rid of her!' he yelled. 'Make her go. I don't want her here any more.'

128

His father paused in knotting his tie.

'Then it's boarding school,' he replied. 'I'm not going to the trouble of finding you another nanny and I can't be tied to a child. I have business.'

'Fine!' Benny shouted. 'Boarding school is fine. Just get her out of here right now.'

'Benny, please,' the nanny called from the hallway. 'Let's sit down and talk about this. I hate that we've upset you.'

'It's time for the boy to go away to school anyway,' Benjamin Snr said. 'Pack your things and leave this morning. I'll make some calls and get him picked up.'

'But he's traumatised. He needs to sit down and discuss this. I can't just leave while he's—'

'I said, pack your things and get out. If you're gone within the hour I'll make sure you get a decent reference.'

Benny watched her go, shoulders down, hands hanging limply at her sides. She was pathetic. She'd barely fought for him at all. Not that he wanted her to stay. His father was right. It was time for him to go to boarding school. He didn't want to live at home any more.

As the cab arrived to pick her up, Benny watched from an upper-floor window. She would still have been pretty if he hadn't seen her doing those terrible things. They could still have had cuddles, and read books together, and she could still have made him laugh with her jokes. Now she had ruined everything. She'd given his father all the sick things he'd wanted and ruined herself forever. Benny hated her and cried for her, and felt as lost as he ever had in his life.

'Benny, thank you for sharing that. None of this can hurt you, remember?' Connie said.

'I remember,' he told her.

'We're moving forward now,' Connie told him. 'On to when you saw the girl in the cinema, the one who made you feel good but bad. Tell me what happened with her.'

'Oh, I liked her,' he said. 'I liked her a lot. I knew I might not see her again at the cinema. Some people don't come for a whole year. So I left my shift and I followed her. My manager wasn't happy. I nearly lost my job!'

'What happened when you followed the girl home?' Connie tried to keep him on track.

'She said goodbye to her friends and went into her house. The light went on so I could see she was on the ground floor. The kitchen was at the front. After a while she went to the back so I couldn't see any more and there was a man walking his dog so I had to leave. The next night, I found an alleyway, figured out which one her house was and at about 11.30 p.m. she went to bed. I waited a while and her window was locked so I had to wait until the next day. While she was at work, I got some tools and broke the lock. Good planning, right? That night I went to see her.

'I was polite and I didn't want to hurt her, but she hit me and tried to run out. She wouldn't even talk to me, and she didn't like me stroking her hair. She didn't like that at all.' He sounded surprised and stopped talking as he considered it. 'It got worse when she grabbed her mobile and tried to make a call. That meant I had to tie her up so she couldn't do it again, but she screamed and I had to put something over her mouth. It wasn't at all like I thought it would be. I really liked her, but she was mean.'

'What happened to her, Benny?'

'By the time I realised she was not a nice girl, I figured I might as well see if she would do those bad things like my nanny did with Father. That made me feel good for a while but then it made me feel bad and I didn't like that, so I tried

130

to stop her crying and she just wouldn't and then she wasn't breathing any more and I got scared so I left.'

'Thank you for telling me,' Connie said. 'Moving forward in time, were there other girls who reminded you of your nanny?'

'I lost count. The police said there were eleven. I never meant to hurt any of them, you know? I just wanted to find someone who would love me the way my nanny did before she did all those horrible things.'

'With your father. What's your relationship like with him now?'

'When I got caught, he came to see me once. He said he never should have married an older woman. He thinks it was because her eggs were so old when she had me that I came out all messed up.'

It was Connie's turn to sigh. 'We're coming back in a minute to the hospital and to now, but I want to ask you something first. Can you make sure you tell me the truth?'

'Of course,' Rubio said. 'Have to tell the truth or we get in trouble.'

'Is there anyone at the hospital who reminds you of your nanny? Anyone here whose hair you've wanted to touch?'

Rubio shifted in his seat and seemed to struggle, as if tied by invisible ropes. Finally he collapsed back against his seat.

'I like Nurse Cameron's hair,' he said quietly. 'I miss her. Will she be back soon? She's kind. Will you ask her to come see me? Not everyone is kind like her.'

'Who isn't kind?' Connie asked.

'That's enough,' Tom Lord said.

'Who's that?' Rubio cried out. 'Who's here? I don't like it. That's a mean voice. I don't want to be punished again!' He was back into baby mode, fists bunched up, shoulders huddled.

Connie put a palm up in Tom's direction.

'It's all right, Benny. We're going to stop now. You've done enough,' she said and Tom tutted. 'Benny, if you look around you'll see the doors you came through. The other side is the corridor, but this time it'll be more brightly lit like the first light of day. I want you to walk to those doors for me. They'll open automatically for you, no need to do anything at all. Just make your way back along that corridor. I'll count the doors as they open. As you walk, you'll feel more and more refreshed. You'll feel like you've had a good sleep. You'll be looking forward to the rest of your day, and you won't be worried about anything at all. Let's go, Benny.'

'I'm at the doors,' he said, his voice husky and quiet once more.

'Well done. Go through them and keep walking: 10, 9, 8, 7, 6. You're halfway now, Benny, and it's fully light; 5, 4, 3. Well done. You've managed this so well. Everything is fine; 2, 1.' She snapped her fingers again. 'You can open your eyes now, Benny.'

He sat upright and gave a tiny bounce on the seat. 'Was I good? Did I do what you wanted?'

'You were great. How do you feel now?'

'Hungry.' He grinned. 'It's weird, like I was asleep but not asleep. I could hear you the whole time but I couldn't open my eyes even when I tried.'

'You did a good job. With some people it takes lots and lots of tries to get them to relax and engage with it. Well done. Maybe Tom could take you to get some lunch now?'

Tom stood and folded his arms. 'Stand outside the door, and don't move. I'll just be a minute,' he said.

Rubio disappeared, almost skipping. Tom shut the door.

'What is it exactly that you're trying to do here?'

She remained in her seat. There was no point reacting to him.

'I'm trying to establish whether or not Patient B will be both safe and comfortable here. PTSD that manifests itself as psychosis is hard to manage and requires some sensitivity.'

'Your client is a killer. Wrap it up any way you want.'

'He's a very damaged man. Seeing military action can be devastating to mental health. He served his country.'

'Honestly, lady, I don't give a fluttering fuck about any of that. Stop asking about the staff here. You want to see kindness, you chose the wrong profession.'

He left, slamming the door behind him, ordering Rubio away to the common room.

Connie stood and stretched, wishing she were closer to a shower so she could wash off the feeling Benny Rubio had left her with. He was revolting but predictable, also untreatable and incurable. With some serial killers you never truly uncovered the source of their rage or derangement, but Benny Rubio was textbook. Hates mother for abandoning him, longs for mother figure. Finds mother figure, puts her on a pedestal, needs to possess her in case she leaves him again. Feels betrayed when he finds out she's only human, feels vulnerable when he realises he's not her priority. Can only feel anything at all while he's punishing women who remind him of those key women in his life, as he tries to externalise and work out his experiences of trauma and rejection.

Not difficult, not complex, mainly reactive and unsophisticated. More importantly he was no match for Tara's killer – ice cold, controlled and precise. Benny Rubio wasn't the killer she was looking for, which was a crying shame because more than half the second day was gone already and Connie was brimming with the frustration of being no further forward.

Chapter 12

Nurse Madani was still with Baarda when Connie quietly entered his room.

'How did he cope with the sedation?' Connie asked.

'No ill effects. His breathing is steady. Good pulse. He's stirred a few times but not come round. ECG was normal. I'm not concerned. Listen, I'm due off on my lunch break. Will you be staying in here a while?'

'Absolutely, you go. I was supposed to be with Patient B all afternoon anyway, so you can go back to regular duties after lunch.'

The nurse didn't need telling twice. She disappeared and left Connie with a still-sleeping Baarda. Connie shut the door fully, made sure no one was loitering in the corridor near the room, then went to do some checks of her own.

'Brodie,' she whispered. 'It's me. There's no one else here. You're okay. Let's get these restraints off.'

If he could hear her, he didn't move. Connie gently undid each restraint and shifted Baarda's limbs to a more relaxed

134

position, then she pulled up a chair next to his head and reached out to take his right hand in hers.

'I wish I'd never dragged you into this,' she said softly. 'But I need you to wake up. There's just no time.'

She reached out her foot and kicked the electricity switch that fed the monitor. Baarda looked like death. They'd met in Edinburgh on the trail of a man who believed himself to be dead. It had taken another year for Baarda to finish up his contract with the Metropolitan Police in London, and then Connie had pursued him relentlessly until he'd finally caved in and agreed to work with her full-time. Together they made a formidable team, much in demand, both in the private sector and as consultants to government agencies across the world. But this was a giant leap outside their comfort zone. True, Baarda had done undercover work before, but here they were subject to other people's rules and command. Connie was starting to get a very bad feeling indeed.

'Okay,' she said. 'Buckle up.'

Sliding her thumb over his, she bent hers to a ninety-degree angle and shoved her nail tip hard into the white half-moon lunula at the base of his nail. Baarda's arm jolted, his hand flying out of hers as he made a strangled noise at the back of his throat.

'Shit,' she said. 'I can't believe you're going to make me do that to you twice. Don't hate me.'

That time she leaned over and used his left hand. Baarda cried out and thrashed his arms before turning a shade that Connie knew could only be green. She ran across the room to the trolley with the medical supplies and grabbed a sick bowl.

A few minutes later, she handed him a cup of water and a cold flannel while he composed himself.

'What happened?' Baarda asked, settling himself back in his bed as Connie cleared up and pushed the monitor trolley into the corner.

'You were sedated, brought back to your room, restrained, and I've been waiting for you to come round. I'm afraid I reached the point where I couldn't wait any longer, so I decided to help.'

'I feel like I drank fifteen pints, each with a whisky chaser. Why was I sick?'

'That was just your body trying to get rid of the chemicals. It's the same as anaesthesia. You need to rehydrate and shortly I'll find you some food. You shouldn't stand for a while. Your blood pressure might be a little unpredictable.'

'I don't understand. Why did they sedate me? I thought you agreed last night that it wouldn't be necessary.' He sipped cold water and bashed his pillow into a more comfortable shape.

'I was hoping you could answer that question,' Connie said. 'What do you remember from the time you woke this morning?'

'It's a bit hazy now, but someone banged on the door and said it was time to get up. I showered, got dressed, my door opened automatically and one of the nurses was in the corridor ushering us towards the common room. Then breakfast, which was some sort of cereal, during which I was told Dr Ong wanted to see me.'

'Who was in the room with Dr Ong?'

'It's all a bit confused in my head. I know at some point that I saw the larger of the two orderlies.'

'Tom Lord,' Connie said.

'Yes, him. I was answering questions, all standard stuff: education, family, medical notes. Then some Rorschach tests. He asked a series of questions about how I'd respond in various different scenarios, how I handle stress. It all seemed fine. Then Tom brought in coffee for us both, I was offered a biscuit, Dr Ong did some eye tests.'

'What eye tests?' Connie asked.

'Checked my retinas, I think, with a light. He was chatting the whole time, very polite. Saying he should be able to find me a trust position on the ward, which would give me extra freedom. That's the last thing I can remember. Then my thumb felt like someone had plugged it in and I woke up.'

'Yeah, that last bit was me. Signature move, sorry. So you don't remember threatening anyone, getting physical, being aggressive?'

'Is that what they said I did?'

'Tom felt it necessary to punch you in the face in order to get a needle in you.' Baarda put a hand up to his face and winced when he found the spot. 'Ong put out an alarm call in response to your behaviour. Says he asked you questions about your children.'

'I have no memory of any of it. As far as I was aware, I managed to stick to my brief, gave the answers from my alibi pack. Are you all right? You look like I feel. Maybe not quite that bad, but . . .'

'You sure know how to compliment a girl.' She gave a half-hearted smile. 'Progress is slow. What was your impression of Dr Ong?'

'I wouldn't want him in charge of any of the criminals I've put behind bars. It's an unpleasant British phrase, but I'd be minded to call him a do-gooder. I applaud his desire to see everyone here as healable and reintegratable, but you and I both know that none of these men can ever go free.'

'I get the impression that his staff doesn't respect him either,' Connie said. 'They laugh about him calling the patients "guests" and ignore any of his rules that they deem ridiculous. Dr Roth has a much more brutal approach to patient care.'

'So did you learn anything new this morning?'

'Professor Saint told me not to trust anything anyone here

says. I think he's only borderline psychotic. I suspect the judge had just never seen a man from such a high academic and social class offend with an extended spree killing, and decided on a hospital order out of caution. The alternative was a traditional prison environment that he'd never have survived. It would have been in the university's interests too, to have him committed to a mental health institution rather than accepting that one of their own was just pure evil. After that, I tried some hypnotherapy with Benny Rubio, which was surprisingly successful. It usually takes several sessions to get as far as I got with him, but maybe his childishness and desire to please allowed me to cut through a lot of the borders fully functioning adults put up. He was under pretty deep, and he was clearly of the view that Tara Cameron was still alive and that he wanted to see her. No suggestion from him that he knew she was dead.'

'All right. I'll concentrate on the patients you haven't met yet, see what I can get out of them. Apparently this evening is games night. Chess, chequers and cards. Should be entertaining.' Baarda tried to sit up but sank straight back down into his pillows.

'I'm not sure you'll be up to it,' Connie said. 'Whatever they gave you packed one hell of a punch. And given that you're not naturally one to get feisty without a good reason, I'd say someone in here is already suspicious of you. Maybe there was something in that coffee that set you off. It would explain your loss of memory. You think it was Tom who brought in the coffee?'

'He brought it into the room but there were several voices in the corridor so I can't be sure who prepared it, or if someone didn't slip something extra into it on the way,' Baarda said.

'I'll check it out. I haven't eaten since I got onto the ward today so I have an excuse to visit the kitchenette at the back of the common room. I can't bring my mobile in – it's too risky – but I meant to ask, is there anyone I can call to let them know you're okay? You'll be in here a week. What did you tell your wife and kids?'

'Ex-wife,' Baarda said. 'The divorce finally came through. Financial settlement is all agreed. And it's term time so the children are at boarding school. My wife insisted that worked best for her, and with me travelling so much for work I could hardly argue.'

'Shit, I'm sorry,' Connie said. 'Do you want me to tell you again that you're better off without her?'

'No, I want you to stick to our previous agreement and not apply your considerable expertise as a psychologist to my life. Some toast, though, would be welcomed.'

'The end of a long marriage is a complex maze to navigate, Baarda. Even that British stiff upper lip is going to wobble at some point. She had an affair with one of your colleagues. It's going to have an effect on your future relationships. We should talk about it at some point.'

'Apparently I can't stop you from talking about it even when I've told you specifically not to.'

'You want me to shut up and get you some food? You know, in most cultures you taking that approach would be considered misogynistic.'

'In the last twenty-four hours, I've been committed, punched in the face, drugged, restrained and sedated,' Baarda reminded her.

'Toast it is.' Connie walked to the door. 'Don't eat or drink anything anyone else brings you until I get back, okay? Professor Saint was right about one thing: we really can't trust anyone in here at all.'

139

Chapter 13

The common room was empty as she walked through. Connie took the time to peruse the books on the shelves, the jigsaws in their tatty boxes, the board games that had seen better days. There were art supplies and paper for origami, modelling clay, stencils for making greetings cards and a large box labelled 'basket weaving'.

The lack of natural daylight made the space claustrophobic in spite of the several rows of overhead strips, and the comfortable furniture was showing its age, but there was never going to be any budget for such niceties.

Running a high-security mental health facility was expensive on a scale that was hard to comprehend. Doctors and nurses had to be properly trained, the environment had to be largely self-contained, the drugs alone were extortionately priced, and that was before you factored in food, bedding and the basics like heating and water. Most taxpayers didn't like the idea of funding a normal prison let alone paying hard-earned cash to house serial killers where they could watch movies, paint watercolours and learn a musical instrument as part of their therapy.

'Lost?' Dr Vassily Sidorov asked, close behind her.

'No. You?' Connie replied. She chose not to step away from him, assuming that was what he was expecting. Backing away was almost always a mistake, whether you were dealing with mountain lions or any other predator.

'I need some food for one of the patients. He's on long-term painkillers and the effect on his stomach is problematic.'

'Joe Yarowski? The one who needed an endoscopy?' she asked.

'Yes,' Sidorov said, taking a deep breath through his nose. Connie got the impression he was smelling her. 'How did you find your accommodation last night? I'm afraid the mattresses here are a travesty. I had my own shipped in, same with my bedding. There are some hardships I'm not prepared to tolerate, however much I'm being paid.'

Connie turned her back on him and made her way to the security viewing area where she waved her pass at the door and waited for it to click open. Vassily Sidorov was right behind her.

'Why are you here, exactly, if the accommodation isn't to your taste and it's all such a hardship – the food, the wine, the thread count?'

She walked directly through the viewing area into the small kitchen, looking around for some bread to make Baarda toast.

In one corner was a trolley on which sat six plastic plates, plastic knives, forks and spoons, serviettes, paper cups and a large metal jug. It made Connie's heart sink. One of its wheels jutted out at a different angle to the others and she could already hear the squeak-thump it would make as it attempted forward progress.

Sidorov opened a large fridge and took out a loaf of processed bread and a pack of ham.

'You really want to find out more about me? Take me up

on the offer of a drink,' he said. 'Tonight, when your precious Patient B has been locked in for the night. My shift ends at eight.'

Connie considered her options as she took two slices of bread from the pack and popped them into a battered old toaster. No one was going to be letting their guard down on the ward during their shift. Perhaps a more intimate setting with alcohol involved and some ego rubbing would be more fruitful.

'Just a drink,' she said. 'I wouldn't want you getting the wrong idea about what was on offer.'

'Never say never.' He grinned. 'Where's the fun in that?'

Connie looked around the kitchen. There was a double sink, the usual cupboards, two large bins, a microwave and a dishwasher. 'Where's the oven?'

'Why would we need an oven?' Sidorov asked.

'It's a long way to the kitchens. I just didn't think hot meals would be transported all that way. There's lifts and stairs, and the catering block is across the other side of the compound.'

He shrugged. 'We have a waiter for that.' Sidorov finished making Joe Yarowski's sandwich and gave her a wink as he walked out. 'Nine o'clock, room S82. Just bring yourself.'

Connie buttered Baarda's toast as she contemplated Sidorov's waiter comment. It wasn't until one of the kitchen walls began rattling that her brain finally kicked into gear.

The dumbwaiter was a feat of engineering. Hidden behind a door that matched all the others in the kitchen, which was why she hadn't initially noticed it was there, the void in the tower walls must have been built into the original structure, albeit manually operated back then. Connie pressed a button on the electric side panel and waited by the accompanying flashing light.

A rumbling grew in intensity beneath her feet until she could hear the dumbwaiter arriving in its dock and stopping. The light flicked to another next to it. Connie assumed it was now showing green for go. She pulled open a metal door to reveal a large compartment featuring three shelves with perhaps five inches of space between them. Plenty of room to stack covered metal bowls of hot food for transportation between floors and wards.

Connie ran her fingertips into the dumbwaiter and across its shiny surfaces. With its metal doors shut, a cabinet door across for added security and a fast route down into the very bottom of the building, it could carry anything just as long as you had the right person waiting at the bottom to receive the package.

Her stomach tightened as she contemplated the alternatives.

Heaven Ward had one main access for staff, past Dr Ong's office and the security room, past the staffroom and laundry room. That meant anyone carrying anything like, say, a baby, was running an enormous risk going out of that door. With all the staff living on site, you might bump into anyone on the stairs down.

The dumbwaiter though – the thought of it left a bead of cold sweat running from Connie's neck towards her coccyx – could have provided the most perfect means of transporting a baby from the highest ward in the tower to a place incredibly near an exit point for the building.

Connie stuck her head further inside, looking for anything at all, any sign that the dumbwaiter might have been used for more than just transporting food. But what would there be? Baby Aurora would have been swaddled, probably put in a duffel bag or something similar, slid into the dumbwaiter, and sent on her way. The controls allowed only for the waiter to go to the ground floor or be called upwards. It wasn't possible to order a stop at any other floor. Simple, clean, efficient. The perpetrator didn't even have to attempt to smuggle the baby out of the ward. No tiptoeing down the stairs hoping the infant didn't start to cry.

No CCTV camera in the kitchen and the one in the common room was out of action. None of the patients should have been in the common room area in the middle of the night. Much less likely to get spotted moving from the medical room to the kitchen than any other part of the ward. It all made perfect sense.

Connie closed the dumbwaiter door then shut the cupboard door over it, grabbed Baarda's toast and made her way back through to his room, timing the walk.

'One minute,' she said, bursting back through Baarda's door. 'That's all it—' Nurse Madani looked up from her position at Baarda's bedside where she was taking his pulse. 'That's all it will take for you to finish this toast, and then you'll start feeling better.' She handed Baarda the plate.

'You undid the patient's restraints,' Nurse Madani said. 'You should have waited until there was an orderly in the room with you for that.'

'He was about to be sick,' Connie said. 'That was a risk while he was secured on his back. I had no choice, but I take your point. Next time I'll make sure I inform another member of staff.'

'Next time you won't do it at all,' Madani said. 'You may feel safe with Patient B, but his assessments on this ward have only just begun. The men we treat here are extremely dangerous. If you don't care about your own safety, at least be mindful of everyone else's. The rules exist for a reason.'

'I'm actually very glad you're taking ward safety so seriously,' Connie said. 'And I apologise. It won't happen again.'

Nurse Madani gave a small nod, acknowledging the truce, and Baarda took a tentative bite of toast.

'Patient B's vital signs are good. He doesn't seem to be suffering any ill effects from the sedation. Dr Ong has said he appreciates the incident was probably down to the new environment and some preliminary stress. He doesn't want to impose an exclusion from tonight's community games. All he's asked is that Patient B is accompanied for the duration by one of the orderlies. I think it'll be Jake on duty.'

'That'll work,' Connie said. 'How long until games night starts?'

'Straight after dinner,' Nurse Madani said. 'I think it would do Patient B good to get up and stretch his legs, also to shower, beforehand.' She wrinkled her nose slightly as she said it. Connie didn't think she'd even realised she'd done it.

That was the thing about working in mental health. It didn't take long to start talking across a patient rather than to them, just as Nurse Madani had done. A patient would suddenly find themselves the subject of a conversation going on around them without their input being requested – or in many cases, toler- ated. They became, in all the ways that mattered, less than.

That was true of all patients in mental health facilities. It was a fact of institutional life that Connie was painfully aware of, but never more so than when dealing with the criminally insane. They weren't just less than so-called 'normal' people. They were less than human, talked over in the same way a vet and a pet owner would talk across the head of a sick animal.

'Patient B,' Connie said, 'does that work for you? Finish your toast, try getting up to make sure there are no residual effects from the drugs, have a shower and change your clothes?'

'It does,' Baarda said. 'Thank you.'

'Good,' said Madani. 'Then I'll leave you to it. I need to ask you to lock Patient B's door as you leave, Dr Connie. Patients aren't generally free to wander around the ward, unless they've been given permission and we know where they're going and why. You should have locked it the last time you exited.'

'Again, apologies,' Connie said. 'I guess I'm still getting used to working on a ward. I'm usually in a more therapeutic setting.'

Madani left, and Connie waited a moment after the door was shut to speak.

'There's a dumbwaiter,' she said, her voice hushed. 'I'm absolutely certain that's how the baby was transported from here to ground level. At that time of night it would have been risk-free. With the thickness of the stone walls, even if the baby had been crying on the way down, no one on the wards below would have heard it.'

'Do we know who was on duty during the evening in question?' Baarda asked.

'The orderly was Jake. Dr Sidorov was on call for medical emergencies, but from his staff quarters and contactable by phone. Same as Dr Roth, who was on call for psychiatric emergencies.'

'So they should have known if anyone else had come or gone,' Baarda said.

'In a perfect world, yes, but there are only six patients on this ward and they're all in locked rooms overnight – and some are probably sedated. The staffroom up here comes equipped with sofas and a large TV. I'm guessing that the night shift is simply a matter of locking up, doing maybe one late patrol, then snoozing in front of a movie knowing the alarm will wake you if it goes off. Easy enough to walk past and let yourself in if you have a pass and the code. So what if you're seen? You just say you're checking on someone, or you think you left your notes in the ward. No one would suspect a thing, right?'

'So we know where Tara was killed and we're pretty sure we know how they got the baby off the ward. But we still don't have a good grip on who's involved, and that's what we need.'

'Looking at it from a traditional profiling perspective, I'd be surprised if it was Professor Saint,' Connie said, wandering across to look past the bars at the view from the window. 'It's right that we're looking for an organised, non-chaotic offender with an above average IQ, and the crimes the professor committed were meticulously planned. However, he kept his offending very hands-off. Hit his victims around the back of the head with an old chair leg. One hit, very hard, to each of them. Remarkably little blood, nothing that involved him getting his hands dirty. It's a unique fingerprint for a mass killer. Most lose control at some point. The exception is snipers and bombers, and those are incredibly rare. Saint's profile just doesn't fit the sort of up-close, hands-on trauma Tara's killer inflicted.'

Connie stood and began pacing back and forth in the tiny room.

'On top of that, I think I can exclude Benny Rubio after hypnotherapy.'

'The guy who acts like a toddler the whole time? He strikes me as utterly deranged, and gives me the creeps. Are you sure he's not a candidate?'

'I hear ya, and whilst the baby thing is undoubtedly play-acting based on early years trauma, it seems to me to be deeply ingrained. His whole personality is chaos-based and reactive, and there's no hint that there was anything amiss in his relationship with Tara. The idea of him having the bandwidth to soak up the information required to perform the caesarean doesn't work for me. It's like he's chosen to disconnect his maturity from the reality of his life. So that's two suspects discounted, from a profiling point of view. I'm going to leave a note on Dr Ong's desk asking for access to Joe Yarowski and Harold Haskin tomorrow.'

Baarda rubbed his eyes and flexed his neck. 'Are you absolutely sure one of the patients is involved? Wouldn't it have been easier for the staff member to have used the medical room at night but done it themselves?'

She took a slow breath in then huffed the air out. 'You know, I've thought about this a lot. What was done to Tara takes a genuine psychopath in the diagnostic sense. This is, at its heart, a crime about money. It took two distinct personalities to see it all the way through. I can't envisage any staff member – whose criminal record and professional history would have been checked carefully – being able to kill in this way. More importantly, they didn't need to. If anything went wrong, they had a helpful serial killer to blame. Serial killer says, "Dr X or Nurse Y told me to do it" – who's going to believe them? Using one of the men in here was almost foolproof.'

'Making the staff member involved very manipulative indeed,' Baarda added.

'Agreed. And definitely a sociopath, but not a psychopath. They needed a patient to do this. Someone who could be manipulated, tempted or threatened into it. Someone not at all squeamish, and either desperate or deluded enough to believe they were going to get away with it, and who doesn't even see a baby as a real human.'

'Maybe a patient who had already expressed an interest in Tara – not in a good way,' Baarda offered. 'Then all they had to do was fuel that obsession, get them fantasising, and make them an offer they couldn't refuse.'

'Such as a positive review recommending a move to a more open facility with more freedom?'

Baarda nodded. 'Exactly.'

'I'm not sure they needed me here. Seems like you could have figured this out all by yourself,' Connie said, smiling at him.

'I suspect you're rather more tolerant than me. I'm not sure either the professor or Rubio would still be alive if I'd had to sit and listen to them pouring their hearts out to me. I don't know how you do it.'

She shrugged. 'I tell myself I'm studying a dangerous virus, like in one of those labs where you put your hands through the long rubber gloves and deal with substances in their own airtight room. It's a learning environment but best never to let them actually touch you.'

Baarda smiled. 'I like that. Anyway, I have a chessboard with my name on to look forward to. What's on your agenda for this evening?'

'I'm having drinks with Dr Sidorov. See if he'll let anything slip after a couple of glasses of wine.'

Baarda slid his legs round and off the bed, rubbing his hands where the dark curls on his head used to be. 'Was that your idea or his?' he asked. 'Seems risky.'

'I'm spending my days on a locked ward with a bunch of serial killers and you're worried about me having a drink with one of the doctors?' She laughed.

'I've heard the way Sidorov talks to female members of staff in the corridor. I don't like him. At least when someone has a conviction for multiple murders, you know not to trust them with a corkscrew.'

He moved slowly into his bathroom and splashed cold water on his face.

'How long have you known me?' Connie asked when he reappeared.

He thought for a moment then said, 'Two years, give or take. Why?'

'Haven't you figured out yet that I don't need you to worry about me?' Connie put the question gently but kept her tone serious.

'How long have you known me?' Baarda asked her.

'Funny,' she said.

'Haven't you figured out yet that I was brought up to care that women don't get hurt by men? And that you, in particular, are someone I really don't want to lose?'

She tipped her head a little to one side, her mouth flickering into a smile. 'Are all old Etonians such gentlemen?'

'Frankly, I'd be more concerned about you going for drinks with an old Etonian than almost anyone else,' he said with a wry smile. 'How much do you know about Sidorov?'

'Not as much as I'll know a few hours from now. What I need is your eyes and ears open at the community session. There's no point me being there too. I'm going down to check out where the dumbwaiter lands, then I'm off to have dinner with Boy – I'll check out the gossip about Heaven Ward staff – and finally drinks with Sidorov. Can I trust you not to start another fight while I'm away?'

'I'm not so sure I did,' Baarda said. 'I have no memory at all of anything after the end of the psychometric testing. I mean, a complete blank. If I was drugged in a way that made me angry enough to lose my temper, surely I'd have some memory of getting aggressive and Tom punching me in the face?'

She paused, thinking over the options. 'You think you were slipped a Mexican Valium?'

'Should I know what that is?'

'Right, you Brits call it a roofie. Anyway, Rohypnol. Used perfectly legally in psych units for things like treating insomnia or as a pre-med before surgery. Strong enough dose and you'd have no memory of what happened. Mix it with cocaine and it could have made you aggressive, with no conscious idea of what you were doing.'

Baarda frowned, gave a small shake of his head and clenched his jaw. 'So either Dr Ong wanted more information than he was entitled to, or someone else got suspicious and wanted me to say something that would expose my purpose here.'

'Or someone wants me out of the picture and kept busy looking after you. That's no real surprise. Whoever was involved in Tara's death knows Director Le Fay lied about her going on emergency maternity leave, and our arrival was way too sudden to be a coincidence. The culprits are going to be trying to get rid of us however they can.'

'No more coffee for me, then.'

'Just make sure you're either drinking from your tap, or from a large jug that someone else has drunk from before you.'

'That's it? You didn't come armed with a helpful knife or a gun that I can slip under my mattress in case of attack?' Baarda asked.

'Dude, if I'd known you were gonna be this much of a bellyacher, I'd have brought my grandma along to help instead.'

'I doubt you'd have listened to her advice either,' Baarda said, resigned. 'Now go. Apparently, I'm in desperate need of a shower.'

'Yeah, well, I'm afraid she was right about that. I'll see you in the morning. And no eating any puzzle pieces, okay?'

Chapter 14

Back in her room, Connie saw that she had a voicemail from the detective heading up the investigation beyond The Institution's walls, asking her to call. The phone barely rang before it was snatched up.

'Dr Woolwine, this is Detective Houlihan. I've been waiting for a call from you.'

'I was on the ward. It's been eventful, to say the least. Is there progress your end?' Connie asked.

'We've identified fourteen vehicles that left The Institution during the period between Tara Cameron's death and when we were alerted, at which point we put up a roadblock purportedly checking for illegal traffickers and so have been able to search vehicles. The fourteen that got away have all been traced and every driver and the home they went to is now under constant undercover surveillance. We've managed to get into eight of those homes with hidden listening devices. We can't go in hard and question people because it might impede live recovery of the baby.'

'Aurora,' Connie said softly. 'Her name is Aurora.' She sighed. 'There's no chance anyone could have got away on foot? By boat even, across the lake, to access a different route out?'

'On foot it would have been suicide. Boat is possible but there are no alternative roads for miles so they'd have got to the dam then had to climb down into the valley, a perilous feat in itself. We've also checked the air traffic control reports for the district and nothing went overhead during that twenty-four-hour period,' Houlihan said.

There was a moment's silence, during which Connie thought furiously. Where do you go once you've excluded all possibilities? Then a final, impossible option occurred to her. 'What if Aurora's still here?' she asked.

'We had our undercover officers assess that initially when they recovered the victim's body. There are no infants allowed there, no mother and baby unit, no nursery facilities. Given that all accommodation is within the actual prison hospital, it would be unfeasible to keep a baby there. There would be too great a risk of the baby being discovered if left unattended during a work shift, and a premature baby like Aurora would need constant feeding and monitoring.'

'Of course,' Connie said, deflated at hitting another brick wall. 'Have you found any reports from Tara before her death? No complaints, suspicions, nothing she mentioned to any friends or family?'

'Nothing. The forensic pathologist confirms there was no rape or obvious vaginal or anal sexual assault. Death would have been fast once the baby – Aurora – was removed.'

'And yet still not fast enough,' Connie muttered. 'Listen, I have what I think may be our first lead. I believe Aurora was moved off the ward in the dumbwaiter to someone waiting at

153

the bottom. I need to follow that up. Call me as soon as you find anything concrete. We're losing time fast.'

Connie followed the steps all the way down to the ground floor of the central tower block only to find that the dumbwaiter didn't open there. Instead, she was on a corridor that led to reception at the front and Le Fay's office at the rear. She wandered in the direction of reception to find someone who could help her and found Boy bringing luggage in from the car park.

'Hey, you.' Connie gave him a broad smile.

'Hi, Dr Connie, you okay? Need anything?'

'I do, actually. I put some dirty crockery in the dumbwaiter last night from Heaven Ward, and now I can't find one of my rings. I've been checking everywhere, and I wanted to look around the exterior of the base of the dumbwaiter in case it got knocked off when the staff took the dirty plates out.'

Boy frowned. 'That's bad. Is it a pretty ring? I don't want you to be upset.'

'It is a pretty ring, and it's important to me, but there's still a chance I might find it. Could you tell me how to get to the bottom of the dumbwaiter for Tower 2?'

'I can show you!' He beamed. 'We have to go through the staff block and the kitchens but they won't mind. They might even give me a treat. Come on.' He'd already begun walking and waving a follow-me hand in the air. Connie was reminded of a pantomime hero, always cheery, always keen to help. It made her happy and sad at the same time. The Institution was no place for a teenager, however much of a retreat it offered from a miserable home life.

She was going to speak with Director Le Fay when the investigation was over, see what more could be done. The very least had to be some formal training, perhaps an apprenticeship, that would allow Boy a pathway to a brighter future.

Connie followed him as he chattered away, regaling her with stories of people he'd met that day and a patient who was due to leave, clearly an event rarely seen.

The kitchens were full of men and women chopping, stirring and cleaning up. A few looked up briefly as Boy and Connie wandered through but most simply carried on with meal preparation.

He tapped a tall, wiry woman on the shoulder then ducked to the other side of her as she looked over, pealing with laughter when she caught the trick, but meeting Connie's eyes in a way that said, *We do this all the time. It's our thing and I love it.*

'How's my Boy?' she asked, ruffling his hair in a way that would have driven any other teenager to a sulk, but that Boy seemed to enjoy.

'Hungry,' he said hopefully.

'Of course you are.' She handed him a bread roll from a vast, steaming tray of them.

He took a bite, careless of the heat, and talked through a mouthful of delicious-smelling dough.

'Get that kid out of my kitchen. He's a health and safety hazard, hands everywhere, no hairnet, and he distracts everyone.' The shouter was a chef of sitcom proportions, filling his whites until they were straining, sweating, hands covered in flour.

'He's just going. Would you give him a moment?' the woman snapped. 'Now who's this?'

'This is Dr Connie,' Boy explained. 'She's my new friend. Dr Connie, this is Maeve.'

'Good to meet you,' Connie said.

'Dr Connie thinks she might have lost a ring in the

155

dumbwaiter,' Boy said. 'I'm just taking her to look. Has anyone found a ring?'

'Not that I heard, but I'll ask around,' Maeve said. 'You just be careful,' she told Boy. 'You'll have to sneak out when chef's not looking. He hates people going down there when they don't need to go.'

'Why not? Is it off limits?' Connie asked.

'Health and safety, he reckons, but I've seen him going down there when he's not on a shift. Boy will tell you all about it. Just remember, those dumbwaiter doors'll have your fingers off if you're not careful. Go on, now. I need bread left for dinner. Nice to have met you, Dr Connie.'

They left Maeve to her cooking, and Boy led Connie quickly out between hanging strips of yellowed plastic, into a corridor filled with huge metal doors as the temperature dropped notably.

'These are the cold stores,' Boy explained. 'I don't like them at all. Warm is better. I don't like the sound the ice makes when the metal containers have stuck to it, like they're screaming.'

'That's quite the image,' Connie said. 'So tell me, is there anyone in the kitchen late at night?'

'How do you mean?' he asked.

'Say I'd done a late shift and I was really hungry before bed. Is there anyone in the kitchen to cook for people who've missed dinner on the wards, or can I go and make myself some food?'

'Well, the kitchen closes after dinner, so I guess you'd have to cook for yourself in the staff kitchen area. You can always ask them to put a plate of food with your name on it in the staff fridge if you know you're going to miss dinner.'

'Great idea,' Connie said. 'So the kitchen gets locked up then at night?'

'This way.' He indicated for her to go with him around a bend, taking them down a level beneath the kitchens and back into the heart of the facilities. 'I'm not sure if they lock it. I don't think they'd need to. Did you want a key?'

'No, I was just wondering,' Connie said. 'Gosh, the lighting down here is terrible.'

There was no natural light at all in the low-ceilinged area beneath the main body of the buildings. The cold from the refrigerators had permeated from above and the natural chill of the mountains and the lake was adding to the inhospitable atmosphere. Every few metres, a light bulb hung in a wire cage, casting pools of sickly illumination. Corridors ran in grid formation beneath the buildings in a mixture of old stonework and new metal supports.

'Maeve told me this used to be the bottom of the castle. They built the new bits on top when it became a hospital. I don't come down here alone if I can help it.' Boy lowered his voice and leaned in to her dramatically. 'Sometimes I think it might be haunted.'

Connie reached out an arm and slid it around his shoulders, giving him a half-hug. 'You know, most scientists agree that if ghosts really existed, we would have found some hard evidence of them by now, been able to record them or identify data about them. I think you need to be more concerned about not tripping over something down here and breaking your ankle.'

Boy leaned his head against her shoulder for a few seconds. 'I wish you were staying longer,' he said. 'Most people don't bother to talk to me for more than a few seconds.'

'Well as long as I am here, while I'm not working, I promise to talk to you as much as I can,' she said. 'Now which way's the dumbwaiter?'

'From here you just have to follow the line of lights. Back

under the kitchens is the waiter for Tower 3, Tower 2 is in the middle, and at the very end is Tower 1. I'll show you.'

Connie followed him, wishing she'd worn a coat, horribly aware of the weight of the buildings above them.

'Here it is,' Boy said. In front of him was a thick wall with a metal door and a familiar electric panel.

Connie reached out and pressed the button. The light indicated that the unit was already on the ground floor and Boy effortlessly pulled the door wide so she could see inside.

'What's it like?' he asked.

Connie gave a brief glance inside. 'What do you mean?' she replied.

'Your ring? It is silver or gold or, once, there was this really cool art teacher here, and he and his wife had matching glass rings. When I get married, I'd like a glass wedding ring.'

'It's silver,' Connie said. 'With a pale blue stone.'

'Like a sapphire?' Boy asked, eyes wide.

'Aquamarine, in fact. My grandmother gave it to me.'

The ring was real, as was its history. Her grandmother had passed it down to Connie for her sixteenth birthday present. Whilst her brain could no longer see the colour, her memory could recreate it perfectly.

'Sounds special,' Boy said. 'I'll look on the trolley.' He walked across the vaguely constructed corridor and pulled a large trolley out from behind one of the structural pillars. 'We put all the dirty crockery on here until the trolley is full, then we take it back to the kitchen. Each dumbwaiter has its own trolley.'

He searched each shelf of the trolley while Connie made a point of looking on the floor around the base of the dumb-waiter.

'Nothing,' he said. 'We should go back to the kitchen and

ask the other porters, then we could go to reception and see if anyone handed it in. People here are pretty honest, I think.'

Connie was glad Boy couldn't see the irony on her face.

'Sure. Out of interest, what's this way? Could someone have picked it up and left in a different direction than the kitchen?'

'I don't see why they would,' he said. 'I mean, if you're down here, you've either come to drop off some food for the towers or to get the dirties. There's nothing else to do.'

'I guess the building maintenance team comes down and maybe security do a tour now and then?' Connie said.

'I never really thought about them,' he said. 'They'd probably come from the far end where the vehicle depot is. There's another ramp there like the one we came from out of the kitchen. I saw some animal traps down here a while ago when there was a problem with rats, and every few days they'd get emptied. It was gross. Rat droppings smell dis-gust-ing!' He held his nose as he said it.

'I tell you what, you go back up to the kitchen the way we came and see if Maeve won't give you another one of those hot bread rolls. I'm going to take a walk this way, see if I can find any of the building management team and ask if anyone has found my ring.'

Boy shrugged unhappily. 'You don't think we should stick together?' he said.

'It'll be fine. I can see your exit from here, and I'll be okay. I've just got to follow this line of lights, right?'

'It's dark,' he said. 'You don't mind about the rats?'

'I promise they'll be more scared of me than I am of them,' she said. 'You go first and I'll watch. Give me a shout when you're at the ramp.'

'I would like another bread roll,' he said. 'Will we meet up again for dinner?'

159

'Not tonight. I have a meeting. Tomorrow though, I promise.'

'Could we play a game after?' he asked. 'I haven't had anyone to play with in ages.'

'I'm sure I could manage that,' she said.

Connie watched him as he went, trudging at first then speeding up as he neared the ramp.

'I'm okay!' he shouted.

'Me too. See you tomorrow, and thanks for your help.'

Boy hadn't been entirely wrong about the other-worldly atmosphere of the lower level of the building. Alone, Connie was aware of every noise. The scratching of rodents, the flapping wings of birds who had sought refuge there, the cold draught that ran like a river between the concrete pillars and metal struts. Most of all, the looming threat of gravity.

Here and there debris had been left on the floor – a lighter, a pillow, a playing card, a condom, food wrappers, a shoe. Such were the dubious treasures of dark places. Connie stopped to consider the shoe. It was a woman's right pump, the leather still glossy in places, well worn inside. That shoe had, at one time or another, been loved. She disliked the movies her brain was directing unbidden inside her head. Why only one shoe? Who could have limped or hopped out of here, a single shoe on their left foot? Maybe they'd crawled. Or maybe they didn't leave at all.

There were spaces in the world that people found in their hour of need, whether that was to hide or let off steam, to do things illegal or hidden. Places to sell your soul.

Baby Aurora had come through here. She had travelled down in that dumbwaiter, no more important to her kidnappers than dirty dishes and food trash, in the first shocking minutes of her life, to be met in the depths of The Institution by whatever grim co-conspirator could separate their conscience from their love of money. From there, bundled up, perhaps packed into a sports bag or a cardboard box for transportation.

Connie continued the inhospitable walk towards daylight, aware that even the sounds of her own footsteps were lost on the crumbling concrete beneath her feet. No risk, no possibility at all in the small hours, that anyone would hear a thing.

She turned as she walked, looking around, uncharacteristically spooked. Not that it was ghosts she feared. The killers she was profiling were so much worse than the spectres of myths and legends. Ghosts were simple in comparison.

It took her a full ten minutes to walk to the far end of the building, past the final dumbwaiter for Tower 3, up another curved concrete ramp and at last to the contractors' vehicles depot. There were three abandoned vehicles in docking bays, one delivering medical supplies, another collecting recycling, and the last was a minibus, the decal on the side a fading attempt to make The Institution look more like a private school, with three towers in an oval. It was hard to imagine where such a vehicle might take staff members or patients for a day out.

In a small cabin, light bulb flickering, a lone man sipped a mug of something hot as he read a newspaper. Connie found it strangely reassuring that he was reading a print publication rather than simply scrolling through social media on a screen. He looked up, raised a hand in her direction, and gave her a curious smile. She walked over to the cabin.

'Come on in, love,' he said. 'Don't you stand out there. It's colder than Siberia with the breeze coming off the lake. You'll catch your death. If you don't mind my saying, you're looking a bit lost.'

There was a tiny heater in the hut. The man was right.

161

Connie hadn't realised how quickly she'd got cold until she put her hands over the rising hot air and her fingers began itching as she warmed up too fast.

'I'm not exactly lost,' Connie said. 'But I'm low on information and I need help.'

She left it there, not to be mysterious, but to gauge the man by his reaction. He was in his sixties by her estimate, grey-haired beneath his woollen hat, a little out of shape by virtue of a job that kept him stationed in a six-by-six-foot hut for hours at a time. But his face was kind.

'I'm Jock,' he said. 'I see you've a name tag but my eyes aren't good in this light.'

'Connie,' she said. 'How're you doing, Jock?'

'My back's aching and I'd like a better radio. Reception out here is subject to the weather, and the geography makes up its own rules about that. Other than that, can't really complain. Still have all my teeth, if you know what I mean.'

Connie smiled. 'I do know,' she said, leaning against the little heater and folding her arms.

'You looking like you're carrying a weight,' he said. 'Would a cup of tea help? I don't have much, but I've got a kettle and a spare mug.'

'If you've got coffee, I may never leave.'

'That doesn't sound good,' he said, flicking the switch on the kettle and opening a jar of granules.

'Do you like working here?' she asked, as he offered up a sugar bowl and she shook her head.

'Don't mind working outside the building, not sure I'd feel the same if I had to be inside all day. I'm a firm believer in pollution, Miss Connie. Comes across the land and trickles into water. Floats through the air into our lungs. I believe it also moves between people. Spend your day among those people

162

with all their terrible thoughts, some of it can't help but infil-trate your brain. I'm security detail, and I can be called on in there, but mostly I just work here where things seem simpler.'

'What did you do before you worked here?' she asked as he poured boiling water into a mug.

'Carpenter,' he said. His face lit up. 'Worked for myself making whatever people asked me for. It's honest work, but hard. In the end, my hands gave in to arthritis and that was that.' He handed her the coffee and she breathed in the delicious steam. He picked up a tiny, perfect wooden snail from his desk. 'I still make a few things. Helps the time pass while I sit here.'

'That's beautiful,' Connie said. 'Truly. You're wasted here.'

'Pays the bills,' he said. He handed it to her and she ran her fingertips over the polished surfaces, tracing the curve of the shell and the little ball of its head.

She liked Jock. There was something about his ability to create beauty from nothing that spoke to her. Connie made a decision. Time was passing. Without help, without trust, she was going to get nowhere.

'Jock, were you working this weekend just gone?' she asked.

'I was, indeed,' he said. 'I work ten days on then five days off.'

'Are there records for vehicles that come and go? Presumably the drivers have to be identified in advance.'

'Every vehicle is booked in. No one comes in unannounced. Drivers too,' Jock said, giving her a closer look. 'There was bad business here this weekend. I've been wondering when someone would come to speak with me about it.'

'You know?' Connie asked.

'I know very little and I'm not asking for the details. I'll tell you what I saw with my own two eyes. The laundry pick-up truck came. Roger, the driver, is one I've seen come and go

163

regular as clockwork for the last two years, give or take. Nice chap. Share a coffee with him every now and again when he has the time. I wouldn't call him a friend, but he's a good acquaintance. He arrived on the Sunday. Did his thing. Opened up the roof of his vehicle, attached the chute and opened the trap from the laundry room above. It was early in the morning, maybe 5 a.m. and I was busy dealing with a food delivery truck driver who didn't have their paperwork in order. All I knew was that Roger was running late and he's prompt as a rule. I might not have noticed, except that Director Le Fay suddenly appeared. I've seen him perhaps once in the contractors' bays, and then only when a man got hit by a reversing lorry, so I knew something was wrong but no one asked me to get involved so I kept my distance.

'A car arrived an hour later, a dark sedan. Didn't go to the visitors' car park. Came here instead. They went to do something with the director and Roger. An hour later Roger drove out of here again. Didn't stop to say goodbye, didn't say what had happened. Didn't even wave. Man had a complexion the colour of a freshly peeled potato. If I didn't know better, I'd say he'd been crying.'

Connie sipped her coffee. 'No one else left that day via the contractors' vehicles? No one other than the usual trucks, regular drivers? You saw nothing out of the usual?'

'No. And I was watching, after that. I know that look, Miss Connie. My son was a paramedic for a decade. Some days he was fine. Others he had that same blank stare, when he'd seen something so awful he was gone in a different world while he processed it. Some things aren't meant to be witnessed. You pay too high a price for it.'

'Were there other vehicles that went before Roger arrived, during the night?'

164

'Give me a moment. My shift didn't start until midnight. Let me check the records.' Jock picked up a clipboard and flicked a few sheets of paper backwards. 'Nothing after 9 p.m. the night before. Probably not much help, judging by the look on your face.'

Connie made a point of rearranging her face into a grateful smile, but Jock was observant – which was a good thing. 'It is what it is. Out of interest, can you walk from here round to the visitors' car park?'

'No, it's on a different level although the roads converge further up. Either you'd have to walk past me on foot – and I'd have noticed that, for sure – or you'd have to go back through the hospital building to the main reception area and go out that way.'

Connie sighed. 'I get it,' she said, finishing her coffee. 'Another dead end. Thank you, Jock.'

He took the mug from her hands. 'I wish I'd been able to help. Whatever it was that happened, it was nothing good. I don't like the feeling it left here.'

The sadness in his voice caught in her throat. It was a relief in a place where empathy was in such short supply, to be with someone so kind. Connie gave him a slow, gentle smile and put her hand on his.

'Thank you, Jock. I don't even need to say it, do I?'

'You don't. Not a word will leave my lips about our conversation. Will you be able to put it right, do you think? The thing that happened?'

'Not entirely. Hopefully I can make part of it better. I should go, Jock. If you see anything or hear anything, I'm working on Heaven Ward.'

She dropped her hand from his, reluctantly left her place near the radiator and stepped to the door.

'Here,' he said, slipping the snail into her hand. 'Take him. I have a feeling he was waiting here for you.'

Connie felt a rush of warmth that had nothing to do with the coffee or the heater. 'I needed that,' she said. 'Stay well, Jock.'

She slipped out of the cabin with the precious wooden snail clutched tightly in her palm, grateful for the gesture and for the sense that there was a force for good at The Institution. Hopefully it would prove strong enough to balance out the evil at work there.

Chapter 15

Having left Director Le Fay an update on his personal mobile's voicemail, Connie stepped into the shower for a blissful two minutes then dressed again, deliberately avoiding the application of any make-up and choosing loose-fitting jeans and a hoodie. The signal to Sidorov, she hoped, would be crystal clear.

Wishing she'd made time for a meal before going to share a bottle of wine with a man she didn't trust as far as she could throw him, Connie paced through the maze of staffrooms until she reached S82. The doors on that corridor were further apart, the carpet newer. It seemed there was a hierarchy at work, which presumably went from consultants to lower-tier doctors, to nurses then to auxiliary staff.

Vassily Sidorov opened the door, glass of wine already in hand. She glanced around to find a lounge area with a tiny kitchenette, a bedroom through an archway, and what Connie assumed was an en suite beyond that.

'Nice place,' she said, choosing an armchair and accepting an overly full glass from him.

167

'I decorated it myself,' he said. 'The pale grey walls were a shade of peach when I first moved in. Left me feeling like I was living in a children's nursery.'

'Not so different from the truth here,' Connie said. 'Do you miss home?'

'No. I still have family in Belarus but I go back there as rarely as I can possibly manage. Too much corruption. Too much politics. I became a doctor to avoid all of that. How did you end up in this line of work?'

'Therapeutic psychology appealed to my desire to make the world a better place, I guess,' Connie said.

'And yet you work with the military.'

'Can you think of a body of people who are prepared to sacrifice more, who witness some of the worst mankind has to offer, and who are more deserving of therapy after all they do? The developed world has largely ignored the psychological effects of warfare on soldiers. We've paid it lip service, sure, but former military personnel still suffer some of the highest rates of relationship breakdown, suicide, homelessness and unemployment. What we offer them in no way reflects the scale of the damage we do those men and women.'

'Did you write that speech yourself or did someone do it for you?' Sidorov asked.

Connie took a slow sip of her wine. 'Which part of it do you disagree with?'

'The part where Patient B is military.'

She'd mentally prepared for someone on the staff to question the veracity of Baarda's past, but this was a more blunt approach than she'd anticipated. Sidorov was an expert in being passive aggressive. It was unsettling. Connie put her glass down on a side table and watched him watching her. He was relaxed enough, leaning back on the sofa, the edges of his lips raised in a simulation of a smile but the tip of his chin was raised an inch higher than was natural and the flirty tone was gone from his voice. She decided to brazen it out and turn the tables on him.

'Is this your way of trying to force details of his offending out of me? You know I can't give them to you. These are matters of national security.'

He smirked. 'Fine. We'll do it your way. I come from a country where men are still expected to do a compulsory eighteen months of national service in the army or air force.'

'Which did you choose?' Connie said.

'Air force. Before I decided on medicine, I toyed with the idea of becoming a pilot as a career. Unlike many of my friends, I enjoyed my time. But I watched the men who'd been in the military long-term and they all seemed so jaded and institutionalised. But do you know the one thing they all had in common? I mean every single one who'd been in a decade or more?'

Connie injected some mock fascination into her voice. 'You're going to tell me, right? Because the suspense is killing me.'

'Tattoos,' he said, and now his smile was genuine if not entirely friendly. 'I conducted Patient B's preliminary medical. He has a couple of scars, a few nasty ones, but military? I don't buy that.'

Fucksticks, Connie thought. The observant bastard was absolutely right.

She matched his grin with cool indifference. It wasn't true that every single solider in the world had marked their body with their unit insignia or some special brand, but it was a good catch and something neither she nor Baarda had thought of. Had they had more time, they might have done.

'You know I can't answer any specific questions. You're right about the tattoos and I accept that most of the personnel I work with have marked their bodies in the same way. It just wasn't the right thing for Patient B. Consider, for example, how much of a giveaway such tattoos would be if he were taken prisoner by a terrorist group.' She paused, and he continued to peer at her, giving nothing away. 'Surely this isn't why you asked me here this evening, because we could have talked about this in the ward kitchen. It's really not that big of a deal.'

'Why did you think I invited you here?' The smile was completely gone now.

'I suppose I wasn't too concerned about your motives. I saw an opportunity to get better acquainted with a member of staff in whose care I'll be leaving my patient. It seemed like a chance to get some work done in a more relaxed environment.'

After a moment, he said, 'I don't believe you. Not a word of it.'

Connie made a point of issuing a small, bored sigh – exactly the opposite of what she was feeling. Sidorov was smart and didn't suffer fools. She was going to have to stay on her toes when dealing with him.

'Fine, but I'm going to have to be vague. Patient B has no tattoos because he was on repeated special assignments. He was the military's equivalent of an undercover officer. He was put in and out of varying regimes, often posing as a gun for hire. Not the sort of job where you want to have permanent marks on your skin indicating your true allegiances or identity.'

'So he'd have seen a lot of action in the Middle East, maybe Africa, South America, those sorts of places, right?'

'I cannot confirm or deny,' Connie said lightly, picking up her glass again.

'Those are all very hot places, and yet his skin is an even

170

shade of white without the ingrained tan marks and wear and tear that sunshine causes. Did he stay indoors for the whole of his military service?'

God, the man didn't quit. If he weren't a suspect in a horrific murder/kidnapping, Connie thought ironically, he'd make a good addition to her team. She changed tack and went for charming instead.

'Vassily, what is it you're so concerned about? You seem . . . unsettled. Maybe I can use my professional therapeutic skills to set your mind at rest.'

Sidorov drained his glass and reached for the bottle to refill.

'You're not wearing a wedding ring,' he said. 'Are you married, engaged, living with someone?'

'You know, you've been interrogating me since I walked through the door. Want to lighten up?'

'Want to actually answer one of my questions?' he countered.

Connie glanced around the room. No photos, nothing personal, no signs of a life beyond the facility.

'Shall we start again?' she asked gently. 'I accept that it must seem strange having me here. There's so much I can't tell you about Patient B. But Director Le Fay has authorised our presence on the ward, and we're here because it seems like this facility is the best place to house him longer term. Ask me about something I'm allowed to talk about.'

'Finish that glass of wine and let me pour you another. I don't trust people who hesitate to drink in social situations.'

'That's not the healthiest of judgements,' Connie said. 'Most doctors think it's a good idea not to flood the body with alcohol.'

'Most people don't live here.'

'Touché.' She drained what was left in her glass and held it out for Sidorov to refill, Baarda's warning echoing in her head even as she ignored it. Connie wished she could pretend she was only playing a role, but the truth was that The Institution was starting to get to her, and the wine was a welcome, if incredibly temporary, diversion.

'Okay, one for one,' he said, setting the bottle back down. 'You clearly don't mind working with men who've done terrible things. What was it that made you able to empathise with serial killers?'

Connie considered his question. The truth, hard as it was for her to tell it, was the only thing likely to get him to trust her. Sidorov was clearly adept at seeing through subterfuge. She steeled herself. The sacrifice of opening up about her past and her private life was worth it, if it brought her a step closer to finding Aurora. She sat back in her chair, and drew up her legs.

'It's not that I'm able to overlook the terrible things they've done,' she began. 'But I understand how it feels to be committed to a mental health facility. I was eighteen years old when my parents were persuaded by a psychiatrist to sign me in to a hospital in Boston. I'd been involved in a car crash on my way to a date on a beach at night. Martha's Vineyard is a great place for a late-night rendezvous next to a campfire with a cold beer and all the stars you can count.' She paused, taking a long drink and abandoning herself to the memory.

'Go on,' Sidorov said.

'I was driving through the woods, crashed my car, never made it to the date. After the accident I couldn't talk.'

'Head injury?'

'Not from the crash. That might've been obvious enough to keep me on a medical ward rather than a psych unit. My elderly but very senior psychiatrist decided that the scan indicated no injury, diagnosing instead that I was exhibiting teenage

172

hysteria. His hypothesis was that I'd been planning on losing my virginity that night to a boy I was obsessed with – some of that was correct, by the way – and that I wasn't ready, so I self-sabotaged by deliberately hitting the tree. That part's not true. He decided that my refusal to speak was bound up in guilt, attention-seeking, sexual frustration and immaturity. By the time I hadn't spoken or communicated in writing properly for a month and my place at college had been revoked, my parents felt they had no choice but to lock me up for treatment. The phrase "for her own good" was used with alarming regularity.'

'Why couldn't you communicate?' Sidorov asked.

'I'd taken a ball to the temple in a lacrosse match previously. I wasn't diagnosed with concussion, being too stubborn to go to the hospital. A blood clot lodged in my brain at the worst possible moment. It was small but positioned somewhere hard to spot.'

Sidorov forgot his former anger and leaned forward. 'What did it feel like to you?'

Connie shrugged and tried not to get sucked too far back into the memories of that time.

'It floored me.' She gave her head a small shake. 'I could think clearly, understand everything, but my mouth wouldn't form the words my brain was thinking and I couldn't get my hand to make meaningful symbols on paper. God, I even tried mime but I think that just persuaded them even more that I was hysterical.'

'What happened to you?'

'Private hospital, my grandmother was wealthy enough to be able to afford it. That was part of the problem. The psychiatrist in question was in her social circle and she assured my parents he was the best that money could buy. He was old-school, thought he always knew best, really didn't like teenage girls. Didn't like me. I think he thought that taking away my privileged lifestyle and teaching me a lesson was going to get me to "snap out of it". I was there a while. Best work placement ever. There were people with psychiatric conditions, psychological conditions, good medics, bad medics, kindness, laziness, bullying. The usual cocktail.'

'That's when you decided on this as a career?'

'Two things happened. The first was that another patient managed to avoid lockdown one night, and came into my room apparently responding to the commands of the alien voices he was hearing in his head. He bit off part of the cartilage from my upper ear. He swallowed it.' She pulled back her hair to show the missing chunk.

Sidorov's mouth dropped open.

'After that, the universe decided to balance the scales with a second car accident. My psychiatrist was put out of action and replaced by someone much younger, who reviewed all his cases from scratch. For me that meant new scans, a closer look, the blood clot was spotted and operated on. I woke up talking normally and the rest is history.'

'If that had been me, the last thing I'd have wanted was a career in psychology,' Sidorov said.

'I think I felt like I couldn't let anyone else go through what I'd gone through. I wanted to find a way to communicate with the people locked up in places like this. Try to find their truth – mad, bad or otherwise. I wish someone had tried harder for me. I have a level of insight that I think escapes most people, lucky for them.'

Sidorov stood, crossed the room to a wine rack where he turned a few bottles to look at labels, before choosing one then picking up a corkscrew.

'I hate wine sold with screw-top bottles. It's not the point, you know?'

'See? I knew if we talked for long enough, we'd find something we agree on,' Connie said, smiling at him as she held out her glass. 'Your turn. Why are you here? It's inhospitable, harsh, and quite honestly rather joyless. I get why the specialist psychiatric staff are here – it's a bit of a feather in the cap, working with such notorious serial killers. But for a medic? You could be anywhere. There are a number of Caribbean Islands hospitals who'd happily offer you a placement.'

'I don't do hot climates,' he said.

He chose not to return to his comfortable place on the sofa and sat on the coffee table instead to fill Connie's glass, their knees touching. She tried to shift back in the armchair to find there wasn't enough give in the cushions to put any additional space between them.

'You know, life here isn't so bad. There's a gym with a sauna, a steam room and a hot tub. No pool and it's not five-star-hotel quality, but it's good enough. The food isn't terrible and there's a weekly delivery service so you can order whatever you want and it all gets brought in on a Saturday, hence the wine collection.'

'That's not enough quality of life for me,' Connie said.

'The money's good. For me, it's about four times what I was earning in Belarus. Most of that is simply to make up for the location and the environment. I'm able to send some cash back to my family each month, which helps with the guilt of having left. Professionally, it's a challenge. We do our best to avoid sending patients out for treatments. It's a security nightmare and takes up too many resources, so we handle almost everything on site except transplants, midwifery, or specialisations like maxillofacial. That means I get to practise more minor surgeries, gives me the time and scope to extend beyond what I'd do in a normal hospital environment.'

'Do you find it lonely?' she asked.

Sidorov reached out a hand and took her glass from her.

'When I first came here, I was running away from a relationship that got very complicated and very messy. It's not as lonely as you might think. In some ways it's quite liberating being somewhere that everyone has the same needs and doesn't feel obliged to start a relationship to fulfil them.'

He leaned in, starting to close his eyes, sliding his left hand up her thigh and his right onto her shoulder, mouth heading for hers.

Holding up a palm to his chest and moving her head back, Connie stopped him.

'That's not what's happening here,' she said, low but firm. 'I'm here for work and I'm not looking for anything else, plus twenty minutes ago you were accusing me of . . . I'm not actually sure what you were accusing me of, but the atmosphere in here was kind of unpleasant for a while.'

'Really?' Sidorov stood. 'You did the whole "Do you find it lonely?" thing. Letting me fill up your glass, sharing details about our private lives.'

'You don't get to play the guilt card with me.' Connie was stuck between genuine outrage, trying to figure out what her undercover character would do, and assessing what the best reaction for Aurora's sake would be. She settled for showing genuine emotion. Sidorov would surely see through anything else. She got to her feet. 'I told you when you invited me that a drink was not going to be a prelude to anything more, and I don't care what normally goes on here. I've known you for all of twenty-four hours and this is a work environment, not a nightclub.'

Sidorov shrugged. 'My mistake,' he said.

'Yeah, it definitely was.' Connie made her way to the door.

'So what actually is the deal with Patient B?' Sidorov asked, his voice rock-hard once more. 'It's all anyone can talk about on the ward.'

She turned back to face him, one hand on the door handle. 'Really? What are the various theories?'

'The most popular is that he's a police officer.' Connie kept her face neutral as her heart sank. 'We think one of the patients is under suspicion for some unsolved murders and that Patient B is going to try to get a confession out of whoever it is.'

'Interesting,' Connie said lightly. 'What else?'

'Internal audit. Maybe Patient B is a professional plant to assess the treatment of patients on the ward.'

'Is that all?'

'Or that he really is ex-military, got caught spying, maybe he went rogue and did some double-agent stuff. Shove him in here, make sure no one can visit him, or that no one will believe a word he says because he's on a psych ward. It's a much better way to dispose of a threat than in either a civilian or a military prison.'

'Now that's more interesting,' Connie said. 'Is there a prize for the winner, when you're all convinced that the truth has finally come out?'

He smirked. 'What do you think?'

'I think this place leaves you all with too little to keep your minds busy, and that there are going to be a lot of disappointed people on Heaven Ward. Goodnight, Dr Sidorov.'

Her cell phone rang as she entered her room, requesting a video call from a number she didn't recognise. It was after midnight, she'd been drinking, and the day had taken its toll, but there was a chance it was Johannes Cameron or the police. Connie took the call. A woman's face appeared, grey-haired, prominent cheekbones, looking as if she'd just had a solid eight hours' sleep and was ready to run a marathon whilst cooking dinner. Connie's first emotion was envy.

'Dr Woolwine, I'm Leona Black, the consultant paediatrician advising Johannes Cameron. Is it a bad time? I've been trying to call for the last couple of hours.'

'I'm so sorry,' Connie said. 'I had to turn my phone off while I was seeing someone from the ward. Give me a moment, would you?' She went into her bathroom, the furthest she could get from the corridor, and shut the door to make sure she couldn't be overheard. 'Thank you for getting in touch. I've been given a lot of information already but I felt it important to speak with you directly.'

'I couldn't agree more,' Leona Black said. 'What did you want to know?'

'We're on the clock, and I'm very aware of the ticking, but I need to know more about what a foetal abduction means for Aurora. How would it have been, taking a baby from a living woman, like that?'

Leona Black looked her deep in her eyes through the screens and the technology that separated them and said, 'Absolute fucking horrific, my dear. That's the truth. I don't need to comment on what Tara went through. I've seen your credentials, and I know you'll be familiar with that trauma already. But for baby Aurora – and please don't be fooled into thinking she won't have any awareness of her own discomfort – it will have been a shocking and painful birth. All I can say is that Tara was fit, healthy and strong throughout her pregnancy. Aurora was already a good size and her scans showed no abnormalities. Nonetheless, she was removed from the womb prematurely.'

'What are the risks associated with that?' Connie asked.

'The increased risk of neonatal death comes really from four directions: malnutrition, dehydration, a weakened immune system, and low temperature. On top of that, because of the trauma Tara suffered, Aurora will inevitably be in shock. There's every chance she won't have got enough air during the birth and her brain might have been deprived of oxygen for a sustained period. I'd be worried about asphyxia, respiratory distress syndrome, and heart or lung defects.'

'There's been a video and an audio file. What did you make of those?' Connie asked.

'The cry was strong enough to give me hope – that's if it really was Aurora's, of course. The skin tone suggested dehydration, and I think that's almost a given. She might not be taking enough milk after a shock like that. Aurora would have an increased need for warmth, observation, probably medication and stimulation, and she'll be getting none of those things.'

For the first time, the strength in the doctor's voice weakened. Connie felt the same. The picture was grim. Baby Aurora was suffering.

'Worst-case scenario?' Connie asked quietly.

'Possibly pneumonia, sepsis. There may well also have been injuries occasioned during the abduction that her kidnappers are unaware of. Listen, Dr Woolwine, I believe you've been told you have a few days. The truth is that every minute counts. The clock you hear as you investigate can suddenly stop. Giving you an average survival time for a newborn without proper care was rather misleading. It was done to give the family hope more than anything else. I've told the police this and I wanted to look you in the eyes and tell you, too: find Aurora. If you don't get to her soon, it won't just be a matter of whether or

179

not she's still breathing. The physical damage done now might stay with her forever.'

'I hear you,' Connie said, and she did. All of it. The plea, the science, the subtext that hope was not just dripping away but cascading like a waterfall. She felt it like a punch. 'I'm doing everything I can.'

Dr Black gave a curt nod. 'I knew Tara,' she said. Connie saw her fight to hold back tears. 'She was a gentle soul with a warrior spirit. Her daughter will be good for the world. Aurora's death would be a tragic waste, and we've all seen quite enough of that.'

'Haven't we just,' Connie agreed.

Chapter 16

'Patient B,' Jake called at the door of his cell before unlocking it. 'Dinner and community time. Let's go.'

Baarda didn't bother to answer, keeping his eyes neutral as they walked the corridor to the common room where the other patients were already seated for their meal. They ate quickly and largely without bothering to talk, but every plate and bowl was cleared.

It was amazing how valuable food became when you couldn't just go to the fridge or pop into a store to grab a snack to keep you going. What they were given wasn't exactly gourmet, but as facility catering went, it wasn't terrible either. Tonight, they'd been served spaghetti bolognese with a side of green beans and a bread roll, orange juice to drink and fruit salad for dessert.

Announcements came from inside the staff viewing area. Only Jake stayed in the common room. Once the crockery had been cleared, Dr Ong, Nurse Lightfoot and Senior Ward Nurse Samuel Casey also entered the room.

'Good evening, everyone,' Dr Ong said. 'You now have four hours of community time. The first section of that will be spent as free recreation, and you have a new guest so please make sure to include him in any games. Thereafter Nurse Casey will choose a film for you all. If you choose not to watch it, do make sure any activities are conducted quietly so as not to disturb anyone. Community time is important. Make sure you're using it wisely and remember our core values please – friendship, support, growth, progress.'

It was a well-rehearsed speech, although given with a surprising degree of enthusiasm. The five men around Baarda sighed as they moved to pick up whatever activity they'd chosen for the evening.

'You play chess?' The man who'd invited him was smiling broadly. Good-looking with exuberant rom-com charm, he waved a tatty box invitingly.

Baarda nodded and followed Vince East to a table. He and Connie had taken a different approach to research before entering Heaven Ward, largely because it was Baarda who was going to be locked into a ward with five serial killers. He'd taken the journey time to read the publicly accessible information on the people he would be boarding with. Vince East, the unit's newest resident, was also its most unusual.

They set the board up together.

'You get to choose as it's our first game. White or black?'

'Black,' Baarda said.

'Damn, I wanted to play black!' East slapped the table happily enough.

'We can swap,' Baarda said.

'I was fucking with you, man,' East said. 'What sort of a psycho would get upset over which colour they played? Between us, in here, that's everybody.'

East made the first move. 'So what are you in for?'

'Let's just play,' Baarda said.

'Wow, you're getting the special treatment with the nice lady sent all this way just to hold your hand and you're not even going to share the gossip. Come on, man. I've been locked up in this place for four years. At least tell me what the outside world's like. Is there anything new on the McDonald's menu?'

Baarda sighed again and pushed one of his pieces into a new position.

'If I'd known you were going to be this much of a grouch, I'd have asked the professor to play. Word of warning, he's going to ask what you think of smartphones and the best thing you can do for your own sanity is to say you never had one.'

'I'll remember that,' Baarda said. 'Your move.'

'And avoid Benny Rubio when he starts having one of his tantrums. If the staff don't manage to calm him down in time, the shit will start to fly. I don't mean that metaphorically. That fruit loop enjoys a dirty protest.' He pushed a chess piece with his little finger without paying attention to the board, and leaned further in towards Baarda. 'So I'm supposed to call you Patient B, right? That's so cool. You got some kind of James Bond thing going, jetting all over the world to assassinate evil dictators?'

'Are you about to ask me if I could kill you with my bare hands?' Baarda asked, staring at the board.

'Oh, I'm sure you could. That's sort of a prerequisite for being allowed residency in here. You know about Joe Yarowski, the basketball team mascot? He never came to terms with not making it as a pro player. Killed a whole lot of people who abused him in his costume at different games.' He dropped his voice even lower and whispered, 'He's a strangler. That's pretty unpleasant if you think of the mechanics of how that really goes down: bulgy eyes, protruding tongue. Gross.'

183

'I thought you wanted to play chess,' Baarda said.

East grinned, and they played a few more moves before he couldn't contain himself a second more.

'At least tell me about your personal chaperone. I mean, she's gorgeous. Is she military too? What does she look like in a uniform? Does she always keep her hair in a ponytail? Because I'm thinking naked with her hair loose, it would probably go down to just below her shoulder blades, those blond highlights catching the sun—'

'What are you in here for?' Baarda asked abruptly.

'I, my friend, am in here because some very powerful people on the outside thought the optic was better if I was portrayed as insane rather than as someone who had practised justified vengeance.'

'So you're innocent?' Baarda asked.

'Shit, no. I killed a whole bunch of people but each and every one of them had it coming.' He dropped his voice again. 'You know the thing about being in here? You're never getting out. There's no end to your sentence, no target for you to focus on. A whole bunch of people have to say you're sane again, that you understood what you did, that you no longer have any form of psychiatric or psychological illness. The list goes on and on, and yet there seem to be no really hard-and-fast rules. I'd have taken prison any day over this head-fuck.'

Baarda took the opportunity to look around. The professor was sitting alone on a sofa doing a crossword. Harold Haskin was doing a jigsaw with Jake the orderly leaning over his chair, talking quietly to him. In the far corner, Nurse Lightfoot was overseeing Joe Yarowski and Benny Rubio as they played a board game and argued over who was going to use which colour plastic pieces.

'Watch, this is the best part of games night. Any minute now Rubio will start pretending to cry, Nurse Lightfoot will tell Joe that he has to hand over the blue pieces, and everything will go flying. I give it about a minute.'

As much as Baarda wanted to look away, he found it impossible. Joe Yarowski had started jabbing a finger hard onto the tabletop as he argued his right to have the blue pieces, and Rubio's voice grew louder and higher-pitched with every word. Other conversations around the room had begun to stall as all eyes made their way to the argument, and Nurse Lightfoot rolled her eyes to the ceiling.

Yarowski's finger jabbing moved up to the air, pointing in Rubio's general direction. Benny Rubio began to screech. Jake made his way over, in no hurry. At the precise moment Rubio began hammering his fist on the table, Yarowski's finger took its first jab into Rubio's upper chest and less than a second later the game board went flying. Red, blue, yellow and green plastic pieces flew into the air. Both men were on their feet in a heartbeat, screaming into each other's faces.

'What's his deal?' Baarda asked Vince East, motioning with his head towards the male nurse, Samuel Casey, who stood leaning against the door to the staff viewing area, his face devoid of expression, as if the altercation weren't happening at all.

'Casey? He's the senior nurse. Never seen him laugh, never seen him lose his temper. Never seen him stay a second later than his shift. He lets the other nurses and the orderlies deal with the messy stuff, not that I blame him for that.'

Nurse Lightfoot was picking up game pieces from the floor as Jake was talking Benny Rubio down. Yarowski had sat back down in his chair, perfectly calm once more. Baarda watched him. Rubio might have lost control, but Yarowski hadn't, not really. He'd known exactly when to stop. Yarowski's hands were at his sides, flopping over the edges of the armchair, fingertips brushing the floor, as if he hadn't a care in the world. He fit the global stereotype of a basketball player precisely. Black, at least six foot five, shaved head, muscles well defined even through the pyjama-style soft hospital wear.

'Yarowski's huge. Has he ever stepped over the line with Rubio?' Baarda asked.

East gave up watching the main entertainment and stared at Baarda instead. 'Whoa, that's the sort of question I'd expect from someone who was scoping out the competition. You looking for someone to fight? I would not take on Yarowski. Not at all. I mean, you're big, like six-three right? But Yarowski's strong and he's still got a few inches on you. Take my advice, leave that alone.'

'There's no access to a gym on the ward. How does he stay so fit?'

'Yoga – I kid you not. He's the only man I know who's strangled enough people to fill a minibus and who can stand on his hands, perfectly still for like, I don't know how long exactly, but it's impressive. One-handed press-ups, ten-minute planks, uses his own body weight to work out. I like to keep in shape, you know, but that's a step beyond.'

Benny Rubio was calm again, clutching game pieces in his hand and counting them, one to four, over and over again. Nurse Lightfoot was still checking the floor for bits of the game. After a minute she gave a resigned huff, threw the lid on the box and shoved it back onto a shelf.

'We're going to start the film,' Casey announced, looking at his watch. 'You can all thank Mr Rubio and Mr Yarowski for the loss of game time. Pick a seat and stay in it.'

'Gotta move fast,' East said. 'Follow me.'

Before anyone else could take it, East was on a sofa against the very back wall, furthest from the television. Baarda took his time joining him, settling himself stiffly into the sagging couch as the professor closed his crossword book and set it down, turning in his armchair towards the large screen. Rubio began bouncing up and down into the sofa. Haskin raised a hand in Samuel Casey's direction and was allowed to go and speak quietly with the senior nurse while Lightfoot put on that evening's movie.

'What is it? What is it? What is it?' Rubio clapped his hands in anticipation.

The titles flicked up on the screen.

'Fuckers,' East whispered. '*Groundhog Day.*'

'What were you hoping for?' Baarda asked him.

'Anything except a film about how someone lives the same day over and over again. It's Casey's little mind-fuck, and this isn't even a bad week. When he really wants to punish us he chooses a musical,' East said.

'What constitutes a good week?'

'An old war movie. Nothing too exciting or revolutionary, obviously. They don't like giving us ideas. *The Great Escape* is out for obvious reasons but *The Bridge on the River Kwai*; *Overlord*; *Merry Christmas, Mr Lawrence*; *The Battle of Algiers*; *The Dirty Dozen* – we get all of those.'

'Not *Papillon* then,' Baarda murmured.

East stifled a laugh. They watched in silence for a few minutes as Bill Murray kicked off with a weather report, and Nurse Casey led Joe Yarowski out into the main corridor.

'What's up with that?'

'Must've asked to be allowed to go to his cell early. One less of us to look after so there's no way Casey would say no. Yarowski'll be locked in for the night. Guess he didn't

187

fancy another rerun of this, even with Andie MacDowell on offer.'

Rubio settled down, laughing louder and more often than anyone else, but the atmosphere was less charged. Even the professor seemed distracted by the entertainment. Casey wandered back through and indicated to Lightfoot that she could take a break. The two of them disappeared into the staff viewing area, leaving Jake alone to maintain discipline in the common room. He chose an armchair and began dozing. East left it a sensible amount of time before starting a new conversation.

'You mind me making an observation?' Baarda kept looking at the screen. 'You don't seem crazy. I say that as someone who has a number of reports detailing my supposed psychosis. What's your story?' He nudged Baarda with a collegiate elbow.

'I can't discuss that,' Baarda said.

'Bull. If it's the military you're worried about, they can't both pretend you're so mentally incapacitated that you've got to spend the rest of your life in here with the batshit brigade and at the same time expect you to be responsible for not giving away any state secrets.'

On the screen Bill Murray was punching an insurance salesman in the face. Rubio responded with a howl of laughter and even the professor gave a satisfied smile.

'Was there something specific you wanted to know?' Baarda asked East, keeping his eyes on the screen.

'Seriously? You'll answer me? God, that's so exciting that I don't know what to ask first.'

'Make it good,' Baarda said. 'You've got one question before I get bored.'

East folded his arms purposefully and settled himself back in his chair, a slight frown crinkling his forehead. He was quiet for nearly five minutes.

'How did you justify to yourself the pain the people you killed experienced?'

Baarda glanced briefly at East. His face had lost its childish grin; his voice was calmer. The question, Baarda realised, was steeped as much in the things East had done to his victims as the desire for knowledge of what Baarda was supposed to have done.

'I've never taken any pleasure in killing anyone. You only need to justify killing if you're enjoying it. I was trained to do the things I did,' he said. 'There aren't a lot of staff here for a ward that's supposed to house prolific serial killers. Is it always like this?'

'There was one more nurse before you came but they're saying she's off on early maternity leave, if you want to believe that. I guess as we're locked in the top of the tallest tower in the middle of fucking nowhere, they figured a skeleton crew would do it. It's not like anyone's actively trying to rehabilitate us except Ong. This is throw-away-the-key territory. And you changed the subject. You must have killed people you weren't supposed to if the military didn't like it. Why do that if you didn't have a personal reason?'

'Hey, shut up,' Rubio shouted across at East. 'I'm watching.'

'You're right, I'm so sorry!' East shouted back. 'You need absolute silence to watch the ending you've already seen a thousand times when he does all the right stuff, breaks free of the pattern he's in and gets the girl.'

Rubio gave a long, loud wail that was more chalkboard than child.

'Fuck's sake,' Jake muttered. 'You've set him off again.'

East sighed. 'Okay, Benny, I'm sorry. I'm going to be quiet. It's all good. I didn't mean to upset you.'

Rubio swallowed the remainder of his tantrum and settled

189

back down to watch. Jake gave East a single nod of either thanks or forgiveness and went back to resting his eyes.

'You were saying . . .' East prompted Baarda.

'I wasn't. Why was there a pregnant nurse on this ward? Surely that was dangerous.'

'You killed people for a living but you're concerned about the well-being of one pregnant nurse you never met?' East joked.

Professor Saint shushed them.

'I never killed a woman, pregnant or otherwise,' Baarda said. 'Did you?'

East wagged a finger at him.

'You do that every time? Soon as we get talking you turn it back on me. You're good, buddy.' He moved across the sofa to get that bit closer to Baarda. 'Let me tell you a couple of things about Nurse Cameron. No one here was ever going to hurt her. Two reasons. First was that she was the only good thing about this place. Good-looking, great body, kind, didn't always toe the party line, you know what I'm saying? The rest of them apply the rules for their own reasons – you don't get to finish what you're doing cos Dr Roth's a bitch and she likes fucking things up for you. Dr Ong likes his routine, says his guests need self-discipline to ready themselves for outside life. Sam Casey just doesn't give a shit, wants to get back to his room. The other two nurses are okay but Madani is only working here to support her family back home, so she's all about the paycheque. Nurse Cameron seemed to actually want us to be happy. She was trying to make a difference. If she knows what's good for her, she'll stay well away from this hellhole. She deserved better.'

'Deserved?'

'From a job perspective, you know? I used to ask her at the

190

start of every shift: what's a nice girl like you doing in a place like this?'

'What was her answer?'

'Keeping herself grateful.'

Jake the orderly was snoring now, mouth gaping. The professor was staring at him, eyes narrowed, fingers curled into claws. Baarda watched as Professor Saint leaned forward towards Jake's chair, lips drawn back, teeth bared.

'You think we should intervene?' East asked.

'Not my job any more,' Baarda replied. 'I don't like that other orderly, Tom. Think he put something in my drink this morning. That ever happen to you?'

'You kidding? They medicate us with extra shit all the time. You think anyone ever gave baby Rubio over there a suppository without slipping something extra in his juice first? They do it to all of us when they want to, most often on a Saturday night when whoever's on duty wants to do something other than sit up here alone for hours.'

'What about for other things than just putting the ward to sleep?' Baarda asked.

Professor Saint had pulled out one of the heavy cushions from the seat of the sofa and was approaching Jake steadily with the cushion held at face height. Whatever the other staff members were doing inside the viewing area, they weren't keeping an eye out front.

Baarda watched and waited. If he alerted the orderly, he might as well leave the ward straight away. Whether his cover was blown or not, there was no way anyone was going to trust him enough to open up again. Doing nothing was equally impossible.

'Whatever they need, they do. There's an inspection once a year, sometimes spot checks too. You're too boisterous? They

191

give you something to chill you out. Sitting in a corner staring at the wall? They give you something to pep you up. Joe Yarowski once pissed Roth off so badly she gave him a shot of something that had him begging for death for three days straight. Drug cupboard on Heaven Ward is a dealer's paradise.'

The professor had positioned his legs apart for maximum stability, the cushion no more than an inch from Jake's face.

Baarda stood.

'Don't do it,' East warned. 'There are rules in here. We don't fuck up each other's fun.'

'You think I care?' Baarda asked. He took a few steps across to the viewing area window and hammered on the glass. 'Hey, I have to piss.'

The professor froze, Jake's eyes opened blearily, then Lightfoot came charging out of the viewing area, Casey walking behind her.

'Get up!' Casey shouted. Jake did as he was told, snatching the cushion from the professor's hands.

East and Haskin both stayed where they were as the professor was bundled out of the door by Jake and Nurse Lightfoot. Rubio was still staring at the TV.

Casey stood in the middle of the room, hands on his hips. 'Dr Ong has a community responsibility regime here. You watch something like that happen and do nothing, you're all responsible. Back to your rooms for lock-in.'

Rubio opened his mouth and started crying again. Casey walked over and slapped him hard across the face.

Baarda checked East's reaction: boredom with a side of amusement. Rubio lowered his head and decided it was time for silence.

'Go,' Casey said.

One by one they went. Baarda could hear Jake yelling at

the professor inside his room. Yarowski was silent as they went past, no light slipping from beneath the door. They disappeared into their allotted spaces, doors slamming behind them, and finally Baarda was alone.

The viewing slot on his door had been left open. Little by little the light from the corridor dimmed as the staff exited for the night.

He lay on his bed, staring up at the ceiling, wondering where Connie was. Wondering how she'd managed to survive in an institutional environment for so many months, only to decide to dedicate her life to dealing with people like Professor Saint and Benny Rubio.

Somewhere, someone was crying, their breath hitching every now and then. It didn't have the childlike, exhibitionist quality of Rubio's earlier outburst. The noise was haunting as it echoed down the stone hallway.

Chapter 17

It wasn't daylight that woke Connie, nor was it sound. It wasn't that she was either too hot or too cold. It was the simple sense that something was wrong. Her heart was pounding before her eyes opened, and one hand was already reaching for the light switch.

As her eyes adjusted to the pool of light from the lamp, she got her body under control and tried to capture the end of what must surely have been a nightmare. Her brain came up blank. She swung her legs out of bed and sat for a moment, listening, breathing hard. No footsteps from the rooms overhead. No early morning music from a nearby shower in preparation for an early shift. No one making food noisily having just got in from a late.

Connie gave herself a shake and made for the bathroom, turning on the light in there too as she splashed cold water on her face. Last night's wine had left her with a distant headache, but nothing she would categorise as a hangover. She thought back to the bizarre evening. Sidorov was an oddball, but he had proved easy enough to handle. More fishing expedition than genuine aggressor, and she had expected an amount of curiosity having turned up so suddenly, under such a cloud of secrecy. Much worse than that had been her conversation with the paediatrician, and the growing feeling that Aurora was taking her last breaths right now, wherever she was. And that Connie's failure to make rapid progress was going to cost her life.

In the mirror, her face was pale and drawn. Connie tried pinching her cheeks to get some blood into them, but the damage went deeper than the superficial. She could see her exhaustion mapped out in the lines and shadows. She needed a trip home to Martha's Vineyard when the case was concluded, some time on a beach with the sun on her face, the rhythm of the waves and a good book for company. A shower would make her feel better. Hot water. She hadn't had the chance to exercise for days and the walls were starting to close in. She dialled up the heat and stepped into the half-hearted stream.

The sensation of the hot water hitting her skin helped, but not enough. Perhaps it was the past leaving her disconcerted. She'd chosen a career in psychology not expecting to ever spend another night in an institution, even if her current stay was as professional not patient. Still, it was bringing back memories long since buried. The invasive nature of treatment provided without your consent. The knowledge that you were being watched, judged and assessed twenty-four hours a day. The smallness of your world and your life. That was the worst of it. It was a place of never-ending conflict, where both insufficient assistance was given to those who needed it and too much latitude was allowed for the truly evil.

Easy to understand, in the context of a ward housing only

six patients, kept separate from the general population, that it might have been easy to tempt one of them into doing something terrible, if only to relive the sense of power and release killing gave them. And what more could be taken from them? Certainly not much in the way of liberty. The end game for the kidnappers might have been to get their hands on baby Aurora, but Connie was sure whoever had murdered Tara did it purely for gratification.

It flew in the face of her knowledge and profession, the concept of evil, and yet there it sat, a slothful toad in her heart. Those with serious psychiatric illness or psychological disorders could hardly be held responsible for their actions, and yet they perpetuated such monstrosities that it was hard to see how they could avoid the label themselves.

Connie knew she was disappearing inside her own head again. It happened when she was stressed. The shower wasn't working. More sleep wasn't an option. The only cure was to get on with her work. It was early, but the ward was beckoning. She dried off and went to find clothes, choosing black jeans and a linen shirt. The shirt had fallen off a hanger and was crumpled on the base of the wardrobe. Connie considered taking the time to iron it and decided not to. She acknowledged her decision as indicative of her psychological state, but didn't care enough to fight it. What she needed was to figure out where baby Aurora was as quickly as possible and get out of there. Nothing else. It didn't matter if she wasn't perfectly presented for a day with serial killers.

She slid the chain off her door and made for the dining hall to grab something quick from the staff breakfast buffet, before changing her mind and heading straight across the campus towards the lifts. She could get coffee in the staff kitchen on the ward. Her stomach had turned sour at the mere thought of food.

Ten minutes later, taking the final set of stairs at a jog to pump some blood around her veins, she was letting herself onto the ward. There had been no one in the ward security area and the staffroom had been equally empty. The clock bore the legend 5.45 a.m. Connie released a slow breath. She'd failed to check her mobile for an update from Director Le Fay, and now she would need to go all the way back down to get it. A flush of uncharacteristic fury flashed through her at the inconvenience.

'Baarda first,' she counselled herself aloud. 'Then coffee and food. Give yourself a damned break. The cell phone can wait.'

The peep slot to Baarda's room was open. He was sleeping. Connie was unsettled enough to stand watching his chest rise and fall before feeling able to walk away, relieved that he was seemingly fine. Through the common room and into the staff viewing area, and from there into the kitchen with the dumb-waiter she went. Inside the dumbwaiter there were freshly baked croissants, a large bowl offering a selection of fruit, a carton of milk in a chiller and a separate dish of ham and cheese on an ice bed. Better than a motel offering, she thought. When she'd been committed by her own parents and grand-mother, breakfast had consisted of porridge, cold toast, unsweetened plain yoghurt and either bacon or sausages at the weekends because weekends were the only days visits were allowed. The optic of a cooked breakfast made for good family relations.

As much as she resented the memory of desperately looking forward to the pathetic treat each week, Connie's stomach betrayed her and growled. She reached for one of the croissants and dipped it in the instant coffee she'd just made, making a mental note to tell Baarda she'd stolen his pastry and that he would have to make do with something else instead. As she finished eating, relieved that no one had come in and found her taking food from their patients, Connie rinsed her cup and considered her to-do list for the day.

First up was getting some time with Joe Yarowski. The best option seemed to be another hypnotherapy session. It had worked well enough with Benny Rubio. Interviewing the patients one by one like that was slow going, but it was important work and she had to take care when she did it. Rush it, ask too many direct questions, and she'd blow her cover and put Baarda at risk. Maintaining the sense of a skilled patient therapist was vital, however frustrating.

After Yarowski, she'd scheduled her daily session with Baarda to see what, if anything, he'd managed to find out and to talk him through her assessment of the various potential conspirators. That would take her up to lunchtime, when hopefully Director Le Fay would be available for a face-to-face. Finally, she needed to see Harold Haskin, also known as the Blindfold Killer. Everyone who'd had access to news media in the previous decade had heard of him. His capture had been the result, in part, of some excellent profiling work, not by her but by someone Connie had partnered with previously. That profiler had chosen a new career path soon after Haskin's arrest. It was one of those cases that marked you forever.

'You know, there's always breakfast available in the staff canteen, even if you're on an early,' Dawn Lightfoot said as she walked in and grabbed a coffee cup.

Connie turned and smiled at the nurse. 'I was up here before I realised I was hungry,' she said. Keen to take advantage of the opportunity to dig, she continued, 'You know, a handful of people have found out I'm working on this ward and asked if I'm replacing Nurse Tara. The way people talk about her, it's like she was some sort of saint.'

'Is that right?' Lightfoot asked, throwing some coffee granules into the mug with what Connie thought was unnecessary force, and putting the kettle on.

'In the military, especially when we're profiling candidates for certain positions or missions, we're always wary of those kinds. We pretty much live by the creed that if someone seems too good to be true . . .' She let it hang.

Lightfoot raised her eyebrows and busied herself getting milk from the fridge.

'Were you two close?' Connie asked.

'Aren't you just full of questions today? What is you want, Connie? You don't mind if I drop the "Doctor" do you?'

'Just passing the time, but also wondering what she'll be like assuming she comes back to the ward after maternity leave. Tara's the one member of staff I won't be able to assess while I'm here.'

'If you heard she's such a saint, I'm sure she'll prove good enough to change your pet serial killer's sheets.'

'Ouch. You pissed at me, or Tara?' Connie asked, stopping in the doorway so Lightfoot couldn't walk straight out.

'Oh, fuck you,' Lightfoot said, sounding tired and irritable. 'Don't come in here and try to psychoanalyse me. I've worked with a hundred psychiatrists better at this than you.'

'And yet you haven't been promoted to senior ward nurse. Why is that?'

Dawn Lightfoot wrinkled her nose and pinched her lips together. Observing her, Connie realised that she was trying not to say something, a memory that was distasteful, but was finding it difficult to resist. Connie waited, fascinated to see which side of the nurse would win out.

Lightfoot flexed her hands in and out of fists for a few seconds then grabbed the neck of her uniform and wrenched it downwards to reveal a raised scar on her upper chest comprised of multiple thick lines tangled together. Connie felt the missing tip of her ear tingle in phantom sympathy. Scars were always more than just physical marks. They were war stories, misjudgements, regrets, the source of blame. Emotional time bombs that went off again and again each time they came into view. Connie's was no different. Dawn Lightfoot's was a source of fury, Connie thought, judging by the nurse's face.

'This was Tara's fault,' she said, her voice so low it was almost a growl. 'I was disciplining a patient during dinner and he wouldn't do what he was told, so I asked Jake to get the taser. By the time he came back with it, Tara was standing in the way, promising she could get the patient to go quietly. She told me I was over-reacting, for fuck's sake. Does this look like I over-reacted?'

'How did it actually happen?' Connie asked.

'While Tara was wasting time playing Florence Nightingale to a mass murderer, I lost my moment to get him to comply. He went over Tara's shoulder with the fork and shoved it into my chest.'

'I thought they only used plastic forks. That scar is deep.'

'Great observation skills,' Lightfoot said sarcastically. 'He shoved it in so far that some of the plastic prongs snapped off inside me, then he turned it and scraped the rest of my skin off.'

'Jesus, that must have been painful. I'm so sorry you went through that. Which patient was it?'

'He's gone now. He was transferred after it happened,' Lightfoot said.

Connie's fingertips itched with the desire to experience the wound first-hand, to feel what Lightfoot felt every time her hand brushed it. She knew other people didn't operate the way she did, constantly needing physical contact to take her inside emotions, to make her experience of the world more visceral and real. She knew other people found her strange, and were put off by her methods and her lack of boundaries. But she needed what she needed.

'Can I touch it?' Connie asked.

'Are you fucking insane?'

Quite possibly, Connie thought. The Institution was certainly making her feel like she was losing the plot. 'Not yet,' was what she said, stepping forward to lay cool, gentle fingertips on the scar tissue.

Lightfoot stood her ground, mouth agape, eyes furious.

'What's worse for you? The way it looks, the pain it still gives you, or the memory of how it happened?' Connie asked.

Lightfoot's eyes fluttered shut momentarily. Like it or not, she was trying to figure out the answer to Connie's question. Brains did that. It was almost impossible to be asked a personal question without the answer popping into your mind, unbidden or otherwise.

'Why are you doing this?' she whispered, eyes still closed.

'The scar is slightly warmer than the flesh around it. The tips of it are hot and raw. I'm guessing it itches sometimes, which stops you from moving past it. I suspect you find yourself touching it sometimes when you're alone. You don't even realise you're doing it, then when your conscious brain catches you at it, you're furious with yourself. You're a nurse. You know the state of the scar could have been improved with surgery. Why haven't you had it looked at?'

Lightfoot finally slapped Connie's fingers away. 'Because I prefer to remember what these animals are capable of.'

'And because you want to remember never to trust anyone again, even if they're supposed to be on the same team as you?'

'This job might as well be in a zoo. We clean the animals'

cages. We herd them to where we need them to go. We get the vet in to take a look at them as necessary. But ultimately all we're doing is keeping the public safe from the danger they present to the outside world. Better never to forget that.'

'And Tara? You must have been pleased when she went off on maternity leave. Are you hoping she won't come back?'

'She shouldn't,' Lightfoot said, picking up her mug of coffee and stepping around Connie. 'A place like this really isn't safe enough for such a delicate soul, especially one with a baby to take care of.' She took a couple of steps forward until she was at Connie's side. 'And if you ever touch me again without my consent, I'll tell Director Le Fay you assaulted me. Just imagine how that would look on your precious CV.'

'I apologise,' Connie said.

Lightfoot was right: she shouldn't have touched her without consent, but it was only in the extremes of behaviour that you ever found out what someone was really like. Overstep a boundary and true colours showed within seconds. But Lightfoot hadn't moved Connie's fingertips off the scar straight away. She'd wanted Connie to know how it felt, how horrible it was. She'd needed someone else to understand her pain. There had been an element of smug satisfaction to it. Dawn Lightfoot hated Tara; that much was absolutely clear. The question was: why Tara had stood in the way to protect a patient from a nurse? Perhaps because she hadn't liked the way Lightfoot was behaving. Perhaps, more to the point, because the use of the taser was not, in her view, justified.

Connie waited until Lightfoot had gone through into the common room then considered where the new information got her. Nurse Lightfoot was not just angry, she was furious, perhaps with some justification. The scar on her skin was nasty, but the scar it had left on her psyche was much more dangerous.

202

So why reveal the incident at all if Lightfoot had been involved in Aurora's abduction?

'In case I find out anyway,' Connie muttered to herself. 'Plain sight is a far better place to hide.'

She made sure the kitchen was left tidy and went back through the common room into the ward corridor. It was still early, but worth checking on Joe Yarowski to see if he was awake. Maybe she could persuade the duty nurse to let him have breakfast before the other patients and start her session sooner rather than later.

Opening the peep slot in Yarowski's door as quietly as she could, Connie looked to see if he was sleeping. Apparently not as his bed was empty. The light spilling from the en suite and gentle burble of a running tap said he was up. That was the first thing that had gone right for her that morning. Connie stepped away to give Yarowski some privacy as he returned to his bedroom.

Five minutes passed. It wasn't the shower Connie could hear in Yarowski's bathroom; she was certain of that. More likely just a tap left running. Perhaps he wasn't in there at all. He certainly wasn't humming or talking to himself. It was possible there had been an incident that had resulted in Yarowski being sent to the quiet room, in which case she was going to have to rethink the shape of her day. She considered going to find the duty nurse to ask, but that meant explaining herself and witnessing yet more eye-rolls. Connie looked up and down the corridor. There was no sign of anyone. If Yarowski was in the bathroom, she could just call to him. If he wasn't, she could take the time to look through his personal effects for anything that might help her reach him in the hypnotherapy session. It was a win-win situation. Connie flashed her security pass in front of the electronic lock and opened the door.

'Hello? Mr Yarowski? This is Dr Connie.'

His shoes were pushed under the neatly tucked-in bedclothes. His shelf displayed a miniature soft basketball, various photos of in-game action, a packet of gum and a neatly folded letterman jacket.

'Whenever you're finished in there, I'd like to see if you're ready for a session with me this morning.' No response. 'Joe? You okay in there?'

Connie stepped forward to the bathroom and put her head slowly round the corner.

'No, no, no.' She was running forward, skidding onto her knees before she'd even thought about it. 'Joe, can you hear me?'

Yarowski was naked and face down, legs out of the shower, upper body beneath the dripping shower head.

Connie slid her left forearm under his neck, palm forcing its way under his chest, and with her right hand she got a firm grip on his right upper arm, bracing herself to take his full weight and flip him over.

Yarowski's body was cold even in those folds that usually preserved heat in the most hostile of environments. Connie began moving him into position for resuscitation. The moment of realisation dawned when she took hold of his face to open his mouth.

'Shit,' she murmured, the urgency draining from her as she felt his stiffening muscles. The face went into rigor mortis first, and whilst the rest of his body hadn't yet had a chance to follow suit, it wouldn't be long before rigidity set in.

There was no need, now, to go screaming off down the corridor for help, no need to breathe oxygen into Yarowski's mouth. Even the natural sadness that would follow was tinged with the knowledge that Yarowski's victims' families might now get some peace and a sense of closure.

Taking stock of her surroundings for the first time, Connie's attention was drawn to the darkened rim of water around the edge of the shower tray, the darkly glistening drops of life that had splashed upwards to stain the wall tiles.

She looked around the bathroom. There was no blood elsewhere. Yarowski had bled but only in the shower, which made no sense because she'd been up close to his face and head. There was no injury there.

She began at the top of his head, double-checking for a wound, running her fingers down his neck, along his shoulders, across his chest, then to his arms, finding the culprit in his right wrist. A long slit had been made lengthwise along the wrist, deep and raw, with multiple tiny cuts coming off one main slice. Taking a closer look, it appeared that something had been inserted into the cut to hold it open and prevent the wound from clotting.

Connie considered what she was about to do, settled for prioritising the needs of her own investigation above standard procedure, and dug her thumb and forefinger into the wound to pull out whatever foreign object had been inserted there.

Connie's stomach complained, and she swallowed the gagging noise that threatened to turn into full-on retching. She screwed her face up as she worked, her eyes half closed as if that would help block out the memory later on.

The object didn't want to move at first, entrenched in flesh, made evasive by the sticky liquids of death. It clung on a while before popping out then flying from her fingers to skim across the shower tray and stick at the outer rim of the drain.

Connie grabbed for it, slipped, and came crashing down herself, smacking her chin on the unforgiving reinforced plastic and slamming her teeth together. She winced, reeling against the pain, and gave herself a moment to recover before holding up the object and rubbing away the organic matter covering it for a better look.

'Fuck. That took some doing, Joe,' Connie said.

Yarowski must have been a southpaw, having opted to use his left hand to first cut with the plastic shard then insert it into his right wrist. What followed must have taken the most extraordinary desire to die, but it explained why she'd found him face down. Connie imagined the scene.

Yarowski waiting until lights were out and the corridor was quiet. Putting the shower on at nothing more than a drizzle to avoid attracting attention. Kneeling on his bathmat, elbows on the shower tray as he performed the amateur surgery on himself. Waiting in the stream of hot water as he bled out, knowing that if he took his wrist from the shower, clotting would almost certainly save his life.

How long had it taken? The average adult human had to lose around forty per cent of their blood to die. From a single wrist wound that took some doing. The wrist had to stay lower than, or level to, the rest of the body, the wound had to remain open, and Yarowski had to stay silent in spite of the pain. He had literally lain there, head over his wrist, watching his life flow down that drain. It might have taken an hour. Possibly more.

The plastic shard that had been used so effectively was shiny and hard with a slightly rounded edge and a vaguely triangular shape. Connie was pretty sure that elsewhere in Yarowski's room would be found another section of a small plastic cone normally used in board games for marking players' places. An unexpected wave of sadness swept through her at the irony of it. Had Joe played that very game as a little boy, enchanted by the bright colours of the playing pieces, excited at the thought of winning, pleased just to be spending time on such a simple pleasure as a board game? She knew she had as a child. Such a pretty, innocuous, innocent thing put to such devastating use. As weapons for self-harming went, it was one of the least likely she had ever encountered.

Connie stood, deciding that it was time to notify the ward staff and Director Le Fay. At least now there would be a valid reason to have the police on site and on hand. Baarda would be that bit safer having the authority of officers on the scene should they need to get him out of the ward fast. It was an uncomfortable sensation, to find benefits in a man's death, but emotion and truth rarely ran on parallel courses.

She tucked the plastic shard tightly in her fist and stepped over Yarowski's body, looking down as she did so and noticing his own left fist in the same shape as hers. Even in death he hadn't released his grip, and she knew with absolute certainty that there was something wrapped within his curled palm.

'What have you got there, Joe?' Connie asked, sensing, knowing, that whatever he was holding had been destined for her all along. 'Come on, share.'

It took some force to prise open his fingers. Whatever secret he was clutching, he'd wanted it to remain his alone.

Even the object seemed to want to hide, sneaking into the folds of his huge palm, blood-speckled and sticky. Connie knew what it was before she had it in her fingers. That twinkle, the way the light reflected from its round cut. She rinsed it in a droplet of standing water.

A precise match for its beautiful twin, Connie held Tara Cameron's missing earring up to the light and marvelled at how such a thing of beauty could have been dug from the rock, polished, shaped and cut, then engineered into a metal seat to sit happily in a hole falsely crafted in a body part. Ripped away amidst a bloody and terrible battle for power and dominance. Held by yet another hand in death. Tears rose, unbidden, in Connie's eyes. She hated crying over tragedy and injustice. Far better, she always thought, to use her energy seeking out resolution. And yet Tara deserved to have people cry for her. The earring wasn't just an earring, after all. It was something precious Tara must have believed she would be wearing for years to come.

She dashed the droplets from her cheeks and slid the earring into her pocket. The piece of plastic she would hand over. The earring was hers until she could pass it safely into police custody. One day it would be returned to Tara's husband. Not that he would want it. What on earth did you do with the earrings your loved one was wearing the day they were murdered? Bury them, perhaps. Return them to the earth from which they came.

Gathering her wits, ready to go back into character, Connie put on her most shocked face and ran out into the corridor.

'Emergency!' she shouted. 'I need assistance in here right now!'

Chapter 18

It was Dr Sidorov who responded first, running out of Harold Haskin's room at full pelt. Connie didn't speak, just pointed through the open door towards Yarowski's bathroom.

She left him to it and jogged to the ward security room, where she found Dr Roth and Nurse Casey.

'Yarowski's dead,' she panted. 'I just found him. Dr Sidorov is with him now.'

'You're fucking kidding,' Casey muttered, grimacing and grabbing his security pass, pushing past Connie to get into the ward. 'Deal with the admin would you, Verity?'

Verity Roth nodded, continuing to eat toast as she dialled a number into the internal phone, hitting the speaker button as she picked up her cup of tea.

'Director Le Fay's assistant. How can I help you?'

'Reporting a cold one on Dr Ong's ward. Medical exam in progress. Director will need to report it to the authorities as a death in custody.' Dr Roth's consonants were softened by partially chewed breakfast.

'All right,' the assistant said. 'Could I take the patient's name and number, please?'

'Yarowski, Joseph. Patient number . . .' Roth paused to look up at a chart on the wall '. . . T2/880061.'

'Thank you,' the assistant said. 'Are you requesting police or pathologist services at the present time?'

'Won't be necessary,' Roth said. 'Dr Sidorov will carry out a post-mortem investigation. Anything that needs further assessment after that, he can contact the necessary authorities.'

'What should I tell Director Le Fay was the cause of death?' the assistant asked.

'One second.' Roth hit the mute switch so she could talk privately to Connie. 'What did it look like to you, suicide or natural causes?'

That's it? Connie thought. *That's her reaction to a death on the ward, to the loss of a patient in her care?* Holy fucking shit, Roth was unbelievable.

'That's really not for me to say,' Connie snapped at her. 'I'm a therapist, not a medic. Aren't you even going to bother examining the body before commenting on cause of death?'

'Listen, snowflake. Yarowski was locked in his cell alone. That leaves two options. You must have seen a dead body before. Help me out here,' Roth huffed.

'Suicide,' Connie said. 'He cut open his wrist and held it in warm running water until his heart stopped.'

'That wasn't so hard, was it?' She hit the speaker switch once more. 'Suicide, clear evidence. We'll undertake a ward systems and security investigation and provide a report to the director. Should be ready in thirty days. We'll need a second medical opinion for the death certificate and could you have the chaplain do the usual rounds?' Roth ended the call and swirled her chair around to a filing cabinet, dragging open a protesting drawer.

'Is there much mess?' Roth asked, flicking through sections until she located the file she was looking for.

Connie studied the scowl on her face and watched the speed at which her fingers worked. Dr Roth was ruthlessly efficient and completely unfazed by the news of the death of one of her patients.

'Are you going to answer me?' Roth barked.

Connie moved to stand behind her before answering.

'Hardly any mess at all,' she said.

Roth didn't bother turning around to make eye contact before continuing the conversation. 'Good, that's one less call to make. The specialist cleaning crew hates getting called up here.' Tom Lord walked through the door. 'Just in time, clean-up on aisle 3. Sidorov and Casey might need a hand with the body, also take the camera, would you? I doubt Yarowski's got anyone left who'll ask questions, but we should cover our arses.'

'Fuck,' Lord grumbled. 'Ong is going to be all over us for this. Have you called him yet?'

'Not until it's all sorted out. You know what he's like when he loses one of his precious guests. Moron was deluded enough to think he was actually making progress with Yarowski.' Roth finally turned to look at Connie. 'Don't repeat anything you hear. These are private conversations.'

'Of course,' Connie said. 'Oh, here you go, this was the piece of plastic Yarowski used to cut his wrist. He lodged it in the wound to prevent closure and clotting.'

Lord picked it up and inspected it. 'He must have taken it during the community session last night.'

'Bag it and label it. It'll have to form part of the report,' Roth said. 'This is exactly why I keep telling Ong that these crazy motherfuckers can't have nice things.'

'Was there anything unusual about his behaviour recently that suggested he was a suicide risk? Any trigger?'

'You mean other than the fact that he was a deranged killer who was facing the prospect of spending every minute for the rest of his life looking at the same view and walking in and out of the same few rooms?' Lord laughed.

'Tom, get to fucking work. I want that room spotless before Ong gets here for his rounds. Tell Sidorov I want the post-mortem done this morning. All other procedures are to be cancelled. Paperwork on Ong's desk by lunchtime. Delay all the breakfasts until the corpse has been moved. They'll all lose their shit if we give them an excuse.' Tom Lord walked off without another word. 'And you, focus on your own patient and stop asking stupid questions. It's a psych unit. These people are contemplating suicide from the second they arrive. Yarowski just saved the taxpayer one hell of a lot of money. That may be the only good thing anyone will ever say about him.'

Roth carried on filling out paperwork, intermittently tapping details into the computer.

Connie hurried to Baarda's room. He was showered, dressed and doing press-ups when she entered. They took the precaution of going to stand in Baarda's en suite to whisper about the events of the previous night. Connie held out the diamond earring for Baarda to see.

'You're sure it's Tara's?' he asked.

'Absolutely. It was in Yarowski's fist, real tight. He must have been holding it as he passed. Rigor was starting to set in. My guess would be that he died around midnight, but that's not precise.'

'There was a fight over those games pieces last night. Rubio got himself in a state over which colour he wanted and Yarowski made it worse. Looking back now, I'd say it was deliberate.

The game set ended up going everywhere, Rubio got hysterical and when the movie was put on, Yarowski asked to go to his room.'

'Who escorted him?' Connie asked.

'The head nurse, Samuel Casey. I spent some time talking to Vince East. Careful around him. He's noticed you,' Baarda said.

Connie ignored the observation, knowing Baarda had made it with no expectation that she would show the least bit of concern. She liked that Baarda cared about her, but even more than that, she appreciated it when he didn't push it. 'Did you get anything from East?' she asked instead.

'He said Tara Cameron deserved better than this place. Past tense. I got the impression that he genuinely liked her, but also that he knew she wasn't coming back. Whether that's because he believes she's resting in hospital before the birth or because he knows she's dead, I couldn't say. So tell me, what happened last night?' Baarda asked, folding his arms and looking her straight in the eyes.

She knew he was looking for any sense that she might be lying to him or deflecting. She combatted with humour, raising her eyebrows and giving a sly smile. 'Why, you jealous?'

'Of you being able to leave this ward, lock your door, wear normal clothes, drink wine and eat with metal cutlery? Yes, absolutely.' Baarda turned to the sink and splashed cold water on his face.

Connie moved to stand behind him. He turned immediately.

'What are you doing?' he asked. 'Dare I say it, but you're behaving even more strangely than normal.'

'First of all, that's rude. More importantly, the way you reacted is normal. I just did the same thing to Dr Roth and she didn't even flinch. Didn't feel the need to turn to see what

213

I was doing, how close I was to her, even managed to carry on the conversation without establishing my position. Spoke to me as if whatever I was doing was completely insignificant. It pretty much defies the usual boundaries of human nature to have someone close behind you like that and not check to see what's going on.'

'Granted that's odd behaviour, but what's the relevance?'

'You've got kids. Do you remember when they were back in nursery school – I know it's some years ago now—'

'You're so rude,' Baarda interrupted.

'Embrace it. Older men are much more attractive than twenty-somethings. Anyway, when kids are in kindergarten we watch all this stuff really carefully. We register when they aren't interacting normally, you know? Not making eye contact, misunderstanding the need for personal space, failing to think baby animals are cute, squashing spiders. We identify those signals and talk about them to parents. This is one of those kinds of things. Roth has a part of her that doesn't function normally. Her triggers aren't set within standard limits.'

'Does she scare you?' Baarda asked quietly.

That was the real question, wasn't it? Baarda always managed to condense everything down to the one simple thing that needed to be addressed. Connie adored him for it.

'You know, I think she does,' she said. 'Madani doesn't, Lightfoot doesn't, Tom Lord's a bully and Jake's a misogynist but even they don't scare me. Roth does, though, and I can't even put my finger on why.'

'Give me some specific examples of her character then,' Baarda suggested.

'Okay, so I'm not sure if she's become jaded by her time working in high-security psychiatric care, or she was attracted to the position because she shares the sociopathic qualities of her patients, but she didn't miss a beat when I told her Yarowski was dead.'

'You think she already knew?' Baarda asked.

She considered it. 'Nope. Her reaction was too cold. Anyone wanting to cover up knowledge of an event like that would have found it hard to resist acting shocked. I think Roth just genuinely couldn't have cared less. Zero feelings, except for being pissed at having to do extra paperwork and bitching with Tom Lord about how annoyed Ong was going to be.' Connie handed Baarda a towel. 'God, these are scratchy. Good thing this is short term.'

'What's your theory about Yarowski having Tara's earring?' he asked.

'You're going straight for the million-dollar question? No warm-up? You're no better than Sidorov, thinking he could move in on me after a paltry two glasses of wine on the first date.'

Baarda bit his upper lip with his lower teeth and raised his eyebrows at her. 'Connie, what did Sidorov do?'

She waved a hand at him and shook her head. 'Relax, it was nothing I couldn't handle. Honestly, he was a bit obvious and clumsy about it. And it came out of nowhere, right? Like it was just something he thought he should do, then he blamed me for giving him the wrong signals. Men are so traffic-focused in their metaphors.'

'The earring?'

'Yeah, I know, I was buying time.' She walked to Baarda's shower and stared down into the tray. 'He was face down, right wrist slit, left fist holding the earring.'

'Fiddly thing to do with such a small piece of plastic. He'd had to have been incredibly careful with the earring, perfecting the wound first, turning on the shower, positioning his body.

Then picking up the earring after that to clutch it until he died. It's all rather staged.'

'Unless he was obsessed with her or guilt-ridden about her death, perhaps wanting to send someone a message about what happened. Yarowski was obsessive anyway. I didn't have a chance to hear his version of his crimes but it was all vengeance-based. Ego killings. There really should be a new profiling category for it. The professor's the same.'

'Speaking of which, you should have seen Professor Saint last night. He was about to kill the orderly, Jake, until I alerted the other staff members,' Baarda said. 'I think it was because Jake was snoring during the movie.'

'That's new, not his M.O. and not what I'd have thought of as his type of trigger,' Connie said. 'Saint only ever killed those students who left him a bad review. No criminal convictions beforehand. No track record of violence. Sounds like his mental health is going downhill in here, or maybe he's evolving. That's really fascinating. I wish I could've seen it.'

'He's not the only one,' Baarda said. 'If I don't eat soon, I'm going to kill someone too.'

'Oh, about that. I ate your croissant. Although thinking about it, there'll be one spare now that Yarowski . . .' She trailed off.

'I'm literally eating a dead man's food now. How charming,' he said. 'So tell me, where are you up to with profiling Aurora's abductor?'

'I've got all the inputs I need – access to the location, working knowledge of the modus operandi, I've seen the body – and yet not much of that is helping, apart from the fact that I know for sure now that every suspect had access to all of it. The hardest profiling aspect of it is the fact that the murder was the secondary motive for whoever stands to gain financially, but it might have been the primary motive for whoever ended Tara's life and took Aurora. Everything that happened was by necessity because it all hinged upon keeping Aurora alive, so I've got no signature aspects of the crime to differentiate between suspects.'

'Is there anyone you can definitely exclude yet?' Baarda asked.

'Yup. Our main suspect found holding the earring. Yarowski's kills were messy, frantic, distraught. His IQ doesn't seem high enough for the surgery performed when you factor in the clean-up afterwards and the lack of an evidence trail leading to an obvious perpetrator. Whoever did this was both cunning and skilled. Yarowski killed a number of people, but in a short time.'

'East told me Yarowski was a strangler. Is that right?'

'Oh yeah. A failed almost-pro basketball player who couldn't make it onto a team but who couldn't break away to find a job outside the industry. He snapped one day, got sick of having drinks thrown at him, getting kicked by teenagers, being mocked. He killed several times in a three-month period, showing severe loss of temper, using extreme violence before finishing his victims off by strangulation. There's some suggestion that he was out-of-body while he killed. His memories of all the interactions were third person, like he was seeing it all from over his own shoulder. Diagnosed schizophrenic. The police investigation was able to conclude it was him fairly easily. He had a dysfunctional personal life and no self-control.'

'And yet he's the one the current evidence superficially favours as Tara's killer. The earring, the suicide. That's not a coincidence, right?'

'No coincidence at all,' Connie said. 'He makes a great scapegoat, doesn't he? Very convenient.'

217

'I really don't like it. Now we have a dead nurse, a missing baby, *and* an inmate who was either murdered or persuaded to kill himself. Someone is prepared to do anything to cover their tracks.' Baarda thrust his hands deep into his pockets. 'So what are you going to do now?'

'I need to speak with Director Le Fay. I didn't see him yesterday. I was hoping Roth would call in the police after Yarowski's death but it looks like they'll just sign it off as suicide and file a half-hearted internal investigation. Ong's going to agree to protect his own reputation. Apart from Le Fay, I'd like to see Harold Haskin today. You speak with him last night?'

'No. I heard someone crying in the night, though. I couldn't be sure who it was or which cell it was coming from. Quiet sobbing. Could have been Yarowski, I suppose.'

From the corridor, Tom Lord called five minutes until doors were unlocked for breakfast, which had to mean that Yarowski's body had been moved and his cell tidied.

'I'm going to have to go and eat, but I had a thought last night. Police on the outside are doing their best to trace the emails from the kidnapper and follow the money trail, but with cryptocurrency that's not going to be a quick fix. Digital wallets can be hard to identify and if the servers are based in a different country, it could take weeks to get the necessary legal authorities to find any information,' Baarda said.

'What do you suggest?'

'When you and I first met in Edinburgh, I spent some time with the Major Investigation Team. They had a case where money was being moved via the darknet. Murderers for hire. Nasty stuff. Someone on the squad found a hacker who helped out. Not exactly legal, and under normal conditions I wouldn't suggest it but—'

'Name?' Connie said.

'Can't remember but someone in the squad will have it.'

Connie racked her brains. 'I consulted on a case for them last year. They owe me a favour. You think this hacker will be able to trace the wallet the newly purchased crypto coins are going to?'

'It's worth a try. You always have to follow the money.'

Baarda's door opened and Tom Lord stuck his head inside to yell. 'Breakfast. We're running late, so get moving!'

'Right, I'll see you later,' Connie snapped at Baarda, who stood to attention. 'And when I return, I expect your bed to be made. Just because you've been transferred to a civilian facility does not mean that normal military standards can be allowed to slip.'

'Yes, ma'am,' Baarda replied. 'Whatever you say.'

Chapter 19

Connie left Baarda and headed for the Tower 2 stairs to go first to her room, then to Director Le Fay's office. Passing the staffroom, she could hear sobs followed by the sound of a nose being blown. Someone was crying. She couldn't help but look to see who it was.

'Hey, you okay?' Connie asked Nurse Madani.

The nurse crumpled up a tissue, tossed it in the waste bin and shook her head. Connie gently closed the staffroom door and went to sit next to her.

'It's a difficult thing when a patient dies in a place like this. When you're around someone all day, all week, whatever they've done, you're bound to form a sort of bond with them. You're allowed to feel conflicted,' Connie said.

Madani gave Connie the sort of look usually reserved for waiting staff to throw at a table of twelve who each want to pay only their portion of the bill down to the last penny.

'We're back down to five patients, and if Patient B leaves that's only four,' she said, the tears starting again. 'I need

220

those overtime shifts. It's not as if I'll get a promotion on this ward. Dawn Lightfoot is senior to me, and she's already saying she wants a pay rise. I have a big family to support, and my sister's sick.'

'It's a lot of pressure, supporting your family,' Connie said.

'It's bad enough that I have to live and work in this horrible place,' Nurse Madani said. 'But my younger brother was encouraged to become a doctor because he's male. My father said nursing was a more appropriate job for a woman because sooner or later I'd leave and have babies. Now my brother is going to be studying for years while I pay for everything.'

'What's wrong with your sister?'

'Does it matter? They just send me the medical bills and expect me to pay them. Never a thank you. They don't even really want me to visit. My mother says it's a waste of money paying for me to travel, and then they'll have to cook for me when I get home. Might as well stay here with the free food.'

'Have you tried explaining that you can't afford it? Surely your brother can get a loan to help with his studies?'

She glared at Connie. 'I have a responsibility. Family is family. And what do you care? It's not your problem.'

'Well, I'd like to think the staff treating Patient B are content, and doing a job they're genuinely invested in,' Connie began, buying time with the soft-soaping as she figured out the best way to get Madani to confide in her without sounding too desperate for information. Sidorov had already come way too close to tripping her up. She had to be more mindful of the role she was supposed to be playing. 'But also, this place is dangerous. You need to be focused on what's happening around you. If you're busy worrying about money, that's when something is likely to go wrong.'

Madani laughed. 'You know, you talk like the men on this

ward actually matter. Where I grew up, we still have the death penalty. There, none of these patients would have made it any further than the end of a rope.'

'Does capital punishment not bother you?' Connie asked. 'There are documented cases where the wrong person has been executed for a crime. Certainly where an offender has an identifiable mental illness, it seems problematic to let them face the death penalty.'

She shrugged. 'Watching someone you love die when you can't afford the treatments the West has to offer bothers me. Knowing you can't afford meat that week because you have to pay your heating bill bothers me. Children walking miles to school barefoot bothers me. Killers dying quickly rather than spending their lives in a room with a comfortable bed, three meals, a hot shower – does that bother me? No. Walk a mile in my shoes, Dr Connie.' She stood, smoothed her uniform and neatened her hair. 'And don't try to make me feel bad about innocent people dying. That happens every day.' Nurse Madani left.

There were cultural issues at play that Connie couldn't even begin to understand, and a lot of what Madani had said made perfect sense. It was all very well to be concerned with human rights and outraged by the death penalty, Connie knew, when you had the luxury of a safe space from which to contemplate such things, but Nurse Madani's family clearly didn't. Stuck in poverty whilst trying to walk a tightrope towards a brighter future was a difficult balancing act. Difficult and pressured. Connie felt for her. She herself had come from a family that was financially stable, and was grateful every day to have a career that meant she could pay her bills. Living hand to mouth took its toll, destroying relationships, families, futures. Little wonder Madani was so waspish.

The pity she felt for Maysoon Madani aside, it was impossible to conclude anything other than that Madani had all the necessary skills to have performed a caesarean on Tara Cameron, and also to have made sure the baby was fit enough to survive the time it would take for the ransom to be paid. All she'd have needed was some assistance overwhelming Tara physically, getting her to the medical room and onto the operating table. Connie hated the vision of it in her mind, one nurse betraying another, one woman assaulting another woman like that. But it had happened before and it could happen again. What didn't sit right, though, was the idea of Maysoon Madani doing something so cruel to a tiny baby, when her priorities were to take care of her own family, particularly her sick sister – if what she'd said was true.

It was still only 8 a.m. and already Connie felt like she needed another shower. Her hands smelled of death. Back downstairs in her room, she stripped off her clothes, threw them into the laundry basket and headed for the bathroom again. A shorter shower this time and she didn't bother to wash her hair, but the soap got rid of the bloody residue that had managed to slither beneath her fingernails. The relief she felt at being clean once more was palpable.

Connie dressed again, keeping it casual but a little smarter given her intention to head for Director Le Fay's office, then reached for her cell phone where it had been charging on the bedside table. The charging cable lay redundant across the water-marked wood.

'Goddammit,' she murmured. 'Where the hell did I put it?'

She checked the bathroom first, then under her bedclothes, behind the bedside table. After that she was reduced to going through the dirty laundry and checking in the pockets of any trousers she'd worn since arriving. It wasn't under her bed. It wasn't in her wardrobe. It hadn't mysteriously found its way inside her suitcase.

It wasn't anywhere.

'Shit,' she said, her right palm almost itching with the need to hold it.

Then came the sickening realisation that she might have lost everything. Contacts, messages, photos, professional documents. It wasn't like her to misplace something as vital as her cell phone. Connie sat on the edge of her bed and retraced the last place she'd had it in her head.

Yesterday. She'd definitely had it then. She could remember plugging it in to recharge. And the alarm woke her every morning so it had to have been by her bed then.

Only that wasn't right. She'd woken far earlier than normal and not turned her alarm off. At least, she didn't remember turning the alarm off. In fact she wasn't sure she'd looked at her cell phone at all since waking up.

'Did I just slip it into my pocket this morning and not even realise?' she asked her reflection in the mirror that was attached roughly to the back of her door.

No, that wasn't right. She'd realised she'd forgotten it on the way up to Heaven Ward. Connie stood and looked at her bedside table from the door, imagining herself in bed, asleep, cell phone charging next to her as it always did.

Her mind reconstructed the sense she'd had of feeling something was wrong. The minutes that followed as she'd wandered around her bedroom and en suite checking windows and door. And yet here she was, cell phone gone, no explanation for that unless she was imagining things. Had she left it somewhere? Dropped it from a pocket? Connie checked the bathroom one more time then stripped her bed completely. No joy.

Her room had been locked from the inside, chain and all.

Windows all firmly shut against the punishing wind that howled down the mountainside and across the lake. But later, after she'd left for the ward that morning, anyone with a master key could have entered. The cleaners had keys, as did the maintenance staff. Security too. There had to be multiple sets around the complex. The truth was that as soon as she'd left, absolutely anyone could have entered.

Connie sat on the very edge of her bed, her heart pounding as she thought through the implications of her cell falling into the wrong hands. It had security. She couldn't do her job and be careless about that aspect of her life. Getting into her files required facial recognition, a twelve-digit password and a thumb scan. Three unsuccessful entry attempts meant that the cell had to be accessed from remote software and unlocked. Only she could do that from her laptop. The thought of it took her breath away. Where had she put her laptop?

Standing abruptly, Connie pulled the tip of her nail clean away. She stopped, checked herself. The last time she'd bitten her nails had been when? It was a fake question. She was playing for time as she came to terms with what she'd just done. The last time she'd chewed her nails was when she'd been committed to the hospital in Boston. The day she was finally released, she had vowed never to do it again.

'Get a grip,' she told herself. 'The laptop is on top of the wardrobe.'

She saw herself in the mirror, talking out loud, feeling the need to reassure herself. Other people found it strange that she spoke to dead bodies. Connie thought that was perfectly reasonable. She had no idea what the reality of having a soul was, but she was fairly certain that even the dead benefitted from kindness and reassurance. Talking to herself, however, was a step too far. And still, even as she tried to calm herself, she found herself saying the words she hadn't said since she was eighteen years old.

'You're okay. Just breathe.'

Back then, inside the ward, those words could only be spoken inside her head. Now she was saying them aloud. If nothing else, it seemed to work.

Her heart rate began to slow as she pulled the chair from the small desk and stood on it to reach the decorative ledge on top of the wardrobe behind which she'd pushed her laptop. It was still there, just as she'd left it.

Opening the cell phone locator app, she searched for a signal, certain she would feel foolish when the location was within her room, in a stray shoe or a drawer. She hadn't been herself since she'd first walked the corridors of Heaven Ward. That wasn't an easy admission to make, but it was important to recognise that she was struggling. There was a lot to unpack from her time as a patient. She'd always thought her choice of career had been all the therapy she needed. Now she was having to re-examine just how much damage it had done.

There was no signal from her cell phone. She tried relaunching the app and searching a second time. Still nothing.

In her laptop, Connie changed all her passwords to any software that would be open and running on her cell then checked her emails. There was one from the lead detective on Aurora's case. Connie clicked it open.

Dear Dr Woolwine,
Update re the case of Aurora Cameron
   Our enquiries through Director Le Fay and the administrative offices have revealed that the ward staff rotas are set by Senior Ward Nurse Casey together with Dr Roth, and approved by Dr Ong. However, it seems

that staff often swap shifts to facilitate longer breaks away from The Institution. During the weekend of Tara Cameron's death, Nurse Maysoon Madani had swapped her shift informally with Tara. This was permitted practice as both were working at the same grade in the same job description. In addition on the night in question, the orderlies Tom Lord and Jake Aldrich also swapped their shifts to leave Jake on duty. No reason has been recorded for that swap.

With regard to those people we are currently surveilling, we are pursuing four active leads. One person has a substantial amount of gambling debt and is being sued. Another was seen purchasing baby clothes and accessories. The third has made several unsuccessful attempts at IVF and recently been refused an adoption application, raising the possibility that the ransom request might be a cover for a desire to keep the baby. The fourth has strong links to a criminal gang, though her husband and brothers were not flagged on her application to work at The Institution as she only performs an auxiliary music teaching role. We are hopeful that the next forty-eight hours will lead us to locate the baby. Do not hesitate to contact us before then should you require any further information.

Regards, Detective Houlihan

For the scheme to work, one of those people had to have access to Heaven Ward's patients, Connie thought. And not just access, they also had to have something valuable and credible to offer them. Surely that should be an easy connection to make. The wheels were turning infuriatingly slowly and it was driving her crazy. She clicked reply and began typing.

Dear Detective Houlihan,

Thank you for the information. Please be advised that I need you to backwards-trace your four main suspects' links to staff members on the ward as a matter of urgency. Please notify immediately should you find any relevant links.

Yours, Connie Woolwine

She closed her laptop and lay down for a minute, feeling as though someone had taken a pneumatic drill to the inside of her skull.

It wasn't like her to rest during the day. Even the worst of illnesses rarely broke her. She would walk or swim, sit up reading or clean. All she wanted now, though, was quiet and stillness. The safety and comfort of bed. She pulled the covers over herself and felt herself begin to relax. It would be just a few minutes until the headache went, and she would be able to think straight. There were plenty of hours left in the day. Connie closed her eyes.

She lurched awake, panicked, disorientated. Her bed felt strange and the light wasn't right for morning. It took her several seconds to remember where she was before she reached for her watch: 3 p.m.

What the fuck? How could that have happened? She wasn't a daytime sleeper, never had been. She felt sick with her stupidity and laziness. She'd slept the day away. Baarda would have been wondering what had happened to her, Dr Ong probably had questions for her given that she'd found Yarowski's body, and she hadn't yet managed to speak with Director Le Fay. And Aurora . . . what might have happened to her in the hours she'd lost?

Connie scrambled to get changed again, more exhausted than when she'd crawled into bed, and she hadn't thought that would be possible. The headache had gone but now her back was aching and she guessed the mattress had seen better days. She didn't dare lift the sheet and the topper to take a look at the state of it. She'd made that mistake once in her old room—

'Shut the fuck up!' she yelled, hands over her ears, screaming at her own brain. 'Be present. Stay present.'

She rammed her feet into shoes, grabbed her security pass and stormed out of the residential area across the block to Director Le Fay's office. His assistant was tidying her desk as Connie approached.

'I need to see the director,' Connie rushed. 'It's urgent. We didn't talk yesterday.'

'I can check his schedule.' She paused to look while Connie did her best not to drum her fingers on the desk. 'I'm afraid it will have to be next week. Would Monday at 10 a.m. suit you?'

Connie stared at her. 'Monday? I'm supposed to have full access. Is he in now? I just need a few minutes.'

'Dr . . .' the assistant took a quick look at the security pass '. . . Connie. Is everything all right?'

'What?' she snapped. 'Why?'

'You look rather – please don't take this the wrong way – dishevelled. And flustered.'

Connie saw the concern on the woman's face. Genuine and kind. All of which made her feel substantially worse. She looked down at her clothes, seeing herself as though through the other woman's eyes. Her top was tucked in one side but not the other, she hadn't brushed her hair since getting out of bed, and her laces were undone. She felt her cheeks redden.

'Sorry, of course. I was out for a walk and I lost track of

time. I do need to tidy up. Thank you for letting me know. So is the director in?'

'He was served with a court summons to give evidence at a trial – that happens a lot here – and he had no choice but to comply. Forgive me, though, are you part of the military placement? Director Le Fay did ask me to let you have access to any facilities you needed. I understand that your confidentiality requirements are particularly high.'

'That's right.' Connie tried not to sigh with relief. 'I've been an idiot and misplaced my cell phone. Could I use the director's desk to make a call? It's important.'

'Of course. Would you like me to bring tea or coffee? You look rather in need.'

Connie wanted to say no. It had been her policy to make her own drinks rather than ever treat support staff as waiters, but at that moment there was nothing in the world she wanted more than strong, hot coffee. 'Coffee would be lovely. That's very kind of you,' she said.

'Not at all. Go and make your call. I'll knock before I bring the coffee in. Just press the button labelled EXT to make the call out.'

The smile she gave Connie made her momentarily weak. Alien tears began to form in her eyes and she headed for Director Le Fay's office to hide.

Sitting in the director's oversized leather chair, Connie did a quick self-assessment. The diagnosis wasn't good. She was experiencing anxiety and a sense of panic, failing to cope adequately with the stress, and having flashbacks. It reeked of post-traumatic stress disorder. She had suffered with it for a year after her release from hospital in Boston, but that was to be expected. Everyone could see it in her and knew what it was. This, however, was an ambush by a band of psychological

230

mercenaries that had been lying in wait for more than a decade and a half.

The only choice she had was to push it away as hard as she could until her job was done. Connie wasn't naive enough to think she wouldn't need to deal with it at some point. PTSD had to be handled with respect. It was a serious problem. The thing was, she just couldn't deal with it that week, not with everything that was riding on the results of her work.

Taking a deep breath, she dialled through to main reception and asked them to find her the number for Police Scotland in Edinburgh. From there, it was only a matter of minutes before she was talking to Detective Chief Inspector Ava Turner, who gave her the name of the infamous hacker, and a mobile number. With it came a warning that Ben Paulson was trouble but Connie, past caring, barely registered it.

The mobile she called rang with one dial tone, appeared to cut out before dialling with a new tone, then finally went to a recorded message where Connie had to leave her own name and a brief explanation as to how she came by the number before hanging up. Director Le Fay's office phone rang within thirty seconds without going through his assistant first.

'Full name and date of birth,' Paulson said.

Connie gave it and waited.

'Social security number.'

Again she gave the information, listening as he typed at the other end of the line.

'Who do you work for?' he asked.

'These days I work for myself, but I was with the FBI. If you're in Edinburgh, I handled the Shadow Man case a while ago, and I consulted on the Edinburgh Bomber investigation.'

'I know you did,' he said. 'My friend DI Luc Callanach told

me all about it. Before you say anything else, you're aware this isn't a secure line, right?'

'I'm not exactly calling from the White House,' she said. 'I'd assumed you'd be Scottish.'

'California born and bred. Moved to the UK after a brief altercation with the CIA.'

'I heard that about you.' There was a knock at the door. 'One second,' Connie said. 'Come in,' she called to Le Fay's assistant who entered with a tray bearing a cafetière, a jug of milk and a plate of assorted cookies.

'What's that?' Paulson asked.

'Someone bringing me coffee,' Connie said, nodding her thanks at the assistant and waiting for her to leave before continuing. 'Tell me about the CIA problem.'

'Oh no. If you're the sort of person who has coffee brought by an assistant then you and I will not get on, and it's a fundamental requirement that I trust you.'

She felt a dart of panic. 'Wait, please. Just hear me out.' She sighed. 'Ben, I'm having the day from hell. I can't really even tell you why. I started the day waking up feeling as if someone had been in my room. Now my cell phone has disappeared. After that I discovered the body of a man who had supposedly taken his own life. I think I'm . . . no, I'm definitely having an attack of PTSD. And if I don't do my job properly a baby girl might never be found.'

'Gonna say it again, this line is not secure,' he said.

'I don't care. If the bad guys are listening then they already know this. I need your help. If we do it the legal way it'll take far too long.'

There was a long pause. Connie could hear a pen tapping against a desk.

'What did you think of Edinburgh?' he asked.

Connie recognised the question for what it was: a moment to figure out her personality, to decide whether or not he could trust her, to assess his feelings about helping her. She'd have done the same. What seemed like him wasting time was, in fact, more like an instant interview.

'Not enough sushi but the Indian restaurants make up for it. The pubs are too hot and the coffee's too cold, but the architecture makes even Boston look like Legoland and the people use expletives in the most creative way I ever heard.'

Another pause. 'Tell me what you need.' She'd passed his test. Connie could hear the smile in his voice and for a few moments she felt better.

'Ransom is being paid in Crater Coins.'

'Crypto,' he said. 'Welcome to the future.'

'Yeah, well, the police already know they won't be able to follow the trail fast enough to identify the beneficiary. That could take months depending on which jurisdiction the relevant servers are in. It could involve international applications for legal disclosure.'

'Good luck with that,' Paulson said. 'Listen, this stuff isn't easy, even for me. The security involved in cryptocurrency is tight, and digital wallets are designed to stay off the database and exist independently.'

'I know. But I need help. Anything. Can I email you the details?'

'Sure,' he said. He gave her his address.

'And, Ben, about payment—'

'Let's talk about that if I manage to help you. In the meantime, try to find your cell. You don't want the sort of information that's on there floating around in a place like The Institution.'

'I didn't tell you where I was,' Connie said. The line was

233

already dead. She stared at the phone for a moment before putting it down, hoping beyond hope that Paulson could get her some information that would help, because if he didn't the chances of finding Tara's baby felt like they were crumbling into dust.

Chapter 20

Dr Ong was holding court in the staff area when Connie got back up to the ward. Connie slid in quietly and took the nearest chair.

'To summarise, I appreciate that this was a peculiar set of circumstances. I understand that certain patients who are so inclined will use any means at their disposal to do themselves harm, but proper procedures dictated that Mr Yarowski should have been checked on during the night. Had he been spotted missing from his bed, we might have caught this in time and prevented the tragedy. Jake, you were on night duty. At what hours did you do your rounds?'

'The problem isn't that he wasn't checked on during the night,' Jake argued. 'It's that he wasn't checked for contraband when he asked to leave the common room early. Nurse Casey gave permission to Yarowski to leave the group session.'

All eyes turned to Samuel Casey, who gave a slow shrug. 'Nurse Lightfoot was overseeing the game. She should have checked that all the pieces were returned to the box. If I'd known there was a piece missing, I'd have done a contraband check on Yarowski.'

Dr Ong sighed. 'You see, everyone, this is the problem. Instead of collectively taking responsibility you are all passing the buck. We have a ward review pending. I am loath to write a report that explains we had failings at all points in our process. But more than that, I feel very strongly that I owe an explanation to Mr Yarowski's family – and that should be the truth rather than some cover-up to avoid repercussions. The people who stay on this ward cannot be responsible for their own safety. We must do that for them. When we fail, the consequences are terrible as we've seen today.'

'We've been short-staffed,' Samuel Casey protested. 'With Nurse Cameron missing, everyone is working longer shifts and that makes it difficult to avoid slip-ups.'

'Then I can only wish Nurse Cameron a speedy return,' Ong said. 'I don't believe this would have happened if she'd been on shift last night.'

Samuel Casey murmured something to Dr Roth that Connie didn't quite catch.

'Is Tara coming back?' Nurse Lightfoot asked. 'How long's she taking for maternity leave?'

'I don't know yet, but I will be discussing that with human resources. Dr Connie will be making a decision next week, I understand, about Patient B's suitability to remain in this unit. Should Patient B leave – and I very much hope we'll be able to provide him with a long-term home here—' he gave Connie a brief, earnest glance '—we will be down to only four guests, which should make all your lives substantially easier. Until that decision is made, I'm sure you'll find a way to cope with five patients, even with Nurse Cameron absent. So, notes in today from everyone who was on duty last night, please.' Without

236

further ado, he turned to Connie. 'Dr Connie, I understand you found Mr Yarowski this morning. I wonder if we might have a chat.'

He exited and she followed him two doors down the corridor into his office. It was the only room in the staff area she hadn't entered before, and there was a moment when Connie felt like Alice falling down the rabbit hole. It was as if the room didn't belong there at all. The sudden luxury was extraordinary. Director Le Fay's room had all the usual trappings of CEO-style grandeur from the huge desk to the bottles of twenty-five-year-old single malt in a cabinet, but this was something else.

Ong's walls had been painted a deep, rich tone, although Connie couldn't tell which exact shade. The overhead strip lights had been taken out in favour of a variety of lamps, tall and small. The paintings were all originals, modest in size as the room was lacking in scale, but they were beautiful. His desk held a few photos of him in lush landscapes, horse riding through a vineyard, walking on beautiful beaches, sunning himself on boat decks.

'Your yacht?' Connie asked, pointing at one photo where he was laughing in the breeze as the yacht ploughed forwards into a crystal sea.

He gave a bark of good-natured laughter as he sat down behind his desk. 'Goodness, no. Salaries here are generous compared to other hospitals but I'm afraid I'm not in that league. I was holidaying with friends. You like the sea?'

'I grew up sailing. That's what happens when you're born on a small island. I can't remember a day of my childhood when I wasn't on a beach.'

He nodded and gave her a warm smile. 'Sounds idyllic. I grew up in Seoul, South Korea. My father was a salesman. I didn't visit a beach until I was at university.'

'Your parents must be very proud of you,' Connie said. It was a hard enough fight to become a doctor, she knew, but to rise up out of poverty to do so took the most enormous effort. She admired him for it.

Ong looked down at his desk and interlaced his fingers. 'My father, yes. My mother died when I was a baby. I like to think she'd approve of the work I do here.'

Connie took the studded leather armchair facing Dr Ong. There was a light panel on the wall behind him, which he set on a remote control to a pale glow.

'That's clever. Makes up for the lack of natural light I suppose,' she said.

'It does indeed. As much as I appreciate the history of this building and the security of its position, the architecture has left us needing to be imaginative when it comes to our environment.'

'You see patients in here?' Connie took a moment to study the rest of the artwork and photographs.

'I do,' Ong said. 'Bringing them off the ward for an appointment with me is a milestone. It happens when they've earned trust. It's a sign that we think they are showing improvement. More importantly, it's the first step towards reintegration into a more normal, more human world. I don't think we can help these men behave better unless they are also being treated well.'

'You actually think they can be rehabilitated? Made safe? Some psychiatric or psychological conditions can't be cured, particularly if they're the result of conditioning,' she said. It was a subject Connie had strong views about, some of them not exactly mainstream. The world, in her opinion, was a better place without some of the killers she'd dealt with, but it seemed that Ong would disagree.

'Is someone who chose to kill with no psychiatric condition

238

less dangerous, less likely to kill again? I would argue that they are not. Most modern social systems imprison murderers for a period, suddenly decide they're safe for the outside world then simply release them back into society, and yet those offenders understood the constraints of law and society but chose to disregard them. The people we treat in here at least had a reason to do what they did. It was not a choice but a compulsion. I believe we can retrain the brain, Dr Connie. Between medication and therapy I think progress is entirely possible. If I didn't, I'm not sure how fulfilling a career this would be.'

Connie faked an agreeable smile to mask her contrary view on the matter. 'I take your point, and it's good to know you have faith in the profession. What did you need from me with regard to Mr Yarowski?'

Ong's face fell. 'Poor Joe, he was hard to work with. Very resistant at first. His crimes were motivated by anger and he did not relinquish that willingly.' Ong reached out a hand as he spoke and pulled back a ball on the Newton's cradle that sat on a corner of his desk. It chimed as it hit the other balls and they all chimed back quietly, ringing like distant church bells.

'I've never come across a chiming cradle like that. What a beautiful sound,' Connie said.

'I'm so sorry. I often set that off when I'm thinking about a problem. I didn't even realise I'd done it. It's hard to lose a patient, and even worse to see how little it affects the staff. Sometimes the abuse they get and the conditions they work under make it difficult for them to see our guests as human at all. Dr Sidorov has listed the cause of death as heart failure caused by extensive bleeding resulting from suicidal self-wounding. Given what you saw, do you agree that was the case?'

'I can only tell you that the room was locked when I entered, Mr Yarowski was alone, there were no signs of a struggle in the room, and he had positioned himself to lie in the shower to keep the wound free from clotting. So yes, from what I saw, I wouldn't necessarily disagree with Dr Sidorov.'

Ong sat back in his chair and laced long fingers across his stomach, tilting his head to one side.

'Is something wrong?' Connie asked.

'That's what I was wondering. You said necessarily,' Ong told her.

'Did I?'

'Yes. You said, you wouldn't necessarily disagree with Dr Sidorov. A conditional turn of phrase. Do you have reservations?' Ong asked. Connie watched the Newton's cradle swing back and forth. Dr Ong reached out and stopped the momentum of the balls. 'Connie, if you have concerns about my ward, I would rather hear them. You don't have to sugar-coat anything for me.'

She hesitated for a few seconds, finding the right words, making sure they sounded deliberately vague. 'I'm not sure. Perhaps the scene seemed a little staged. Too obvious,' she said, shrugging. 'And if I had any comment, it would be that whenever someone tries to present me with a very clear picture of something, it's often an attempt to cover a less desirable set of circumstances.' She rubbed her forehead, warding off the headache's attempt to reignite.

'Agreed. Was there something more specific? You seem troubled. I'm not asking you to reveal any information about Patient B – I respect military confidentiality of course – but I welcome feedback about my staff. It can remain between us and you don't have to name names.' Ong leaned forward and watched her closely.

Connie was suddenly uncomfortable, too aware of her crumpled clothes and mussed hair. She shifted in her seat to straighten up.

'I found it concerning that everyone was able to reach a conclusion about the death so quickly, before an investigation. Just assumptions being made. That's all. Nothing specific.' She gave a bright and hopefully reassuring smile. 'And as you mentioned, there's the fact that Yarowski wasn't checked on. If I hadn't gone in, he might have been left like that for another couple of hours.'

'You had planned an early conversation with him, as I understood?' Ong asked. 'Your appointment was on the staff board.'

'So everyone knew I'd be the first to see Mr Yarowski this morning?'

She frowned and Ong looked concerned.

'Did we do something wrong? Was it important to keep your timetable confidential?' he asked.

'No, I suppose not. Speaking of appointments, I really should get on. I'm seeing Harold Haskin this afternoon.'

'Interesting case,' Ong said. 'Exercise caution. Haskin can be sexually aggressive and explicit if triggered. I'm going to start compiling my report on Yarowski's death. Can I give you a call later if I have any further questions?'

'Yes . . . actually, sorry, no. My cell phone disappeared from my room. You could always email me instead.'

'Your phone disappeared from your room? How do you mean?' Ong asked.

Connie stood. 'I phrased that badly. I meant it disappeared sometime. I thought it was in my room but when I went to look for it, I found I'd lost it.'

Ong frowned. 'You've reported it to reception then? I'm sure

241

it will be handed in. The Institution is usually fairly community-minded.'

'Great idea,' Connie said. 'I'll be sure to do that this evening. Thank you, Dr Ong.'

Connie exited, kicking herself for sounding so paranoid. Ong was already concerned about his staff's professionalism and the upcoming review. He certainly wouldn't want any other potential loose cannons on his ward.

Tom Lord walked past her as she let herself in through the main doors.

'Bad habit, that,' he said.

'Sorry, what?' Connie asked.

'Your nails,' he said. 'Looks like someone's feeling a bit nervous.'

She dropped her hand from the edge of her mouth, a fragment of nail lurking on the tip of her tongue.

'I'm fine,' she told him. 'It was just a hangnail.'

Chapter 21

The sky outside the barred window was rolling with ever-darkening cloud. Harold Haskin had agreed to talk to her but only on his own terms and that meant him remaining in his room and lying on his bed as they spoke. Connie was on a chair at the far end of the bed and Ward Nurse Samuel Casey stood with his back to them, his elbows resting on the window ledge, staring out into the approaching dusk.

'What do you want to know?' Haskin said, running long fingers up and down his chest as if he were playing some sort of strange instrument. He was well-muscled in spite of the lack of exercise, with a high forehead from which his hair was receding in a straight line, and a wide jaw, giving his face the look of a large, pale box.

'I thought we might try some hypnotherapy,' Connie said. 'I'd like to see the world through your eyes.'

He can see that I'm lying, she thought. She couldn't think of anything worse at that moment in time than actually seeing through Haskin's eyes, and he knew it. He was instantly dislikeable and disconcerting.

'Fuck that,' Haskin growled. 'I don't want you inside my head. Not you, not Ong and not that bitch Roth. Ask your questions; I'll answer if I can be bothered.'

'Okay. Let's start with the basics. Name, age, where you're from, family set-up, education, career.'

'I'm fifty-two. Been on this mind-fuck ward now for fourteen years. I've outlasted every staff member and every other inmate. I guess I'll be here to the day I die. Unlike Joe, I intend to stay alive as long as I possibly can.'

'Are you upset about Joe's death?' she asked.

'Bored, next question,' he said, studying the ceiling.

'Tell me about your family.'

'My mother was a plumber, and you didn't fuck with her when she'd had her hand down someone else's shitter all day. My father decided life would be more fun with a woman who understood that dressing sexy meant putting on lingerie, not men's shorts complete with stains. Good for him. Left when I was ten, never saw him again. Going to be a speedy psych analysis, right? Missing father, bitch of a mother, killed a load of little girlies because of my dysfunctional childhood. Blah blah blah.'

'Is that why you killed those young women?'

'If I tell you that already, you're gonna go, and I was just starting to enjoy you, so for now let's say there was a bit more to it than that.'

He was absolutely right. The second she could get out of there and away from him, she would be gone.

'How was school for you?' Connie asked, keeping the questions bland. He would tell her everything he wanted in his own time.

'Shit. But that's because I was a perfectly normal teenager. It's those creepy fuckers who enjoy school you need to worry about.'

'Fair point,' Connie said, tilting her head a little to one side. 'You're funny, Harold. Did your friends think you were funny, at school, at work maybe?'

'It would be arrogant of me to say that, wouldn't it? Hey, do you think the girls I killed thought I was funny? Never heard any of them laughing. They screamed a lot though.'

You sick fuck, Connie thought. *Those girls must have been pleased to get away from you, even if their only escape route was straight into the arms of death.*

'Does it make you feel important, that you made those girls scream?'

'Important? No. Excited, would be a better word.' He took one hand and began to run it down towards his crotch.

'Touch it and you'll be confined to this cell for seven days, personal items withdrawn,' Samuel Casey said sternly.

'Killjoy,' Haskin said. 'Do you know they're making a movie about me? Not just one of those true crime mashups with interviews and stock footage. Dramatised. Scripted. A-list actors and everything.'

'You won't be watching it. Not ever,' Casey said, seeming to relish the fact.

Haskin drew in a deep breath, turned his head in Casey's direction and let out a feline hiss.

Casey took a taser off his belt and held it in the air.

'That's your last warning. One more and it's fifty thousand volts and the quiet room. This will be Dr Connie's only opportunity to interview you. Dr Ong won't authorise a second visit if you don't behave.'

Haskin's eyes were daggers but he was already settling down and fixing his attention back on Connie.

'Education? Went to college but they didn't seem to like me very much and asked me to leave. I was eighteen when I got my first job in a mall as a security guard.'

'Why were you asked to leave college?' Connie asked.

'I drilled a hole through from a stationery cupboard into the girls' changing room. They said it was an invasion of privacy,' Haskin said.

'You didn't agree?'

'Most of them should have been paying me to watch them undress, they were so disgusting,' he sneered and she wanted to slap the smile off him. 'It was a janitor who found the hole. The principal set up a camera to see which student went in there, like it was some big deal. We agreed that I would leave quietly without a stain on my record so they could just seal up the hole without the female students finding out. Avoided the college being sued. Meant I could get a job.'

'Is your mother still alive?'

'Relevance?' he demanded.

'I'd like to know how she came to terms with the things you did, after you were convicted?'

'Changed her name. Moved to another city. I never heard from her again, which wasn't a shock.'

Sensible woman, Connie thought. 'Do you regard yourself as someone who hates women, Harold?' *Tara,* she wanted to say. *Did you hate Tara? Did you do something terrible to Tara?*

'Don't you want to hear what I did to them before you ask me that? I mean, from my own lips. I'm a profiler's wet dream and we have all evening.'

The words sent her stomach shrivelling. She forced herself not to react as she wondered if that had been a mere throwaway phrase or an intended barb. 'But I'm not a profiler. I'm a psychologist and a therapist. I'm here to help Patient B settle

246

in and to establish whether or not this is the place for him. Part of that involves finding out more about the people he'll be hospitalised with.'

'I was told you were a profiler,' Haskin said.

Holy hell, Connie thought, arranging a bemused look on her face, slight frown combined with amused smile. *What the actual fuck?* How had Haskin come by that information?

Connie looked at Nurse Casey, who had gone back to staring out of the window.

'That's strange. Who told you that?' Connie asked gently.

Haskin slid his eyes sideways at Casey, made sure he wasn't looking, then made a zipping-up movement across his lips.

Connie shrugged and gave him a bored look. 'No matter. It's not true. We were talking about whether or not you see yourself as someone who hates women.'

'Why don't you just ask if I hate women or not?' He sat up.

'I'm assessing your self-perception. The best way to understand it is by giving the example of a man who beat his wife. If I ask him whether or not he hits his wife, he might admit it and say yes, but believe he has cause. That's a different thing from him understanding that he's a domestic violence abuser.'

After a long pause, Haskin said, 'I don't hate all women.'

'Okay.' Connie sat back and waited.

'You want to know how I chose the women I killed?' Connie said nothing. 'I didn't rape any of them.'

'You say that as if that lessens your culpability. Is that what you think?' she asked.

'No way I'd have fucked any of those pigs.'

'Is that why you killed them? Because they had some physical attribute you disliked?'

'You want to hear it or not?' he snarled. 'I'm not answering any more of your dumb-ass questions until you let me tell it.'

247

Connie felt herself die a little inside. She didn't want to hear it. At that moment, she didn't want to be in that glorified prison cell listening to a monster call young women derogatory names. What she needed was a walk. A long one. A few miles along the mountain road high enough up that she could look back down on The Institution and get it in scale. She needed some perspective.

But Aurora needed her.

'Go on then,' she said dully. 'Say the things you want to say.'

The lead detective on the case would never speak about the things he saw and found once the case was concluded. When Haskin's lawyers managed to convince the court that their client was mad not bad, that same detective would unload on those lawyers outside the court building so ferociously that he was detained and held in the cells until he'd calmed down twenty-four hours later.

The Blindfold Killer, as Haskin had been dubbed, went to the trouble of sending the police a video of each young woman whose life he stole. Not of the victim herself, nor of the things he did to her. The video showed a different woman altogether, tied to a basic wooden chair, wrists around her back, ankles tied to the legs. There was audio. Too much audio for most to tolerate.

When police received the first tape, they watched and waited, horrified, to see what would happen to the girl in the chair. Then they heard the sound of a baseball bat hitting a body. The unmistakable dull thump, the odd crack, the spatter of liquid being expelled under pressure. Laughter. Grunts of physical exertion.

The girl in the chair began to scream and closed her eyes. Blood hit her body, her face. It went on for longer than it could possibly have taken to kill the victim. Until the young woman in the chair was unconscious. Until Harold Haskin was all laughed out.

The detectives had hoped and prayed that the video would be the first and last. Of course, it was the first of many. A calling card, a clue, the ultimate showing off. More young women disappeared. The dots on the map formed no coherent pattern; there was no centre point to focus on. They were taken at all hours of the day and night.

This was how profilers in the case had come to decide the killer was either unemployed or a shift worker. It had been a bird watcher keen on noting the progress of a pair of mating eagles who had seen a chance encounter with one of the victims and a man who had bundled her into his car. He hadn't seen the licence plate or any facial features but he had the impression that the aggressor had been wearing all black with some detail on it. The uniform had given police a potential shortlist of careers. Security guard was on that list. But it was one of Haskin's female co-workers who'd made the call.

All the missing girls were a larger than average clothing size and all were taller than five foot six. They all had short hair. A couple were lesbians, one was known to be bisexual, most were heterosexual, so that wasn't the thing. It was just that particular look. The look, Haskin's co-worker said, he called 'plumber girls'.

The police took their time. Arresting him while he was still holding hostages would likely end in them never being found. They searched his home while he was away, but the three-room apartment on a fourth floor was no place to hide so many victims and certainly not soundproof enough for what he did to them. He was careful when driving, checking his mirror constantly. In the end, they'd hidden a tracking device on his car and waited for him to visit.

What they found when they broke into the cellar of the deserted, condemned motel, was a circle of six young women, each tied to a chair. Haskin had blindfolded himself and was in the middle of the circle spinning himself around, baseball bat in hand.

No one died that day, but the number of bodies they found was greater than they had been searching for, each so devastated that only DNA identification was possible.

Thus the Blindfold Killer was born. He didn't need to watch what he was doing, he had explained to the judge. The bloodshed itself wasn't the point. Hearing the screams, having the young women experience the randomness of life and death, making them feel terrified but at the same time grateful that they had survived another week, *that* was the buzz.

There were survivors. Some had lost track of how long they'd been there. They were kept in the basement together, Haskin explained, so that when they had to watch one of their number die, the emotional impact was all the more poignant. Fate decided who would live and who would die on each occasion, Haskin was quoted in the press as saying. Not him. He had never specifically elected a single girl to die. It was simply whoever his baseball bat had found first.

'Are you done?' Connie asked. The question was too blunt to be professional in a therapeutic session, but she was past caring. She didn't want to spend another second in a room with Harold Haskin. It was a miracle any of the female staff in The Institution ever did.

'Are you?' Haskin replied.

Connie's right foot was bouncing up and down. She badly wanted to kick him with it.

'Why did you kill those women?' Connie asked.

'The psychiatrists said I was angry with my mother for being so unattractive that my father left. They think I was punishing anyone I found who looked like her. The blindfold, they hypothesised, was because I couldn't bear to see their faces as I hurt them. I would have had to come to terms with their humanity and with the monstrosity of my own actions.'

'Were they right?' Her voice was steely now, all pretence of interested therapist gone.

'I'll tell you if you call me Daddy,' he said.

Connie put the lid on her pen and flipped her notebook closed.

'Why are you running away? I'm no threat to you. You don't look one little bit like my mother.' He grinned.

'That's it, I'm on my break,' Samuel Casey said. 'Time to go, Dr Connie.'

'Just one time, call me Daddy. I dare you.'

'Fine by me,' Connie said to Casey. 'I've got all I need.'

Casey opened the door and held it for her. They exited together and Casey locked the door behind them, leaving Connie standing outside listening to a still-talking Haskin.

'I did it for fun,' he said. 'They really should have called me the piñata killer. That's all any of those women were to me. You know, I never had a birthday party, not one. I'd see all my school friends with their party hats and games, some even had a clown and a piñata, full to the top with sweets, hitting it with that stick 'til it broke and they all fell out. The funniest thing was when one of the kids missed with the stick and hit another kid and they'd cry and I'd laugh . . . It was all just for fun, Dr Connie. I did everything of my own free will, and I enjoyed every second of it.'

He walked to the door of his locked room. Samuel Casey

disappeared up the corridor whistling. Connie watched Haskin through the viewing slot.

'There's no such thing as free will, Mr Haskin. Human beings like to believe there is but studies, proper neurological studies with scans providing endless data, show that we make decisions at a very physical level. We've made decisions before our conscious self ever realises. From the second your father made the terrible decision to blame your mother's physical attributes for his decision to leave, everything you did afterwards was just you following your pathway.'

'That's not true,' he said. For the first time since they'd begun speaking, there was an edge of neediness to his voice. 'That's not true.'

'The thing you liked about the piñata wasn't the sweets, it was the stick. Because you wanted to hit someone. You already knew the person you wanted to hit was your mother. Your brain knew you were destined to kill women years and years before it gave you the green light to start doing so.'

Connie watched until Samuel Casey turned a corner, making sure he was beyond earshot before she spoke.

'Who told you I was a profiler?' Connie asked.

'Who told you I was a profiler, *Daddy*?' Haskin widened his mouth to form a distorted grin.

'Not content with being a serial killer and having a documentary – I apologise – a dramatisation made of your life, you also feel the need to play stereotypes with me? One that doesn't even fit the pattern of your offending?'

'I just want to see if you'll do it,' he said smugly.

'Why?'

'Because if you do it, then it's true and you need the answer. If you don't need the answer, you'll walk away.'

Connie had never wanted to push her thumbs into another

human being's eyes as badly as she did at that precise moment in time.

Instead she stepped closer to Haskin's door.

'You're right,' she said, her voice low, keeping eye contact. 'I do want the answer. You haven't lied to me yet. Are you going to lie to me now?'

The grin faded a few kilowatts. 'No,' he said.

'I didn't think so. I'd like to know about Nurse Tara. Was anyone watching her? Anyone a little bit more interested than they should have been?'

'Something happened to her,' he said.

Connie studied his mouth. A slight downturn. Grin gone.

'Is that a question or a statement?' she asked.

'I thought she'd gone into labour,' Haskin said. 'I heard her scream once, loudly, outside my door. Then I thought I heard her fall. Something happened out there but I couldn't be sure what. The next day she'd disappeared. Nurse Casey told us she'd gone because she needed to rest before having her baby.'

'Has anyone else been talking about it?' Connie asked.

'We all heard her scream. Everyone except Yarowski, who was in the quiet room that night. If he'd heard it, he'd never have shut up. He was obsessed with her. He's been gutted since she left.'

'He was obsessed with Nurse Cameron?'

'Poor bastard. I don't think anyone has been nice to him since he got arrested. The way he used to look at her.' He gave a slow shake of his head.

'Harold, have you told me any lies in the last couple of minutes?' Connie asked.

He returned her eye contact, didn't waver, but it wasn't forced or rebellious. 'No. But it's true isn't it, what I heard about you?'

'Who told you I was a profiler?' she asked again.

'Call me Daddy,' Haskin said, 'and I'll tell you.'

His head was tipped slightly to the side now, his lips parted.

'No, I'm not going to do that. Because now you're playing with me, and I don't like to be played. Goodnight, Mr Haskin. I appreciate you talking with me.'

She began walking up the corridor.

'Visit me again tomorrow,' he shouted after her. 'I might have remembered something else. Dr Connie!'

She walked away. The lights in the hallway flickered momentarily. A second later everything was back to normal. Connie stopped, leaning against the wall to process everything she'd just been told. Haskin was, in many ways, the most boring species of serial killer. A simple woman hater who took out his personal frustrations in brutal violence whilst harbouring feelings of superiority. He was, Connie was certain beyond doubt, untreatable. She felt no sympathy for him and no curiosity about him. It would have been better if the police had shot him during his arrest, no questions asked. And yet he was the one person who knew who she was. Did that mean he was involved or just that he had his ear to the ground?

Reasonably intelligent, tick. Some level of emotional intelligence even if he misused it, tick. No doubt able to follow instructions, tick. Never getting out of the ward, so would be desperate for a route to the outside world, tick. Psychopathic, sociopathic, completely lacking in empathy, hates women. Haskin should have been her prime suspect. But annoyingly, infuriatingly, Connie just wasn't feeling it, much as she wanted to believe he had been responsible for the murder. Harold Haskin had been playing with her the whole time, right up until he started talking about Tara. Then his voice, his stance, his whole demeanour had suddenly changed. He was being real.

Vassily Sidorov exited the medical room and glared at her.

'There you are,' he said. 'You're wanted downstairs. Campus announcement in the dining room for any staff not on night duty. You'd better hurry.'

Chapter 22

The dining hall was as full as it could have been, every seat taken and plenty of people lining the walls, arms folded, looking resentful that their free time was being used for announcements. Connie squeezed in and remained near the doors, anxious to get away again as soon as she could.

'Quiet, please,' an administrator said. 'As those of you who have been with us for several years will be aware, we occasionally have to deal with weather warnings.' The lights flickered once more as she spoke and a ripple of nervous laughter went through the crowd. 'Well, that was timely. I'm sure you'll all have noticed the conditions today and we've been given a severe warning. This will involve very high winds, flying debris, rain and possible hail. As always when a threat to life warning is issued, the mountain pass will be closed. Anyone here now will have to stay. No one can enter via the mountain road. No helicopters can access The Institution until the restrictions are lifted. All medical procedures must be dealt with on the premises.'

256

'Can we get through if we leave immediately?' someone asked.

'No, sorry, that's too much of a risk. If you get stranded, emergency services will not be able to reach you. I appreciate this sounds dramatic to newer members of our community, but we go through this a couple of times a year. However, we have enough food to survive a zombie apocalypse.' That one got a bigger laugh. 'And backup generators, so you can all still binge your favourite shows.'

'How long will it last?' Connie asked.

'It passes when it passes, but best guess is that we'll be home and dry seventy-two hours from now.'

Connie made fists in her pockets. The thought of being stuck there unable to leave even if she closed down the case immediately, was making her crazy. The dining room was too small for so many people. The low ceilings and strip lighting were an insect buzzing in her head, leaving pixelation at the edges of her vision. She wanted to hit the sides of her skull to get rid of it.

No, not crazy. People had used that word about her before and she hated it.

A hand grabbed hers. She flinched and pulled away.

'Dr Connie, are you all right?' Boy asked. 'You don't need to be scared of the storm. We have them all the time. There's usually a party with dancing. Will you come?'

Connie shook her head. She wanted to tell him she was all right. She wanted to tell him it wasn't the storm that was scaring her but something that hadn't yet taken shape in her mind – a vague, lumpy form that she was certain had been in her room the night before and taken her cell phone. She wanted to reassure the teenager who was doing his best to be kind to her.

Instead, she backed away, giving him a sad smile, before flying up the corridor from the dining room into the reception area where one woman sat idly by the reception desk phone.

'Keep it together,' Connie ordered herself, tensing her muscles hard before making them relax one by one, then shaking her hands out at her sides. She decided to make the most of there being no one else around. It was time to get a grip, and that meant an hour of self-care. First things first.

'Hi,' she said to the receptionist. 'Could I leave my name and room number with you in case anyone hands in a cell phone? I'm not sure exactly how and where it got mislaid, but—'

'Thick plastic case with a hexagon on the back?' she asked.

Connie breathed in sharply. 'Yeah, that's right.'

'You'll need to turn it on and show me you have all the security codes. Just a second.' She reached down into a drawer and pulled out Connie's phone. 'Here you go.'

'Who found it?' Connie asked as she went through her layers of security to prove ownership.

'One of the catering staff, I think. They said it fell out of your pocket as you were going down a corridor and by the time they'd got to it, you'd disappeared around a corner. They didn't know you or we'd have found you and returned the phone. I hope it didn't get damaged in the fall.'

'No, it seems fine,' Connie said. 'Do you know the name of the person who handed it in? I'd like to thank them personally.'

'I'm sorry, I don't. It's chaos here in the mornings. I can't even remember my own name half the time!' She gave a cheery laugh.

'Okay, thank you. It's good to have found it.'

'Especially with the coming storm,' the receptionist said. 'You'll want to warn your friends and family that you'll be out of contact for a while. It can be upsetting for people who don't understand what it's like here when they're unable to get through.'

'I'll be sure to do that.'

Connie pocketed the cell phone and considered her options. She wasn't hungry, couldn't face returning to her room, and Baarda would be eating now so she wouldn't be able to get him alone to talk. Beyond the glass doors to the staff car park, there was nothing but water and fresh air. The storm meant it might be the last opportunity Connie had to clear her head. Cool air in her lungs and wind in her hair were the only things that would make her feel normal and alive again. She needed to reconnect with the world. She needed a coat too, even took the first few steps back towards her room, but the two minutes it would take to get there and back again were too much. She had to get out, was on the verge of just running for the door. The best she could manage was to walk speedily towards the outside world, the extra layer of warmth forgotten in favour of her sanity.

Nothing more than a short stroll, she told herself. Just enough to blow away the cobwebs. Connie went out into the night. She crossed the car park in the direction of the lake, slipped under the security barrier and followed a footpath that took her closer to the water.

The air was strangely still. The little light that hung heavy in the distance was no more than a layer of melted butter on the horizon. The rest was black. All around the edge of the lake was a wall as thick as the ramparts of a medieval castle and higher than her head. The wall along the front of The Institution was dramatically spike-topped, but along the sides of the lake, the wall was flat. The dam itself had an overflow system she'd seen from the helicopter to stop water spilling backwards into the grounds of The Institution. The body of water posed no threat, but it was alluring. The temptation to swim in the long, hot summer months must have proved too much for some.

Connie longed to see the stars reflected on the surface. She walked, trailing the surface of the wall with her fingertips, letting its roughness guide her and steady her. Its slow, smooth curve led her away from The Institution, and with every step her heart lightened, the misery of the walls, doors, alarms and locks at her back.

A solo gust slapped her face and left Connie staggering backwards. She came back at the wind grinning, embracing the ever-dropping temperature. She couldn't go back yet. Inside, there was nothing but deception and despair. Out here, the environment was at least honest. Brutal, but honest.

Ahead of her now, there were steps. At the bottom of them was a metal chain at waist height designed to keep idiots at bay with a swinging sign declaring – when she got close enough to peer through the murky light – 'Danger, Engineers Only'.

Connie stared at it a while. She did so want to see the lake. It was safe enough for engineers to climb up there and she wouldn't be more than a minute. Climbing over the chain, she kept one hand on a side rail, making her footsteps count on the concrete steps to the top of the wall, allowing for another gust if it came.

It was worth the risk. The obsidian water was flawless. Barely a ripple marred its surface as the wind dropped obligingly. Atop the wall, Connie could feel the weight of water below. It deadened sound and soaked up time. Behind, the lights from the windows of the looming towers were nothing more than decoration. Ahead, the dam sighed in the night as cold air rushed down into the valley.

Lifting her face to the sky, Connie watched as the moon fought the surrounding clouds to rise undimmed in the night sky, casting a sallow light across the waterscape. It was a bad moon rising, her grandfather would have said, and it was bringing the storm. He was from Louisiana where they knew a thing or two about hurricanes. She missed him. He'd been taken from her when she was too young, when he was too young, in fact. His sense of humour was bordering on slapstick, and he'd tickled you until it was half past funny, but he knew how to love. Connie hadn't thought about him in an age. She wondered what advice he'd give if he could see her then, feeling as lost as she had in years.

Lightning struck the far side of the lake and for a second she was back at home on Martha's Vineyard, watching Fourth of July fireworks from her family's boat sparkle and bloom over beautiful Edgartown. The heat of it crackled, sending tendrils out towards the few trees that dared line the bank. She could smell the electricity in the air.

'One, two, three, four, five, six, seven . . .' The thunder rolled through the wall beneath her feet, rising up through her legs to rattle in her chest. With it came the wind again, not gusting now, but a long, low, insistent howl.

The time had come to get off the wall, but there would be no view of the light show from the footpath and another minute couldn't hurt. Connie felt powerful up there. Free.

She scanned the horizon for more lightning. There had to be another strike. Every hair on her body was standing on end. Sure enough it came, a sheet of fire this time rather than the drama of a fork. And in its light, she saw a man silhouetted further along the wall, towards The Institution. Between the pitch dark and the blinding light she couldn't tell at first if he was facing her or looking away, but a man it certainly was, moving now.

Moving towards her, in fact. Her eyes had adjusted to the dark enough to be able to see that. *Engage him in conversation?* she wondered. *Just run? Prepare to fight?* Her heart was

261

performing a drum solo in her chest and her breathing was suddenly worthy of a marathon.

Go back down the steps and onto the footpath below the wall, and he'd be above her. She didn't like that at all.

What was he doing out here with the storm coming in? Why was he on the wall and headed in her direction? What were the chances of them meeting in that time and place unless he'd followed her? The thunder came again and its fury made her gasp.

She turned and headed along the wall, away from the man, away from the towers. The dam was still too far in the distance to concern her. If the man was no threat to her, he would stop soon enough and head back. And if he was trouble, then she was sure-footed enough to keep some distance between them.

At first she walked, until the lightning struck again. He had gained on her, Connie saw, as she whipped her head around. She broke into a run. The wall was broad enough for it, she told herself. It was a good metre across, and flat, no loose stones. There was just enough milky moonlight for her to see her feet. As long as the wind played fair, she could move safely.

Thunder again, and sweat trickled down her back as she flew along. Connie kept running. Now the footpath below her began to dip and divide from the wall. Beneath her, the drop grew, and she could make out the chaos of wild greenery. If she jumped now, who knew what she would land in or on, but she couldn't go back.

The man would be at the steps by now. Standing to fight him was not an option with the certain death of the freezing depths to one side.

Heading for the dam was the only option, hoping she could make it all the way across before he caught up with her. Across, loop around on the far wall, and head back. Back to her room, a locked door, and safety.

Connie turned again, but the moon had been overtaken by cloud and now there was barely enough light for her to see her hands in front of her face, and certainly not her feet. She squatted, gripping the wall with her hands as she listened for the thump-thump of the man's feet heading for her.

Nothing.

She turned her head this way and that, listening more carefully.

Nothing.

Then the lightning came again, and she had nowhere left to hide. He would see exactly where she was and, worse, know she had lost her nerve. Connie searched the wall for him as the world lit up.

Still nothing. He was gone.

Gone from the top of the wall, at least. He could have left via the steps, and be hiding in the undergrowth. Waiting for her to give in and head for home.

Or perhaps – she hated herself for thinking it – perhaps she had imagined him. Perhaps the thunder and lightning, the wind and water, the day that had started and ended with death in one form or another, had conjured a demon in her mind.

She was shaking now. The effort of concentration was taking its toll and the adrenaline was making her nauseous. Connie told herself to stand, but her legs refused.

Aurora appeared, the image so clear in her mind that Connie gasped. The baby had long since ceased her crying. Her little breaths were so feeble that her chest hardly moved. Connie reached out a hand in the dark as if to touch her. What mucky blankets she'd been given had fallen away to leave her shivering with cold. Connie knew with a blinding certainty that there was no time left. 'What the fuck am I doing?' she whispered to the void around her.

She dangled her legs over the edge of the wall, footpath side. There was no choice but to jump. Height unknown, terrain unknown, but she couldn't stay on that wall all night and she was out of options. After rolling onto her stomach, Connie lowered herself as far as she could until she was holding on with just her fingers.

The drop was terrible, but not long. It was a bush that she hit, prickly and angry with her, but she was in one piece. It took a while to manoeuvre her way out of the shrubbery. However scratched up she was, at least it had broken her fall.

Connie walked slowly back, stopping every now and then to listen for footsteps. She picked up a stick that was neither as heavy nor as long as she'd have liked, but it was enough to strike with if that was required, and it had one end sharp enough to seriously damage an eye if it came to that. She did her best to keep her ragged breathing to herself, forcing one foot in front of the other. Back at the steps, she slunk against the wall, her skin crawling as she brushed spider webs and the husks of their desiccated meals.

Connie willed herself to move to no avail. The darkness was absolute now, and she longed to bathe in the pool of lights in the car park. There was something scratching in the undergrowth a few metres from her, maybe closer, she was losing her sense of space. Then came a louder noise and Connie bolted, stumbling the first few uneven paces, slipping in a patch of mud, before finding her stride.

She'd gone further than she thought, and The Institution was still punishingly distant. Above her, in the centre of it all, was Heaven Ward and, as she ran, she made herself think of baby Aurora, of the arms that held her at that moment, Connie's footsteps echoing the beat of the tiny heart that surely could not go on much longer.

Down she went, the crooked paving tripping her then slicing her screaming knees. Connie slapped the tears of self-pity that washed her cheeks.

'Get up,' she told herself. 'Get up and get inside.' She picked up the stick once more, held it firmly in her right hand, and went more slowly. She couldn't afford to fall again. Next time she might break an arm and hit her head, and where would Aurora be then?

As the car park drew nearer, the voices in her head quietened. From there, she could call for help. So close to reception, surely she could now be seen through the glass frontage? She turned back only once, palm horizontal over her forehead to block the glare of the lights, searching for any sign of the man who had chased her.

There was none.

And suddenly, she was inside.

As the panic subsided, she became aware of people staring at her. Inside the reception area, Connie wished herself invisible.

There were bits of twig in her hair, rips in her clothing, blood dripping down her shins. If she'd looked unkempt this morning, now she looked like – she hated to even think it – but like she'd just escaped from one of the towers.

As she advanced, more people stared. Someone asked if she was okay. Connie didn't bother answering. Instead she headed for her room, for her shower and for her bed.

She plugged her cell phone in, checking it over and over, making sure she wasn't just imagining its comforting presence. Her door was locked and chained. Her windows were locked. Everything was as she had left it.

Finally, exhausted, Connie slept.

Chapter 23

Connie woke from a dream where she was in a maternity hospital but couldn't identify baby Aurora from one hundred other crying newborns, to find her cell phone ringing.

'This is Kenneth Le Fay. Dr Woolwine, is that you?'

'Yes, sorry.' She sat up and willed her mind to clear. 'Are you back on site, Director?'

'I'm not.' Connie's heart sank. 'You received the storm warning?'

'Of course. I hadn't realised you didn't make it back here in time. Is there any news?'

'The post-mortem didn't reveal any substantial new information. The final crypto coin deposit is due to be made into the kidnapper's digital wallet at midnight tomorrow night. There has been no new footage of baby Aurora and I have to say, Tara's parents and husband are starting to lose hope. What progress your end?'

'Joe Yarowski is dead. I found him yesterday clutching Tara's missing earring in his hand.'

'You think he was responsible for her death?'

266

'I don't know,' Connie said. 'I didn't have a chance to speak with him before he died, but it all just seems too . . . neat.'

'Any progress finding out who moved the baby from the ward?'

'No, but I believe Aurora was sent down in the dumbwaiter to the level below the kitchen where someone was waiting for her. It would have been too much of a risk to take a baby down the stairs, in the elevator and across the hospital to transportation.'

'I agree,' Le Fay said. 'So any other forward progress? Have you at least been able to exclude anyone?'

'Only hospital support staff, administration and the like. Now that I've spent some time on the ward, it's become clear to me that anyone involved must have had close involvement in patient care. No one else ever has access to the ward, not even security, cleaners or caterers.'

'Well that's . . . be it . . . have news ab . . .'

Rain began lashing Connie's window and Le Fay's voice sputtered in and out.

'I'm sorry, I didn't hear that last part. Could you say again?'

'I said we have some news. Sidorov's previous employer reported that he'd been involved in a violent incident at the hospital. He expressed concerns, but said a deal was negotiated where Sidorov agreed to leave. I don't have any of the details. My phone is going out of range. There's a lot of noise on the line. I'll be in touch . . . I can . . . tomorrow . . . the police.'

'You keep cutting out, Director.' Connie got out of bed to stand next to the window and away from the thick walls, but the noise of the rain bombarding the glass made hearing him even more difficult.

'. . . think you should . . . criminal conviction . . . got to update . . .'

'Shit,' Connie muttered. 'Director, I'm not catching most of this. Could you email me—'

'I can't hear you.'

'I said, it might be better if you email me,' she shouted.

'I'm travelling . . . vital that—' The line went dead. Not just fuzzy with white noise but completely dead.

'Damn it,' Connie hissed. 'Fucking godforsaken place, middle of frigging nowhere.'

She waited a couple of minutes before checking her emails to see if Le Fay had managed to get anything through, but his name didn't appear in the stack of messages needing her attention. The only one she opened was from her mother, telling Connie not to worry about them. That they'd be fine without her. That she really shouldn't feel bad for choosing to put work first. Nothing more guaranteed to make her feel guilty than telling her not to.

As if to reflect her ever-darkening mood, the rain stepped it up a notch and the glass pane began rattling in its frame. Connie grabbed a hoodie from her wardrobe and pulled it over her head. A cruelly cold draught of air was playing around her room, but it gave her the incentive she needed to dress fast and get moving.

The next requirement was food. She'd been too lax about her body's needs. Now she was aching from the previous night's run, her face and body were covered in scratches, and she was ravenously hungry.

Connie didn't allow herself to think about anything as she hurriedly threw together a plate of eggs and hash browns with a mug of black coffee.

As she ate, she thought about Boy. She needed to put things right from the campus meeting. Boy was always around in the mornings, running errands. He hadn't made an appearance in the dining hall so she put her head around the kitchen door. Still no sign of him.

'Have you seen Boy?' she asked a passing porter.

'In the changing rooms having a fuss made of him.' He gave a braying laugh then motioned over his shoulder with his thumb.

Connie followed the general direction until she saw a door marked 'staff changing'. Down that corridor were two options: male and female. She heard and recognised Maeve's voice long before she reached the doorway.

'You have a responsibility.' Maeve's voice was low but urgent. 'I keep covering for you but I can't much longer. While you're here, you have to act like an adult.'

Connie put her head round the doorway and gave a smile.

'Hi, sorry to interrupt. I was told you were in here and I think I have an apology to make to Boy.'

Maeve was sitting next to Boy on a bench, one arm around his shoulders. Boy was staring at his shoes. 'I'll leave you to it,' she said, 'although he does have work.' She raised her eyebrows in Boy's direction. 'Just a couple of minutes then. Don't keep the doctor too long. I'm sure she has work to be getting on with as well.'

Maeve headed back towards the kitchen. Connie waited until she'd heard the far door shut.

'You okay?' she asked gently.

'Sure,' he said quickly. 'Sometimes I get a bit distracted and then I don't get everything done that I should on my shift. Someone complained about me talking too much and being too loud.'

'That's awful. You'd think people would enjoy having someone as cheerful as you around. How come Maeve was left dealing with it?'

'She's my . . .' He broke off, frowning, and punched himself in the leg. 'I forgot the word.'

'Your mentor?'

He sighed and then grinned. 'That sounds right.'

'Take my advice. Be who you want to be. Follow your own goals. Don't follow the herd and don't be told how you should behave.'

He shook his head. 'That's easy to say, Dr Connie. Not everyone's like you.'

'You're right. And maybe I don't know enough about your life here to be giving you advice, but I don't like you being told off. Can we be friends again, Boy? I was upset last night and you were being so kind. I'm sorry I ran out and missed our dinner together.'

'I'm sorry, too.' He hung his head even lower. 'I followed you. I knew I shouldn't have. Maeve always tells me to leave people alone and let them have their privacy, but you seemed upset and I was worried about you. Are you cross with me, too?'

Connie breathed a sigh of relief. 'Cross with you? Never. I'm so pleased it was you.' She gave a shaky laugh. 'Oh my goodness, I was so scared. I was just trying to get some air then all of a sudden I'd gone further than I thought and the storm started and I saw you. I was so stupid. I started running along the wall and I don't know what I was thinking. I couldn't seem to stop—'

'I didn't leave the car park,' he said. 'I found you at reception, then you went out of the doors so I followed to see you were all right and I thought you just wanted a walk. I wasn't on any wall. I'm not allowed to go near the water. You shouldn't have either. It isn't safe. You can slip. They told me the water's half a mile deep in places. No one who goes in ever comes out.'

'Oh,' Connie said, her voice suddenly no more than a dry crackle in her throat. 'Oh, right, sure. It wasn't you.' She shook herself. 'Hey, listen, it's nothing. Say, do you want to have dinner together tonight to make up for yesterday? I could use the company.'

He grinned.

'Yes,' he said. 'Yes please, Dr Connie. Will you tell me a story? Something exciting, like last night with the man chasing you.'

'Sure.' Her heart sank at the idea of losing more time but even so she didn't feel able to say no to the lonely half-child before her. 'But not that story. That was just me imagining things. See you at seven o'clock, okay?'

'Okay. I'd better go. Maeve'll slap my ears if I'm late anywhere else today.'

Connie took the elevator then hurried up the final staircase back to Heaven Ward. Baarda had finished breakfast and was waiting for her in his room.

'I was getting worried about you,' he said, as she shut the door behind her and collapsed onto his bed. 'Is everything all right?'

'No. Either someone knows exactly who I am, which means they'll have figured out who you are too, and they've found a way to get into my room, or I'm losing my mind. Right now, I'm honestly not sure which of those options scares me the most.'

'Slow down,' Baarda said. 'Tell me what happened.'

Connie explained it all then sat, biting her nails, waiting for his judgement.

'You're the psychologist, not me, but it's clear that being back on a ward like this is putting you in a difficult place. If you can't carry on, no one will blame you. The director has the option to simply bring in police units and do this the old-fashioned way, or wait until the ransom is paid and hope they deliver baby Aurora as promised.'

'So you think it's all in my mind then,' she said, 'the missing cell phone and the man on the wall last night?'

'I didn't say that. What worries me more is that you can't be sure exactly where you lost your mobile or if someone did actually break into your room. You shouldn't have been walking in the dark along that footpath last night, certainly not climbing up onto the wall. You're taking risks. Unnecessary ones. I know that's partly who you are, but it feels as if this place has got under your skin. Maybe you should call it quits now. We can both be out of here today.'

'They haven't told you then,' Connie said.

'That doesn't sound good.'

'Apparently there's a storm approaching, hence the horror movie thunder and lightning last night and biblical levels of rain currently trying to wash us all away.'

'How bad's it going to get?' Baarda asked.

'On a scale of one to ten?' She closed her eyes. 'More than ten.'

'Damn,' he said. 'What does that mean in practical terms?'

'The mountain road is shut. No one in, no one out. No helicopter access. Power might go out but I'm told there are backup generators, so lucky us.'

'What does Director Le Fay think? Does this change the operation?'

'Yeah, that's the other thing,' she said, sitting up and rubbing her eyes. 'He was off campus when the news broke about the storm. I spoke with him this morning.' Connie relayed the snippets of information about Sidorov. 'That's all I got before we were cut off. I'm waiting to see if Le Fay emails me – it sounded as if he had more for us – but I'm not that hopeful.'

Baarda crossed his arms and leaned with his back against the door. 'So the only person within The Institution who knows our real identities and who could get us out in the event of an emergency, isn't here?'

'That would be correct,' she said. 'But it's just for a couple of days, Brodie. After that there's no point carrying on anyway. We can stay out of trouble for forty-eight hours, right?'

'I'm sure I can stay out of trouble for that long, but I've known you a while now and I'd say twenty-four hours is your limit.'

Connie smiled, but it didn't reach her eyes. 'I know I seem a bit flaky, but I feel like we're making progress.'

'All right. Let's run it,' Baarda said, taking a seat.

'I don't like the earring in Yarowski's hand. My appointment with him was written up on the board in the staff area so there was a good chance I'd be the first person to go in there. I was told Yarowski was obsessed with Tara, so why kill her?'

'Men often kill the women they're obsessed with,' he noted.

'Fair point, but that's on the outside. Life inside changes everything. There are only six rooms on this ward. That's not a lot of socialising with fellow prisoners, almost no visitors. Same old staff and, honestly, the ones who are here aren't exactly the people you'd want to spend an evening drinking with. Tara may have been the only light in Yarowski's life.'

'That's rational thinking. These are serial killers who've been diagnosed with serious mental illnesses. What if Yarowski simply lost control?'

'That doesn't work for me. The person who did this didn't lose control. They planned, prepared, researched or were trained, then carried out an operation to remove a baby and hand her over still alive. This wasn't a crime of passion. If

273

Yarowski really was obsessed with Tara then he'd have been the last of the prisoners anyone would approach to perform the foetal abduction. He might just as easily have told her what was going to happen to gain favour with her,' Connie said.

'So the earring was, what, planted on him after he died? Are you saying he was murdered?'

'No, something much simpler I think. Yarowski's never getting out of here. Nurse Tara was the only light in his otherwise utterly miserable existence. Suppose someone told him she was dead, convinced him that she'd had an accident, died in labour, whatever. Maybe they even managed to show him a picture of her dead body, then suggested a way to end his own life. Talked him through it. He's got nothing to live for, he's an easy target, and he's known to be obsessed with Tara. Give him a reason to kill himself, give him a way, then plant the earring in his hand so the first and most obvious conclusion is that he took the earring as a memento when he killed her.'

'If you're right, that puts us both in a very precarious position indeed,' Baarda said.

'Agreed, but we knew when we came in here that the guilty parties would be suspicious of us straight away. Nothing's really changed. Also, Haskin told me that he heard Tara scream the night she died. Said everyone on the ward would have heard it. They assumed she'd gone into labour or had an accident. That's why none of them were surprised when she was no longer working the next day.'

'Was it also Haskin who told you that Yarowski was obsessed with Tara?'

'It was,' Connie said. 'But someone also told him I'm a profiler, so he's getting reliable information from the outside world somehow. Given that no one has my surname, they did some pretty good research.'

'Or they took a photo you were unaware of and used facial recognition software.'

She stared out of the window as she thought about that. It made her feel sick to think someone on the ward might not just suspect but actually know everything about her. Every case she'd been involved in. Who her family was. Where they lived. 'It's possible,' she agreed hesitantly.

A whiplash crack of lightning struck close to the towers and the lights went off. Connie counted to four in her head. The darkness was absolute in that time, a dead zone. She felt suspended in mid-air, as if the whole tower might crash to the ground without warning. At the count of five the light came back on.

'Convenient of Haskin to have opened up to you like that. Do you think he might have been involved?' Baarda said, apparently unaffected by the blackout.

She recounted her assessment of Haskin, including her final sense of the truth of what he'd told her about Tara.

'That's not evidence, Connie. It's not even a deduction. Don't hate me for saying it, but you're not on your A game at the moment.'

She looked Baarda straight in the eyes and took in a shaky breath. 'I don't hate you for that. If anything, I kind of love you for it. Thank God you're here. I know I'm not at my best right now. But this is all I've got. I don't believe it was Haskin.'

He gave her a long stare in response, gentle, concerned. 'All right,' Baarda said eventually. 'Talk it through for me. He's the most dangerous prisoner in here. He killed young women and made other captive women watch while he filmed it. Also, he evaded capture for a sustained period. He's smart and he's good at killing without leaving a trail.'

'Yeah, I know. He matches the killer's profile. He'd have

275

been perfect in many ways. I just think . . .' She shrugged. 'It's sort of that he's so fucking arrogant, he wouldn't have been a good choice to be used as someone else's pawn.'

'Okay,' Baarda said. 'I get it. So where are you with staff members?'

'I have to investigate Sidorov more thoroughly. There's something under the surface that's making me uneasy. Nurse Madani is desperate for money and she swapped her shift with Tara the night she died, so she's a possible. Roth is an absolute bitch, and I suspect she disliked how popular Tara was with everyone. Tom Lord is a bully and a fool, but I don't think he's bright enough to have masterminded it.'

'I don't like him,' Baarda said, scowling suddenly. 'I still think it was him who drugged me on day one.'

'There's that, too,' Connie said. 'I haven't had much to do with the other orderly, Jake. What's your take on him?'

'Lazy. The man fell asleep in front of the TV in a room full of murderers. If you want my opinion, he's too relaxed to be involved. If he were in the middle of something like a murder, kidnap, ransom and he suspected you and I were here to investigate, I hardly think he'd have been so off his game.'

'Nice deduction. So the others I'm not sure about yet. I need to talk with Vince East. I've met him briefly but I have yet to form any opinion about whether or not he's capable of involvement. What's happening with you this morning?'

'Group therapy session with Dr Ong. I think they want to help us all process our grief over Yarowski's death and answer our questions.'

'Grief counselling in a high-security psych unit? That's like asking people with no sense of smell to try different perfumes, but all power to Dr Ong for trying to address these sociopaths' humanity,' Connie muttered. 'Good luck. I'm going to check in with you again this afternoon.' She stood. 'We're getting there. I can feel it.'

'That's good, but I'm worried about you, Connie. Any more trouble or if you feel like you're struggling, you should just stay off the ward until Le Fay's back. Promise me.'

Connie stood on her tiptoes and gave him the lightest of kisses on the cheek.

'I like it when you worry about me, Baarda. You're not such a repressed, English stick-in-the-mud after all.'

'High praise from you.' He smiled.

'Don't get used to it,' she said. 'I'll be back to my old self before you know it.'

Connie began to exit. Baarda took hold of her right arm and pulled her back into his arms, hugging her hard. She wanted to stay there, safe, protected by him, and that feeling made her push him away. It was too difficult to let herself be vulnerable. Too scary.

'You don't need to worry about me, Baarda,' she said. 'I'm gonna be fine.'

'I know you are,' he said. 'Sometimes you need reminding of your own humanity, that's all. You're flesh and blood. Don't be so hard on yourself.'

Connie turned before he could see the tears in her eyes, and headed for Vince East's room. Sometimes Baarda seemed to be able to read her better than she could read herself. She was stressed and scared, feeling out of her depth, but there was no time to unpack any of it. She put one hand on East's door handle, cautioning herself not to let her rising sense of panic around finding Aurora cloud her clinical judgement. All she needed to do was get results.

Chapter 24

'I was feeling a little left out,' East said as she entered his room. 'You decided to leave the best till last, huh?'

'Good morning, Mr East,' Connie said. 'It's a little loud in here with the rain trying to break through the window. Shall we go somewhere else to talk?'

'Brunch? Where do you want to go? I know a great little place that does pancakes with maple syrup and bacon that's perfectly crispy but not burnt.'

'Sadly the mountain road is closed, so that's not an option,' she said. 'The therapy room is in use for a group session.'

'Yeah, I wanted to say thanks for getting me out of that. Dr Ong getting us in tune with our emotions is not my thing. Have you seen Benny Rubio cry yet? Fuck me, that man can bawl.'

'Sounds entertaining. Listen, I know it's not the best place to chat but let's use the medical room. If nothing else, it'll be a change of scenery for you.'

East fell silent for a few seconds before contouring his face into the semblance of a smile. He was working hard to appear laid-back and friendly, Connie thought. She wondered if his attempt to make her like him came from loneliness, a need to manipulate, or because he had something to hide. 'Sure,' he said. 'A change is as good as a break, am I right?'

Connie hadn't been into the medical room since discovering Tara's earring. Vince East hung back behind her. Connie turned to study his expression as he went in but his poker face was too good for her to figure him out.

'Well, it's private but not exactly warm and welcoming,' East said. 'Tell me you don't want me to lie on the couch.'

'Would it be a problem for you if I did?' she asked.

'I'd prefer to stand,' he said.

'Won't be necessary. There are a couple of chairs in the side room. I'll fetch them.'

East stayed where he was and let her bring the chairs in. He wasn't pushing his luck with her, which was good as she hadn't bothered to arrange a chaperone, but East was all façade. Breaking through it wasn't going to be as easy as it had been with the others.

They sat facing each other, a couple of metres apart. East put his right ankle over his left knee, as if they really were old friends meeting for a coffee and sitting in the sunshine.

'Come on then, hit me with it,' he said.

Connie knew a little about him from her preliminary police briefing, but she hadn't had the time to study the case statements or the psychiatric assessment in detail.

'You were convicted of eight murders over a period of five months. You didn't plead guilty to any of them. You made the prosecution prove their case, and yet you declined to defend yourself and gave no evidence at your own trial.'

'What can I say? I'm a private person.'

'Your hands are shaking, Vince,' Connie said. 'You good?'

'Not often I'm in a room with a beautiful woman.' He instantly rubbed one hand across his eyes and cringed. 'Sorry, that was on the creepy end of the compliment spectrum.'

'Are you concerned how that comment might affect me, or how I might perceive you because of it?'

'Um, both, I guess, and I suppose when a man talks to a woman like that, it's – you know – a sort of low-end violation.'

'I see. Let's go back to the question. You were fine before we walked in here, but since we sat down your hands have started shaking. Is there something about this room that you don't like?'

'You got any idea how many needles I've had put in me without my consent since I was committed?' he replied.

'Some idea, yes. Let's move on. You killed six men and two women. That's relatively unusual. Most serial killers either stick to one sex, or the kills outside their normal pattern are effectively collateral damage. People who were in the wrong place at the wrong time. Was that the case with you?'

'No,' he said. 'Everyone I killed, I chose specifically.'

'And a range of ethnicities too.'

'You already know the answer to the question you're about to ask,' he said.

'I know how you were caught. Is that the real answer to the mystery or is there more to it?'

'Does it matter? I killed all those people. I've already admitted it to you. Yes, either sex, different ethnicities, different age groups.'

'Would you tell me about it?' Connie asked.

'No. I didn't talk about it at trial, I won't talk about it to Roth or Ong, and as much as it's nice to have a new face on the ward, I won't talk to you about it either.' It was said politely

280

and with an odd passivity, but East's expression was all business, neutral but still engaged and focused.

'Can I talk about what I know, hypothesise about it, without triggering you?'

'My defence lawyers asked about six months of questions. They never did get any answers, but they're all still alive if that makes you feel any better.'

It actually did. 'Still alive is kind of a low bar, but if that's all you got, then I'll take it.'

'Before we start, just in case you and I fall out, I like your man. We bonded over *Groundhog Day* and a near-death situation earlier this week,' East said.

'He's my patient, not my man. Language is important. And yes, he told me you'd met.'

'Wouldn't tell me what he'd done, though. Loose lips sink ships and all that. Seemed sane though, which is unusual in here,' he said.

'I can't answer your questions about him, as you know. You ready to start now or do you want to try to delay this again?'

'I'm all ears.'

Connie got herself comfortable, made sure she was settled back in her seat, legs crossed at the ankles and tucked under her chair, and hands held loosely in her lap. Nothing tense or aggressive. Nothing defensive.

'If you're not okay with any of this, you can stop me.' East nodded his understanding but stopped short of another flippant quip. She was glad. It was hard to read him when he kept up the act. 'The first four people they found dead, the police had no idea what the link between them was. By the time the next death occurred, they'd been able to do a deeper dive into the victims' pasts and found that at some time or another, they'd all worked at a boys' home. It took police a while but eventually they were able to obtain records of all staff and students over the decade that boys' home was operating.'

Connie paused, giving East the chance to interrupt or challenge her. He opted not to.

'It was what they used to call a home for wayward boys aged from seven to seventeen. That's awfully young for anyone to label a child as wayward, whatever that's supposed to mean. I don't believe a seven-year-old is ever bad enough to justify sending them away from home. If a child that young is displaying really bad behaviour, it's usually the parents who need looking at, not the child.'

She could imagine the scene, children who were causing trouble at their normal school, parents who couldn't be bothered with them any more, parents who couldn't afford to look after their children any more, dropping them off at the boys' home.

'Anyway, after they had the list of possible suspects, when the final victims were taken, the net began to close. Victim number eight was killed differently to the others. There was some speculation about that, but it looks as if you were running out of time, and what mattered was to make sure he couldn't survive, more than the slow, painful death you served on all the others.'

Above them, the tiled roof of the tower took a direct hit and the air smelled of burning as the lights went out. In the internal room, there was no light at all. Connie waited.

A hand touched hers, fleetingly. She did her best not to flinch.

'It's okay,' he said. 'Happens all the time, here. The lights will come back on soon.'

The surgical implements were all locked inside cupboards, and most of the equipment was secured, but the reality of sitting there in that small room, with a man who had killed so many people in cold blood, was making her heart race.

'Are you scared of me?' he asked.

'A little,' she said. 'Probably not as much as I should be.'

'That's based on an assumption. You're assuming that just because I have killed, I have no conscience about killing and therefore might not hesitate to kill again.'

'No,' she said. 'All the people you killed previously had something in common that I don't share. I'm concerned that you have an illness that might blur the boundary between right and wrong, and that you might use me to escape the ward.'

'Wow, you're right. I hadn't even thought of that. You think that would work? I mean, probably it would for a couple of hours. I reckon I could make it out of the tower, even as far as outside, then I'd be forced to let you go or you'd slow me down. The weather would get me before security. Best-case scenario, I'd find shelter but the temperature would leave me hypothermic. Still, at least I'd die outside of this place.'

'Is that really the best-case scenario for you?'

'Would you want to die in here?' he asked.

'I would not. Do you believe you're going to?'

'I do. The medical reports, compiled by three leading psychiatrists, say I am paranoid and delusional, and narcissistic with a god complex. They believe childhood traumas caused the initial breakdown, which was followed by repeated bouts of self-harm. Finally, I evolved into full suicide attempts. They also say I'm schizophrenic: one minute cheerful and behaving with normal boundaries, the next I'm psychotic and unable to function normally. That's enough to keep me here a very long time.'

Connie wished the lights would come back on.

'What's your opinion of your mental health?'

'I say let them have their opinions. The jury decided I

killed those men and women. The doctors decided I was ill rather than criminally culpable. My feelings on the matter are irrelevant.'

The legs of his chair scraped the floor and she heard him walk to the far side of the room.

'I'd prefer it if you'd stay seated. Or we can go back out into the corridor and talk in your room,' she said.

'So you really are scared of me. What took you so long to suggest changing rooms? Did you not want to appear weak?'

'Actually I thought we were getting on reasonably well, and I didn't want to change the environment and burst the bubble.' The light sputtered back on.

East was standing in the far corner, leaning against the wall, arms crossed, as far from her as he could get. She couldn't be sure, but his eyes looked irritated and watery. Connie tried not to stare.

'What's it to be? This room or back to yours?' she asked.

'You're really going to pursue this? I assumed you'd be getting bored by now.'

'You hate this room.'

'Every inmate in here hates this room. The ankle and wrist straps on that bed aren't just for show.'

Connie knew that was the truth. Electroconvulsive therapy under anaesthesia wasn't some Gothic tale to conjure images of Victorian asylums. It was real and used regularly as a treatment for severe depression or bipolar disorders. Her memories of it were cloudy and vague. She remembered trying to say she did not consent, not that it mattered. Her parents had consented for her. She recalled the bee sting of the needle and the chill of the liquid in her veins. Then a sensation as if her world was on fire. It had been like dreaming her own death.

Tara's dream had been all too real, on that very table. That's

284

what Connie needed to focus on. She pushed her own memories back down into the trash compactor of her brain.

'You've had ECT?' she asked.

'Everyone has it, sooner or later. Dr Roth tells us it "takes the edge off" which I guess means it makes us easier to deal with. Except Benny Rubio. Every time he comes out of the frying pan, he gets more and more screwy. You want to watch out for your James Bond guy. Patient B will be next on Roth's list for sure.'

Connie didn't like that. Not at all. Sadly, it was a move she could believe Roth might make. East walked back to his chair and sat down.

'Why did you crucify seven people and cut the throat of the eighth, Vince?'

'I thought you were going to tell my story. You're asking questions again.'

His voice was different. Harder. Connie watched the Gatsby-esque transformation, from Hollywood good looks to cold, intense purposefulness, and wondered what conversations he'd had with his victims, if he'd bothered speaking with them at all.

'The school, I'm guessing, had religious affiliations. The crucifixion is too obvious to be anything else, and would have been an awful lot of work to construct. They found the structures in your garage. The seventh victim was still nailed to her cross, the eighth at her feet, having been left to bleed out as you prepared for the arrival of the authorities.'

The earlier bodies had been found dumped back in their own homes having been crucified. That was where her factual knowledge ended.

'A school for wayward boys. To me that sounds like the sort of place abusers would be drawn to. I wasn't informed that the victims were priests or from one particular faith. Usually when that happens, there's an investigation from a church or sect.'

'It was non-denominational,' he said, clapping his hand back over his mouth and making round eyes momentarily.

'That's okay,' Connie said. 'Speak if you like, don't speak. You're not betraying anyone. Not even yourself.'

East sat on his hands, and now he was neither intellectually playful, unstoppable Gatsby nor temperamental and bitter. For the first time, he was just a vulnerable man in a hospital.

'Non-denominational is interesting. It suggests a lack of control and oversight from a wider organisation, and it means there probably wasn't much hierarchical structure. No one to answer to. No inspections. Working there would have appealed to a whole range of teachers, caretakers, support staff. All types. I'm guessing the school survived on charitable donations. Probably also money from authorities glad not to have to keep such difficult students in their own schools. How long were you there?'

East had gone quiet again.

'Probably a few years,' Connie continued. 'Hopefully not the whole decade. I'm aware that those places were at times as hard to get out of as this one. Perhaps the thought of The Institution was something like home to you. I imagine you hate that this is something you're familiar with. If it helps, and by helps I don't mean that it will lessen your experience, but to show you're talking to someone who knows, I'll tell you a bit about my time living in a place like this. Not high security – I hadn't killed anyone – but I was committed there against my will based on a medical condition that hadn't been diagnosed. A little like you, I saw good medics and bad. Treatments I'd sooner not recall. My fellow patients ranged between some of the nicest, sanest people I've ever met, to the truly disturbed and diabolical.'

'How am I supposed to believe this?' East asked.

'You already do, or you'd have called me a liar straight out of the gates. The worst thing about places like this, like the school you went to, is that you get used to them. You don't think you ever will, then it slips under your skin like a splinter and you press it for a while just to feel the pain, because pain is right, it's how you should feel. Then one day you notice that the splinter isn't pricking your skin any more. It's gone all the way in, so deep it's finally painless. You know it's there but it's just normal. Then you wake up one day and realise the thought of being anywhere else is terrifying, and that's the day you finally hate yourself more than you hate all the other people put together, and you hate them a whole fucking lot.'

East nodded.

'It was abusive?' she asked.

He took a deep breath, nodded again.

'Physical or sexual?' East looked away. 'Both, I'd imagine. Sexual abuse in places like that is never about sex. It's about dominance and power, it's about destroying something innocent, it's control and mind games and terror. It's about taking away every single private part of you until it feels like you have absolutely nothing left.'

East laced his hands behind his head and stared off into some safer emotional place.

'That sort of damage makes children incredibly vulnerable, then it makes them almost impenetrably hard. It creates a problem for the brain, because the brain struggles to function as a single unit. It's trying to mature in opposing directions. The resulting internal conflict can be crippling. I can understand the desire to kill the people who did this to you. What I don't understand is why you didn't present the evidence to your lawyers. They might have been able to do a deal with the prosecution.'

She sat quietly for a moment and thought that through. The problem, of course, was that the defence could never have proved the abuse. It was just East's version of events, and even then so many years later it wasn't a defence to the charges. The hospital order made more sense, in the circumstances. A man driven to kill after such terrible damage had been done to him didn't deserve to be in a prison on twenty-four-hour-a-day lock-up, but he did need psychotherapeutic treatment.

'I'd like to go back to my room now, please. As delightful as your company is, it's honestly a bit painful watching you hypothesise.'

'Then tell me,' Connie said. 'Jesus, why is everything such a battle?' She shut herself up, took a breath, mentally kicking herself for losing her temper and blaspheming. It was out of character and unprofessional. She rubbed her temples for a second and regrouped. 'What I'm trying to say is this: you're stuck in here. Admitting that you killed those people can't hurt you. In fact, in terms of getting out some day, it would be extremely helpful. Acceptance, honesty, perspective, change, stepping away from denial and into remorse. All that stuff. Or is wanting to get out of here just another part of your act?'

'Why is this so important to you? None of this is relevant to Patient B settling in, or assessing his threat levels or whatever bullshit you're up to.'

'It matters to me what kind of human being you are,' Connie said.

'What the fuck? I've been treated, assessed, prodded and probed and no one has ever come out with a line like that. Is this a set-up? Are you recording me?' He folded his arms tightly over his chest.

288

Connie sighed and leaned forward, elbows on her knees, trying to create a sense of intimacy between them. 'No. I need to know if I can trust you. I need to know why you killed those people and why you're in here.'

He laughed, and Connie felt like it was genuine. 'You need something from me. You're asking me for a favour. I'd forgotten what that felt like. It's nice, you know, to have the choice, the ability to give or withhold. I'd forgotten it.'

Connie screwed up her eyes against the harsh electric light. The next headache was going to be a bitch.

'Here you go, my gift to you. I got out of the boys' home. Until they stuck me up in this tower, I could get out of, or into, most places. I wasn't prepared to hang around in that hellhole. I was thirteen when I finally found the courage to go, and the only reason it took me four years to do it was because my brother was there too. We shared a room. Oliver was a year older than me.'

'Did he escape at the same time?'

'No.' East shook his head. 'And I didn't take him with me when I went. I couldn't. Oli was special. He was born with both physical and mental disabilities. He spent his life in a wheelchair, and would largely just smile, make the odd noise and wave his head around when you spoke to him. I loved him, though. He was, I don't know, pure. He never got to a point in life where he was tainted. My parents just couldn't be bothered. There were expenses, round-the-clock care. I did what I could but I had to go to school. I started noticing bruises, swelling, what I now believe were fractures. Then they heard about The Redemption School and that was it. They were packing his bags by the end of the day. I begged them not to, pleaded with them. In the end I said that if Oli was going, I was going with him. I overplayed that hand. They were fine about it. Dropped us off, put their house on the market, went on a road trip. The school required a small contribution, and they screwed together the money for that, then they were free.'

'You never saw them again?'

'There was a visit once a year. They came to start with, then I would try to tell them what was happening, warn them about the abuse, the bullying, the restraints.' He gave an unwilling glance at the table. 'They didn't want to hear. If they accepted it, that meant taking us out of school, taking us back. It meant being tied down to parenting again, and realistically a lifelong commitment to Oli.'

'How many boys were at the school?' Connie asked.

'Maybe a couple of hundred. We were housed in different blocks depending on our year groups. The man in charge called himself Pastor Peter. He'd created his own faith, his own church. His wife, who we all had to call Miss Mary, was a sour old woman who never set foot in the school buildings if she could avoid it.'

'You think she knew what was going on?'

'Maybe not the details. Almost certainly not the terrible things her husband was doing. The physical abuse? Definitely. The sexual stuff? I think she just closed her mind and turned away. They lived in a nice house, had a pretty garden, and we'd see the local ladies' circle turn up to take tea with her every Wednesday afternoon. She made a deal with the Devil and kept her mouth shut.'

Connie nodded. 'So your parents left after you told them what was happening, and nothing changed?'

'Oh no, that's when everything changed. That's when I knew I had to leave.' East closed his eyes and the emotions that played across his face were a moving picture of what he was remembering. 'They obviously decided that for them to walk away with clear consciences, they had to pretend to do something. So they had a little chat with Pastor Peter about the things I'd reported to them. He didn't come to me himself that night; he sent the two nastiest teachers of the lot of them, and that was going some.

'Oli was in bed. He got tired easily, and needed a lot of sleep, plus it was easier for the staff to get him sorted early so they didn't have to look after him for protracted periods of time. When Oli went to bed, I went to our room to give him some company, make sure he was okay. Try to keep—' He broke off.

'You tried to keep him safe from the staff members?' Connie offered.

East nodded. 'I couldn't that night. I knew as soon as the knock came at the door that we were in real trouble. They took it out on Oli. That was the worst thing.'

Tears rolled down East's cheeks. Connie didn't think he even knew he was crying.

'They made you watch?'

'Yes. They said they were going to keep on and on until I watched, so the fastest way to get it over with was to do what they said. The things they did to him . . .'

'Vince, look at me.' It took a while, but he met her eyes. 'You need to reprogram your brain to handle these memories. It's important to learn to take their power away. You can't hold all this inside.'

'They dragged him around, used him like he wasn't even human. When I tried to stop them they just punched and kicked me until I couldn't move any more. In the end, I stopped trying to fight them.'

Connie sat and waited.

'When they'd finished with him, they did the same things to me. I ran away that night. I went in just the clothes I was wearing, my only pair of hand-me-down shoes, which were too small the first time I wore them, some food I'd stolen from the canteen previously, and the only photo of Oli that I had.'

'What happened to Oli?' she whispered.

'He never left that school. I don't know exactly what happened, but I know he didn't survive it.'

'There must have been a death certificate,' Connie said. 'Did you try to find it?'

'His death was blamed on his various conditions. Natural causes. The school used a doctor who didn't have a problem turning a blind eye to what went on there. He got paid come what may.'

'Was there a funeral? A resting place you could visit?'

'Cremation. I don't know where his ashes are. My parents saw to that.'

'Where are they now?' she asked.

'No idea. I tracked them for a while then decided I was better off without them. They never even tried to find me. But that's not why it ended the way it did,' East said. 'I drifted around for a long time. Cut it out of my memory, if you like. Sort of scribbled over it with black pen so I couldn't see the detail. I knew there was a hole in me but if I didn't try to figure out what was hiding in there, I could carry on day to day. I had a job in the hotel business; I'd been promoted, was on my way up the managerial ladder. I even had a home if not a stable relationship. That always eluded me.'

'Were you happy in your life, at any stage?' Connie asked.

'I was as happy as you can be when you're trying to pretend that no part of your childhood actually happened. I rewrote my own history, created a new version of myself. Things could have been worse.'

'So what happened?'

'Social media happened. Photos on the internet. Advertising for my hotel. That's how the lawyers found me,' he said.

'I don't understand.'

East sighed. 'A group of boys from the home had got together, started some group online. Compared stories. Decided that they should finally speak out. Of course, by then the home had been closed for years. The change in the need for regulation, accountability, made it impossible for them to carry on. But the group had done their homework and found several staff members. They all remembered Oli and they wanted me to give a statement to support a prosecution.'

'Did you?'

'Nope. Couldn't face it. Didn't want any part of it. I guess I knew my whole life would be impacted, everything I'd built – even if it was just a shell – was going to crumble. But I watched them put themselves through it. They fought to get the police to take statements, and I saw the investigation progress. They had their own lives pulled apart, their characters muddied. Every stupid thing they'd done as kids was used against them. The investigation concluded that all those God-fearing members of staff were being targeted with criminal complaints with a view to suing for compensation later. Not one of them was ever charged.'

'So they got away with it. Your life was disrupted again, and you decided that enough was enough?'

'They killed my brother,' East said. 'They murdered him. I don't know how I wasn't angrier about that for so many years, but when I finally started thinking about it again, I couldn't stop. I just couldn't stop. I mean, the fucking hypocrisy of those people. The sheer scale of the evil in that place.' He caught himself shouting, and stopped. Put his standard dopey grin back on his face. 'So I did what I did.'

'Did you struggle at all with watching them die?'

'No,' East admitted. 'So maybe I am a psychopath after all. I guess it's possible that I'm just as broken as they claim.'

'I suspect they just didn't know what to do with you,' Connie said. 'The murders were clearly linked to your past. The prosecutor must have had some idea about what went on in that home. And, honestly, anyone driven to kill each victim slowly over a period of days, by crucifixion no less, is bound to be assumed mentally ill.'

'So did you get what you want? Only I'm getting hungry.'

'You could talk to Dr Ong, ask for a new assessment.'

'Which lands me in a normal prison, sharing a cell with three other men, twenty-two-hours-a-day lockdown, random violence, bullying and blackmail.'

'At least you'd have a release date,' Connie said.

'If I lived long enough, sure, but the sentence for what I did is going to be so long I'd be a walking corpse before I saw daylight. Can I ask you something?'

'Sure,' she said.

'Why do you have new scratches all over your face and hands?'

Connie raised one hand halfway to her face before she realised what East was talking about.

'Funny story, went for a walk yesterday evening, fell off a wall, made an idiot of myself.'

'Doesn't sound funny at all,' East said. 'Can I ask why you'd come here after what happened to you?'

'I became fascinated with the human condition. Psychology is evolving all the time. One hundred years ago society locked up young mothers with postnatal depression, did terrible things to them. We even hospitalised women who were unfaithful to their husbands, called it moral insanity. The psychiatrist who treated me, the one who failed to diagnose the cause of my silence, claimed I was suffering from teenage hysteria. That's not a clinical diagnosis worthy of any practitioner, but I was young and female, and that old male doctor got away with saying whatever he wanted because my grandmother had known his family for decades. We give doctors a lot of power. Most of the time, rightly. Occasionally, that's dangerous. I guess I needed to work those issues out, so I came back to the place it all started.'

'You like your job?'

'Like is probably the wrong word. It's a good fit for me.'

The building groaned and creaked as the wind wrapped around it, and hail played percussion on the roof.

East stood up and put his hand on the door handle. 'In the interests of full and frank disclosure, if you read my file it's going to say there were three additional deaths they investigated me for after they got me for the school staff killings.'

Connie got to her feet. 'I didn't know about those.'

'That's because they never linked me to them evidentially. Three women died at the hotel where I worked over a period of about five years. Not actually in the hotel or on the grounds, but they were all guests staying with us at the time.'

'All right,' Connie said. 'Do I need to ask if you were guilty?'

'I don't think you'd be very good at your job if you had to do that. Haven't you formed an opinion about me yet?'

'I have,' she said.

'Okay then. Just so you know. I don't want anyone out there turning you against me.'

'I make my own mind up about people,' Connie said. 'Don't let me keep you from your lunch.'

'It's risotto, Thursday lunchtimes,' he said breezily as if the conversation they'd just had was already distant history. 'It's kind of gross, but it could be worse. You do not want to try the tapioca pudding.'

'I'll remember that,' Connie said, a vague smile at the edges of her mouth.

She escorted East back to his cell in line with proper procedure, and waited until the door clicked shut. As they walked, she thought back over the conversation. He was believable, superficially honest. Charming too. It was that last aspect of him that she was least at ease with.

Very organised killers often had a high IQ and good self-control. Beyond that, many of them were good with people, able to persuade and manipulate. Able to make people believe in them. Charming enough, in this case, even to persuade Tara Cameron that he needed something looked at in the medical room. Imagine that – being able to get so close to the end goal without having to lift a finger. Perhaps it was only at the last moment when Tara had a sixth sense that something was amiss, and screamed. Vince East, however compelling his personal story was, ticked every single box of the profile she had outlined for Aurora's abductor.

Chapter 25

'Director Le Fay's assistant was trying to get hold of you. She said it was important,' Nurse Lightfoot said. 'I couldn't find you.'

'Yeah, must have been really hard to find me inside a locked ward with a limited number of rooms,' Connie muttered, regretting the sentence before she was even halfway through it. She wasn't going to make any progress by alienating people. Lightfoot seemed not to have heard.

'You can call her on the internal phone. Extension 1405.'

Connie picked up the phone and waited for Nurse Lightfoot to give her some privacy in the security office. The nurse didn't move.

'Would you mind giving me the room? I'll be quick, only it's likely to be contact from the military base and the conversation will be confidential.'

Lightfoot didn't bother to reply, settling for a deep sigh, grabbing her can of soda and shifting out of her seat, leaving the door to slam shut behind her.

Connie called Le Fay's assistant.

'Yes, Dr Connie, could you come down, please? There was a young man trying to get hold of you,' she said.

'Trying to get hold of me how? Aren't the external phones out?' Connie said.

'We have one satellite phone. These storms happen all the time out here. We have to make sure we have at least one way to keep in contact with the world. Could you hurry? I'm supposed to go off shift soon.'

'I'll run straight down,' Connie said.

A few minutes later, out of breath, Connie was at the assistant's desk.

'Come through to the director's office again,' she said. 'It was lucky I was in there when the satellite phone rang or I might have missed it. He was quite insistent that he speak with you.'

Connie followed her to where the black phone sat in its charging block, the thick aerial pointed skyward.

'Here's the number. I'll be off. Replace it when you're finished, make sure it's charging again please, and pull the door shut behind you. It'll lock itself. They're showing a movie in the dining hall this afternoon and I don't want to miss it.'

'Which movie?' Connie asked.

'*The Hateful Eight*. I do love a bit of Tarantino now and then.' She disappeared, looking excited.

Connie picked up the phone and dialled Director Le Fay's number first, but wherever he was, his phone wasn't reachable. She gritted her teeth. If Le Fay wasn't available, she'd just have to keep going. Next, she dialled the number from the slip of paper. Silence followed, then a distant mechanical warbling and a screeching sound.

'I'm busy, leave a message.' Ben Paulson's recorded voice

came through loud and clear, followed by beeping as the voice-mail service got started.

'For fuck's sake!' she growled.

'Connie, is that you?' Ben's voice came through in real time.

'It is,' she said, laughing as she spoke for no other reason than it was so good to be talking to another human being who wasn't stuck inside The Institution with her. 'Sorry about the expletives. It's hard getting hold of anyone from in here. We're in the middle of a storm. How did you find the number for the satellite phone?'

'I once hacked into the Pentagon's private contact details database,' he said. 'This number is almost publicly listed compared to that.'

'Please don't tell me anything else,' Connie said. 'You seriously are trouble.'

'That's what I get paid for,' he said. 'You okay? Looks like you're going to be cut off a while. I couldn't even get an email to reach you.'

'External phone lines and internet are down. We have backup generators to run the essential systems if need be. There's a lot of rain though.'

'Rather you than me. I'm catching a flight to Belize tonight. Time for a bit of snorkelling, diving and caving. Thought I'd touch base before I leave.'

Connie felt her pulse quicken. 'You found something? Do we have a name?'

'Not exactly,' he said. 'I'm good, but even I can't hack a digital wallet that's being held offline at an undisclosed location.'

'Shit,' she said. 'Thanks for trying anyway. I knew it was a long shot. I hope it didn't take up much of your time.'

'That's not everything,' he said, his Californian accent adding a strange buoyancy to the conversation given the subject matter. 'I was thinking, who the hell does something like this for five million Crater Coins? I mean, kidnapping a baby and killing the mother. That's too much risk versus the reward. Crater are very average coins as far as cryptocurrency goes. You'd certainly be better off investing in Bitcoin or others in the marketplace that are on a better upward trajectory.'

'So how much are Crater Coins worth? Can they just be exchanged for cash?' Connie asked.

'You'd have to sell them through an exchange to get cash. And how much they're worth is the really interesting part of all this. They had to be purchased in batches because sometimes there are restrictions on how many coins you can buy at once. The first batch cost just cents per coin, but as each new batch was purchased they got more and more expensive. Crypto is like any other stock: prices go up and down.'

'Okay,' Connie said.

'But when I started looking into it, I saw the value of the shares was rising exponentially. So say five million Crater Coins were originally worth two million dollars when the baby was first kidnapped. Guess how much those five million coins are worth now.'

'I wouldn't have a clue. Have they doubled in value?'

'More than that,' he said. 'In the last three days Crater Coins have increased in value by a multiplier of fifteen.'

Connie let that sink in. 'So now it's worth thirty million dollars? That's a lot more money to buy accomplices. People will do all sorts of things for that much money.'

'I agree, but that's not where the real profit is. This'll blow your mind. The original miners of these coins and the people who bought them early on for almost nothing have just become multi-multi-millionaires. As soon as the investment money started pumping in, they advertised the fact, made sure everyone was aware of the sudden increase, so the price of the coins rose even more, and bingo. They're rich beyond their wildest dreams.'

'I don't get it. How did it make people so rich so fast?'

'All that money getting poured into their stock acts like a magnet for other investors. People jump on the bandwagon, seeing prices going up and an opportunity to turn a quick profit when it reaches an even higher price.'

'Then what?' she asked.

'Then the clever ones dump the stock and cash out. Stocks that were worth very little a week ago can end up suddenly worth hundreds of millions. People have become billionaires on the back of a rapid rise in crypto coin value. When all the money is suddenly lost from a coin because stocks are sold in bulk, the coin value comes crashing back down again. A few people get very rich; most lose. The tax man rarely gets to hear about any of it, particularly if there's an offshore bank account to transfer funds into.'

Connie sat down in Le Fay's chair to let it sink in.

'So the actual crypto coin transfer might just have been a stunt to get the value rising?' she asked.

'I'd put money on it,' Paulson said. 'Forgive the pun. And we're talking about so much money, the digital wallet the ransom coins were put into might never be claimed. Your kidnapper might have made enough money just from the rising stock value, provided they get out at the right time. Why bother touching the original investment that will ultimately lead the police directly to them?'

Connie whistled. 'If that's right, we may never be able to prove a link to the person who organised this atrocity.'

'I'm afraid it's the one case where following the money, however vast the sums involved, may not get you a conviction.'

301

'Worse than that, it won't get us the baby. I appreciate your help, Ben.'

'I'm sorry I couldn't be more helpful. But money like that, Connie, it buys a lot. We're talking about sums that could tempt almost anyone to break the law. Be careful. Someone has a lot riding on this. There's nothing they won't do to protect this sort of investment.'

Connie headed directly to her room to process the up-to-date information. First, she wrote out the names of the ward staff members on pieces of paper and set them on the floor in front of her. She didn't have the time or the resources to perform the frantic information grab she would normally undertake at this stage of a profiling exercise, but she could still do a rapid immersion and see what floated to the top. She formed a rough triangle with the names.

Dr Ong
Dr Roth – Dr Sidorov – Senior Nurse Casey
Nurse Madani – Nurse Lightfoot – Tom Lord – Jake Aldrich

Those closer to the bottom were on the lowest wages, with more reason to respond to financial stimulus. Nearer the top, the professionals were on better pay, and had either trained longer or had more to lose in terms of professional status.

Then again, what did any of that really matter? If Ben Paulson was right about the value of the Crater Coins rising to a total value of hundreds of millions, then none of the people involved would ever have to work again.

A breeze rippled across her floor, sending the pyramid of papers tumbling and scattering. Connie huffed, irritated. The ancient building offered security for many reasons, but it wasn't the most comfortable or practical of places to live. The window was shut though, and firmly locked. Her door had a draught excluder strip attached to the bottom. She stood, angry that her time was being wasted, gathering the papers and laying them out again but they lifted and tumbled as she set them down.

The papers were moving towards the door and the window. She cast her eyes around. Her en suite featured internal walls only.

Moving slowly, staring in disbelief at her wardrobe, mentally chastising herself for paranoia and time wasting, Connie opened the wardrobe door inch by inch.

The temperature in the room dropped immediately and the draught picked up to a low breeze. She reached inside, feeling like an idiot, and knocked a shirt from a hanger to the dusty wooden base. That was how she'd found her clothes before. Knocked off. As if someone had been in her wardrobe.

'Not in,' she said, her pulse starting to race. 'Through.'

Connie put one careful foot inside, then followed up with the second. She put both hands against the back of the wardrobe and pushed.

Nothing happened. There was no movement at all. The wood wasn't excessively cold, there was no give in it. It was just her standing in an old, past-its-prime wardrobe.

'No Narnia here,' she said, stepping back out, scratching her head and feeling like an idiot.

The base of the wardrobe creaked as she took her weight off it. Connie looked down at it, then knelt on the floor just outside the wardrobe door. Running her hands around the base, her finger identified a wooden lip. Forcing her fingertips under the edge of it, she pulled it up a few inches then it flew open on silent hinges, clearly recently oiled.

'You motherfuckers,' Connie said.

Understanding and fury merged into a blinding moment of clarity. She wasn't losing her mind. Her cell phone had been taken from her room then returned to make her feel foolish. And when she'd woken in the night with the overwhelming sense that something was terribly wrong, that was just her subconscious doing its proper job.

She thrust her feet into trainers, hesitating for only a second before adding a hunting knife that she strapped around her chest and putting her hoodie on over the top. Sitting on the edge of the opening in the base of the wardrobe, icy wind blasting around her legs, she prepared to explore the darkness below.

Her feet found steps as she edged downwards, and she could hear the storm, as furious as she felt, outside the building. As the light from her room grew powerless to battle the gloom, she took her cell phone from her pocket and switched on the torch.

The steps landed in a dark corridor with rough wooden walls, stone pillars here and there, and a concrete floor. There were no lights, no electrics, and at each end the corridor simply turned a corner. Along the length of it, two other sets of steps reached upwards. The steps weren't new additions but part of the fabric of the oldest part of the building, there from a time when access up out of the basement had been for an entirely different purpose. As a fortress, the current basement might well have been the original ground floor, those steps nothing more than a way up to a higher level for soldiers or guards. But someone had ensured that access was possible through the wardrobe, likely not originally for her. She shuddered thinking of the other purposes those steps had been put to in the past. The question was, who had allocated that room to her?

Connie shivered, looked left and right, and knew that simply wandering off into the darkness was the worst possible choice.

If nothing else, she needed to be able to find her way back. Whoever had entered her room knew who she was and why she was there, and the secret to finding them lay in the depths of the building, where the dumbwaiter landed, and where there was access to the road through the service vehicle bays.

Connie needed to leave a trail behind her. Scrambling back up the steps, scraping her shins, threading splinters through her hands, she got back up into her room. The bathroom was her best bet. She loaded her pockets with toothpaste, her toothbrush, deodorant, soap, shampoo, mascara, lip salve and her hairbrush. As she dashed back through her bedroom, the storm stepped it up a notch and did its best to break her window.

Somewhere above her a sound that might have been a bomb blast echoed, sending a ripple of smaller bangs and crashes in its wake. She ducked instinctively, closing her eyes for a moment, her stomach dropping. Five seconds later, Connie flew to the hole in the base of her wardrobe and took the steps in two jumps, falling at the bottom before righting herself and reaching for her cell phone torch app once more. She left her hairbrush on the bottom step to be sure she could make it back into the correct room, then turned left.

The wooden walls were protesting the treatment from the elements, and beneath her feet, her trainers were slapping onto the concrete noisily. Connie put one hand to the floor and felt a slick layer of freezing water leaving the floor slippery. The rain was getting in at the edges of the towers, and finding its way to the basement level. She hurried to the end of the corridor, dropped her toothpaste just inside the corridor that led back to her room, and took another left.

That corridor extended again in both directions, the end of each too distant for her torchlight to illuminate. The grid formation had to be vast. She had of course walked a little of it with Boy previously, but being there alone took her understanding of his disquiet at being beneath the historic stone stacks to another level. Shivering already, her clothes powerless against the cold and damp, Connie stood still to orientate herself with the layout of the building above her head.

Had she been one floor up, she'd have left the corridor of bedrooms and turned onto the larger corridor that led to the staff recreation room and then on to the dining room. Behind her, had she turned right, she'd have been walking towards the staff accommodation area that included Dr Sidorov's quarters.

The floor was getting wetter as she walked, and it occurred to her that she had to be heading towards the front of the building and the staff car park. Given that The Institution was set at the base of the mountain, it was reasonable to assume the foundation had been set into a gradient. The car park would be at ground level and the basement she was in now had to be roughly level to it, allowing for the sloping ground level.

Somewhere in the distant maze of corridors a cat was mewling, no doubt tempted in to shelter from the rain, now stuck alone, lost in the dark. Poor thing. Connie knew how it felt, and tried to tune it out so as not to be distracted by its suffering. There was a crossroads in front of her. Turning left was pointless – she'd have been nearly back where she began. Straight on and she'd be heading for the front edge of the basement and most likely a dead end.

There was another set of steps nearby but no way of knowing which room they led up to, or if they were completely blocked off. The cat again, crying louder now, but definitely somewhere behind her.

She took her deodorant from a pocket and put it on the

floor before she made a decision about the corridor. The only logical thing to do was turn right at this stage and yet—

A desperate wailing sounded from above. Her hand flew to her chest and she held her breath. The noise penetrated the basement corridors and shrieked around the corners, bouncing up off the concrete and leaving Connie breathless. The siren was a two-tone warble. Definitely not the sound she'd heard on Heaven Ward when the alarm had been set off. This was something else.

'Fuck.' Connie looked back at the corridor behind her. 'Fire alarm.'

In spite of the water beneath her feet and the freezing air, it was entirely possible that a lightning strike had set off a fire in a higher part of the building. She breathed in through her nose, her senses giving her nothing but the smell of damp foundations and rotting wood.

She yearned to go on. The answer was down there somewhere – she was convinced of it. But a fire meant a risk to the structure. To be trapped there, no one knowing where she was if a part of the tower went down, was unthinkable. It would be stupid not to go back. And without her there, without Director Le Fay on site, Baarda was at risk too. She owed it to him to go back.

Screeching in frustration, Connie forced herself to turn back the way she'd come, moving faster now, leaving her toiletries where she'd placed them to retrace her steps once she knew it was safe to do so. She ran back to the last junction and took a right, happier running on a route she'd already trodden, knowing there were no hidden pitfalls or barriers. The mewling of the cat was trailing off now. It sounded exhausted. A short distance in front of her were the steps to her bedroom, and the fire alarm was louder in that corridor. Here and there she caught tinny voices and trampling feet above.

Not just a false alarm, then. Something was happening overhead, and she needed to get out of there fast. Her corridor was fully wet underfoot now as she ran to her steps, the water splashing up to dampen the tops of her trainers and the hem of her jeans.

Connie climbed up into her room, blinking as she made it into the full light. Someone was hammering on her door.

'Give me a minute!' she yelled, pulling her legs up and out, then crawling from her wardrobe and slamming the door shut behind her.

She got to her feet then lurched for the door, finding Dr Sidorov there with a security guard.

'Connie? You look terrible. What have you been doing?' Sidorov blurted.

She replied with the first thought that came to mind. 'I heard a cat crying in the basement below my room. I was trying to rescue it,' she babbled.

'We've got to get you out of here,' the security officer said. 'This tower's been struck by lightning. And don't worry about the cat. I guarantee you were imagining it. There's so much poison down there for the rats, no cat could eat anything and survive.'

The realisation hit her like a wrecking ball. How had she ever thought it was a cat? Perhaps because the cry was so reedy and pathetic, such a thin, weak sound.

Of course it wasn't a cat. How could she have been so stupid and so blind?

'It's not a cat. It's the baby. The baby's under the building!' she shouted. 'I've got to go back down.'

'What baby? Do you know what she's talking about?' the security guard aimed at Sidorov.

'No idea – there are no babies on site. She's clearly not rational,' he replied.

She smashed a fist into the doorframe, as her world began to spiral out of control. Why could no one understand her? 'Just listen to me!' she yelled.

'Connie,' Sidorov said. 'You've got to come with us. We're getting everyone out of the block.'

'You don't understand. There are passageways. I found them because someone came into my room that way and now there's a baby down there.'

'Miss,' the security guard shouted, 'I have a lot of people to see to. Get your things together now. Essentials only.'

'You go,' Connie shouted. 'I'll be fine. I've got to go back down.'

She took a step backwards and tried to shut the door but the security guard had his foot in before she could latch it.

'Sorry, this is policy,' he said, sounding anything but. 'You have to come with us.'

'One of the upper floors is on fire. We're trying to keep you alive,' Sidorov insisted.

'Aurora will die!' Connie shouted. 'I have to find her.'

She left them at the door and flew back across to the wardrobe, wrenching open the doors. The security guard was right behind her, and Sidorov was at his back.

'Connie, no!' Sidorov shouted. 'We have to get out.'

'Leave me alone,' she yelled back at them. 'Why are you trying to stop me? Sidorov, are you part of this?'

'I don't have time for this,' the security guard growled as she scrabbled to open the door in the base again, but now the damp had got into the wood and her fingernails were snapping beneath the rim. He slipped an arm around her waist and hoisted her up into the air.

'No!' Connie screeched. 'I know where she is. I have to get to the baby. Put me down!'

'I feel something beneath her clothes,' the security guard said. 'What is that?'

'It's none of your business. I can walk. Just let me go,' Connie demanded.

'Stay still,' the security guard said. 'Are you going to tell me what that is?'

'It's just a small knife,' she panted. 'No big deal. I needed it for . . .' She tried desperately to think of a good explanation but her brain was working overtime and nothing coherent would come.

'You'd better hand it over,' Sidorov said.

Fuck! she was screaming inside. *Not now, not now, not now!* But she just slipped her hand inside her top and withdrew the knife she'd concealed in there before her trip into the basement.

'Personal weapons aren't allowed inside The Institution,' the security officer said. 'I'm going to have to take you to Dr Ong. He's in charge while Director Le Fay is absent.'

'Huge mistake. Don't do this, please! You have no idea what's at stake.'

The men continued their conversation over her begging.

'He's in his office on Heaven Ward, overseeing the transfer of prisoners out of Tower 3 to alternative cells,' Sidorov said. 'Heaven Ward's operating as normal for now. The best thing would be to take Dr Connie there.'

Chapter 26

Dr Ong wasn't at his desk when she was deposited in his office, so Connie sat counting the wasted seconds, hands curled into fists, biting her bottom lip as she waited.

The building had been chaos as she was escorted through. They were evacuating the whole tower, including all the staff accommodation, kitchens and dining hall. The lower-risk male patients from Tower 3 were being transferred to Tower 1, which meant doubling up the female and elderly in their cells to create space. The additional pressure on staff that came with the increased risk of violent incidents and escapes was etching tension on every face.

Connie could just about smell smoke from the reception hall, but they were fighting on two fronts. Those trained to deal with a fire were upstairs trying to put out the flames and preserve the structure of the tower, while other staff members were bringing in sandbags to create a barrier in front of the main entrance. The dam overflow system wasn't coping with the amount of rain the storm was bringing, and the water was

311

breaching the wall between the lake and the staff car park. It wasn't a flood at that point, but it was heading that way, and the high winds were making access outside of the building perilous.

The prematurely dark sky told the whole story. All they could do was wait it out. The building echoed with the fight between thunder and lightning. Every patient had been confined to their room. Lockdown had begun. The auxiliary staff were trying to make themselves comfortable anywhere there was space, while medical staff were headed to their wards to bunk down in their various staff common rooms.

Connie could hear voices in the corridor beyond Ong's room. In Director Le Fay's absence, convinced that baby Aurora was being held in one of the basement rooms with the structure above weakened by fire, the moment had come to trust someone and enlist help. If she could get Baarda released, the two of them should be able to cover enough ground to get the baby out. It wasn't the way she'd planned it, but if she could just get Dr Ong onside, they had a window of opportunity.

The door opened and Drs Roth and Sidorov entered. Behind them was the security guard who'd escorted her up to Heaven Ward, and Boy.

'What's going on?' Connie asked, standing abruptly.

Dr Ong entered last, looking exhausted and concerned.

'Dr Connie,' he said. 'Apologies for the formality of this meeting. Please sit. I can ask Tom Lord to bring you tea or coffee if you'd like?'

Connie recalled Baarda's suspicion that Tom had put something in his drink on the first day, and shook her head.

'Actually you and I need to talk alone, Dr Ong. I appreciate this is a difficult time for you but it's an urgent matter—'

'So I've been told. Dr Connie, concerns have been raised

about your behaviour, and I've asked to hear from the people present to assess what should be done.'

'Is Patient B all right? Did something happen on the ward?' she asked, her voice squeaky with panic.

Dr Ong frowned and sat down in his chair very gently, as if moving too fast might break something.

'I'm not concerned about Patient B right now. My focus is you. The security guard explained to me that he had to escort you here against your will, and furthermore that you had a bladed weapon concealed beneath your clothes, strapped to your chest. Is that correct? Take your time. I think we're all deeply concerned about the storm and the fire, so we should allow for some stress and poor judgement,' Ong said.

'You don't understand the situation. If I could just explain,' Connie said.

'It's not just that,' Dr Roth interrupted tersely. 'Look at your face, your arms. You came in here this morning covered in scratches. Staff members on the ward were concerned and alerted me. I had to ask downstairs if anyone knew what had happened. I tracked down Boy because you were seen behaving strangely to him during the storm announcement last night.'

'I apologised for that,' Connie said. 'It was a misunderstanding.' She was seeing the faces around her more clearly now. Their concerned expressions. The sense that she had become a problem that needed solving.

Not now, Connie thought. *I can't deal with this.*

'She did apologise,' Boy pleaded. 'Dr Connie was just busy. I told you that.'

'Please, everyone, we have to do this in an orderly fashion and I won't have anyone making Dr Connie feel uncomfortable. She's a professional. Let's maintain some decorum.'

'That's great,' Connie said curtly. 'Please just listen. I know

I'm in kind of a state physically, but I can explain all of it. What matters right now is that there's a life at risk. Dr Ong, I'm going to have to insist that we adjourn the hearing into whatever complaint has been made against me. I'll make the necessary apologies at a later date. Right now, I need to use Director Le Fay's satellite phone so that we can—'

He gave a conciliatory smile, arms crossed loosely and resting on his desk. 'Sorry, Connie, can we take it one step at a time? Did you refuse to leave your room even though the fire alarm was going off and both Dr Sidorov and the security officer were asking you to exit?' Ong asked.

She clenched her jaws. 'With good reasons that I can't discuss in front of all these people.'

'And the weapon?' Ong continued.

'Yes, but again, there's an explanation for that,' she said.

Stay calm, she told herself. *Sound reasonable. Don't irritate any of them. Just fix this.*

'All right.' Ong made a note and turned to the security officer. 'I think you can go now. I'm sure you're needed elsewhere.'

The guard disappeared out of the room.

'Now, as far as the scratches on your face are concerned, Dr Roth asked me to hear what this boy had to say about that.'

Roth pushed Boy forward. He stepped up to Ong's desk and hung his head sadly.

'I was worried about Dr Connie. She's always really nice to me so I thought I should see if she was okay and then I followed her and she went out into the car park but it was dark so I didn't want—'

'One moment please, your name again?'

'Boy,' he said. 'It's just Boy.'

'Oh.' Ong peered over his glasses. 'Well, that seems rather

to have missed the point of a name, but at least you are unique. Slowly now, because this is important. You seem to like Dr Connie very much. Is that right?'

'Yes,' Boy said. 'She's kind, and she's funny and she even smells nice. Not everyone here smells nice.'

'Indeed, they do not. Now, you saw Dr Connie go out into the car park. What happened then?'

'I followed but it was dark and I'd been told not to go near the lake wall after dark. Dr Connie just kept going and I was scared to follow so I went back inside.'

'Do you know what Dr Connie was doing out there after dark?' Ong asked.

'Sorry, but I really don't appreciate being talked about as if I weren't here,' Connie interjected loudly.

'Bear with us,' Ong directed at her. 'Boy, do you know how Dr Connie got all those scratches on her face.'

'Oh, come on,' Connie muttered, tensing every muscle in her body and rolling her eyes to the ceiling.

'Let him answer,' Ong insisted. 'Go ahead, Boy.'

'I don't want to answer,' Boy muttered. His cheeks were dark and he was staring at the floor as if he wished he could sink into it.

'No one here is in trouble,' Ong said. 'Least of all Dr Connie. We just want to look after her.'

Connie stood, grinding her teeth. 'You want to do what now?'

'Sit down,' Sidorov told her. 'You're just going to make it worse.'

'Really? Advice from you?' she snapped. 'Dr Ong, I appreciate that Dr Roth has expressed concerns to you, but they're not warranted, and if you'd just hear me out I would be able to explain everything that's happened since I've been here.'

'I fully intend to hear you out. Now, Boy, if you want to help Dr Connie, you must answer my questions. This facility is very good at taking care of people. Can you help me to do that?'

Boy nodded slowly. 'She thought someone was following her. She was happy for a minute when she thought it was me, but when I told her I'd gone back inside, she got worried again. She said she'd jumped off a wall into a bush because a man was chasing her, and that she'd got all scratched up. I didn't think it was right, her running along the top of the wall in the dark like that. It's dangerous.'

'You're right, it is dangerous,' Ong said. 'I don't want you ever trying that, you hear me?'

Boy shuffled sideways to stand nearer to Connie. 'Dr Connie's my friend. Nothing will happen to her, will it?'

Connie took his hand in hers. 'Of course not,' she said. 'I'll be fine – you don't have to worry about me.'

'Dr Connie will be all right now,' Ong said. 'You can go back downstairs to reception and they'll tell you where to go to stay safe.'

Boy hesitated then slung his arms around Connie's neck before dashing out of the door. Tom Lord slipped in as Boy exited and the orderly stood silently at the back of the room.

Connie fixed her attention on Dr Ong and made a concerted effort to sound as calm and rational as possible. 'I can see how my behaviour might seem unsettled. I accept that the walk along the lake was a poor choice. The scratches to my face and hands must look concerning. But I can assure you, I'm all right, I'm in control, I'm not delusional or paranoid.'

'I was told you were talking about a baby,' Dr Ong said. 'I'm sorry to have to ask this, but have you lost a child recently? Miscarried? It's not uncommon for women to think they're past such traumas only to be revisited by them when least expected. Particularly during stressful times, such as spending a period in a high-security facility. You've interviewed each of our guests this week, and although fascinating, their tales can also be disconcerting and emotionally affecting.'

Connie did her best to maintain her patience, but it was like trying to hold water in her hands. 'No, I haven't ever lost a child. And I've spent plenty of time around serial killers.'

'In the military?' Roth interjected. 'That seems unlikely.'

'When I was training in forensic psychology,' Connie said. 'I spent some time in the field with the FBI.'

'Really? So not just top-secret military now but also FBI? This just gets wilder and wilder,' Roth said.

'Perhaps I should undertake a physical check,' Sidorov said. 'To make sure Dr Connie is well. Given the injuries she's sustained and the state she's in—'

'Absolutely not,' Connie said, glaring at him. Director Le Fay had been trying to tell her something about Sidorov and she wasn't prepared to be left alone with him in the medical room until she knew more.

'You're refusing a medical assessment?' Dr Ong asked, eyebrows raised. 'I think that's unwise. I need to be sure that you won't attempt to go back to the areas where there's risk from both fire and flooding. Whatever it is you believe you need to do there, your safety has to come first. I should tell you that it has come to my attention that you've been talking about your own experiences as a patient at a mental health hospital. It does concern me that I wasn't made aware of your past. It's clearly having an impact on your state of mind, and that puts both my staff and our guests at risk.'

Connie sighed. 'Oh, would you stop calling them your fucking guests. These men can't check out or move to a different establishment. They're convicted killers with psychiatric disorders. You might call them patients at best, but they're prisoners and they know it.'

Dr Ong blinked twice and sat back in his chair. 'I see. Thank you for the benefit of your opinion. You do seem agitated. I have to ask you to confirm whether or not you've spent time committed to a psychiatric hospital?'

'It was a mistake,' Connie said, spitting the words out slowly, emphasising the consonants. 'An unprofessional and overly zealous psychiatrist failed to properly diagnose a medical issue when I couldn't communicate.'

'What was the diagnosis, exactly?' Roth asked.

'It doesn't matter, because none of it was real,' Connie said.

'That must have made you distrust psychiatrists a great deal,' Ong noted.

'Not really. It was a psychiatrist who ended up reviewing my case and putting the matter straight. I had neurosurgery, which solved the problem.'

'So you accept you had a problem?' Roth said.

'This isn't about me.' She pointed her finger and thumped it into her chest, accentuating her words, and immediately regretting it. It was a mistake to let them see how angry she was. 'The facts are being manipulated. You're allowing yourself to be manipulated,' she told Ong.

'Thank you. I'd prefer not to be told that I can't make my own professional assessment,' Ong said, his nose pinched, his voice immediately chilly. 'Dr Roth, do you have a temporary recommendation?'

'A period of restraint.' Roth's cheeks were flushing, her pupils dilating. Connie noted a hint of relish in her voice and felt pure loathing for her. 'Dr Connie can't be confined to her rooms at present because of the fire, and I'm not sure she'd be safe from self-harm. I would say sedation initially, then I'll take a look at medicating for the paranoia.'

'Oh no, you don't get to do that to me. This is insane,' Connie yelled.

'That's not a word we use in here, and I'm surprised to hear a fellow professional saying it,' Roth cooed.

'Let's not make this any harder than it needs to be. I'm only prepared to authorise such a course overnight. I don't want this to take a turn for the worse and it's clear to me that Dr Connie has an impressive professional record.'

'You can't do this. There are laws and procedures,' Connie said.

'We're in an emergency situation here, and you're making very little sense,' Ong said. 'By all means, if there's a rational explanation for your behaviour and your state then tell me. I have no desire to follow Dr Roth's plan, but I don't currently see an alternative.'

'I've already told you, I can only speak to you alone.'

'Military secrets again?' Ong asked.

'No,' she said. 'Not military. I'm here as part of a police operation.' There was no harm saying it out loud at that point. Whoever was involved clearly already knew who she was. Perhaps the only safe course of action was to tell the truth in front of everyone, and protect herself. 'You have to release Patient B as well. He's part of this with me.'

Dr Roth laughed.

'I'll have none of that,' Dr Ong said, giving Roth a sharp glance. 'Dr Connie is one of us. Please explain, Patient B is what, a police officer like yourself?'

'No, neither of us is a police officer, but we are here at the request of an investigating police force.'

'Investigating what?' Ong asked.

Connie took a deep breath. 'Tara Cameron's murder and the foetal abduction of her baby.'

Ong looked at Roth then across to Sidorov. He folded his arms and pursed his lips before speaking very slowly. 'I see. You understand that Director Le Fay himself assured me of Tara's transfer to a specialist maternity unit. When I enquired after her, I was told she's doing well. I think I'd know if there had been a death on my ward.'

Sidorov excused himself and left the room.

Where the hell is he off to? Connie wondered. *Is he making a call to the kidnappers? Getting ready to run? Destroying evidence?*

'Everyone in here, everyone on this ward, is a suspect. This is why you need to speak with the director as soon as possible. He can validate what I've told you, then Patient B – whose name is Baarda – and I can find baby Aurora.'

'But you're not a police officer. You're not from the military. You have no legal authority. And you're now saying you shouldn't really be on my ward at all.'

'I'm a profiler,' Connie said. 'That's why I was sent. Baarda is a former police officer who specialised in kidnapping cases.'

'But I've seen Patient's B's medical and military records. You told me about him yourself,' Ong said.

Connie wanted to scream and kick. The only thing that stopped her was the certain knowledge that it would make her situation – and therefore Aurora's – even worse.

'I know this has come as a shock to you, but if we don't find that baby soon she'll die. We're running out of time. I believe she's down in the basement corridors under the staff accommodation. Someone broke into my room at night and stole my cell phone to make me doubt myself, but then I found a door in the base of my wardrobe.'

'Someone broke into your room now to make you feel paranoid? You know that is actual paranoia, right? We need to get on with this,' Roth said. 'I've heard enough. I'm happy to sign this off.'

'Reluctantly, I've reached the same conclusion,' Ong said. 'But I want six-hourly reviews for the next twenty-four hours. Dr Connie is not to be held for a second longer than is strictly necessary. I intend to speak with the director about it as soon as the crisis here is contained.' Tom Lord was suddenly at her back, Roth to one side. 'I'm taking nothing for granted, I promise you. The second I can refer this matter externally, I will make sure your case is looked at again. If there's no improvement, I will have you transferred as soon as it's practically possible to a lower-grade facility but for now I can promise you that The Institution will prioritise the very best care we can give you.'

'You're fucking kidding,' Connie barked. 'Do this and you'll have a child's blood on your hands.'

'It would be better if you walked out quietly,' Lord told her, uncharacteristically hesitant. 'I don't want to restrain you.'

'Lay one single finger on me and I swear it'll be the last digit you ever put anywhere near a woman.'

Lord snorted and reached out to take her arm. Connie blocked his reach with a downward forearm swipe and stepped to the side.

'Look me up on the internet. My name is Dr Connie Woolwine. I worked for the FBI for years. I've consulted on cases for police forces around the world. Brodie Baarda was a member of the Metropolitan Police Force. Call them and ask them.'

Lord looped an arm around her neck from behind. Connie elbowed him in the ribs, and he let out a satisfying whomp of air but kept her in his grip.

'Pick her up if you have to,' Roth said.

Ong remained at his desk as they manoeuvred her out of his office and into the corridor, her feet dragging along the tiles, her hands flying out to grab anything she could, but in vain. Lord was far too big and well trained for her to win the fight.

Panic as dense as quicksand was threatening to devour her. *Get a grip*, she told herself. *Figure a way out of it. Stop reacting and start working the problem.*

'Could you find Director Le Fay's assistant?' Connie heard Ong say. 'Tell her it's extremely urgent. I'd like to use the satellite phone.'

Roth gave Sidorov a thumbs up as they walked past the security room. He got up from the chair and watched them go through the doorway onto the ward.

'If you can't get hold of Le Fay or local police, call Ben Paulson. It'll be the last call made from the satellite phone!' Connie shouted back in Ong's direction.

The ward door swung shut behind her and Tom Lord pushed Connie into the quiet room.

Chapter 27

'If you don't calm down, I'm going to have Tom put you in a restraint jacket,' Roth said. 'Is that what you want?'

'Fuck you,' Connie said. 'This is bullshit and you know it. I can see the smile on your face.'

'Tom, fetch a jacket please,' Roth said.

'Don't,' Connie told him firmly. 'You know it's not necessary.'

He looked from Connie to Roth and back again, then left the two of them alone.

'Are you going to swallow the sedatives willingly or do I need to inject you?' Roth asked.

'Was it you?' Connie asked her. 'Did you conspire to kill Tara Cameron?'

'You're a profiler, apparently, so surely you can tell me if I have the right personality to be involved in a crime like that.' Roth grinned.

There was a lot at stake, not least her own personal safety, but ultimately Aurora's life. She needed to prove to Roth beyond all doubt that she was who she said she was. Flattery wouldn't

323

work. Roth was too long in the tooth for that. All Connie had left in her arsenal was naked truth. She kept her voice matter-of-fact and her tone professional, as if delivering a report.

'You're an alpha personality type and you dislike being challenged. You're constantly shifting position, fiddling with a pen or a piece of paper. Your body seems to be moving almost all the time. You find it hard to settle. The lack of ease makes you snappy and irritable. I'd say you have chronic insomnia. I think you suffer from mood swings. Your confidence and the way you speak to fellow staff members suggests you came from a middle-class background, but not upper class. You speak down to everyone almost all the time, so I'd say you have a level of resentment that you haven't reached the heights you wanted to at this stage of your career. You've been in the middle of everything all your life, never quite at the top. Did you get fed up with always being second best?'

Tom Lord walked back into the room with a restraint jacket over one arm. He hung near the door watching the exchange.

Roth's face flushed and her bottom lip stuck out a little. Connie could see petulance written all over her.

'A few lucky guesses. But none of that gets you anywhere near me being involved in some fictional conspiracy. You're not well, Connie. We need to make sure you don't self-harm,' Roth said.

'I haven't finished. You took this job because you thought it would look good on your résumé but you found that actually this is a final stop for almost everyone who comes through the front door. The work is lacking in substance and challenge. You're bored. You're not interested in psychology, your tone of voice and reputation for pettiness suggests you don't like the patients, and you certainly don't like being told what to do by Dr Ong. You won't look at him while he speaks. You glance slightly off to the side every time. It's a quite deliberate act of defiance that involves an amount of smugness and a dislike of authority.'

Tom smirked.

'Are you done now?' Roth asked.

'Not quite.' Connie's tactics had changed. Now she was playing to an audience, hoping her take-down of Roth would appeal to Tom. 'You hate it here,' she continued. 'Which makes me wonder why you can't leave. Is Dr Ong aware of how little genuine love you have for your job? Because if he is, you're not going to get the sort of reference you need to transfer anywhere prestigious, which is what you think you're owed. Or is it your private life? Maybe you have nothing to move to or for, and so you're still here, counting the days until a miracle happens and everything changes.'

'I'm assuming you'll need forced sedation,' Roth said loudly. 'I'm going to organise that now.'

'You hated me from the second I walked in,' Connie carried on talking as if Roth hadn't issued the sedation threat, hoping against hope that she was winning Tom Lord over. 'I think that was because you knew I'd be leaving, unlike you. You feel like this place, your colleagues, even your boss, are beneath you. Even the way you breathe, that huff every time you have to answer a question, is disdainful. Did someone offer you a way out? Enough money that you'd never have to work again?'

'You're right, actually,' Roth said, her voice suddenly lighter, mocking. 'I don't like working here. If you'd actually read the files on the things these sick fucks have done, you wouldn't like it either. But that doesn't bother you, given that you're going back off to your life as what, an FBI profiler or an undercover pretend cop or some sort of military secret weapon? Which is it now?'

Connie folded her arms and said nothing.

'I can handle this from here,' Tom told Roth. 'You don't need to stay.'

Connie didn't dare hope for too much, but just the fact of Tom dismissing Roth was progress.

'Fine,' Roth said. 'But I want her properly sedated. And the jacket goes on. Any issues, call me. You have a lovely night,' she directed at Connie.

Roth left. Connie stared at Tom and he stared back.

'You dislike her, too,' Connie said.

'I do,' he said. 'But if I don't do what she told me, I'll get fired.'

Connie tried to ignore the nausea that was swamping her, but it won out. Sweat was not just trickling but running down her back. Her bravado with Roth had taken its toll. Panic was setting in once more. 'Please, Tom, you can't sedate me. You know I won't be safe,' she said.

'Dr Roth doesn't like it when people disobey her. She can be . . . cruel.'

'Has she been cruel to you?'

He considered her question for a moment. 'She has a tendency to mock. I don't appreciate it. But Dr Ong's orders were to follow Roth's treatment plan, so I don't have a choice.'

Connie kept her shoulders down and her face neutral. Showing fear was the worst thing she could do.

'I'm going to be in here alone. I can't communicate with anyone. I won't tell anyone you were kind to me. But I need you not to sedate me. I have to be able to think clearly.'

He frowned, shrugged. 'You lied to all of us.'

'With good reason,' Connie said.

'You were asking all those questions. Talking behind our backs.'

'Tom, were you involved in Tara Cameron's death?'

'I'm not even sure she is dead,' he said. 'I don't know who you are. How am I supposed to trust anything you say?'

'You don't have to trust me. I'm stuck in here. I can't fight you, and I won't try. But you can answer the question anyway. It can't hurt.'

He took a look behind him to make sure no one was looking through the viewing slot.

'I wouldn't hurt Nurse Tara. I liked her. She never spoke to me like I was just muscles without a brain. That's what the rest of them think of me.'

His voice was steady. If he was acting, Connie thought, it was an impressive performance.

'If you liked Tara, then help me. You need to let me out. I have to speak with Patient B and get word to the director. Every minute I'm stuck in here, things get more precarious.'

He shook his head sadly. 'I can't,' he said. 'I won't. I don't know you. I'll lose my job. Even if you are who you say you are, Roth will make sure I don't work here any more.'

'I'll deal with Dr Roth when this is all over, Tom. She shouldn't be working in psychiatry.'

He held out the restraint jacket. 'You have to put it on,' he said. 'She'll be coming to check, and she'll see if you don't have it on. It'll only make things worse for you.'

'I don't think I can,' Connie said.

Memories she'd crushed, buried so deep they hadn't even been accessible before that moment, threatened to swamp her.

'I won't do it tight. You just have to put it on,' he said.

'If I put it on—' she swallowed hard '—will you agree not to sedate me? I'll just stay quiet until Dr Ong reviews me in the morning. By then he'll have spoken with Director Le Fay and it will all have been sorted out.'

He thought about it for a moment. 'You have to pretend, if Roth comes in, I mean. You can't get all smart with her again and keep answering back. She'll know.'

Circumstances weren't on her side, and she knew it. There weren't going to be any lucky breaks or unforeseen rescues. She hated the thought of being so vulnerable, but keeping her wits about her and listening to what was going on was the better option.

Hold your goddamn nerve, she told herself. *It's only for a few hours. You've been through worse than being in a room with your arms tied around you.*

Connie took a steadying breath. 'All right. But be kind? Not tight.'

She let him put the jacket on her. It was a leap of faith. If he'd played her, she was about to face the consequences. He could sedate her now without her putting up any sort of fight. He didn't, and the gratitude she felt for that took her to the edge of tears. The jacket was tight enough to do the job given her slight frame, but not painfully tight.

'Tom,' she whispered. 'I know you've already gone out on a limb for me, but could I ask one more favour? Please? I swear it'll be the last thing.' Her voice was shaking as she pleaded with him, and Tom responded with a pitying look. He nodded. 'Speak to Patient B – Baarda – for me. Let him know what's happened. He'll be worried, and I need him trying to figure out what to do.'

'You know I can't do that,' Tom said. He buzzed the door lock.

'No, wait!' Connie begged as he began walking up the corridor. 'Please, it's so important, and it can't hurt. He's locked up; I'm locked up. I just need him to understand that I haven't abandoned him in here.'

Tom walked back and whispered to her through the slot. 'It's not that I don't want to help, but it's too late for that. Patient B was moved by Dr Sidorov. I have no idea where he is or what they're doing to him, and they wouldn't tell me even if I asked.'

Connie felt a tsunami of bile rush upwards from her stomach. She just made it to the far corner before she was sick.

Chapter 28

The quiet room . . . wasn't. Connie could sense the storm trying to get in from behind the padded walls and supporting bricks. She felt the vibration of every slamming door along the corridor, and heard the shouts and moans of the men on Heaven Ward who demanded answers to their questions: What was going on? Why could they smell smoke on the wind blasting through the edges of their windows? Why were they on lockdown? Benny Rubio was squealing and giggling. Harold Haskin was punctuating his shouts with repeated kicks of his door. Gregor Saint was yelling about the lake: Was anyone checking on it? Couldn't they see what was happening? Some of the staff car engines were flooded. But by far the worst of all the noise, the loudest, the most awful, was coming from inside Connie's head.

She could hear a baby crying in the distance. Connie wanted those cries to stop but she knew that the moment they did, it would be too late to save Aurora. She also knew that from the heights of Heaven Ward up in the tallest tower, those cries were all in her imagination, and still she couldn't separate them from reality.

Voices crept in, too. Voices she'd hoped never to hear again. The most dominant of them was the psychiatrist who'd instigated her own committal where she'd spent too much time in a room indistinguishable from the space she now inhabited.

'In you go. It's for your own good. If you won't speak to us, then we'll have to assume that silence is what you're after. I think you should understand that a silent place is a very lonely place. It won't take you long to start communicating after this.' She could see him, clear as the day she'd first met him, in his pinstripe suit, floral handkerchief poking out of his top pocket, looking around at his medical entourage for admiration as she'd hunkered down in the corner, quietly weeping.

It had never occurred to her that she might revisit that terrifying corner. That it could all go so horribly wrong. And was she crying again like she had all those years ago? She thought so, but she couldn't raise her hand to check, and stuck between the then and the now she wasn't sure what she was remembering and what she was actually experiencing.

Someone was sitting on Connie's chest. It was hard to breathe and she couldn't understand why she couldn't fight them off. The pain in her ear was excruciating and she was sure she could feel blood, hot on her face.

'No,' she muttered. 'That's not real. That was before.' But she was alone again. That was real. Her parents had left her there, under the authority of a man who couldn't be trusted. He was a bully, and he was mean, and Connie thought the fact of the matter was that he hated women, especially young women.

She wanted to go home, only it was hard to visualise where home was. Clarity came. She could hear the water. Home was

Martha's Vineyard. A warmth spread through her. There was sunshine and fresh lobster, cold beer and ice cream. The ice cream sparked a particular memory and she fought through the dense underbrush of adulthood to reach it. She'd been working at the ice-cream parlour on Circuit Avenue, Oak Bluffs, when he'd come in for a vanilla cone. She hadn't been able to take her eyes off him. They'd been planning to meet on the beach, but then a tree had hit her. No, not right. She'd hit the tree. She remembered crying as she waited for help to come because she couldn't move and she'd wanted to scream but something was wrong with her mouth and it wouldn't make any noise. She wondered if it was working again now. But of course it wouldn't be working. She was in a hospital. Hospitals were places that prevented her from talking.

Connie tried to stand but found that she had no arms to push herself up from the floor. She couldn't recall how she'd ended up down there, but her arms were gone. Had she lost them too, when she'd lost her voice? Who'd done that to her?

Wake up wake up wake up.

Her eyes flew open. Standing over her were Dr Roth, Nurse Casey and Nurse Lightfoot.

'Oh Christ, she's pissed herself,' Roth said. 'Get her up.'

'Don't touch me!' Connie screamed at them. 'Don't you fucking touch me. They told me I could go home. I'm not supposed to be here. I can talk now!'

'What the fuck's she on about?' Casey asked.

'No idea. She's got a long history of mental instability apparently, and given the noise she was making just now and losing control of her bladder, I'd say some intervention is necessary,' Roth said. 'Move her to the medical room.'

Casey dumped her into a waiting wheelchair as she struggled and kicked. A waist strap put paid to any thought of escape.

The short trip along the corridor gave Connie time to catch her breath. She wasn't eighteen any more, and this wasn't Boston. If she could just calm down, she'd be able to communicate properly.

'Did you want to get Ong to sign off on this beforehand?' Lightfoot asked.

'Not necessary,' Roth said quickly, skipping over the words. Her excitement was unmistakable. 'With Le Fay absent, Ong is the senior member of staff on site. He'll be downstairs controlling the emergency response. It's 2 a.m. and I'm not going to bother him with this. He said my treatment plan was to be actioned. This patient is distressed, confused, agitated and suffering delusions. We'll start on minimum voltage for two seconds.'

'Stop,' Connie panted. 'Please. I'm good. I was just having a nightmare.' The words felt slow and sticky coming out of her mouth.

'Get her on the table please,' Roth ordered. 'I'm going to sedate her.'

'You're supposed to call Sidorov for that,' Lightfoot said.

Roth frowned and gave a dismissive flick of her hand. 'I've done this procedure a thousand times. We just need her nice and relaxed, and not struggling.'

Casey lifted her out of the chair and Lightfoot undid the straps on the restraint jacket. Desperate now, Connie tried to bolt from the room but her legs were jelly. She landed face down, sprawled on the floor, panting and sobbing.

'The two of you can't control a single woman who's already been sedated once tonight?' Roth hissed.

'I haven't. I persuaded Tom not to sedate me. I'm suffering PTSD from previous mistreatment – that's why I had the nightmare. There's nothing wrong with me. I want Dr Ong to

333

do a review.' She tried crawling towards the door but Casey hoisted her up as if she were a child, placing her on the treatment table and holding her as Lightfoot did up the straps around her wrists and waist.

Connie was there again, imagining Tara on the same table, baby Aurora weighing down on her abdomen. The same strap being tightened on her body to prevent their escape. Her escape.

'Don't,' she pleaded.

'These are just to keep you still during treatment. They're for your safety. You've seen this before, right?' Nurse Lightfoot said.

'You can't do this. You need a detailed assessment with a full medical, an MRI scan, bloodwork,' Connie said.

'Your brain needs some help to break out of old patterns,' Roth said. 'Blood pressure and heart monitors on her please. Also, make sure there's a mouthguard ready.'

'You can't do this!' Connie shouted. 'I don't consent and you have no authority over me.'

'In fact, two fully qualified psychiatrists have assessed you and decided that you need emergency psychiatric intervention. You've accepted a history of mental health issues, so you know the score. If you're a danger to yourself or others then—'

'I'm not a danger to anyone, and I don't have a history of mental illness. I had a blood clot lodged in my brain,' Connie said, doing her very best to lower her voice and sound reasonable.

'Monitors are on,' Casey said. 'Lower clothing is coming off. We'll use incontinence pants for speed.'

'Leave my clothing alone,' Connie snarled, too late. There were hands in places she didn't want them, making her feel helpless and hopeless, violated and weak. Part of her wanted to give up. To just lie there and stop fighting. She was more exhausted than she ever had been in her life.

Thirty seconds later they were tying up ankle straps as Roth prepared a syringe of sedative.

'I'll sue and I'll prosecute. Every one of you will lose your practitioner licence. I doubt you'll ever work again,' Connie threatened impotently.

'Do you have any idea,' Roth said, leaning over and shining a light in Connie's eyes, checking her pupils, 'how many times I've heard that in my career? How many threats I've had to listen to? How many promises of retribution? It's a psych ward. The only surprise is when a patient doesn't threaten me.'

'Did you hear about the Shadow Man case in Scotland?' Connie asked, garnering what little strength she had left.

'I did,' Nurse Lightfoot said.

'I profiled him. He was suffering from Cotard's delusion. I was brought in by the Major Investigation Team, who I also assisted in the case of the Edinburgh Bomber. We saved lives.'

'Hero complex as well,' Roth directed at Samuel Casey, who rewarded her with a laugh.

'Or maybe,' Casey said, 'you just read about those cases.'

'Ask yourself what I'm doing here,' Connie said. 'How I got the necessary authority to come here. What is it I'm doing on a high-security ward with full access to all your patients granted by Director Le Fay himself? There are two possible answers to that question. Either I am with the military and Patient B is a priority prisoner, in which case the full force of the military is going to come down on all your heads if you do this to me. Or I really am working with the police and they established my position here for undercover purposes. There's no option that ends well for you. You could simply secure me in a room – Joe Yarowski's is available – where I cannot harm myself or anyone else, until Director Le Fay can be consulted. The wrong decision here will be life-changing in professional terms, I guarantee you. And that is not some empty threat.'

Nurse Lightfoot took a step back. 'Maybe Dr Connie's right. We should wait and speak with Dr Ong. She does sound okay now, definitely better than when we found her.'

Connie felt a rush of relief worthy of a death-sentence reprieve at Lightfoot's intervention, and found herself holding her breath as she waited for Roth's response.

'May I remind you,' Roth said, 'that this woman was ranting about searching for a missing baby in the basement, and claiming that Tara was murdered.'

Samuel Casey gave an uneasy shrug. 'If she's right about any of that, you don't think it'll make us look guilty – involved, even – if we do this now?'

'You sound as feeble-minded as she is,' Roth sneered. 'This conversation is happening way too late in the day. We agreed what we were going to do before we picked her up off the floor.'

'Who agreed?' Connie asked, leaping on the chance to sow more division in the ranks. 'Because it doesn't sound like there's agreement any more.'

'I don't want to be in here,' Lightfoot said. 'I'll send Tom. He'll be more help in case she needs lifting afterwards.'

'Don't you go anywhere,' Connie told Lightfoot. 'You know this isn't right. You can feel it.'

'Nurse Lightfoot and I will discuss it later,' Roth said tightly. 'Right now, I need you to relax. Once you're sedated you'll feel virtually nothing and remember very little. This isn't the Dark Ages. Electroconvulsive therapy has proven benefits and is used in psychiatric facilities across the world. If you really had all the experience you claim, you'd know that. Insert the mouthguard please, Nurse Casey.'

'No!' Connie shouted, doing what little she could to thrash against the restraints. Lightfoot exited quietly and closed the door behind her. 'Don't you fucking dare!'

He put it into her mouth anyway as Roth applied a neck brace and head band, tightening it to keep Connie completely still, then wheeled the machine closer and began flicking switches.

Connie thought the room had begun to move until she realised her own body was trembling so hard she couldn't see straight. Her thoughts were too jumbled to be coherent. They bombarded her, one after the other, with questions. Would it hurt? Would she remember it? Would she survive it? How long would it take? Would she be the same when she woke up? Was Roth going to set the dose too high and make it look like an accidental death? She was looking for something . . . what was that? Aurora! Where was she? Would anyone ever find her?

'Her blood pressure's too high,' Casey said.

'It won't be once she's sedated,' Roth said, picking up the syringe. 'Now, Connie.' She adopted a husky attempt at a soothing voice. 'I'm going to give you an injection. It'll just be a little scratch followed by a cold sensation in your arm. After that, just count down from ten inside your head. I guarantee that by the time you get to five, you'll feel perfectly happy. Nothing to worry about. When you wake up, you might feel a little groggy, and calmer. Much calmer, in fact. You may not feel like chatting or moving for a day or so, but don't worry, that's perfectly natural.' She patted Connie on the cheek. 'Right, let's do this.'

'You fucking bitch,' Connie tried to say through the mouth-guard. 'If I live through this, I'm going to slice you open and rip your heart out.' She knew that all Roth would hear was a strangulated gurgle.

337

Casey wheeled the blood pressure monitor to the side of the room.

'You're sure about this?' he asked Roth quietly.

'I can do without a second nurse questioning my professional judgement today,' Roth said, superiority and irritation oozing from her.

Casey fell silent.

Connie tried one last plea, no more than a sob that came from deep in the back of her throat as she breathed desperately through her nose, tears leaking from the corners of her eyes in spite of her fury.

Roth put the tip of the needle in Connie's arm. The sting brought fresh tears to Connie's eyes. She squeezed them shut, both longing for and dreading the coming numbness. There was a crack of thunder loud enough to make Roth jump. The needle went in too far, too fast. And the lights went out.

'Fuck,' Roth muttered, pulling the needle out again. 'Now we'll have to wait until the emergency generators kick in.'

Connie had been waiting for the cold sensation to flood her arm but felt nothing. She opened her eyes into the darkness, hardly daring to believe it. Roth and Casey were trying to feel their way in the dark. She heard the plink of Roth dropping the syringe into a surgical tray, Casey swearing softly as he stubbed his toe. The squeaking wheels of the ECT control cart as Roth pushed it to the side.

The storm had saved her. The same storm that had cut off communications and struck the tower with lightning. Was it all just a game for some higher power? Render her helpless then save her at the last possible moment? It didn't matter. For now, she was safe, however long it lasted. Connie held back a cry of relief, determined not to give Roth the pleasure of hearing it.

'Why aren't the fucking lights coming back on?' Roth said. 'God, the infrastructure here is about on par with Bedlam a hundred years ago.'

'We should take the mouthguard out,' Casey said, reaching clumsily for Connie, running his hands over her until he reached her face, then finally taking the rubber from between her teeth.

She breathed hard as it came out, giving a desperate, choking gasp.

'We'll wait. It'll get fixed,' Roth said.

'Thank God they evacuated Tower 3 so fast. I should go and check on the other staff members. I can't have any of them left wandering around the ward in the dark.'

'Fine, I'll go to the security area and see if the internal phone lines are working to get an update.'

To her right, Connie could hear Roth making her way towards the door. *Go on,* Connie thought. *Just fucking leave and don't ever come back.*

'What are we going to do about her?' Casey asked.

'Leave her. I don't want to take her back to the quiet room and it's not like she can do any damage in the meantime.'

'Fine,' he said. 'But you're the one making the decisions. If Ong doesn't like any of this, I'll tell him you gave me no choice.'

'Fine with me. Let me know when your balls drop.' Roth opened the door and let it slam shut behind her.

Casey removed the contraption from Connie's head and released her neck from the constraints.

'Please, just take me back to the quiet room,' Connie croaked. 'I don't want to be left alone on this table in the dark.'

'Doctor's orders,' he said quietly, but there was no mockery in his voice.

In that moment, Connie saw it all. Dr Ong was just a figure-head. A useless, ineffectual manager. Wherever he'd come from before this posting was probably pleased to get rid of him, and this was certainly the end of the line for him professionally. Roth was the power behind the throne, ruling through bullying, mockery and fear. Unlike Ong, Connie suspected she was perfectly aware of her own likeability and limitations, and never expected to take another posting. The sorts of personality traits she was showing were lifelong, most often formed in her early years. Every colleague she'd ever worked with had prob-ably found her difficult and obnoxious. The Institution might well have been a lifeline in terms of her career.

'At least release my ankles. You can't expect me to lie here like this. I don't even have a sheet over me. I'm cold.'

There were a few seconds of silence then a hand on one ankle, releasing the restraint strap followed by the other.

'That's all you get,' he said. 'Wrist and waist straps stay on. Don't make me regret it.'

He shuffled across the room and Connie heard a key in a lock somewhere high up. A minute later, a light paper sheet landed on her. It wasn't much, but at that moment it seemed like an extraordinary kindness.

'Thank you,' she said. 'Could you call Dr Ong? I know he's dealing with a lot, but he should know what's happening. Just tell him. I'm not asking for any special favours. It might help you, too, in the long run.'

Casey didn't say a word. She heard feet heading away from her, then the creak of the door and the firm click of it setting back into its frame. Connie was alone once more.

Chapter 29

Baarda heard his door being unlocked, then Sidorov appeared. He gave Baarda just seconds to put on his laceless trainers and a soft grey hoodie for warmth, then he used a cable tie as a makeshift restraint for Baarda's wrists and marched him out of Heaven Ward and down the stairs.

Baarda asked where they were going, to be met only with an order to be silent and a demand to move faster. At the base of Tower 2, Sidorov took stock of the people running around shouting at one another, and pulled Baarda closer to his side.

'Stay quiet, keep your head down. Walk next to me and maybe you won't get hurt.'

Baarda knew he could fight his way out of it. Even with his hands tied behind his back, he had enough strength in his legs and years of training that he could have kicked Sidorov into submission, probably into unconsciousness. But that would defeat the object. It finally felt like he was about to figure out what was going on behind Heaven Ward's clinical façade. He played along.

341

They went through the building towards the mountains at the rear, away from the reception area where staff were storming through with fire-fighting gear as others built increasingly high sandbag walls to keep out the incoming water.

They came to a set of wooden doors where Sidorov first knocked, then rattled the handles, and finally kicked the wood in a desperate effort to enter. The doors held firm.

'Where are you taking me?' Baarda asked.

'Somewhere for your own good. Just be quiet and let me figure this out.'

'I'm supposed to be on the ward,' Baarda said. 'The military hasn't authorised me to be held anywhere else.'

'The military? You're sticking with that? Stop wasting my time,' Sidorov said. 'I've got it. Don't move a muscle.' He walked to a desk situated across the corridor and picked up the two-way radio. 'Security? This is Dr Vassily Sidorov. Meet me outside Director Le Fay's room immediately.'

There were boots along the corridor, incoming at speed. 'I was just around the corner, Doctor. What is it you need?'

'You've got a set of master keys, right? This is a high-security military prisoner. I've had to move him from his ward given the current threat to building security. I'll wait with him, but it seems the best place to keep him is in the director's office in case I need access to the satellite phone.'

'Very good, sir,' the security guard said, 'but I hope you'll be okay without backup. I'm needed to help transfer prisoners out of Tower 3.'

'I understand,' Sidorov said. 'You can lock the doors behind you. That will help.'

The security guard let them in, watched as Sidorov escorted Baarda to a chair and made sure he remained there with the use of an additional cable tie threaded through the one already connecting his wrists and extras around his ankles and the chair legs. With that, the double doors closed, and a key turned in the lock.

The lights flickered, everything went dark for a few seconds, then the electricity won the battle.

'I want to know who you really are and what you're doing on Heaven Ward,' Sidorov said. 'And let me warn you, it would be very stupid to lie at this point.'

'I was in the military for two and a half decades. I was found guilty of criminal conduct after a posting in Afghanistan.'

'And yet the woman who originally told me that story is currently upstairs telling a very different tale,' Sidorov said. 'So now I'm not sure who I should believe.'

Baarda glared at him. Sidorov was perched on the edge of Director Le Fay's desk, arms crossed.

'Dr Connie was engaged by the military prosecutor. She's not here for my sake.'

'I get it. You're going to stick to the cover story. But don't you even want to know why she's busy with Dr Roth and Dr Ong?' Sidorov glanced at his watch. 'Actually that was a while ago. By now, the lovely Dr Connie will have been moved to the quiet room, changed into a gown and most likely sedated.'

Baarda tried to stand, forgetting his bound legs, and crashed straight back down, baring his teeth.

'You seem very upset given your purely clinical relationship with Connie,' Sidorov said.

'Why would they do that to her?' Baarda demanded.

'Because she has been acting increasingly strangely. Running away from some unknown assailant along the lake wall at night. Injuring herself. Claiming there's some sort of passageway beneath her cell. Something about a lost baby. And she was open with me about her past experience as a patient in a mental health facility. Dr Roth made the assessment that your "doctor" is a danger to herself and others, and that whilst The Institution is in emergency mode, she needs to be locked up.'

Baarda breathed heavily through his nose for a few seconds as he studied the room. There was a letter opener on the desk. The blade wouldn't be sharp, but it was something. There were irons by the large fireplace that would have the weight he needed for a blunt instrument, but they would be harder to reach. On a small table in the corner there were crystal glasses that could be smashed and used for sharps.

'What has this got to do with me?' Baarda asked.

'Dr Connie suggested that you're not a convicted killer at all. The new version of events she gave Dr Ong is that the two of you are undercover, investigating the murder of Tara Cameron and the kidnap of her baby. If that's true, then with Connie under Roth's care, you have just found yourself in an extremely vulnerable position.'

Baarda ground his teeth. Sidorov, quite simply, gave him the creeps, and Connie's experience of the man hadn't been any better. Down here, he was separated from Connie and off the ward with no way to verify what he was being told. Telling Sidorov the truth might put Connie in even worse danger.

'Why did you bring me down here?' Baarda asked sharply.

'Because, Patient B, I can't overrule Roth, and Dr Ong is too worried about what's happening in the rest of the prison with the director away, so he's in no state to listen to protracted arguments.'

The lights dipped again. That time Baarda counted to twenty before the power went back on.

'What does it matter to you who I really am?' Baarda asked.

'You don't matter to me,' Sidorov said. 'But I worked with Tara Cameron and I respected her. I want to know if she was killed on the ward. The timing of your arrival makes me think that Dr Connie was telling the truth, but you're right – I saw your military file and the director vouched for you. Is he in on it as well?'

'I can't answer any of these questions,' Baarda said, stalling as he assessed Sidorov some more. The man was hard to read. 'I'd like to go back up to Heaven Ward and see Dr Connie now.'

'I never believed you were military,' Sidorov said slowly. 'I told Connie that. You have no tattoos. She said you're ex police. If you can confirm that to me now, I'll let you out of that chair. I brought you here to keep you safe while Connie no longer could.'

Baarda drew himself up in the chair. Connie would only have told Sidorov that as a last resort. If he didn't respond correctly, he might blow her last chance of getting to safety. Get it wrong and Aurora was as good as dead. 'What if you were involved in Tara's death?'

'You're wasting time. Roth is a bitch. She regards herself as the superior authority on the ward. She doesn't care what anyone else says, not even Dr Ong, and he doesn't argue with her because Roth reduces the amount of time he spends on the ward when he'd much rather be in more pleasant environments. I'm only going to say this once. I wasn't involved in Tara's death, and I'm here to help you.'

Baarda sighed. He couldn't leave Connie alone and vulnerable, to be subjected to God knew what treatment from Roth. He knew it, and apparently Sidorov knew it too. 'How, exactly, can you help us?' Baarda asked.

'So it's true,' Sidorov said, standing. 'Tara's really dead. And your colleague's surname is – I can't remember – something beginning with W?'

'I can't discuss that. You need to cut me loose,' Baarda said.
'I think I'm entitled to know what I'm dealing with first.'

Baarda clenched his lower jaw and spoke fast. 'Bloody storm,' Baarda growled as the lights went out completely. 'Why now?'

'There are backup generators,' Sidorov said. 'They normally kick in within a couple of minutes.'

'What if they don't?'

'I'll leave you down here and check what's happening. Once Roth has left the ward at the end of the night shift, it should be possible for me to get Connie out of the quiet room and move her somewhere safe.'

A key turned in the lock. Baarda gave him a pointed look.

'Stay still and stay quiet,' Sidorov told him. 'Let me handle this. It's probably just the security guard checking in.'

'Is there a torch in here?' Baarda whispered. 'Cut me free right now.'

The door opened. A silhouette of a man was just visible in the doorway. He entered, shut the door behind himself and walked in.

'Hello?' Sidorov said. 'Who is that? This is Dr Vassily Sidorov from Heaven Ward and I'm using this room as a temporary secure base.'

There was a metallic scraping followed by a dull thump. The sound of a body hitting the floor was unmistakable.

Baarda was on his feet again, pulling the chair up behind him and swinging it against the wall to smash the back of it.

As the lights finally decided to illuminate the room once more, Baarda looked into the face of the man who had struck Sidorov, caught the movement of the fire iron through the air, and had a fraction of a second to hope that Connie was going to find a way out of the quiet room before his attacker got to her too.

Chapter 30

Connie allowed herself a moment to recover from how close she'd come to having voltage put through her brain. Half a minute, not a second more. The world was exactly as it had been before she'd been strapped to that table, yet it felt immeasurably different. Nothing and everything had changed. There was no shame in the terror she'd felt, and the things she'd promised herself she'd do to Roth were a perfectly normal response. Her desire to live, though, had exploded within her. How was that possible? You walked around all day thinking you wanted to live to the same extent that everybody else did. But fear – primal, bestial, savage fear – turned your whole world upside down.

'Enough,' she said aloud. 'You're still in one piece. No harm done. Move on.'

However badly affected she'd been, the most pressing need was to figure out a way forward. There were forces working against her, and no allies in sight. Her first job was to get out of the restraints, and figure out where Baarda had been taken. If Roth had felt able to make such a drastic decision about

347

the treatment of a fellow medic, then Baarda really was at Sidorov's mercy. And she still had to find baby Aurora, as if that were an afterthought. The worst-case scenario was that now Connie had revealed her true identity, whoever had been responsible for Tara's death might well have decided to end the baby's life sooner rather than later.

Connie rattled her wrist restraints, but they were too tight to allow any movement at all. Bending her knees and planting her feet higher up the table, she was able to achieve some movement with her torso, but that wasn't enough to find a way to get free. She tried driving enough motion through her body to get the table to start rocking right and left, but it was too solid and well balanced, and there was always the prospect that she could get badly injured.

Screaming was her other option: attracting the attention of a different staff member who might be kinder, more sympathetic. But that was a double-edged sword. Scream and she would be confirming the allegation that she was hysterical and out of control. Scream, and she might attract the attention of someone who agreed with Dr Roth's chosen course of action, and restrain her even more soundly.

All she could do was wait in the dark. Wait, and hope it was Tom Lord who came in first or Jake, even Nurse Lightfoot. Best-case scenario was Dr Ong, although the power outage and continued failure of the backup generators made the prospect of Ong arriving back on the ward less likely any time soon.

Breathe in slowly, centre yourself, breathe out. Use the time to assess the situation.

All right. There were staff members around who were seriously short of money. Nurse Madani was one of them. Tara Cameron's family were going to fund whatever was necessary to get their granddaughter back. That gave Connie the option to offer whatever bribe was needed.

Breathe in, centre yourself, breathe out. Decide on the priorities.

She needed access to the satellite phone, and to find out where Sidorov had taken Baarda. She wasn't going to be able to email or text anyone. With the power out, the internet would inevitably be down too.

Breathe in, centre yourself, breathe out.

After that, the imperative was making sure Ong knew what Roth had planned for her and stopping the treatment in its tracks.

Breathe in, centre yourself, breathe—

A loud, heavy clunk came from the door, echoed several more times a fraction of a second afterwards in the corridor beyond the medical room. Connie held her breath, hoping beyond hope to hear the noise a second time, wishing she was wrong, desperate, suddenly, even for Dr Roth to re-enter the room.

Holy crap, no, Connie thought, widening her eyes as if that would somehow help her see through the darkness. The sound she heard surely couldn't be the fucking door locks.

Her mind raced through everything she knew about emergency procedures. If all else failed, she'd been told on the first day, the prisoners had to be released from their cells because of the fire risk with keeping all the doors locked. *Not good,* she thought. What else had she been told? Staff would evacuate the corridor to keep themselves safe. Then they would wait it out, only manually opening the main ward door if the actual tower was on fire.

Lightning never strikes twice, Connie told herself. *You're being paranoid. It'll all be okay.*

Her heart was thumping so loudly, it was dizzying.

She tried to listen. Everything was muffled. Vague. She could hear voices somewhere, but they might have been on the ward below. No footsteps. No sign that any of the prisoners had left their rooms. Not yet.

Had any of them been aware that she'd been taken into the medical room? That didn't bear thinking about, but she'd been protesting, loudly, at points. Crying. Someone would have heard her. Even if the patients didn't come looking for her specifically, there was nowhere to go on the ward that gave them access to anything exciting except the common room – also completely dark with no electricity for the television – or the medical room to search for weapons or drugs.

If Baarda had still been on the ward she'd have been fine. He'd have been at her side by then, releasing her, ready to do whatever needed to be done. And it had been Vassily Sidorov who'd taken him away. Was that just coincidence? Was it all part of a larger plan? Sidorov had been the first to leave Ong's room as soon as she'd admitted her real purpose at The Institution. Had he also fanned the flames of Ong's belief in Connie's declining mental health? She'd told Sidorov about her past as an in-patient. It had to have been him who passed the information on.

Footsteps now, quite clear. Connie wasn't imagining them. Those went straight past her door and continued into the distance then faded, presumably around a corner.

Nurse Lightfoot knew she was there, as did Sam Casey. Even if Roth was a truly vindictive bitch, there was no way she could just leave her there.

Breathe in, centre yourself, breathe out.

She just had to wait it out. Stay calm, stay quiet. Refuse to let fear and panic override her vital brain functions.

More footsteps. They went past the door. Stopped a few steps along the corridor, began retracing. She heard the door handle grind softly, little by little, as she hoped against hope that for some reason her lock was still in place, knowing she was grasping at straws. All the locks must have been sprung in the emergency procedure. Including hers.

The gentle thud of the door handle hitting its lowest point met her ears. She froze, every nerve in her body screaming. Connie felt the motion of new air entering before she heard the first footfall on the medical room's tiled floor.

She wanted to say something. Surely that was the best course of action. To be unafraid. To ask for help and reassure whoever was in there that she meant no harm and that they could work together to ensure their mutual safety. That she would vouch for them afterwards, tell Dr Ong and Director Le Fay how sensible and responsible they'd been, and how much that might assist in their future reviews. But the words wouldn't form in her mouth. Even her lips wouldn't move. In fact, she couldn't breathe at all.

Shuffling feet moved further inside. The door shut so softly behind the incomer that Connie knew he had held the door quietly until the very last second. No one would know he was in there. Lightfoot and Casey wouldn't be safe either if they came back for her. No number of torches would be enough to fully illuminate all the rooms and corridors at once. Entering now would be suicide.

A body part collided with one of the cupboards on the walls. She heard the metal doors shake. Feet shuffled again, closer now. She tried to run through the facts in her adrenaline-flooded head. Someone in here had helped kill Tara Cameron. That someone wanted her dead too. If that had been Joe Yarowski then thank God because it was one less problem, but even so, she was on a ward of serial killers and strapped to a gurney.

Closer now, banging into the trolley with the ECT unit on it. Whoever was in the room with her had the presence of mind not to call out while barking their shins. But they seemed to be looking for something. Checking cabinets was a good thing.

That meant that they might have no idea she was there. Perhaps, if she stayed absolutely silent, they would go away. If she could just hold her breath a tiny bit longer. Just another thirty seconds.

Hot fingers touched her knee and the breath burst out of her. Connie screamed. It was short and brutal. The fingers slid upward and gripped her thigh.

'Quiet.' It was a whisper, a man's voice, fierce and commanding.

'Please let me go,' she blurted. His free hand was over her mouth before she could get any more words out.

'Shhhh!'

More footsteps now outside the door – slow, heavy and deliberate. She was shaking and sweating. Was she better off with the man inside the room, identity still unknown, or calling out to whoever might be passing by?

The decision was made for her as the footsteps trailed away and a nearby door slammed.

The hand remained in situ over her mouth but the other one felt for her wrists and began undoing the restraint.

'Stay quiet, you stupid girl, and perhaps you'll survive. Make a noise and I can't guarantee that at all.' Professor Gregor Saint took his hand from her mouth. Connie stayed absolutely still. 'I heard Roth and the others bring you in here. What I don't know is why they're doing this to you. Tell me and don't lie.'

'Let me up first.' He was leaning over her. She could feel his breath on her neck and chin. It made her skin crawl.

'No. The waist strap and other wrist strap remain on. If I have to, I'll simply knock you out and leave you here.'

Connie could tell that he meant it, and that left her no choice. She began to speak.

'They said I was paranoid and irrational. They think my previous alleged history of mental health problems have been exacerbated by my time here. Roth says I'm hysterical. Ong told her to leave me in the quiet room for my own good until he could review me in the morning, but I was having a nightmare and apparently that was enough reason for her to recommend a dose of ECT.'

'Are you paranoid and irrational?'

'What do you think?' she asked, careful to keep any confrontation from her voice.

There was a pause and then the professor began undoing the remaining restraints. Connie felt a heady rush of relief spoiled only by the suspicion that the professor had something even worse up his sleeve for her.

'Why are you helping me?' she asked softly.

'Primarily because I don't like Dr Roth,' he said. 'I'm not alone in that, of course. No one likes Roth. She uses treatments as a punishment if you do or say anything that annoys her. A quick session of ECT is her favourite. Up you get. Just sit for now. Your legs will be weak.'

'I'm okay,' Connie said. 'I need to get out of here. God only knows what they've done with Baarda.'

Connie swung her legs over the side and tried to stand. The professor had been right. It took a moment for her body to belong to her again and follow her commands.

'Who's Baarda?' the professor asked. He was still standing close to her, his legs pressing against hers, one hand on her shoulder. Connie didn't like it, but she was in no fit state to fight. Regain strength first, assert herself later.

'Patient B,' Connie said. 'His surname is Baarda. Dr Sidorov took him somewhere before the power went out. Do you know anything about that?'

'No. He didn't go past me to the common room so I'm assuming he was indeed removed from the ward.'

'I have to get off the ward too,' Connie said. 'Can you help me to the ward door?'

'You're not going anywhere,' he said, his intonation suggesting he thought her utterly stupid. 'The cameras are out so they won't be able to see that you're standing at the door. Everything is soundproofed.'

'They'll be able to hear me if I shout at the door,' Connie said.

'No. There's normally a little speaker so they can hear sound from inside the ward corridor but that will be out of action too.'

'But the door locks disengaged. There must be some backup supply of power somewhere for absolute necessities.' She stood shakily, but it felt much better to be on her feet.

'The door locks are on a separate battery system. Emergencies only. One-way function. Just enough to prevent us all from being burned to death in our cells.'

Connie rolled her eyes in the dark.

'I have to try to leave. Come with me to the ward door. If they've got a torch, they'll be able to see my face at the viewing slot. They'll have to let me out.'

'But it's not in my interests for you to get out right now,' he said. 'I have some requirements. A negotiation seems to be a good way forward, and one should always negotiate from a position of relative power.'

She couldn't push past him and run for the door. He would grab her in a heartbeat, and Baarda's tale of the professor being about to kill the orderly in the common room was surfacing in her mind. The professor was smart and he could be sensible, but he was no pushover and there were things he wanted. Playing along was her best option.

'Okay. You released me from the table and it seems only

fair that you should get something out of it. I'd be happy to help. What's on your list?'

'I want a lawyer-verified guarantee of an annual review, with a psychiatrist brought in from a different facility to give an independent diagnosis.'

'I'm sure that's possible,' Connie said. 'Is that it?'

'I'd like access to a proper academic library, not just the low-grade genre paperbacks they have here.'

'Also more than feasible. Continued education should be part of any hospital programme. If we move to the ward door, I'm sure I'll be able to persuade the staff to listen.'

'Nothing's going to happen until the power's back on and emergency status is lifted. I need Director Le Fay to get the lawyers on it and give me a cast-iron guarantee. I know what they're like here. Ong has made promises before that he hasn't kept.'

'You've asked for these things on previous occasions?'

'Yes, and been told it will happen. But I never had a hostage before, so things are different now. I suggest we make our way to my room. No one will bother us in there. I can hide you but I won't be able to keep you safe from the likes of Haskin. He's a monster.'

She thought through his proposal quickly. It worked for her. If the power came back on, Roth would be unable to find her, and if it didn't, she wasn't completely alone. 'Makes sense,' Connie said. 'Let's go.'

Professor Saint took her arm, gripped it tightly enough that she was under no illusions as to either his physical strength or the strength of his intentions, and together they inched their way to the medical room door.

'We'll turn left out of the door, hold on to the wall, walk until we go round the corner then my room is the next on the

355

right. Don't call out, don't run away, don't do anything unexpected. Whilst I have nothing against you personally, I'm intolerant of poor behaviour as I hope you've realised.'

'Got that message loud and clear,' Connie said. 'You want to open the door or should I?'

The professor answered by pushing her slightly to one side and easing the door open inch by inch. There was only stillness in the corridor beyond, and finally the relief of the faintest patches of light issuing from the moon beyond the patients' windows, spilling through the viewing slots of their doors, not enough to see by but sufficient to detect a shimmer in the air along the passageway.

As Connie stepped into the hallway, the professor bringing up the rear, a separate shaft of light was visible, source unknown, back in the direction of the main door to the ward.

'What's that?' she whispered, pulling Saint's arm to get his attention.

'Doesn't matter,' he said. 'Come on.'

'No!' she held her ground. The beam of light was shining across at floor level. It was dim but definite. 'It has to be a torch. There's no floor-level lighting in here. We could use that.'

'We need to move, now!' he growled.

She had a split second to make the decision, and she was done playing good girl. Twisting on the toes of her left foot, she brought her right knee up hard and spiked it into the professor's stomach. He doubled over, instantly letting go of her arm. Connie leapt over him as he went down, reaching an arm out for the wall to guide her and going as fast as she could towards the beam of light from around the corner.

The professor was cursing behind her, already getting up. Connie jogged along, knowing that if there was anything unseen in her way, she would fall, but she was more scared of waiting around.

'Get back here,' the professor rasped.

Connie was within a few feet of the corner. Whatever was waiting for her around the next bend, she would just have to take the risk. The beam of light was clearer now. She took the ninety-degree turn, determined to run for the ward door, and sprawled face down. She pushed herself up. Whatever was beneath her gave way a little before she felt solidity beneath the soft upper layer. She didn't need to run her hand over any more of the surface to know it was a man's body, and that there would be no bringing him back to life.

The ward door suddenly seemed miles away.

The beam of light had come from a torch, apparently dropped during the attack. Connie reached across the body, all too aware of the professor's rapid approach, and grabbed the torch.

'Careful,' she whispered at Saint.

Shining the light into the face of the fallen male, she noted the dark liquid staining his front. The man's throat had been cut, presumably from behind given the length and angle of the gash. Bracing herself, Connie checked the face.

'Nurse Casey,' the professor announced. 'He must have been coming back for you.'

'Someone in here has a knife with a pretty substantial blade, looking at the depth of that cut.' She checked Casey's hands and patted down his pockets. 'His emergency keys are gone and his electronic pass cards are both gone. You have to help me attract attention at the ward door.'

'No. This changes nothing other than the fact that I am not prepared to remain in this corridor a second longer.'

Connie cast the torchlight up towards the end of the corridor where the ward door sat in the distance. The reflection of the

357

beam of light on glass was missing. Someone had closed the viewing shutter the other side. How long until a staff member realised Casey was missing and ventured in to find him? Maybe minutes, maybe hours. Given the various emergencies in other parts of The Institution, there might be no other staff on the ward until morning.

The professor grabbed the neck of the gown she'd been put into, and twisted until it was tight around her throat.

'I'll take that.' He snatched the torch from her hand and pushed Connie in front of him. 'My room, fast.'

It was easier to go at speed with the torchlight ahead of them, both of them veering away from any doors that might open unannounced. At the professor's room, he told her to get onto the bed and face the wall while he checked for any unwanted presence in the en suite.

He turned off the torch and waited as their eyes adjusted to the natural light from the window. From his cell window, craning her neck, Connie could see the glow of the fire, still raging, in the third tower. It had spread over two floors now, and any use the rain might have been putting it out had been counterbalanced by the wild winds fanning the flames.

'Damned room, every stick of furniture nailed down. We'll have to sit with our backs to the door,' he said.

'Nurse Casey didn't come onto the ward without his keys. With the electronic pass system down, the only way in and out is manually. Whoever cut his throat can open or lock any door on this ward, and even exit the ward completely if there's no one in the staff security area.'

Professor Saint shone the torchlight into her face.

'What are you suggesting?' he asked.

'Only that the stakes have changed. There's a dead body in the hallway. I know I didn't kill him, and Patient B was removed from the ward earlier, so that leaves four of you as suspects.'

'I was with you,' he barked.

'Depends when Casey was killed. I was alone in that room for several minutes. I don't know where you were at that point in time.'

'That's ridiculous!'

Connie's mind was racing. She needed to take control, and fast. 'What's ridiculous is thinking that keeping me hostage is a stronger bargaining point than getting me out, potentially saving my life, reporting Casey's murder at the earliest opportunity, and making yourself the hero of the piece. Do you seriously think anything will be the same when the power comes back on? Everyone on this ward will be moved to different towers, probably into solitary confinement, while the events of tonight are investigated. The staffing of Heaven Ward is bound to change. Whatever assumptions you're making right now about who you'll be dealing with in the future are foolish. Handle this wrong, and you can forget any chance of more regular reviews or increased privileges. You have one way of turning this to your advantage, and it's not by making demands while a man lies brutally killed. You're more intelligent than that.'

'I'm certainly more intelligent than you,' he sniped. 'All right, then. How do we get out? We don't have the keys, and whoever does is also in possession of a deadly weapon. I'm not sure how we maximise the potential of this situation.'

'Keeping me alive would be a start,' Connie said. 'For that we need greater numbers.'

'Numbers?' The professor laughed quietly. 'Young lady, you are on a high-security psychiatric ward. Just where are your knights in shining armour hiding themselves?'

'In terms of the threat to me, my assessment would be that Rubio and Haskin present the greatest danger. East's killing pattern, whilst it contains some female victims – similar to your own record – is not gender-driven. If we team up with him, we're three against two. We try to get attention at the ward door, and failing that, we find the easiest place to defend ourselves until morning.'

'Did you also fall for the quick smile and superficial looks? I'm rather disappointed.'

For a moment, Connie was confused. 'Oh, you're talking about East?'

'Indeed.'

'Who else did you think fell for the smile and good looks?' Connie asked.

'Nurse Cameron always had far too much time for East. I myself judge a book by what's between the covers.'

'Nonetheless, East is the best option,' Connie said. 'If you have a better plan, now would be the time to share. That fire over there's not going out any time soon and the storm is still raging, so you're as stuck as I am.'

The professor huffed. 'All right, but I'm in charge. Not you, and not that juvenile East. The plan is mine: you'll do as I say, and I get the credit. Agreed?'

'Agreed,' Connie said.

'And you'll support me, once we get to safety. You'll say I saved you and that it was my plan to get you out.' They were questions, but he said them like statements.

Connie gave it a few moments' consideration. 'Sure.' She stood, pulled the gown more tightly around herself and prepared to leave.

'And it's your considered professional assessment that East isn't dangerous. Not as bad as Rubio and Haskin, at least.'

It occurred to her for the first time that perhaps the professor hadn't come to find her in the medical room to negotiate at all. That all the talk of more regular reviews and extra books had been to save face. The man asking her opinion now was scared, looking older and less sure of himself than he had before. All of which meant that he might not be a threat to her, but he might well turn tail and flee if faced with a fellow psychopath holding a knife. East was undoubtedly the better prospect as a fighting partner.

'We should go,' Connie said gently. 'But it would help if I could put something more substantial on first.'

The professor pointed at a shelf. 'Jogging bottoms and a sweatshirt. They'll be too long for you, but the bottoms are elasticated.'

Connie grabbed them, slipped into the en-suite shower for privacy, and pulled them on. It felt better straight away, being less exposed.

'Okay, Professor, let's move.'

A creak sounded in the corridor beyond, someone trying – and failing – to be silent. Connie held her breath. The door handle complained as someone set their hand on it. Connie reached out instinctively in the professor's direction, wanting to tell him to move, to get down to hide. Not that there was anywhere to go. Too late she was stepping up to the door to get her weight behind it. Before she could make it, the door flew open, leaving Connie directly in front of the incomer.

'Don't even try to fight me,' Harold Haskin said. 'I have a syringe in my hand and you don't want to know what's in it. You're both coming with me. We need to get a few things sorted out.'

Chapter 31

'Common room,' Haskin said, taking the torch from the professor's hand and waving them in the direction that took them as far as they could get from the ward door. 'Go all the way in, sit on the floor in the centre of the room,' he directed, shining the torch around, checking the corners.

'What exactly do you hope to achieve?' the professor asked him.

'Keep the snooty out of your tone, Professor,' was Haskin's reply. 'You think an old man and a girl are any match for me?'

Haskin checked behind himself twice, looked back at them, did another sweep of the room. 'Why was she in your room, Professor? What were you two talking about in there?'

'I was in the medical room when the lights went out,' Connie said. 'The professor was going to walk me to the ward door, to see if I could be let out. That's all.'

'That wasn't all,' Haskin shouted. He was thumping his free hand, fist rolled, into his thigh. 'I heard my name. Why were you talking about me?'

'Nothing bad,' Connie said. 'We were just trying to figure out who was still on the ward and unaccounted for.'

Benny Rubio burst through the double doors into the common room to join them, crying hysterically.

'I don't want to be in the dark any more. I'm scared. I don't like it. Can I come in here with you? I'll be good. I won't talk and I won't break anything.' He wiped an arm along his nose and it came away visibly wet.

Connie tried not to let the revulsion show on her face.

'Shut the fuck up,' Haskin said, taking a step to the side so Rubio didn't touch him on his way past. 'Sit down there with them and stop fucking sobbing.'

Rubio sat down uncomfortably close to Connie who did her best to hide her disgust at the smell of a man who had plainly taken the obsession of nappy wearing too far.

'Should have just stayed in my room and kept quiet. All your fault,' the professor muttered next to her.

Rubio began sucking his thumb complete with loud, wet lip-smacking noise and reaching out sticky fingers to stroke Connie's hair.

She fought her desire to slap his hands away, grimacing at Rubio's touch even as she tried to focus on Haskin.

'I didn't do it! I didn't, and you're not going to frame me for it,' Haskin told her.

Connie's head felt like it might explode. 'You didn't do what, exactly?' she asked.

Haskin dropped his voice to a whisper. 'I didn't kill Casey.'

Rubio had a handful of her hair now and was rubbing it between thumb and forefinger in time with the rhythmic thumb-sucking. Connie wanted to shove him as far away from her as she could get him, then sprint for the nearest shower. The professor was tapping both his feet on the floor in a frenzy.

The syringe in Haskin's hand was shaking and there was sweat running down his face.

'You didn't kill Casey,' Connie agreed. 'No one knows who did. The whole of The Institution is chaos. We don't know what's going on. Now's not the time for accusations. We need to stay calm and wait until help arrives.'

'I know who did it! I know!' Rubio stuck the soggy-thumbed hand in the air and looked like that child in school who was always desperately trying to please teacher.

Connie stared at him. Was it just more Rubio theatrics or did he actually have valuable information?

'I told you to shut the fuck up, Benny,' Haskin snarled. 'You don't know shit.'

'But I do!' Rubio pulled Connie's hair to get her attention. 'I saw someone with the keys.'

'Okay, Benny,' Connie said softly, discreetly pulling her hair from his grasp. 'Who's got Nurse Casey's keys?'

He leaned in towards her, his eyes huge in the near dark, his childlike voice an excited squeak in the quiet.

'Vince had them in his hand. He opened the door to the quiet room. I guess he was looking for you, right?' He clapped his hands together. 'Did I do good? Am I your favourite boy now?'

'I did warn you about East,' the professor said smugly.

'Dr Roth said Mr East is a bad man,' Rubio said, wrapping his arms around his knees and rocking backwards and forwards. 'She told me he killed some ladies. Nice ladies. She said he never got caught for it like I did, but that he was just as naughty as me, maybe worse even.'

'Fuckin' East,' Haskin said, dragging out the words. 'He's going to get us all killed. They'll find Casey's body, come in with the tasers and fry us. And if that doesn't finish us, Roth will zap all our fucking brains again.'

'Benny,' Connie said. 'Was East carrying anything else when you saw him?'

Rubio shrugged dramatically. 'I can't remember.'

'Think hard. You saw the keys. Which hand were they in? How was he carrying them? Could you see his other hand?'

'Ummm, I don't know. I guess I could see it, but it was kind of closed, like in a fist. The way I eat pudding.'

'She's trying to ask if he was carrying a knife, you moron,' the professor snapped.

'Well I didn't see a knife, but there was something in his hand. I just don't know what. Dr Roth said he used a knife to kill all those pregnant ladies too. She said East is the baddest person here and he should never be let out, and that no woman will ever be safe near him.'

Connie's stomach shrivelled. 'Did you say pregnant?' she asked.

Rubio nodded enthusiastically. 'Yes! Dr Roth says East didn't just crunchify all those people on the news. There were other ladies too.'

'Crucify,' the professor corrected. 'So were those other ladies in East's file? Did you know about them?'

'He told me about them,' Connie said softly.

And he had. He'd told her there were victims, but denied his involvement. But the word 'pregnant' had never crossed his lips.

'So it wasn't me then! You know now,' Haskin said. 'You've got to tell Ong it wasn't me. I'm not going down for that.' He waved the syringe in their direction.

Another figure emerged from the shadows, remaining in the doorway at Haskin's back. He leaned against the doorframe, arms folded.

365

'He's here! Oh my gosh.' Rubio bounced up and down, clapping again. 'Do you have the keys? Can we go for a visit downstairs?'

Vince East looked grim. Gone was the easy smile and the preppy charm, replaced with watchful tension and shifting eyes.

'Dr Connie, you okay?' East asked.

'I am,' she said. 'Benny says you have Nurse Casey's keys. Is that right?'

Haskin turned sideways, syringe out front. 'You got a knife, East? Because I got a syringe full of nasty shit here, so you don't want to mess with me.'

'Is this your way of covering up what you did, Haskin, by hiding the knife and grabbing a hypodermic instead?' East asked him.

'I don't like it when they argue,' Rubio said, bottom lip starting to wobble. 'Tell them to stop, Dr Connie. They're nasty boys.' She felt his hand back in her hair, clutching at her, and only narrowly prevented herself from slapping his hand away so she could focus on the drama unfolding in the doorway.

'Why don't we all take a breath?' Connie said. 'Mr East, Mr Haskin, no one knows what happened on the ward tonight but it's certainly not going to get sorted out like this.'

'Fine. But you come with me.' Haskin pointed at Connie.

'She's not going anywhere,' the professor said. 'It seems to me that the only fair thing is for all of us to remain here until the lights come back on. There's only one torch and I don't trust any of you.'

'I don't want to be in the dark again,' Rubio said, letting new tears fall down his grubby cheeks. 'There are bad things in the dark. They hide under my bed and they laugh at me at night.' He slid closer to Connie and buried his face against her back, and that time she couldn't stop herself from pulling away.

'Don't let them take the light away from me, Dr Connie. Please don't.'

'Connie, stand up. We're leaving,' East said.

She took a deep breath, kept her movements slow, deciding that whatever the outcome, being on her feet probably wasn't a bad idea.

Rubio gripped her waist and stood with her. 'You won't leave me alone, will you? Not in the dark. I want a glass of milk and my favourite blanket and my night-light. I don't want to be here with them. They scare me.'

'Rubio, I told you to shut the fuck up!' Haskin roared.

'Connie, step away now and come here to me!' East said.

'I found her first,' the professor said. 'And I say she stays with me.'

'Dr Connie,' East was walking closer to her now, ignoring Haskin's syringe waving and the professor's irate declaration. 'I'm not going to take no for an answer.' He got within a few feet of her and held out his hand.

'She won't go with you,' Rubio said. 'I told her all about those ladies you killed.'

East bared his teeth. 'You told her what, exactly?'

'He told me that the women you were accused of killing were all pregnant. Is that right, Vince?' Connie asked. 'Were they?'

'Don't listen to Rubio,' East said. 'He's messing with your head. Walk towards me right now and I'll get you out of here.'

Connie looked from East to the professor, to Haskin, and then to Rubio who was clinging to her and whimpering.

'Benny,' she said. 'Could you let go of me please? I think the best thing is for us all to walk to the ward door and attract attention. Anyone who has nothing to hide will come with me.'

'You know what, Dr Woolwine?' Benny Rubio whispered in her ear, voice deep, gravelly, menacing, no hint of childishness or distress. 'I just don't think that's going to work for me.'

Chapter 32

The knife that was pressed to Connie's throat was tacky, presumably with Nurse Casey's freshly shed blood. She wasn't surprised – not that her prescience made the imminent threat of death one iota less terrifying. It was just that she'd had a sense of it all week, that something had been looming. Waiting for her.

'I should have known it was all too simple,' she said.

'Which bit?' Rubio asked, slipping an arm around her waist to manoeuvre her into position as a shield between him and his wardmates who were frozen in place, waiting to see what would happen next.

'The hypnotherapy. Getting you to open up. It was unusual, a patient being that compliant during the first session, but I see now that I was under pressure and I just wanted to believe. I was arrogant, I guess.'

'Arrogant is a good word for you. All that, "You're in a safe space. Nothing can hurt you here." Did you really think I was going to give you everything with one snap of your fingers? Not my first rodeo, sweetheart.'

'Rubio, let her go,' East said. 'If you hurt her, you die. No one here has anything left to lose.'

'Neither do I,' Rubio said. 'So before your hero reflex gets triggered, I'm going to show you how serious I am.'

He whipped the knife around to the rear side of her neck, low down, just above the rise of her shoulder.

'Try not to scream,' he whispered.

Connie jolted in his grip as the knife went in, the cry she issued a strangled blend of shock and pain.

'What the fuck, man?' Haskin shouted.

Connie was gasping for breath. Rubio held her tight, her back against his chest.

'She's in no danger right now. I'm good with blades. This is just one centimetre into her upper trapezius muscle. Tell the nice men you're okay, Dr Connie.'

'M'Oh . . . kay,' she panted.

'We're walking out of here now and you're all going to stay right here. If any of you hypocrites decide to try to win a few points with Director Le Fay, this knife is going to slide all the way round to the front of her neck, and believe me, this baby's so sharp it'll be like slicing butter.'

Everything on Connie's right-hand side was burning from her eye down to her waist. It was hard to breathe and even harder not to panic. The blade made its presence felt every time she tried to move, as if not just a centimetre of metal but a whole pole had been pushed down through her body.

'You motherfucker,' Haskin growled.

'Wow, from the man who wishes he'd been dubbed the piñata killer rather than the Blindfold Killer. Tell the truth, Haskin, you're just jealous that I got to her first, am I right?' Rubio gave a bizarre, high-pitched laugh.

'Fuck you,' Haskin shouted.

'Yeah whatever, I'm done with all of you. Maybe I'll send you a postcard from the Maldives.' Rubio pushed Connie forward as he spoke.

She could feel the blood trickling down her back. One false move, by her or any of the other men in the room, and she knew he would split her neck in two.

The professor was backing away towards the far corner. Haskin took a step to the side, keeping the syringe firmly out in front. Vince East stayed where he was, hands on hips, his eyes on Connie's.

'Where you going, Benny? There's nowhere to hide. Sooner or later, they're coming for you,' East told him.

'Who, you fucking child? You think I'm alone in this? I have a plan, you moron. I have a future.'

Rubio was guiding her through the common room doors and out into the corridor. Connie did her best to keep her body facing straight forward, not to twist her neck and deepen or widen the wound. The pain was bad, but pissing Rubio off would be so much worse.

'What the fuck are you talking about?' East called from behind them. Rubio didn't bother to answer. 'Connie, what plan is he talking about?'

She kept quiet, all her energy pouring into breathing in and out, keeping her upper body as still as possible, and setting one foot in front of the other in the dark without tripping because tripping almost inevitably meant death, although at least the knife would be ripping out of her back rather than moving forward into the front of her neck.

They rounded the corner to where the patients' rooms had a view of the lake and where the moon, albeit briefly, helped light the hallway.

'I have to ask,' she said, her voice no more than breath on the wind. 'Why did you kill Tara? No one has said a bad word about her. She sounds kind and sweet.'

'You see, that's why you couldn't figure it out. You're still slave to the concept that goodness means nothing bad will happen to you. Two things, Dr Woolwine. Firstly, boredom. There comes a time when the fantasies of things already done just aren't enough to get you off. Oops, look out, another corner coming up and unless I'm mistaken there's a body just around the bend.'

Connie kept her footsteps small and her pace steady.

'What was the second thing?' she asked.

'Means to an end. I was promised some things, you see. You don't need the details. But for the first time in a long time, there was suddenly hope of a world beyond a tower, one room, cycling through the same old movies, and the numbness of medication. Step over him. Don't bother taking another look. That fucker is irreversibly dead.'

Rubio took a closer hold of Connie as together they stepped across Nurse Casey's body. She could feel the muscles in her shoulder pulling and pushing around the knife tip, and the sense of violation was making her more nauseous even than the pain. They kept shuffling along, and now Rubio was releasing her waist and digging in his pocket.

Give the psychopath his dues, his toddler act had been an Oscar-worthy performance, not to mention genius. It had kept him out of a normal prison, which would have seen him relegated to the bottom of the pecking order, and had made him one of those fascinating cases psychiatrists and psychologists loved to comment on. The only believable part of the façade now was his rage, those childlike tantrums, that loss of control. Those things, Connie thought, were entirely real but he was choosing to give in to those aspects of his personality, embracing them, as opposed to squashing them like a functioning adult.

'Here we go. Good of Nurse Casey to enter the ward looking for you. This would have been much harder to achieve without a set of keys.'

Finally they reached the ward door. Rubio left the knife sticking out of her shoulder while he pushed her against the door, his weight against her body, and checked each key until he found the one he was looking for.

'Green key fob,' he said. 'Green for go. Now, just so you know, if we meet anyone on the other side of this door, it's going to be very important that you don't try and run to them; I need you to be quiet and act frightened. I don't have to run this knife to the front of your throat, you see. I can just twist it ninety degrees, lacerate your muscles, maybe even pull it backwards and sever your spinal cord. You fancy a life as a quadriplegic?' He slipped the blade in a couple more millimetres to drive his point home. The pain made her head swim.

'No,' Connie rasped.

'Then you'll behave yourself. Now, I've put the key in the lock but I need you to turn it for me, open the door, and go through. Anyone pulls out a taser, it'll be you taking the charge.'

Connie wasn't going to argue with him.

'I'm coming out!' she called. 'This is Connie Woolwine. Clear the doorway.'

She opened up. No one spoke. In the security area there was only darkness.

'Is it a trap?' Rubio whispered.

'I don't think so,' she said. 'Was someone expecting you?'

'Don't be a smartarse. Get going.' He pushed her along the

corridor past Dr Ong's consulting room, past the staffroom, past the corridor to the laundry chute through which Tara's poor corpse had been shoved, and out onto the staircase.

'I can't make the steps,' she said. 'I feel faint.'

Rubio twisted the knife a few degrees. Connie screamed until bile rose in her throat and cut off the sound.

'The lifts are out of service thanks to the power outage. We're taking the stairs, and you are going to stay with me until I have no further use for you.'

She tried to lean forward to vomit but Rubio wasn't relinquishing his hold on the knife. All Connie managed was a deep retching noise and a stream of saliva down her top.

'Keep it together,' Rubio said, 'and I might even let you—'

He flew forwards, pushing her down as he went, the knife sinking deeper in for a tenth of a second before exiting completely, still in his hand. Rubio hit the far wall at the top of the stairs as Connie was being dragged backwards into the staff corridor then someone was stepping over the top of her, shielding her body.

Rubio got to his feet, snarling. 'Son of a bitch!' he screeched.

'Run while you can,' a man called.

Connie felt herself fading fast, bleeding badly and in too much pain to focus on what was happening around her.

'I want her,' Rubio said.

'Can't let you take her. I've got Haskin's hypodermic. You can cut me, but I'll get the sedative in you at the same time.'

It was East's voice she could hear. Connie fought to speak. 'Don't let him go,' she said. 'Baby.'

'The baby?' Rubio laughed and the sound echoed back as it bounced down the stone staircase. 'No way that fucking baby survived. It was barely alive when I pulled it out. Weak little thing just like her mother. No fight in her at all.'

'Who taught you how to do it?' Connie asked, jamming her left forefinger and thumb over the wound and pressing the sides together.

'It's a hospital, Dr Woolwine. No shortage of doctors in here. And I did that baby a favour. Every mother lets you down sooner or later. They fuck you up and leave, or they fuck your father up and he leaves.'

'Get lost, Rubio. Go wherever you're going. We won't call security if you just leave Connie alone.'

'No, she won't call security because she believes that baby is still alive, and I know how to find it. Call security and I'll have the bundle of joy put out of its misery. I can do that. You know I can.'

'I believe you,' Connie muttered. 'Don't hurt her. Please.'

'He's already gone,' East said. The torchlight was already fading as Rubio leapt down the stairs, his feet clattering down the old stone steps. 'Where's a first aid kit?'

'Security office,' Connie said, 'next to the door. There'll be another torch in there somewhere too.'

East disappeared for a minute. A new beam of light appeared from the office, then he returned, already ripping open a gauze pack and handing her surgical tape.

'That's bleeding a lot. I should get you downstairs to someone who can help you properly.'

'They're all dealing with the fire and the flood. Pack the wound, then stretch a pad over it tight and put on as much tape as you can,' she said. 'Fast.'

'Okay, but you'll need stitches,' East said, doing his best to patch her up.

'Where is Rubio?' a quiet voice called from behind them.

'He's gone. You should go back to your room, Professor,' East said.

375

'I think I'd prefer to take a look around, actually. Why are you the only one who gets to step outside the ward?'

'Have at it,' East said, his voice tinged with impatience. 'Okay, Connie, that's the best I can do, but you need to find Sidorov or someone. How do we notify reception that Rubio is missing?'

'We don't,' Connie said. 'I don't want security to know, not yet anyway. I need to find Rubio myself. He'll be heading for whoever he was working with.'

'You can't do that. He's insane. And yeah, I get the irony of a convicted serial killer who lives on the highest security wing in this place saying that, but truly, Rubio is fucked up. He would have killed you.'

'But he didn't. Professor,' she shouted, 'where's Haskin?'

'In his room, somewhat surprisingly,' he replied. 'Do you know, I think I'll take a little walk. I'm really not concerned about the prospect of being tasered. It seems worth the risk for a little fresh air.'

Connie didn't have the time or energy to fight him on it.

'Promise you won't kill anyone,' she said. 'Even if you see them with a smartphone.'

She wasn't joking.

'Agreed,' he said.

'Vince, could you get me a stab vest, please? There's one hanging on the wall in the security office. Professor, the ward keys are still in the lock. Fetch them and lock Haskin in. I should at least leave the ward with one of its patients inside.' East fetched the vest for her and she dragged it stiffly up over her lacerated shoulder then Velcroed it into place as the professor locked up.

'You'll have to help me down the stairs,' she said, grimacing with the pain. 'The elevators are out. One of you will need to hold the torch, and the other will have to help me. Can you do that?'

The professor folded his arms and lifted his chin.

'For Christ's sake,' Connie muttered. 'I'll speak at your next review, Professor, obviously.'

'Shall we?' Professor Saint motioned to the stairs.

East helped her up, and together they began their descent, the professor holding the torch, East with one arm around Connie's waist as she held the banister for support the other side. She concentrated on her breathing, on the rhythm of each step, on counting the floors as they went, with each passing minute getting the pain under control, acknowledging the agony in her shoulder but separating that from the remainder of her body, which was remarkably unharmed. By the time they reached the ground floor, she was walking unaided. Battery-powered lamps had been left every few metres along each hallway to make the place safer.

The professor handed over the torch and disappeared the second they could hear the voices of other people busy managing the crisis.

'I'm going with you,' East said.

'No, can't do that. If I'm seen with you, whoever is in this with Rubio will have a valid reason to attack me. They'll say I was aiding an escaping prisoner and that they used necessary force. I have to do this the right way.'

'So what can I do to help?'

'You can try to find Baarda – Patient B – for me. Ask around for Dr Sidorov. That's who took him off the ward. I have no idea where he'll be holding him, and it may not be safe.'

'I'm not going to get very far in my grey hoodie and joggers with a patient number printed on them. The first person who sees me unescorted will call security.'

'You're right,' Connie said. 'Come on, there are staffrooms on the ground floor of every tower.' They walked until they found one. She left East outside and reappeared with a set of scrubs.

'Best I could do,' she said. 'The room's empty. Go on in and change then bring me your uniform. I can only spare thirty seconds.'

That was all he used, thrusting the joggers into Connie's arms. She shoved them down behind a nearby plant pot, out of sight.

'Be careful,' he said.

'Vince,' Connie called after him as he walked away. 'Those other women, the ones at the hotel. Tell me you didn't kill them.'

'I didn't kill them,' he said. 'One of them was someone I cared about very much. If I find your friend, maybe one day you can repay the favour and identify the real killer.'

Chapter 33

Connie made it as far as the reception area before needing to rest and get to grips with the excruciating pain she was in. She focused on her breathing as she tried to figure out the efficient way to find Aurora. The building was vast. Aurora's kidnappers had to be inside somewhere though. They would be noticed immediately if they were outside in the storm. But there was no time. If she screwed up, if she went the wrong way now, it would all be over.

Think, she told herself. *Calm down, stop freaking out, and think*.

The view through the front doors showed cars with water over their bumpers. Given that the generators were all out of action, that meant the underground passages where she'd previously heard the baby crying had to be immersed by now.

Rubio would have headed straight for his co-conspirators, which meant they knew Connie was either gathering help or trying to find them herself.

'They could have let baby Aurora drown in the basement,' she talked it through with herself aloud, 'but there'll be a survey of damage once the flood has receded, and a police investigation with potential evidence against anyone involved. If it were me, I'd move the baby. Can't bring her inside with the staff area closed off in case she cries. Someone would hear. That leaves putting her into a vehicle and hoping the floodwaters don't rise any more, or moving her somewhere she can't and won't ever be found.'

Connie stood and watched a stream of people moving like ants between a back corridor and the front doors, lugging yet more sandbags in mute exhaustion.

The kidnappers would be tired by now, she thought. Tired of waiting to maximise the share price, cash in their stocks and bathe in their new money. Tired of caring for a baby. Tired of waiting for it to be over. And they'll need to get rid of the evidence once and for all.

'Shit,' she said, moving her feet towards the front doors. 'Let me out! I've got to get out!'

'No one goes through that way,' she was told by one of the sandbagging operatives. 'The doors are locked. Open them up now and everything we've done will be for nothing.'

'I need to get to the far side of Tower 3,' she shouted. 'How do I get out there?'

'You stupid? There's a lightning storm and a flood outside. You won't make it back.'

'There's a life at risk. So how?'

'Through the kitchens, the ramp out the back that runs left to the basement also goes right across the quad.'

He was talking to air. Connie was already running for the staff areas, past the TV rooms, past the accommodation hallway, on through the dining hall, bumping her thighs and shins on

380

tables and chairs in the narrow beam of torchlight. She took the double doors into the kitchen at a run, her good hand out in front, the doors slamming against the walls and clacking shut behind.

She ran between the metal counters, reaching out to grab a knife from a tray of potatoes that had been left mid-preparation, sticking it into the rear waistband of her trousers as she went. Connie took the exit she'd previously trodden with Boy, turning right instead of left. That pathway took her upwards, leading away from the tower and across a stretch of gravel, now muddy stone soup, with only a single destination at the top of a curve of shallow steps.

Connie slid the torch button to the off position, thanked the moon for continuing to shine through the wind and rain, and ran as fast as she could towards the incinerator block.

It was nothing more than a concrete cube with a chimney extending up into the sky. No windows. No decoration. Not so much as a sign by the front door.

Connie forced herself to slow down. The incinerator block should have been locked. When the power had gone out, normal operations would have concluded for the day. It was inconceivable that anyone would have remained at their work post in such a storm. Best-case scenario was finding it locked, with no light inside.

She reached out a hand and took hold of the doorknob. It gave the faintest squeal as it turned but kept going, and finally the door gave and Connie was able to push it forward.

Perhaps they just forgot to lock up in all the panic, her brain insisted. It might be nothing more than an oversight. Who could have foreseen that anyone might want access to that building during a superstorm?

And then she heard it, that same feeble mewling from the

basement corridors. Connie's heart lifted and sank in one overwhelming second.

Aurora was alive. She'd felt it in her gut and wanted so desperately to believe it, and here she was, finally in the same building as Tara's child with a chance – a tiny but tangible opportunity – to save her. But here Aurora was in the hands of her kidnappers, her would-be killers, alerted to the need to dispose of the baby because Connie had revealed herself to avoid being institutionalised.

Other voices now, and the baby's cries grew weaker still. A man and a woman were arguing, sniping at each other, hissing, accusing.

Connie crept in blind. No windows meant no moonlight, and she couldn't risk the torch. The voices were coming from a different room in the heart of the block, and there was nothing but the faintest glow in the distance, insufficient to light her way. Holding her hands out in front, she reminded herself that she had all the skills she needed to find her way in the dark. Unable to see colour, her world was already reduced to shades of grey. If she could only wait a moment to allow her eyes to get used to the near-black, she would find a way to proceed. What really mattered was not tripping over anything, not kicking anything, not alerting the people in possession of baby Aurora to her presence.

'Just give her to me,' a man shouted, fracturing the silence with his temper. 'I'll deal with it. I'm the one who got her to you. All you had to do was keep her alive for a few days.'

Benny Rubio. Not a shock to find him there, but Connie would rather have dealt with anyone but him. He knew she was injured, and she knew he was capable of absolutely anything. The question was, who was with him?

Connie moved forward inch by inch, feeling her way. Here

was a desk, past that a filing cabinet, after that a potted plant, which seemed both a useless and a hopeful thing to put into a place designed only to burn and destroy.

She was close now, and drew the knife from her waistband. Rubio, the baby, and the unknown woman were in the next room, the door standing a few inches open. Connie considered all the women who might be in there with him: Nurse Madani who certainly needed the money; Nurse Lightfoot, who had disliked Tara so; Dr Roth, who had done her best to disable and punish Connie.

Through the crack between the door and the frame, she could see Rubio now, in front of a vast open metal door with a blackened glass pane in the front, doing his best to light the incinerator manually with matches and a mass of scrunched-up paper while the electric ignition was out of use. *Thank God for the storm,* Connie thought.

Moving slightly to the side meant she could see baby Aurora, blanketed and held in a woman's arms. Connie's heart skipped several beats as she brought one hand to her mouth to stop herself from crying out. The past few days that had felt like a year were suddenly forgotten. Here she was, the child Tara Cameron had died for, the baby Connie had promised to find.

She craned her neck for a better view and didn't like what she saw at all. The baby was floppy, barely moving, its head resting against the woman's chest. Her skin was pale and flaky, one tiny hand fluttering delicately.

The paper firelighters Rubio was using flared and crackled. It was time to move. Whoever the woman was, Connie had no choice but to use her as a bargaining tool, exactly as Rubio had done earlier. A knife to her throat, disable the woman if that became necessary. She put her free hand against the door and prepared to barge through.

'Dr Connie! Dr Connie!' The voice came from outside, and she spun around to face it. The outer door flew open and Boy came dashing in. 'It's not safe in here. The floodwaters are rising too fast. You have to come back into the hospital.' He grabbed her arm and pulled her back towards the door. Rubio came crashing through the interior doorway, snatching the knife from her hand and taking hold of her by her injured shoulder, pushing her down to her knees.

'Let Boy go,' Connie pleaded. 'He won't say a word. This is nothing to do with him.'

'Get in here,' Rubio told Boy. 'I want a word with you.'

Rubio dragged Connie through into the incinerator room and Boy followed without a word. Connie's eyes filled with tears. There was no way of justifying it, saving one child at the expense of another's life. She should never have befriended Boy.

'I'm sorry,' Connie said. 'This is all my fault.'

The woman who'd been holding the baby stepped forward and slapped Boy hard around the back of his head.

'I told you to find a way of stopping her before she got anywhere near us. What the fuck were you doing?' she asked.

Connie's mouth dropped open.

'She was being weird in the reception hall, then she started running and I got caught in the crowd,' Boy whined.

Maeve, out of her kitchen whites and hat, was almost unrecognisable. Connie's cheeks burned with the combined shame of having been fooled so easily and the fury she felt at one woman being complicit in sadistic demise of another. But the knowledge that Boy had conspired, play-acted and befriended her was so much worse, it was nearly unbearable.

'You're part of this?' Connie exploded at him. 'Did you make friends with me on that first day deliberately?'

He grinned triumphantly. 'You believed me! Mum said all I had to do was tell a sob story. I was so nervous but then you were all kind and sympathetic, wanting to take care of me.'

'Enough,' Rubio said. 'I have to finish this and get ready to go. Give me the baby.' He held out his hands for Maeve to pass Aurora over.

'You're Boy's actual mother, right?' Connie said. 'So you know how precious that baby is. Did you really sign up for this? You can't be responsible for a child's death, in front of your own son.'

'Shut the fuck up,' Rubio ordered. 'And don't think any of that psychological bullshit is going to work with her. She's getting paid plenty for her part.'

'Don't do it, Maeve,' Connie said. 'For Boy's sake, don't let him see you do it. He'll never recover.'

'Tell her, Mum,' Boy said. His voice was gleeful. 'Tell her it like you told me.'

'Do you know how much I make per hour?' Maeve asked. 'How much Boy makes per hour? I start work at 6 a.m. every day. Sometimes I don't finish until 8 p.m. if we're short-staffed. That's six days a week. It costs slightly more than ten times my annual wages to keep a single prisoner on Heaven Ward for a year. I've done nothing but work hard and do right, and sick fucks like him—' she nodded her head at Rubio '—get all the money spent on them, after what they've done? Well, enough. And Nurse Tara with her "Don't swear in front of your son," and "Your child shouldn't be working here; he should still be in education." She didn't even need to work for a living, did you know that? Condescending bitch.'

'Fuck's sake, give me the baby!' Rubio shouted. 'The incinerator's ready. Let's do it before anyone notices the smoke.'

'Give it to her. Push them both in together.' Maeve smirked. 'You've got to kill her anyway now she's seen us.'

'I was going to have a bit of fun with her, but there's no time now, so whatever. On your feet.' He pulled Connie up by her hair and Maeve thrust baby Aurora into her arms.

Connie looked down into the tiny face, pulled the blankets tightly around the baby, tucking the ends in, making sure Aurora's head was well covered, checking that she was padded everywhere in preparation for what was about to happen.

'Don't do this,' Connie pleaded. 'If Aurora survives, there'll be less to answer for.'

'Stand facing the furnace door,' Rubio commanded. 'Move!'

Connie held the baby against her stomach with her left lower arm, feeling the heat of the furnace as she stepped closer, smelling the remains of the last load to burn. As she held the child, knowing she was about to do what no good mother might feel able to do, Connie had a millisecond to wonder about her own unborn children. Their faces, natures, their unwritten futures.

'God, I've missed this,' Rubio said. 'First Tara, then you.'

Connie could feel his hot spittle on her neck as he spoke, and shuddered. Benny Rubio was disgustingly excited and out of control. If the worst was going to happen, then the very least she could do was hold Aurora, wrap her up and fill her last moment on earth with love. Connie could be everything a mother should be as they died together. Not that she had any intention of going out without a fight, however unlikely the reprieve.

'Reach out and open the door,' he ordered.

'I want to know what happened to Joe Yarowski,' she stalled. 'Did he really kill himself?'

Rubio snorted his derision. 'Didn't take much persuasion

when he knew his precious Nurse Tara was gone and never coming back. As far as that big idiot was concerned, Nurse Tara died in premature labour and everyone on the staff was lying to him about it. Her earring was all the evidence it took to push him over the edge. That, and a bit of advice about how to open his wrist with a little piece of plastic.'

'You managed to set all that up on your own? You must have had help, Rubio. You can tell me now. Isn't that the least I deserve at this stage?'

'You want some sort of tell-all monologue and confession? Go fuck yourself. This isn't some cheesy movie. Now open the door. It's the fastest death I'm going to offer you.'

'Get out of here, Boy,' Maeve ordered, reaching to push him away. 'Go back to the towers and get our stuff. We're leaving the second the road opens again.'

'Leave me alone,' Boy slapped at her hands. 'I want to watch.'

Connie put one shaking hand on the furnace door handle. It was about twice her width, opening a couple of feet from ground level and went up above her head height, obviously designed to push loads in from trolleys.

'You go in nice and fast, I reckon you'll hardly feel a thing. There won't be any oxygen left in there now anyway. You stop, you pause, I cut your throat and throw the baby in alone. You'd rather do the decent thing and go with her, right?'

Rubio laughed. Connie hated him with a passion that drowned out the terror, soaked up all the adrenaline, and left her with a rage that knew no limits. She opened the door a few inches, letting the first blast of heat out sideways.

'Last chance to save your souls,' Connie told them.

'Too late for me,' Rubio said. 'I'm already destined to burn. Now go!'

Connie took three deep breaths, closed her eyes against the ferocious heat, and pulled the door fully open, bracing against what was about to happen. Rubio shoved Connie hard in each shoulder blade into the mouth of the furnace.

In the same moment, Connie dropped the baby from as low as she could, praying that Aurora's neck and brain would survive the fall. Squatting, Connie reached over her right shoulder with her left hand to grab Rubio's wrist, letting his forward momentum take him over her back and into the mouth of the furnace, rolling her right shoulder down to guide him in then driving his body forward on top of her own, ducking to avoid going with him.

Rubio reached out to grab whatever he could to stop himself. His fingers found the inner rim of the door and he screamed, instinctively pulling his fingers away again at the heat, giving Connie, panting hard, the split second she needed to get upright and shove his body into the furnace, slamming the door onto his legs as he tried to kick his way out. She could see his limbs jerking, shadowy, past the tiny window, hair flaming, as he fought for the few seconds it was possible to survive. Seconds later, his fight was over. Just the roar of the all-consuming flames.

Connie froze momentarily, slack-jawed. It would have been her in there, her body reduced to nothing but a misshapen, charred mass, an artwork of agony, had she not been prepared to do the unthinkable and simply drop the baby. She only hoped she hadn't saved her own life at the expense of Aurora's.

As she turned, Connie saw Maeve's eyes swing to spot Rubio's dropped knife at the same moment she did. As one, they dived for it. Adrenaline and fitness gave Connie the edge. Her fingers hit the target first. She didn't hesitate, slashing out with the blade and tearing it across Maeve's face. Maeve cried out and turned to run, but Connie had already learned what it meant to leave an enemy standing. Lurching forward, she grabbed the back of Maeve's left leg and stuck the knife in, wrenching it across to sever the tendons at the back of her knee. Maeve went down screaming, thrashing and clutching at the wound. She wouldn't be getting up again without help.

Connie staggered to her feet and turned to Boy, who stood in the corner, mouth hanging open, eyes burning.

'You shouldn't have done that,' he said. His voice was flat but his eyes were venom.

'Your mother will survive,' Connie told him. 'Nurse Tara didn't. This baby probably won't.' Too terrified to find out yet whether her efforts had been in vain, she picked up Aurora and slid the tightly packed bundle of baby inside the stab vest without looking to see if she was still alive. 'Why would you get involved in something like this? The lies you told me!'

'And every word you told me wasn't a lie?' he spat. '"Be yourself," you said. "Follow your own goals." We had nothing! All we did was work and live in this shithole. This was just one week, then we would never have to work, ever again.'

'Well, when you get out of prison, you'll have a fine career ahead of you as an actor,' Connie said, but she felt no victory in her words. Boy was a victim too. Loveless parenting and a careless society had conspired to make him what he was, and it broke her heart to witness it. 'You sure as hell fooled me. Stay with your mother. I'll send help for her.'

'Fuck you,' Boy said.

Connie kept the knife out where Boy could see it and shuffled backwards towards the door to the incinerator block, Rubio's fiery body providing enough fuel to light her way.

'Was it you who chased me along the lake wall that night?'

Boy laughed. Gone was the sweet, childlike personality he'd presented before. This was an altogether different version of

389

Boy. More worldly. The laughter was cruel and mocking. 'You were so scared, it was funny.'

'And was it you who came into my room through the passage-ways and stole my cell phone?' she asked from the external doorway.

'It was,' he said. 'You were having a nightmare. I thought about holding a pillow over your face.'

'What stopped you?'

'I thought it would be cool to see you lose your mind,' Boy said. 'My mistake.'

Connie let the door slam shut, then turned and ran.

Chapter 34

Connie made it back into the staff areas before she saw anyone, then she was ushered out of the danger zone with a swift reprimand, the amateur firefighters having given up the fight with Tower 3. They were going to have to leave it to burn, and now they were evacuating everyone from the middle tower too, shifting them across to the far end of the building.

The flooding had worsened in the front section of The Institution, the sandbags too little too late. The only good news was that there was no way the fire would be able to spread at ground level, even if the third tower collapsed entirely. Now it was just a matter of moving all patients, staff and essential equipment to make sure they could survive until the storm ended and the mountain pass reopened.

All too aware of Aurora's perilous health, Connie knew she had to get her to a medic as soon as possible, not to mention a security guard to keep her safe from further threat, but first she needed to get her hands on the satellite phone to call in

391

specialist paediatric care and the police, and that meant accessing Director Le Fay's office.

The door was unlocked. Connie entered quickly and quietly, having picked up a battery lamp from one of the hallways. Inside the doorway, she froze.

Baarda was bound to a chair by cable ties. Sidorov, bleeding from the head and looking badly concussed, was on another chair. Vince East was in the far corner, a gun being pointed into his chest by the security guard Connie had met at the contractors' vehicles exit. His name was Jock, she remembered.

On a sofa, one long leg crossed over the other, was Dr Ong, a taser in his hand. He stood as she entered.

'Dr Connie,' he said. 'I owe you an apology. You tried to tell me there was a plot going on among my team and I didn't listen. Worse than that, I put you in Dr Roth's care who I understand abused the trust I put in her. Rest assured, her appointment will be terminated with immediate effect.'

Aurora gave a feeble cry and fluttered tiny, weak fingers against Connie's chest. Connie took the baby from her top and held shaking fingertips over her chest. Her heartbeat was fluttering and irregular, but she was hanging on.

'My priority is to obtain medical assistance for this baby. I need the satellite phone too. I have to notify the police and Tara Cameron's family. Dr Ong, could you release Baarda? I need his help. Jock, you can lower your weapon. Vince East has done nothing but assist me.'

'I'm sorry, none of that's possible,' Ong said. 'Mr East is dangerous and high-risk. Patient B cannot be released until I've seen the proper paperwork or had a court order. I won't be sued and I won't have my reputation dragged through the mud for making bad decisions. We can, of course, organise whatever medical assistance is required.'

'Dr Ong, this baby's all that matters. I need you to do as I'm asking, and quickly,' Connie said. 'I informed you that Patient B was a colleague of mine placed here by the police. I gave you my full name and explained my position. The fact that I'm holding a baby in my arms should be all the proof you need that everything I told you was correct. Now get Director Le Fay on the satellite phone so that we can release Mr Baarda.'

'The satellite phone is out of action. I came in here to use it, found that Dr Sidorov had taken Patient B off the ward without my consent, became concerned that it was an escape attempt and dropped the phone after calling security for help.'

Connie moved behind the sofa to the base point for the satellite phone, and saw the pieces of it on the floor.

'That's unfortunate,' she said slowly. 'Most satellite phones are like bricks. Takes something to smash them. Baarda, what's the deal with Sidorov?'

'One of ours,' Baarda said.

'Sorry, I must insist that you don't speak with Patient B at the moment. He's under my care, and out of the ward I would be worried about you inciting him to violence.'

Connie clutched the baby closer to her chest and stared at Ong. In the back of her mind she could hear the chime of the bells in his specially made Newton's cradle.

'Dr Sidorov, can you walk?' she asked.

He nodded and made his way to her.

'Are you safe to carry her?' she checked, before handing Aurora over. Sidorov nodded and took Aurora gently in his arms, and stroking her face. 'Do whatever you can for her. She's been through so much already. She deserves to meet her family.'

'She looks badly dehydrated, and I don't like her skin colour,'

Sidorov said. 'I need to get her hooked up to an IV drip immediately.'

'I am still in charge here. In charge of the whole facility, in fact, during Director Le Fay's absence,' Ong reminded her.

'Then you'll want this baby to get medical attention as quickly as possible,' Connie replied, her voice hard. 'Check out her neck and skull with care. I had no choice but to drop her.'

'Come with us,' Sidorov said. 'You need medical attention yourself. You've lost a lot of blood.'

Connie looked down at her clothes. They were a mess and she must have looked terrible, but not all the blood was hers and she had bigger things to worry about.

'I'm good,' she said. 'Just go. And don't let that baby out of your sight. She should be in a locked room with round-the-clock monitoring until we can get an air ambulance here.'

Sidorov nodded and took the baby from her, slipping quickly and quietly through the door.

'I had a chat with Benny Rubio earlier,' Connie told Ong. 'It was strange because he clearly has some experience with hypnotherapy and yet you told me it's not something you use at The Institution.'

'I don't understand the context for you having that conversation with my patient at all,' Ong said.

'Hypnotherapy is a great way to impart information. People who have short attention spans or neurological disorders often benefit from it, because the subconscious is able to give the conscious mind and memory a bit of a boost. Especially, say, in a demanding, high-pressure situation when you need someone to be able to act decisively.'

'That's all very interesting, but I have a facility to manage. Guard, return Mr East to his room on Heaven Ward, and send another officer in to deal with Patient B who will need to remain incarcerated until I'm satisfied of his true status.'

'I want to hear about Benny Rubio,' East said. 'What did he do, exactly?'

'Jack, take East up to his room now!' Ong ordered.

'It's Jock,' Connie said. 'Given that you're currently in charge, you should probably know the names of your staff. And actually the Rubio question is an interesting one. He admitted to killing Nurse Tara. He performed a caesarean on her and left her body in a laundry basket that someone else moved off the ward. Her body was deposited down the laundry chute, working on the assumption that it would go straight into the van and not be found for a day or so. The thing is, Rubio's help was clearly enlisted by someone who didn't have the appetite to get their hands messy.'

'This sounds like something you should be discussing with the police,' Ong said. 'Certainly not in front of other patients. It's very disturbing. Come along, East. I'll escort you upstairs myself while I go and check on Mr Rubio to see what sort of nonsense he's been spreading.'

'Rubio's not there,' Connie said.

Ong glared at her.

She took a few steps in Baarda's direction, keeping the knife she was holding hidden. Ong walked across the room to stand in her path before she could reach Baarda.

'Someone persuaded Rubio to get involved. Someone with all the necessary knowledge, or access to it, of how to perform a caesarean. I looked it up. It's not a difficult operation if the mother's survival doesn't matter and you're not squeamish in the least. Rubio, woman hater that he was, was the perfect candidate.'

'That's enough,' Ong said. 'I suspect you are still suffering from PTSD; certainly you're sounding deranged. Guard, never mind Mr East. Dr Connie needs to be taken to the quiet room on Heaven Ward. I'll have a formal assessment done as soon as possible.'

'Don't do it, Jock,' East said. 'You can tell who the deranged one is, right?'

Jock looked from Connie to Ong to East.

'I have no idea what's going on here,' Jock said. 'But I'm willing to let Dr Connie finish. Don't you move a muscle, Mr East. I haven't had to shoot a gun for years, but I don't suppose triggers have changed all that much.'

'If you don't want to lose your job, you'll do as you're told right now,' Ong said.

'Don't much care for threats,' Jock replied. 'Don't much care for this job either, truth be told.'

'Rubio had to be trained to do what he did. And he had to be told there was something in it for him. It would have taken someone with real authority to persuade him that the offer had legs. Until the storm came along and changed a few things, I'm guessing Rubio thought he was getting out on a review or perhaps the agreement was that he'd be transferred to somewhere low-security. One of your treasured "guests" finally being made better? That narrative would have suited you well. None of the nursing staff had the authority to promise any such thing. And the patients all hate Roth. No one would have believed an offer from her.'

'Amen to that,' East chipped in.

Ong sighed, tutted and backed off to stand next to the fireplace.

'Which leaves you. You with your cosy, private consulting room, with your undoubted knowledge of hypnotherapy, with the chiming balls, perfect for inducing a hypnotic state. Which is why when I tried a different approach, Rubio was not just immune to it, but very well equipped to pretend that he was actually hypnotised. You used the hypnotherapy to train him how to perform the operation.'

'That is the wildest conjecture I ever heard,' Ong said.

'I'd have thought so too, only when I first arrived someone told me to consider why anyone would ever choose to come and work in such a place. You have to want the money to work here. Really, really want it. And you're basically a glorified key master given that none of the patients incarcerated are ever meant to leave. So a dead end in professional terms. I can see why the prospect of being a multi-multi-millionaire might have been tempting.'

'These conspiracy theories are doing nothing to help me believe that you're not delusional,' Ong said.

'You knew what Roth was capable of, but you left me in her care. That was your first mistake. And you recruited two other members of staff who were desperate, people on the bottom rung of the ladder, who honestly believed they would disappear off into the sunset with a lifetime's supply of cash. Here's your problem. Boy came into my room, took my phone, made me paranoid, chased me along the lake wall, then he made sure he was available to give you all the reasons you needed to take me out of the picture.'

'Prove it,' Ong said. 'Prove just one tiny bit of it.'

'Baarda wasn't aggressive with you that first day. You slipped something into the coffee that Tom Lord made, because you knew as soon as we turned up that our arrival wasn't a coincidence. You wanted to see how we'd react.'

'You're desperate,' he said.

'Boy's mother, Maeve, has been disabled and is waiting for help. She can't currently walk. Boy is with her. You think they won't tell the police everything when it's them or you? They're

397

going to cut a deal with the prosecution. Look what Maeve was willing to do for her son's future already.'

There was a moment when no one moved and no one spoke.

Ong grabbed the fire iron faster than Connie had anticipated, arcing it through the air as he went for Connie. She raised her arms in front of her face, dropping the lamp that smashed at her feet, leaving the room in darkness once more.

Then Ong was gone and all they could hear was a choking, gargling noise.

'Come near me or try to shoot, and I guarantee you, Patient B will die,' Ong said. 'Dr Woolwine, if you don't want your colleague's blood on your hands, I suggest you go into the far corner and join Mr East. Talk as you move so I can hear you going in the correct direction.'

'Fine,' Connie said, walking to the far end of the room. 'Don't hurt him. There's no need. Like you said, everything is speculation. It still needs to be proved at trial. It won't benefit you to hurt anybody at this point.'

'Can I talk?' East said. 'Only I'm really angry. I mean, you've been in charge of my care for a while now. And what, all the time you were lecturing and asking me to open up and exploring my mental state, you were planning to murder the only decent person in this hellhole? Jesus, where are they going to put you when they find you guilty? Oh shit, dude, I just realised. There's no way they're going to believe you're sane. I mean, training a serial killer to cut the baby out of a nurse, then holding that baby to ransom? You know, Joe Yarowski's cell is free right now. I'm thinking they'll just change the sheets and get it ready for you to join us. Can you imagine that?'

'Shut up!' Ong screamed.

Baarda's breathing was hoarse, laboured, wet-sounding. Connie could hear the chair being dragged towards the doors.

'Can you imagine if they promote Roth to ward consultant?' Vince belly-laughed. 'Oh fuck, dude, she's gonna fry your brains until you're just sitting in the corner dribbling like the guy at the end of that book. Can't remember the name. What is it, Dr Connie?'

'*One Flew Over the Cuckoo's Nest*?'

'That's the one! You know how Roth likes a cook-out. She's going to be waiting for you with the dial turned up to ten, Dr Ong.'

'No one will believe any of you, and they certainly won't believe that servant and her idiot of a son. I'm getting out of here and—'

The shot rang out directly in front of the doorway.

Connie stopped breathing, and Vince gave a startled cry.

'I'm okay,' Baarda said. 'Could someone please release my wrists and ankles?'

'Open the door,' Connie said. 'There's light in the hallway.'

As the room became visible, the scene revealed itself. Jock had manoeuvred his way around the edge of the room to wait for Ong, making sure he fired the gun directly into his head, up away from where Baarda might have been in the line of fire. Even Vince had helped in his own unique way by distracting him with pointless chatter.

Ong was on the floor, on his side, a chunk of his skull opened up – she could actually see part of his brain, and it didn't bother her at all. What she was even more pleased about was that Dr Antonio Ong, perhaps the most intellectually dishonest psychiatrist ever to have practised, was hanging in there. Still taking breaths, albeit short and ragged, one eye still blinking, mouth opening and closing like some new species of deep-water fish.

'Hey.' Connie lay down and put her head on the floor to

look him straight in his functioning eye. 'I'm glad you're still with us. There are a couple of things I wanted to say to you. I'm not sure if I'd prefer you to survive and spend the rest of your days the way you are now, or if I'd rather watch you die here in front of me, in agony. You know, I genuinely believe Tara was the only person on your ward who thought in the terms you pretended to. She wanted to treat the patients like guests. She had faith that they could be rehabilitated. Nurse Tara listened to you. And the worst thing about all that, granted among a lot of options, is that you didn't even have the balls to kill her yourself. Are you phobic about blood, Dr Ong? Is that why you didn't perform the caesarean yourself?' She thought about it for a moment. 'No, I don't think that's it. I think you believed you were just too good for it. Let someone else dirty their hands, right? Not you, with your photos on yachts. I bet you thought you'd finally be able to buy one of your own – or was it a vineyard you were after? Your own island, maybe?'

Blood bubbled up through his mouth and his breathing became no more than a series of liquid-filled hiccups.

'I hope it hurts,' Connie whispered. 'I hope it hurts so fucking much that you're lying there wishing I would shove my hand into your gaping brain and squeeze the life right out of it. But first, I want you to know that people will study your mental state and conclude that you weren't ill at all. Just greedy. Greedy and vile and soulless and utterly, utterly undeserving of the life you had. And the all-too-speedy death.'

No more blood bubbles. No more blinks. No more twitching fingers. The end when it came was anticlimactic. Connie wished he'd suffered more, but she needed to get to Aurora, to make sure she was all right. Then to phone Johannes Cameron, and Keira and Francis Lyle.

She looked up to see Jock reaching down for her. Gentle Jock with his carved animals – who had taken all the information in, made a judgement, made a decision, and been brave enough to act. He pulled her to her feet, patted her shoulder, then released her and watched as she rushed to Baarda to cut his bonds.

'Brodie, you okay?' Connie asked gently. 'Is your neck damaged?'

'Seriously, you look like death, and you're asking if I'm hurt?' Baarda asked, standing and rubbing his wrists. 'What on earth happened to you?'

'Nothing much. I mean, I was committed, nearly given electroconvulsive therapy, stabbed, taken hostage, captured again, and almost pushed into the incinerator. But I found Aurora and when I realised she was still alive, none of it mattered any more. I can't believe that bastard dropped the satellite phone.'

'Not to worry,' Jock said. 'Storm's passing. Rain's stopped. Won't be long before help comes from the outside.'

Connie stopped to listen. The wind had dropped to almost nothing, and the constantly lashing water was down to a drizzle.

'Thank God for you, Jock. I'm so sorry for what you had to do.'

'That's all right, Dr Connie,' he said. 'It can be my parting piece. Feels like time to retire. Not sure I want to go back to sitting in that hut in the car park.'

'No,' Connie said. 'I think you have better things to do. There are warmer places to carve wood.'

'Indeed. Now I suppose I should go and make an effort to retrieve Mr East. Looks like he slipped out while we were talking. You said he saved your life, is that right?'

'He did, Jock. Mine, which also means he helped save baby

Aurora. He's no threat – that's my assessment anyway. You should probably concentrate on finding Professor Gregor Saint first. He's not exactly stable. Leave East a while until the professor is back in custody. I'm sure there are plenty of other people needing help right now.'

'Very good,' Jock said. 'If you two are quite all right, I'll be getting on.'

He slipped quietly out and left them standing in the half-light.

'Seriously, I thought Sidorov had taken you somewhere to kill you. You scared the hell out of me. Don't do that again!'

'Oh really? How about we make it a policy to always assume that anyone who calls convicted serial killers "guests" is as psychotic as they are?'

'Good call,' Connie said. 'Let's go check on Aurora. And I could use a Band-Aid on my shoulder.'

'You are ridiculously understated,' Baarda said, as they left to find the baby. 'I thought the British had the monopoly on that, but you really are quite skilled.'

'Stop it. You'll make me blush,' Connie said with a laugh.

'I'm not actually sure that's possible.'

Chapter 35

Director Le Fay landed by helicopter at first light on Saturday with a specialist paediatric crew, but first out and running across the landing pad towards the entrance was Johannes Cameron, closely followed by Tara's mother and father. Francis Lyle had his arm around his wife's shoulders. They followed their son-in-law towards the group of waiting medics who would usher them inside to where baby Aurora was awaiting an assessment for fitness to fly, and to be bundled up, monitored and supported as she was transferred to a different hospital. Connie didn't rush to join them. The family had far better things to do than debrief her and Baarda. All that had happened until that moment paled into insignificance compared to the prospect of holding Aurora in their arms.

Connie followed behind at a respectful distance. She was, after all, a reminder of their previous, awful visit.

Aurora might have been waiting for them. She lay comfortably in a nest of soft blankets, the drip and monitor not

403

bothering her at all. As Johannes Cameron stepped inside, everyone else a few steps behind, the room hushed. He walked to his daughter's side, and the only sound was his awed sigh.

'Can I—' he whispered.

'She'll be fine,' Sidorov told him. 'Go ahead and pick her up.'

Johannes' hands were shaking as he bent over the cot, and his tears began falling as he lifted his daughter to nestle against his chest. Aurora turned her face into his warmth and fluttered tiny fingers against the stubble that had grown on his chin since Connie had last seen him. He sobbed, burying his face against the last living remnant of his wife, and Francis Lyle stepped forward to comfort him.

Keira Lyle hung back, keeping her distance. Hers were the only hands not shaking, the only dry eyes. Connie studied the muscles in Keira's jaw and neck as they flexed, her lips barely covering her teeth, her stillness and concentration marking her effort to appear normal.

Connie moved forward and laid a gentle hand on Keira's arm. She flinched. Connie said nothing but nodded towards the corridor, away from the extraordinary reunion. Keira followed her out and Connie found a quiet room across the corridor, shutting the door behind them.

'I can't touch her,' Keira whispered. 'I've spent every second of the last week hoping beyond hope that we'd find her alive, and now I can hardly bear it.'

'Of course you can't,' Connie said. 'Part of your brain is telling you that feeling joy now would be traitorous. How dare you replace your own lost baby with another one? How can you even contemplate feeling maternal again, loving another little girl when yours is waiting to be put into a grave?'

Keira glared at her, made fists with her hands, but the anger only lasted for an instant before it dissolved. Her mouth twisted into an open grimace and she howled, clutching her stomach, bending in half, a lightning-stuck tree of grief.

'Your husband doesn't feel it quite like you do, does he? Not even Johannes. And you can't understand how it is that they're carrying on, that they've found this ray of hope in the wake of so much endless pain. That's making it worse for you, because in the middle of all the loss, you thought you'd hit rock bottom then suddenly you hate your own husband and son-in-law.'

Keira cried harder, saline and saliva mixing and pooling on the floor below her.

'Let it out,' Connie said. 'It's poisoning you, so let's finish this.'

They waited, Keira crying, spewing a river of bile and bitterness and self-loathing.

As her tears slowed, she reached out a hand to the wall for support, and inch by inch, straightened her body.

'I can't recover from this,' she gasped. 'When we heard the baby was safe, I was expecting something to change. To feel relief. Anything. But I still want to die. Even now, with her just in there, all I want is to not feel any more.' She ran an immaculately ironed shirt sleeve over her face, leaving it sodden. 'Am I not human? Am I the same as the monsters in this hellhole?'

'No,' Connie said. 'You're the opposite of them. Many of the men and women incarcerated here find it hard to feel any emotion at all. You're feeling too much. It's like trying to stay on your feet while you're being hit by a tsunami.'

'Why me and not them?'

'You mean Johannes and your husband?' Connie asked.

Keira nodded. 'Because Tara grew inside you. From the second you learned you were pregnant, your brain began an age-old battle between love and fear. Every second of every day. You adored your daughter, you were terrified for her, sometimes you were terrified of her; in the teenage years you'd have been terrified that your bond was weakening. You were addicted to the love you felt for her and resentful of the fact that it over-whelmed everything else you'd ever felt or achieved in your life. And it's not that fathers – men – love less. It's that you grew every cell in Tara's body. She was you, in most ways. How could you not be contemplating death right now when part of you is already dead? That's what the issue is. You're walking around almost physically attached to cells that were once the most vibrant part of you, and now all you feel is their dead weight behind you. Every step must be an agony.'

'Yes,' she sobbed. 'Yes.'

'Would you sit a minute with me, Keira, like we did before?'

Slowly, sloth-like, she moved one arm, one foot, shifted the balance of her body, until she finally collapsed in a chair. Connie moved another seat across so that their knees were almost touching, and took Keira's ice-cold hands in her own. Her pain might be psychological rather than physical, but Connie knew that Keira's own death would not be far away unless she chose to start living again. Dying of a broken heart was not just the stuff of fairy tales.

'The name of the man who killed Tara was Benny Rubio. He was psychiatrically ill, but he was also evil. It's important to acknowledge that because too often society contextualises the bad things people do as somehow outside of the person who does them. Rubio had a deeply troubled childhood, but he funnelled it into something truly dark. Say his name.'

Keira tried to speak but choked on the words.

'You have to do this,' Connie said. 'Say his name. You can't let him have any power over you.'

'Benny Rubio,' Keira said quietly, the words no more than a strangled mew in the back of her throat.

'Good,' Connie said. 'Now clear your mind of everything else and picture the image I'm about to describe to you. I want it in full colour inside your mind. Squeeze my hands if you're ready to do that.' Connie felt her fingertips flex weakly. 'Benny Rubio didn't just take Tara from you. He tried to take Aurora. He put your granddaughter in my arms and he tried to push us both into the incinerator.' Keira gripped Connie's fingers even harder. 'I had no choice but to drop Aurora. I kept her as low in my arms as I possibly could to minimise the fall.' Keira's hands were painfully tight around Connie's now. 'But he failed. The force he tried to use against me to shove us into the incinerator was his own undoing. I felt the weight of him fly forward over my back. That dead weight was terrible just for the seconds I felt it, but ultimately it shifted, Keira. That dead weight will leave you, too. Say it.'

Keira shook her head. It was a tiny movement.

'Stop it,' Connie said. 'Stop insisting that you will always feel so much pain. You're doing it because you think you have to own that pain, but you don't. All emotional pain has to have a time limit. It has to, because otherwise it just becomes an excuse not to live. Now say it.'

'The dead weight will leave me too,' she said. She didn't believe it then, Connie knew, but she would come to, in time.

'Benny Rubio went over my back and into the mouth of the incinerator,' Connie said. 'He knew what was happening. I lifted my back as he went over to make sure I formed an incline so he couldn't stop his body from moving forwards. He tried to grab the lip of the incinerator to pull himself back out but it was too hot and his fingers refused to grip it. Can you imagine that, Keira, can you see it?'

'I can,' she said, her voice tiny and closed off. A child hiding in a wardrobe after a nightmare, too scared to call for help, too scared to open the door.

'But as I shut and latched the door, even as he started to burn, Benny Rubio managed to squirm around in that incinerator. He managed to bang on the glass. His hair was already on fire. So were his clothes. There was no oxygen left and he knew he had only seconds to live.

'Those seconds were a lifetime of agony. He suffered every microsecond of the pain he inflicted on other people, as if it were decades. His scream reached beyond the glass and metal. The only reason there were no tears on his face was because his skin was already melting.'

Connie's fingertips were swelling with the pressure on them, but she had to finish.

'He burned and charred before my eyes, ashes flying from him. You could hear the spitting as the fat flew out of his body. Benny Rubio burned and burned and burned. Say it.'

That time Keira paused for only half a second.

'Benny Rubio burned and burned and burned,' she said.

'Again,' Connie told her.

'Benny Rubio burned and burned and burned.'

'Good,' Connie said. 'Whenever you think of him, you're going to say that phrase, either out loud or in your head. And you're going to remember the image of him behind that glass. What are you going to say?'

'Benny Rubio burned and burned and burned.'

'All right,' Connie said. 'Try relaxing your hands now.'

Keira gasped as she looked down, peeling her locked fingers off Connie's one by one.

'Sorry,' she said.

'No more sorry,' Connie told her. 'That stops too. No more apologies for how you feel or how you need to express those feelings. And don't believe anyone who tells you that healing works best through forgiveness. That's such bull.'

Keira gave a surprised laugh then slammed her mouth shut to cut off the sound.

'Sor—' She stopped herself halfway through the word.

'Laughing is okay, too. Angry laughing. Ironic laughing. Crazy laughing. Sad laughing. All of it. But anger most of all, because that's the appropriate response. Not forgiveness. Forgiveness, understanding, mitigation – that's a crock of shit. Be furious, punch walls, go into the pantry and scream, throw things and break things. But then remember this . . .'

'Benny Rubio burned and burned and burned.' It was the strongest voice Connie had heard her use. Keira took a deep breath and said, 'I'm ready to meet my granddaughter now.'

Keira stood, and Connie followed her to the door, but then Keira stopped and Connie followed suit. 'I hope you don't mind, Dr Woolwine, but would you not accompany me? I'm so grateful for everything you did, including to that evil bastard Ong. The police gave us the details. But I want to remember you here, in this room, just as we are. I need this. I just don't want to take it with me to Aurora.'

'That's a really good idea,' Connie said. 'Aurora's amazing and she's beautiful. It's within your power – you and Francis and Johannes – to make sure she's not affected by too much of it. Keep her free from the past.'

'I will,' Keira said. 'Thank you.'

Connie let her go, and found a place to sit a while as Aurora was fussed over by an adoring father and grandparents who would move heaven and earth for her. The weight of it all began slowly to slip from her. It was impossible to witness so much pain and not absorb some of it, she thought. The human brain was a sponge. Connie tried to focus on wringing hers out, shedding some of the excess stress and fear that she'd been carrying.

The worst of it, even after she'd saved Aurora's life, was that several hours had passed before she'd been sure the baby would survive. She blamed herself, as irrational as it was, for dropping her. Connie knew she would be reliving that moment in her mind for years to come, but the real culprits for the baby's perilous health had been a lack of nutrients, and shock.

Aurora, though, had been blessed with her mother's spirit. She'd clung to life the whole time she was being barely cared for by Maeve, kept alive solely for the purpose of ensuring that the payments were made. She'd fought to survive as Connie had almost given up hope. Sidorov had done his best for her, and it was he who sought Connie out after handing her care to the paediatric team.

'You all right?' Sidorov asked, sitting next to her as she sipped coffee in the staff lounge. 'I was expecting you to come back in with Mrs Lyle.'

'I'm fine,' she said. 'Just giving everyone some space. How about you? It's been a rough few days.'

'It has. I'm not sure The Institution can survive this. The staff exodus has already begun. I think Le Fay's inbox is pretty much flooded with staff resignation notices. Mine among them.'

'I don't blame you,' Connie said. 'I'm sorry we got off on the wrong foot. I didn't know who to trust, and for a while there I thought you were involved. Director Le Fay warned me that an incident had been flagged from a hospital you'd worked at in the past. What happened?'

Sidorov sighed deeply and hung his head. 'Back in Belarus,

during my medical training, a nurse discovered through mutual friends that I was briefly in a relationship with a fellow medical student. A male student. Homosexuality may no longer be illegal in Belarus but that doesn't mean it's not discriminated against. My life was made very difficult indeed, and I ended up in a physical altercation with another doctor who was bullying me. I'm not proud of it. I should never have lost my temper and lashed out, but I'd been pushed to my limits. I was given the option to stay and face disciplinary proceedings and potential criminal proceedings, or to leave quietly with no fuss and a reference. I chose to leave, for obvious reasons, and I ended up here.'

'Is that why you made a pass at me so quickly? Why you make passes at your other female co-workers?'

Blood rushed to darken his cheeks. 'Predictable and pathetic, I know. I suppose I've been over-compensating. I felt conflicted about my past and concerned about how it might continue to affect my professional reputation. Branded, almost. I'm not a violent person by nature, and I have no idea why I suddenly behaved like that. I think it's why I've felt able to work with the patients here. I understand that if you apply enough pressure to anyone, they can snap.'

'I'm sorry for what you went through,' Connie said. 'The world is terribly slow to change, and those sorts of prejudices are generational.'

'And I'm sorry for making a pass at you,' he replied. 'You're really not my type. Too prickly and, honestly, you're slightly odd. No offence.'

'It may be a lost-in-translation kind of thing, but I don't think you've properly grasped the meaning of no offence.' She smiled. 'But don't worry. I get the *odd* thing a lot. We're good.'

An orderly appeared to let them know the helicopter was

preparing for take-off. Connie and Sidorov joined the crowd of people gathering to wave them goodbye as Aurora was wheeled out, still monitored, for transfer.

Johannes Cameron appeared, hugging Connie hard for a few seconds, before racing to catch up with his baby. Francis Lyle was next in line, offering her a sombre hand to shake.

'I didn't believe you could do it,' he said.

'Belief is for fools,' Connie said. 'All I ever do is wait and see.'

He stepped in closer, still clutching her hand. 'Whatever you said to my wife . . . thank you. I've been worried.'

'There's no need for that,' Connie said. 'The women in your family love hard so they lose even harder. Don't be surprised if Keira makes a few holes in your walls along the way.'

'Should I ignore them? The holes, I mean.'

'If it were me, I'd frame them,' Connie said. 'It's no good plastering over emotions. They're like damp walls. Ultimately, they just keep staining the paintwork. Better to celebrate them.'

'You know, you're very . . .' He couldn't seem to find the word.

'She knows,' Sidorov said over her shoulder. 'She gets that a lot.'

They waved as the helicopter took off, and disappeared quietly one by one, in their own directions.

Baarda appeared and notified her that their own helicopter would be arriving within the hour. Jock came to say goodbye to them both, slipping a tiny wooden owl into Connie's hand.

'I'm a little late. Could you send that on to the baby for when she's older? I don't believe in angels per se, but I do believe nature watches over us and does its best to preserve what's good in the world.'

'Thank you, Jock.' Connie gave him a long, tender hug. 'It's beautiful. I'll make sure it gets to her.'

Baarda said nothing, but gripped and shook the hand of the man who'd saved his life.

Connie and Baarda were checked over, patched up, and spent some time with the police providing statements. Over the next week, Connie knew they'd be spending a lot more time explaining how Benny Rubio's ashes came to be in the incinerator, and how Maeve's tendons came to be slashed, but it would all eventually end in justice largely being done.

Jock had found Professor Gregor Saint, and returned him to Heaven Ward. Connie had asked that Saint's assistance to her be recognised in the form of an additional weekly book allowance, which Director Le Fay had agreed. Dr Roth had been fired, and Connie had celebrated that piece of news with a very expensive bottle of wine.

Only two people remained unaccounted for.

Boy was long gone by the time security guards went looking for him. Maeve was telling no one where her son had gone, and Connie doubted they would ever find him. He knew The Institution's hiding places better than anyone, and would eventually have found transport out of the mountains.

Vince East was nowhere to be found when the hunt for him had begun. His patient uniform had been found, ripped and ruined, floating in the lake. There was speculation that he'd tried to swim across the dam and perished in its freezing water and lethal undercurrents. Of course, he hadn't been wearing his patient clothes when he'd escaped, but Connie had forgotten to pass that information on to the authorities. It seemed that Baarda and Jock, following her lead, had suffered the same lapse of memory.

The decision had been far from easy for Connie. Her gut

instinct had proved fallible where both Boy and Rubio were concerned, so she'd started at square one with basic profiling skills. Connie had read the psychiatric files, checked the original police reports, investigated through a frantic information grab as if she were working the case from scratch. That was how she formed an opinion about the level of danger East posed the general public. The other information she'd gleaned during her reading had been the extent of evil done to the boys in the home where Vince's brother had perished. Eventually, she'd decided that the so-called victims of Vince's crime had it coming.

She had no idea if East was alive or dead, but it felt right that he was no longer incarcerated. Given the lives he'd helped save, that was as much as Connie cared to know.

Leaving Baarda with the investigators chasing the financial end of the matter – it seemed there were multiple parties who stood to make an awful lot of money from Crater Coin's sudden rise – Connie had travelled to the mortuary for a visit she had promised to make. She waited until the technician left her alone with Tara, then pulled up a second gurney and lay next to her, flat on her back, staring at the ceiling. Remembering what Johannes Cameron had said about his wife, Connie pulled out her cell phone, and found a Springsteen track to play. He sang 'My Hometown' to them as she reached out and held Tara's hand one last time.

'I'm sorry I kept you waiting so long,' she said. 'You must have been terrified for her. Gosh, Tara, she's so beautiful. In spite of it all, you know? I could feel this fight in her, from the second I took her in my arms. You must be so proud.' She squeezed Tara's hand. 'I'm guessing you were watching over her the whole time. I'm not going to lie, I was kind of scared there for a while. For both of us, not just for Aurora. I'm sorry about that. I should have been the bigger person but I just got lost in it all.'

Connie rolled onto her side and studied Tara's profile.

'Yes, she does, she looks like you. Her daddy didn't even get a look-in genetically speaking.' Connie stroked Tara's hair. 'I wish this had never happened to you. Rubio was evil. That's all there was to it. And Ong was greedy and vile, a spineless hypocrite and a liar. If it helps, and it can never balance the scales, but they're both dead. They can't hurt your family any more. As much as maybe it would have been justice for them to stand trial, I'm glad they're no longer on this earth. They didn't deserve the oxygen. Monsters, both of them.'

She leaned across to press her lips against Tara's cold forehead, kissing it briefly as she'd been unable to before. The forensics didn't matter now. Her killers were dead.

'I'll keep an eye on your girl. When she gets older, if she has questions, I'll make sure she gets the answers she needs. Rest quietly now.' Connie sat up and hopped off the gurney, pushing it away again. 'You'll live on through her. I honestly believe that. Goodness is like any other form of energy. It can be transferred but never extinguished. Goodbye, Tara Cameron. Sleep tight.'

Connie left. There was work to be done to tie up all the loose ends, and she had some work to do on herself too, making sure she finally dealt with the post-traumatic stress disorder she'd left simmering for far too long. And after that there was a cold case she needed to investigate. She'd promised a friend. More importantly, she wanted to do justice to three dead girls who'd died whilst guests of one particular hotel.

Her cell phone rang as she exited the mortuary, relaying a

voicemail message left while she'd been with Tara. It was her mother.

There was a long pause at the start, a rattling breath being taken, the rustle of material near the mouthpiece. A sob.

'Connie, it's your mother. I didn't want to tell you like this. It's your father. He's gone. Last night, in his sleep.' Connie waited as her mother broke off. She could almost see her wiping her eyes and straightening her back, preparing to speak again. 'I'm so sorry to call when you're at work. I hope it wasn't a bad time.'

Connie dropped her cell phone, letting it clatter on the stone tiles. It didn't feel real. All that hard work, saving Aurora, doing her best for Tara's family. Worrying about Baarda. Having a knife stuck in her, for fuck's sake. Nearly losing her mind. All because she'd chosen to leave her own family and put someone else's first.

Now she would never hold her father's hand again. Never tell him she loved him. The opportunity to find some common ground with him was gone forever. Was that the price she had to pay for finding the baby? Did the universe really level the scales so crudely?

She knew she had to pull herself together and get moving. Her mother needed her. There were arrangements to make. Plans to put together. Flights to book to Boston, then a hop to Martha's Vineyard. Plenty of time later for crying and questions and self-loathing. Connie dashed tears from her cheeks, bending down to retrieve her phone.

It rang as soon as she wrapped her fingers around it. The number was unfamiliar.

'Connie Woolwine,' she said. A voice on the other end began to relay details. Two dead, both elderly but unrelated, tortured and left in a freezer with a cryptic and disturbing letter from

416

the killer. 'I understand.' She looked at her watch. 'Sure. I can be at the airport in an hour. Can you book two tickets? I'll be bringing my colleague with me. Email the file and we'll see you in Havana. Make sure I have access to the bodies as soon as I arrive.'

She hung up. It was an easy hop from Cuba up the coast back to Massachusetts. The funeral wouldn't be for several days. Her family would understand. Work had to come first.

Acknowledgements

People contribute to books in a thousand different ways, some obvious, others less so. Occasionally it's just a passing comment from a friend or in a coffee shop queue or at the hairdresser that sparks an idea for a new twist or a line of dialogue. To all the people I simply cannot thank here individually – I'm still grateful.

To those I can name but whose efforts still go relatively unseen, I appreciate you each and every day. Publishing is a tough business. Keeping up the enthusiasm for every book, for every author, for every press release is unbelievably hard. So endless gratitude to Helen Huthwaite, Thorne Ryan, Elisha Lundin, Maddie Dunne-Kirby, Ella Young, Gabriella Drinkald, Samantha Luton, Hannah O'Brien, Tom Dunstan, Oliver Malcolm and Charlotte Brown.

And to my agents, Hardman & Swainson, who continue to stick with me in spite of all the stupid questions, my administrative errors and general author paranoia – I love you guys – Caroline Hardman (thank you is never enough), Joanna Swainson, Thérèse Coen and Nicole Etherington. Also, to Tory Lyne-Pirkis and all at Midas PR for helping spread the word.

And as ever, to the word-dealers. The booksellers, the librarians, the English teachers, the bloggers and reviewers – where would we be without you?

To Margaret Baumber for talking books with me constantly and being my champion. To Ruth Arlow for coming to endless bookish events with me and keeping me laughing. To David, Gabe, Sollie & Evangeline for all the usual stuff. And if I've forgotten anyone – you know me, I'd forget my own head if it wasn't screwed on.

If you loved *The Institution*, then why not try Helen Fields's iconic DI Callanach series?

Available from all good bookstores now.

And if you enjoyed the DI Callanach *Perfect* series, we think you'll love these fantastically twisty crime thrillers . . .

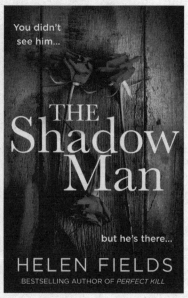

Available from all good bookstores now.